Operation Roadrunner

Operation Roadrunner

A Novel of Nuclear Espionage

Victoria Stevens
And
Jill Rose

From an original story by Richard Miles

SAFE HOUSE BOOKS

www.safehousebooks.co.uk

Safe House Books Ltd
London, England
www.safehousebooks.co.uk

Published by Safe House Books, 2024

OPERATION ROADRUNNER

Cover design by Stuart Polson

A catalogue record for this book is available from the British Library

9781739754037 (paperback)

Typeset using Atomik ePublisher from Easypress Technologies

Foreword

Operation Roadrunner is an enthralling spy thriller inspired by the remarkable true story of British graduates recruited at Cambridge University in the 1930s to work covertly for the Soviet Union.

Drawing on the personal experience of their uncle, Victoria Stevens and Jill Rose have spun a gripping tale of espionage, centered around Lieutenant Tom Davis RNVR of the British Embassy in Washington and set in the tense post World War 2 period.

Operation Roadrunner consciously evokes the style and atmosphere of the great early twentieth century espionage writers such as Erskine Childers (*Riddle of the Sands*) and John Buchan (*The 39 Steps*) as it explores the conflicting emotions of British, American and Soviet officials at the end of the Second World War. The authors have beautifully captured the contrast between the gilded diplomatic lifestyle in the Washington Embassy and the humdrum reality of life in a victorious, but impoverished, Britain still governed by widespread rationing; the departmental rivalries between the various new intelligence agencies in both London and Washington; as well as the simmering tensions, and occasional mistrust, under the surface of the close US/UK cooperation on defence and nuclear matters (so essential for Britain's long term security) at a time when the international power balance was shifting from an exhausted UK to a vibrant and confident America.

But the heart of the story revolves around the conflict between patriotism and personal loyalties felt by Tom and his colleagues as geopolitics shifted so quickly and dramatically from the certainties of the fight against Nazism to the many uncertainties around the start of the Cold War. The authors have done an excellent job in blending these various tensions into an exciting and fast-paced novel.

Sir Mark Lyall Grant GCMG
Former British Ambassador to the UN and National Security Adviser

Author's Note
by Jill Rose

Our uncle Richard Miles was born in October 1917. Although he spent his formative years in England, Richard was raised with a deep pride in his Welsh ancestry, as well as close family ties, a strong sense of duty and service, and the moral rectitude of his parents' faith.

Richard took his degree in PPE (Politics, Philosophy and Economics) from Exeter College Oxford in 1939, and almost immediately enlisted in the Royal Navy. He served with the Arctic convoys before being promoted to Lieutenant, at which point they discovered he had a hearing defect due to a congenital deformity of his right ear that, to his dismay, precluded further active service. In the autumn of 1942 Richard was posted to the British Embassy in Washington, with responsibilities for White House Liaison with the Naval Attaché's Office. He later worked for the embassy's Economic Advisor, and in 1946 he became adviser to the British Delegation to the United Nations and adviser to the UN Atomic Energy Commission.

From early in 1947 until the middle of 1948 the Secretary of the Anglo-American-Canadian Policy Committee on atomic energy matters was a high-flyer named Donald Maclean. He was just four years older than Richard, and their paths would have crossed both socially and professionally. In 1951 Maclean was revealed as a Soviet spy who had for many years been passing top secret information to the KGB, and he defected to Moscow along with fellow-traveller Guy Burgess.

I remember Richard telling me, many years later, that he had known Donald Maclean and that he had written a *roman à clef* inspired by him. More than twenty years after his death in 1997 I acquired the manuscript of this unpublished novel. There were several drafts, as well as many hand-written notes and addenda. My challenge was to meld everything into one coherent version that remained faithful to my uncle's original work.

In 2022 my sister Vicky and I revised and rewrote that earlier edition, and the result is *Operation Roadrunner*.

Chapter One

Tom Davis had never seen a dead body up close before. From the decks of HMS *Athene* Tom had watched the still-smouldering hulks of merchant ships, the ruins of Murmansk run convoys they had tried but failed to protect. Aeroplanes tumbled from the sky and disappeared into the pitiless Arctic waters even as he and his shipmates stood helplessly watching. Once, the frigate had depth-charged a U-boat to its doom. Tom hadn't seen it, couldn't even be certain it was a genuine kill. When a raid had buried Tom and other crew members in the vaulted cellars of their Portsmouth barrack block, they were dug out never knowing how many corpses lay beneath the rubble. In three years of active service during the early years of the war, death had come no closer than this. The destroyed head of Patrick Marsden was the first time he had confronted its physicality, face to face.

He had woken early that April morning in the comfortable little town-house in Georgetown that he had shared with Miles Hansen, the Assistant Air Attaché, ever since he had been posted to the British Embassy in Washington in the spring of 1943 as Assistant Naval Attaché, after leaving active service in the Navy. It was nearly eight months since the war had been brought to an end with the surrender of Japan and there were still days when he woke full of an astonished gratitude that it was, actually, all over.

He rolled over in bed and stretched contentedly. The shimmer of sunlight through the window shade promised a fine spring day. It was Easter Sunday. In England, his parents would have expected him to go to church, but here in Washington, on the other side of the pond, he was under no obligation to do so. Tom was looking forward to a leisurely breakfast and a bath, after which he intended to join in the softball game, the first of the season, against the State Department at eleven-thirty. Charlie Weaver, one of his friends at the US Navy Department, had invited him and Miles for drinks after. How could he begin to explain this world to the folks at home?

Since being posted to Washington there had only been one brief, rushed visit to London. Tom had returned to America feeling almost guilty for his own good fortune. The contrast between the two capital cities could not have been more striking. He saw it in the bombed-out buildings, in the lack of consumer goods in the shops, the pinched faces and shabby clothes of the people, and the stiff and awkward social interactions even with his own family. In Washington, there was an embarrassment of material riches and people you hardly knew were apt to treat you as a long-time friend. Even the little things about life in America gave him pleasure: decent coffee with cream, not strong tea with tinned milk; orange juice – almost unobtainable in England – cold from the refrigerator; plenty of hot water for his bath (sorry, 'tub'). After more than three-and-a-half years in the States he still found the material excess and the language intoxicating.

As he lay back drowsily against the pillows, the telephone rang. It was Boots, the embassy Security Officer. He must have had an official name but was always and only known as Boots. He had served in the Military Police in the First World War and was not inclined to let people forget it.

"Lieutenant Davis? Apologies for the early call on a Sunday." Tom understood the implication that by now, with the sun up for an hour already, he should at least have gone for a five mile run, taken a cold shower and be dressed and ready for church.

"You're needed at 4820 Connecticut, sir, as soon as possible. I'll put you in the picture."

It wasn't going to be a pretty one, Tom realised, sitting bolt upright in bed.

Patrick Marsden, special assistant to the British Counsellor (Information), had been found dead in his apartment. Shot through the temple, a revolver beside him.

"*What?*"

"The police are there now. Clear case of suicide. They, and the embassy, don't want any fuss. Just agree with whatever they say and sign the papers they will have ready."

"But surely this should be handled by one of the higher-ups, Marsden's boss, or someone like Sylvan Ross?"

"Not available," Boots replied brusquely. "Mr Ross suggested yourself. Well, sir, just look as though you know about this sort of thing. It's a diplomatic case, you see. As long as the embassy is happy, they will just record the death. No inquest or any of that stuff necessary. Embassy will inform the relatives. Sir John asks that you report back to the Annexe immediately after you've been there. By the way, sir," he added, "may I ask how well you knew him?"

Not well. Not well at all, really, Tom thought as he headed his old Pontiac into Rock Creek Park, a green oasis meandering through the neatly laid-out city, where the road dipped down and ran along the shallow ravine of the eponymous creek, to surface again near the Zoo to join up with Connecticut Avenue. In fact, he now admitted to himself, not at all. They had exchanged pleasantries when they passed each other in the corridor or the canteen, but that was about the extent of their acquaintance.

Tom had met enough Americans in the past three years to have a good understanding of how vital to the war effort the British information service was, how it had attracted to itself fine brains from the press, radio and the universities. But he had also come to realise how feeble it actually was in relation to the huge task it faced. This was not merely boosting Britain but getting all those only somewhat united states to understand what the war was *about;* the war in Europe in particular and, most difficult and yet most important of all, the sort of world people wanted *after* the war. Patrick Marsden, in Tom's opinion, had not been one of the front runners in this enterprise. He did not travel; never left his desk. He was not to be seen lunching with the press corps or at the salons where the Washington gossip circulated. He wrote reports, surrounded by press cuttings and copies of the Congressional Record.

Tom pulled over at the apartment block where Marsden had lived alone. It was an uncompromising rectangular six-floor building screened by a few conifers and neglected evergreen shrubs. There was no off-street parking, but he decided it was safe to slot in behind a couple of DC police cars waiting there. The janitor took him up in the lift to the third floor where a large, stony-faced policeman checked his credentials and led him along a bleak corridor to the apartment. Two uniformed policemen and another man in plain-clothes filled the little lobby. He noticed the pistols the officers wore in leather holsters on their hips; in England the police carried nothing more lethal than a truncheon.

"Good morning, *Lootenant,*" said the taller police officer. (This pronunciation of his rank was one of the few things about America with which Tom had a problem.) "Your Mr Ross told us to expect you. I'm Captain O'Malley, and this is Captain Forbes from the Diplomatic desk. Perhaps you could sign these documents for us."

He indicated where they lay on the small hall stand.

So, it was Sylvan Ross who had dropped him in it. 'It' being a situation he was not in control of and felt he was being rushed through for some undisclosed purpose.

"I'd better see what happened first," he said, and made to enter the living room.

"Not necessary, unless you really want to; t'aint a pretty sight."

Not a pretty picture, not a pretty sight, thought Tom, steeling himself. He did not want to be accused of ghoulish morbidity, but, deciding he had a duty to do, led the way into the room.

He paused in the doorway trying to look nonchalant, to give the impression to the American police officers (*'cops'*, he reminded himself, *and almost certainly hard-boiled*) that this was not in fact the first time he had seen a corpse, even though he was sick inside with trepidation.

Marsden had been sitting at a desk by the window, and his pyjama-clad body was slumped forward towards the desk-top. After this initial glimpse Tom panned away, taking in the open door to the bedroom, an old and rather scruffy-looking sofa, and an armchair with clothes tossed roughly on it, until his eyes came to the bookshelves where he let them rest on the familiar yellow and black bindings of Gollancz Left Book Club titles while he steadied himself. Then he walked firmly towards the window.

What was left of Patrick Marsden's head rested in a sludge of blackening blood. There was a blueish wound on the right, up-facing temple; the real mess luckily seemed to be on the other side of the dreadful face. A rather pink and hairless face, as Tom remembered, but which now had the texture of a Stilton cheese. The lips were drawn back in hideous tension over clenched teeth. The right hand was curled around a small handgun; in Tom's strange state of heightened reaction he noticed that the nails were bitten down to the quick.

Too many damn guns in this country, he thought sourly. His friend Charlie had told him that the right of every American citizen to bear arms was enshrined in the Constitution and was jealously guarded. *Why?* he had presumed to ask, but as yet, no-one had given a satisfactory answer.

He cleared his throat.

"So the doctor is satisfied that it's suicide?"

"Doctor ain't been yet, sir," said O'Malley

"*What?* Why not?"

"He'll be here directly. But we seen a lot of these. There ain't no doubt about it – even left a note."

Uncertain how to proceed, Tom thankfully looked away and asked: "Who found the… er, body?"

O'Malley opened up a bit.

"Janitor saw the door was ajar early this morning, came on in and finds – this. He called the station. We alerted Captain Forbes here; he called your embassy then came right on over."

"Yeah," said Forbes. "Don't do any good to have publicity with the press nosing around when we get these diplomatic cases. State is notified, of course, and the FBI." He nodded in the direction of the plain-clothes man who had followed them into the room. "But the embassies don't want no scandal and we go along with that."

"Of course," Tom said hesitantly, "if that's the usual form."

He had to collect his thoughts. Forcing himself back to the body, he tried to memorise the details. There was a cup of tea on the corner of the desk, cold now, with a dead fly floating on the surface. In front of Marsden was a sheet of paper, the bottom edge pinned beneath his head as he had fallen forward. Although spattered with blood, the words, in a neat cursive handwriting, were quite legible: *This has to end. I can't go on* – followed by what looked like a tick trailing off into a dark reddish-brown stain.

Tom felt a sense of unease that bordered on annoyance. Why had Sylvan Ross called him in rather than someone more senior, someone who was used to handling sensitive situations? Well, he'd been given authority: he decided to use it.

"I want nothing touched in here," he said. "I'll be back later. I'd like to see the doctor when he's done – and *then* we will deal with the paperwork. But thank you, gentlemen, I'm sure you have it well in hand. The, er, embassy will be most grateful."

As he moved to the door, the FBI man who had not yet said anything, now spoke over Tom's head as though he didn't exist.

"Give me a call at the Bureau, Captain, when these guys are done."

Then he was out the door.

As they waited for the lift, Captain O'Malley offered Tom a cigarette, which he accepted gratefully.

"Don't fret about it, Lieutenant. It'll be as I say. But if you're looking for an explanation, have a word with the janitor."

It was, though, the janitor's wife who appeared, anxious for news, and who had no doubt as to the reason for the tragedy.

"Oh my Lord, that poor young fella. Too much on his own, he was. What they want, I always say, is a woman. It ain't healthy without a woman."

"That's all you need to know," said Captain O'Malley as they parted. "The janitor fella, nor I, couldn't have put it neater."

Chapter Two

Tom drove back through Rock Creek Park. It was still early and there was almost no traffic. The air was a little cool but very pleasant at this time of day and it would be comfortably warm later. He pulled up by one of the picnic sites close to the water, where a large sugar-maple shaded a wooden table and bench. The sounds of the surrounding city were hardly noticeable, only the soft cooing of pigeons and the mindless babble of the little stream. It was a tranquil spot where Tom could take a few minutes to calm down, to think about what he had seen, and to decide on what he was going to say when he reported back at the Annexe.

The sight of death still had him in shock. He was a keen reader of spy and detective novels, but the violence and killing they portrayed seemed generally to leave the surviving characters completely unperturbed as they moved on to the next episode: a kiss and a clinch or a cup of tea or the plotting of bloody revenge. The reality was quite different. Here he was in the King's uniform, at the end of a terrible war, and yet a single death could shake him up so much? Yes, it could.

Pulling himself together, he drove on. It was only a few minutes to the British Embassy on Massachusetts Avenue. The grand Lutyens building – an extraordinary evocation of the English country house that more or less told America what it thought of its vulgar modernism – housed the ambassador's private residence and the Chancery, the business offices of the British diplomatic mission to the United States. Tom drove round the back to the Annexe, a three-floor, box-like structure that had been built during the war to temporarily house the overflow from the overcrowded Chancery. Though the war was over, the need for this additional space had grown, not diminished, and so the Annexe, generally known as the pigeon-loft, remained in place.

The meeting in the Security Office was already in progress when he got there. At the head of the table sat the Minister, Sir John Portent, a man in his late fifties, with thick, greying hair and a roundish, rather forgettable face. His amiable demeanour gave him the air of a genial English squire, but this bland exterior masked a complex and resolute character of formidable intellect. The Minister was second only to the Ambassador, Sir Geoffrey Leeds, himself. Sir Geoffrey was the face of the British mission, but behind the scenes it was Sir John who did the heavy lifting. Tom knew something of Sir John's background: he had taken a First in Greats at Oxford, and had marched into Damascus with Lawrence and Allenby during the Great War. Unusually for British men of his generation, he had subsequently earned a post-graduate degree in Political Science at Harvard in Boston, before joining the Diplomatic Service.

Boots, the Security Officer, was seated at the end of the table near the door, his toothbrush moustache positively quivering; next to him First Secretary Sylvan Ross, Sir John's right-hand man, who had apparently detailed him for this morning's unpleasant duty. Also there were the Military Attaché, and Lord Zender. Seldom seen by the staff, Lord Zender was not formally attached to the Mission, but had a room in the Residence that was also his office when he was in Washington. A Nobel Prize winner for his work on particle physics, Zender had been then-Prime Minister Winston Churchill's scientific adviser during the war.

Sir John looked at his watch and observed, rather irritably, that Tom had taken his time. What had been happening?

Tom told them.

"You went rather beyond your brief, didn't you?" said Sylvan Ross, somewhat unfairly, Tom thought. Over the past three years he had developed a good friendship with Sylvan, who had taken Tom under his wing when he first arrived in Washington.

Boots frowned.

"I told the Lieutenant just to sign the papers and get back here as soon as he'd done so."

Still upset, and irritated by the criticism, Tom retorted, "I went on duty as a Naval Officer. I didn't like what I saw or the rush with which it was being handled. I think I'm owed… you owe… I am entitled to an explanation."

He sat down in a vacant chair, aghast at his own boldness.

It was clear the meeting had not expected this reaction and there was a pause. Lord Zender spoke first in his quiet voice.

"Lieutenant Davis is quite right, of course. And it may be no bad thing to have shown the FBI that we are not merely stooges." Turning to Tom, he added, "It must have been a most unpleasant duty, young man. Death can be a messy business.'

Sir John sighed and said, "Very well, you have a point. Naturally we're all very sorry. Damn shame. Poor chap was supposed to be starting two weeks' holiday on Monday. But please appreciate we are five hours behind London and we must get this report off straight away." He pulled a sheet of typescript from the pile in front of him. "Lieutenant, I want you to read this page. Just this bit which concerns Marsden's death. It is a matter of the highest security and urgency. Please read it and give your assent."

It wasn't a request. It was an order.

Tom glanced over the few lines. Marsden's suicide was recorded with a confirmation from the local police authorities. He wondered for a moment whether to ask what Lord Zender was doing there, but thought better of it.

"Agreed?"

Tom mumbled agreement and signed.

"Now, be a good chap, will you? See their doctor fellow and do what has to be done down there." Obviously relieved that everything had gone to plan he flashed his professional smile and added, "Come up to the house for a drink after. Don't want to spoil your Sunday too much."

It was, again, an order.

Sir John Portent lived near the embassy in a largish 1920s 'Tudorbethan' house, furnished inside by the British Ministry of Works to a standard thought suited to ministerial rank: comfortable but impersonal. A white-jacketed manservant showed Tom into a sunny chintz and flower-filled sitting room where Sir John greeted him and, without asking what he wanted, poured him a drink.

"This first. You probably need it. Chin-chin!"

It was a short dollop of Hollands gin. Tom swallowed it gratefully and gasped. But it dried the cold chill that had lain inside him since he had first seen Marsden's head. He tried to stop seeing it. A longer glass was put in his hand, and Sir John indicated a large and comfortable armchair. Then he sat down himself opposite Tom and proffered an open cigarette box.

"Feeling a bit more up to par? Jolly good. Cigarette?"

He took one himself and lit it, then Tom's.

"Now, Davis, this is Ross's bailiwick really; why he was at the post-mortem — sorry, not a good choice of phrase — the meeting earlier. The Information Department where the lad worked is ultimately his responsibility, but we feel you probably do deserve an explanation so I am going to tell you something in the strictest confidence. I assume you have read the Official Secrets Act? Well, now is the time to remember it."

He paused.

"Marsden was an enemy agent."

Tom couldn't help but gasp.

"A German agent? But the war's over!"

"No, no, Davis," said Sir John reprovingly, "of course not German! As you say, *that* war's over, thank God. But an enemy agent nonetheless. There's a new, cold war now."

Tom recovered himself, slightly ashamed of his impulsive assumption. For him the enemy would for ever be the Nazis.

"Are we talking about our victorious allies, the *Russians*?"

"Well, yes; I'm afraid so. He was transcribing hush-hush documents and formulae onto microfilm. Just a clerking job. Not a principal, just a cog in the machine."

"Atomic data? I noticed a copy of that Manhattan Project Report from last year on his bookshelf; the same binding as the one I've got."

"He was probably trying to understand what it was all about. I don't believe he knew as much about this atomic stuff as I do; certainly not as much as you do. And that Report tells an awful lot about it. You know, sometimes the Americans astound me. They are so hot on security but they published that thing! I'll bet you a pound to a penny that HMG would never have allowed it – *never* – well, at least until it was thirty years out of date. And they are actually going to invite a bevy of VIPs and journalists to the South Pacific to witness their next nuclear tests this summer!"

"Are the Yanks really so hot on security?" Tom asked. "Their Secret Operations lot seem mainly to provide plots for all these war movies they churn out."

Sir John pulled his chair closer and lowered his voice.

"Actually, Davis, they are *bloody* good. Too bloody good, in fact. Their people picked up the trail that led to Marsden. Now they want more from us. Who is behind Marsden? Might it be the ambassador perhaps? Or you? Or me? If Marsden had been picked up by the FBI, which *might* have happened today, God knows what would have come out!"

Tom could understand the Minister's concern. He found the crude 'anti-Red' skirmishing, not only in Congress but in much of the press, unsettling. The shameful spectacle of Congressman Martin Dies, Chairman of the House Committee on Un-American Activities, and his acolytes, seeking glory by 'exposing' 'lefties', 'reds' and 'commies' in public life, in the unions and the Government service, had struck a blow at his idealistic view of America. Anyone who had held a job under Roosevelt's New Deal was liable to be pilloried and slandered and, from what he read, this attitude seemed prevalent throughout the heartlands of America, egged on by J Edgar Hoover, the pugilistic Director of the Federal Bureau of Investigation.

"Yes, Hoover would have a field day if he could expose Reds under our British beds."

"But Marsden must have known they were closing in," Sir John added. "That's why he… well, you know. Took the coward's way out." He leant back and lit another cigarette.

"Frankly, the *scandal* is the side *I'm* paid to worry about; atomic secrets don't come under my remit, thank heaven. So far we are the barely-trusted partner in this atomic business, and we've sunk all we have to contribute into the *American* programme. Already there are lobbyists in Washington for a 'go-it-alone' policy. Can't you just see the headlines if this got out? *Britain Leaks Secrets to Reds*. And that would be the end of our involvement." He shook his head. "Doesn't bear thinking about."

Tom was still trying to process all this. He said slowly, "So Marsden…"

"Yes… as I said, he knew he was close to being rumbled, so he… well, suicide. Nasty thing." Sir John got up, suggesting the session was over. "Can't thank you enough, Davis, for sorting things out for us with the authorities. Signed all the papers, Official Secrets Act too, I hope." He took Tom's glass. "Stay for lunch?"

Chapter Three

Tom didn't stay for lunch. He didn't feel like company. The soft-ball game had gone ahead without him; he phoned Charlie Weaver's wife Gracie and made his apologies for missing the drinks party. Then he drove downtown, parked in a side street off Constitution Avenue and strolled across the green lawns of the National Mall, the stately park at the heart of the city, towards the Washington Monument.

It was a beautiful afternoon. Children and dogs played on the soft grass, while out-of-town visitors gawped at the legendary buildings; even the temporary structures put up during the war could not detract from their grandeur. On a small hill to the east was the Capitol Building, home to the US Congress. To the west, at the far end of a long reflecting pool, stood the memorial to Abraham Lincoln. Across the Tidal Basin to the south was the perfect white neoclassical temple that was the Jefferson Memorial; the cherry trees around it had bloomed early this spring and the trees were cloaked in pale green leaves. And to the north Tom could see the gardens of the Ellipse, and behind them the White House, home of every American President except the first, General George Washington. Although he had become familiar with these symbols of American greatness, so many of which were constructed when the nation was young and full of promise, they never failed to impress him.

The aroma of cooking onions reminded him that he'd missed breakfast and had had only a shot of Holland's gin all morning. He walked over to the vendor's cart and bought two hot-dogs with onions, sauerkraut and extra mustard, then found an empty, shaded bench where he settled down to eat his lunch and think things over.

Tom had left university in the summer of 1939 with an Upper Second in PPE and no idea what he wanted to do with his life. When war with Germany broke out that September he volunteered as an Ordinary Seaman with the Royal Navy, and served more than three years, including several runs through the bitterly cold northern seas to Murmansk, before the higher-ups discovered that he was an Oxford graduate and promoted him to Sub-Lieutenant. At the same time, they determined that a hearing defect in his right ear precluded him from further active duty, and he was posted to a shore establishment. In his more cynical moments, Tom wondered why the same minor disability had not mattered when he was only a rating. A couple of months later he was moved up another notch, to Lieutenant, and assigned to the British Embassy in Washington. He had arrived in America's capital in May 1943 as a complete outsider, well aware that this was a plum assignment. He was determined to make the most of the opportunity.

He was to work for the Naval Attaché, Archie Struthers, and he soon came to realise that a great deal of his job was paperwork. But as he ploughed his way through the reams of memoranda and telegrams copied 'for information' to the Naval Attaché's office, he came to have a much wider understanding of the current global situation than he would ever have learnt on the decks of a warship. It was Sylvan Ross who had later arranged for him to work with Meredith Hobson on what everyone referred to as 'this atomic business'. The job was fundamentally a political one: the vital task of seeing that Britain kept a finger on the trigger of whatever weapon that might emerge and, looking cannily ahead, on the future control of nuclear power. It was not to become an American monopoly. Sylvan, he realised, now he looked back on it, had been a significant feature of his time in Washington.

Now Tom recalled their first meeting. Still new to the job, he was having lunch alone in the embassy canteen, revelling in the exotic delights of Chicken Maryland and coleslaw, followed by ice-cream. A voice in his bad ear made him turn his head.

"You, I think, are the Naval Attaché's new assistant. May I join you? My name is Ross, Sylvan Ross."

Sylvan was a tall man, in his mid-thirties, with a slight Scottish burr to his voice. He wore his hair quite long at a time when the Americans sported crew-cuts and the English short-back-and-sides; a mannerism which was generally considered 'artistic'.

"Tom Davis," Tom replied. "It's a pleasure to meet you, Mr Ross."

Sylvan set down his tray on the table and they shook hands.

"Dear old Archie. Natters on about too much paperwork, but some people wonder what else he has to do all day, what with all the admirals we seem to maintain in Washington nowadays."

Tom knew that Sylvan was a big shot in the Chancery, but he felt he had to stand up for his superior officer.

"I've hardly settled in, but there's a huge amount to do. Largely involves organising shipping to get supplies through back home and also to various fronts globally. We have Army and Air Force missions here, as well as us – well, you know that, obviously – and procuring and shipping supplies seems to be a major part of what we all do. And we certainly need the help. We Brits should really be grateful to America for the support."

Sylvan snorted dismissively.

"Took the Yanks long enough to join in. Your average American saw it as a purely European conflict. America First. Isolationism. It was only Pearl Harbour at the end of '41 that brought them in."

Tom was quick to defend his hero.

"Yes, but Roosevelt did his best to involve them: he was under no illusions what a Hitler victory would mean to the world. Thank God, or Roosevelt or the Japs or whoever, the Americans are in now. Without them – well…"

They were both quiet for a moment. Then Tom added, "Not to mention all this secret stuff…"

"Secret stuff? Oh, this atomic business, eh?"

"Well, if you say so." Tom suddenly felt guilty. "My chief goes on at me about not talking about it to anyone." Although in fact he knew almost nothing about it at the time.

"Quite right, too; forget we ever mentioned it," said Sylvan. But he leant forward conspiratorially. "Archie, though, your boss, is *deeply* involved in it all. Don't worry, everyone knows that. His pals in the US Navy Department are squaring up for the big fight with the other services for which of them will be in charge of the first big bang development; for when, that is, the boffins report that a big bang will really work."

He grinned, leant back in satisfaction and took a large forkful of the shepherd's pie which the canteen also thoughtfully supplied to those who, possibly for patriotic reasons, still preferred a British menu.

Tom was relieved when Sylvan changed the subject and asked him about himself. Still a little uncertain of his footing, he was glad to supply the information, and at the end of the conversation had given his interlocutor a complete profile of his background and life so far.

"Well," said Sylvan, finishing his rice pudding, "most interesting. Oh, and by the way, I assume you have been invited to the ambassador's party this evening?"

"Well, no. I wouldn't have…"

"Disgraceful. Don't worry, I'll get you in. Marcie will give you a buzz this afternoon to say you are on. Know Marcie, do you? Lady Gertrude's social secretary?"

They hadn't been formally introduced, but everyone in DC knew the gorgeous Lady Marcia McKenna, daughter of a Duke, mother from somewhere in the Irish peerage, and known universally as Marcie.

"It will probably *be frightfully* boring," Sylvan continued, "a lot of southern congressmen and their, well, I suppose we must call them ladies; all madly pro-British but slave owners in all but name. They abolished slavery, as you know, but it more or less goes on just the same. Anyway, you should be out there getting to know people – starting with those southern belles; you're a handsome devil and they will just *lurv* your uniform. See you then."

The phone call came through at three.

"Lieutenant Davis? He*llo*. It's Marcie McKenna," she continued needlessly. The voice alone was enough to identify her, with its drawling aristocratic vowels, although there was an essential vivacity and friendliness to it which captivated him.

"Sylvan tells me there's been an oversight. *So* sorry!"

"Well, I wasn't expecting…" acutely embarrassed.

But she continued as if he hadn't spoken. "Anyway, it's all arranged. You're on the list. See you there, sweetie."

When Tom arrived at the Residence that evening, a couple of dozen guests were already milling around in the exquisite formal gardens. The roses were just coming into bloom and the air was scented with jasmine. Liveried waiters circulated discreetly with trays of champagne and canapés. As so often since his arrival, Tom was awed by the abundance of everything in America. Reading between the lines of his mother's letters, he knew that his family in England struggled with the restrictions of rationing. It made him almost angry to see a woman take a small bite from a cracker topped with smoked salmon and casually discard the rest; don't you know there's a war on, he wanted to shout at her.

He could see no one he knew and, being a very junior member of the Embassy staff, he was at first reluctant to push himself forward. Until, like his fairy godmother, Marcie McKenna appeared, wearing something long and slinky in black velvet with a necklace of baroque pearls. Her dark hair was swept back from her forehead, and her lipstick was very red against her perfect pale complexion.

"Darling! Lovely to see you. Tom Davis, isn't it? I'll introduce you to your hostess."

Lady Gertrude Leeds did not show well beside her glamorous social secretary. She was angular, with tightly permed hair and wearing a frock that looked as if it had been made from a pair of curtains. But she was very welcoming, asked Tom about his family, and when he said the roses reminded him of England, she said, "Aren't the gardens quite delightful? They were designed by Lady Elizabeth Lindsay, you know, the ambassador's wife in the thirties. People tell me the garden party reception held here for King George and Queen Elizabeth in 1939 was the most coveted social event in the city's history!"

"Gosh!" said Tom. "Was it really? How, um, splendid!"

He caught Marcie's eye and she moved to the rescue.

"You mustn't monopolise this gorgeous young man all night, Gertie dear," she said, and propelled him towards a group of American politicians.

He had forgotten about the legendary American friendliness. People didn't wait to be introduced, but introduced themselves, and Marcie abandoned him happily chatting with his fellow guests. They did not seem to be the Neanderthals that Sylvan had implied.

"Charlie Weaver, US Navy Department," said a short but wiry-looking man with a cruelly short crew-cut of sandy hair and a welcoming grin. "Don't think I've seen you here before."

"Tom Davis, Assistant Naval Attaché," replied Tom. "No, I've only been in Washington for a few weeks."

"I knew a guy called Davis at Oxford – Welsh – Herbert Davis. Any relation?"

"No, not a relation; there's a lot of Welshmen named Davis, but Herbert Davis was my tutor, at Exeter College."

"Well, son of a gun, whaddya know! I was a Rhodes Scholar at Exeter College, way back when. Say, is that pub I used to go to on The High still there… Haystack, Wheatstack, or something?"

"The Wheatsheaf… yes, it's still there. But they demolished The Vine a year or two before the war started."

They chatted animatedly for several more minutes, until Weaver said, "Sorry, Tom, I've got to go, but it's been great talking with you." He pumped Tom's hand. "I expect we'll see a lot of each other in the future; one of the hats I wear is as Liaison Officer with your Naval Attaché's office."

As Tom turned, he accidentally bumped into a woman standing close behind him. Her glass fell out of her hand and rolled on the grass.

"Oh, terribly sorry," he apologised, reaching to pick it up, "jolly clumsy of me."

"No need to apologise, Mr…?"

"Davis, Lieutenant Tom Davis, Assistant Naval Attaché. Let me get you another drink."

"Some ginger ale would be nice. Quite frankly, the wine is not very good."

Her voice was low and husky with a trace of an accent that Tom couldn't place.

Tom spoke to one of the waiters, then hurried back to the woman.

"They don't have any ginger ale, so I got you something called Coca-Cola – I hope that's all right, Mrs…?"

"Masudi," she replied, "and I am guessing you have not been long in America if you have not tried Coca-Cola."

She was a large, striking-looking woman in her mid-forties, wearing a good deal of both make-up and jewellery, and Tom guessed her clothes were expensive.

"No, just a few weeks, actually."

"So, we are both newcomers. My husband and I also arrived just a short while ago. He is a doctor; he trained in London with the brother of Sir Geoffrey Leeds, who arranged for us to come to America when Libya was liberated in the spring."

"Are you Libyan?" asked Tom.

"No, I am Lebanese and my husband is Egyptian, but we lived in Tripoli for many years."

"That must have been rather difficult, while the Germans occupied the place."

"We managed," she said in a flat tone.

"Ah, there you are, my dear," said an elegantly dressed man, coming up to Mrs Masudi and taking her arm in a proprietorial way. Tom surmised that this was her husband. The doctor was about ten years older than his wife, heavy-set with a receding hairline. "Come, I want you to meet the ambassador."

"Goodbye, Lieutenant," said Mrs Masudi as, with a brief nod to Tom, her husband whisked her away. He looked around and noticed Sylvan Ross, wearing a very American lightweight cream linen suit and a blue-and-white spotted bow tie, holding the floor to a group of earnest young men. Intrigued, Tom helped himself to another glass of Californian red from a passing waiter, despite Mrs Masudi's warning about the wine, and made his way across the room.

"Our political masters at home set a stiff agenda," Sylvan was saying. "They're naturally desperate to maintain Britain as a full partner, but they also believe, in a very British way, that they know best how to handle Johnny Foreigner, whether he be friend or foe. And so they seek to exert a restraining hand on what they fear is American… shall we say exuberance? *Exuberance,*" he continued, waving his full glass rather dangerously for emphasis, "exuberance over the terms to be offered the enemy, plans to unite the nations of the world, and, above all, their plans for those parts of the world marked red on the map and claimed by the British Empire, over the dissolution of which our Prime Minister, the great, the one and only Winston Spencer Churchill, has famously declared he does not intend to preside."

He gulped back some of his wine.

The Americans all nodded earnestly, and one of them attempted a riposte. "Well, OK, but don't you think…"

But Sylvan had spotted Tom.

"Where do you stand, dear boy, on the defence of Empire, and the question of how far we should kowtow to our American masters?"

"I hadn't thought a great deal about either. I suppose there are bound to be geopolitical changes when the war ends. As for the Americans," he glanced apologetically at the listeners, "are you suggesting they want to take over the Empire?"

One of the men guffawed and another turned away to greet a parting acquaintance.

"Not only the Empire, dear boy," said Sylvan, "but also the world."

The rest of the group had decided not to pursue the discussion and drifted away. Sylvan took Tom's arm.

"How did you get on with Senators Gaylord and Beauregard?"

"Who? Oh, the southern Senators. They were fine, I thought. Not too antediluvian."

"Didn't bend your ear about the outcome of the Civil War.?"

"No, not at all. That was in 1865, wasn't it? Why would they?"

"Lucky you. There are a great many Southerners who still believe they were in the right. The Lost Cause, you know, very romantic."

Tom laughed. "Like the Cavaliers in *1066 And All That*: 'Wrong but Wromantic'."

"Funny, isn't it," mused Sylvan, "the way we talk about right and wrong sides, so very black and white, as it were. My country right or wrong. And would you die for it?"

"Of course! I've proved that, haven't I?"

"Idealist, are we? Very commendable, no doubt, but you need an open mind as a shield against the devouring dragons of ideology, whether religious, political or just faddist that beset us."

"Maybe, but you couldn't have an open mind about the Nazis. There had to be one – and one only – right course to take."

"You can become confused about long-accepted loyalties, you know. What you would once have died for can become an abomination. Any of us may, by luck or virtue, be given exciting jobs, but we can get out of our depth, cannot make the best of them. We cannot make the key decisions, except…" He paused and gazed without focus into the glass in his hand.

"Except?"

"Except when we have an ideological commitment."

Marcie appeared in a swish of velvet at Sylvan's shoulder. "Darling," she said, "Stop hectoring poor Tom."

"Of course, Ma'am. Anything you say."

"Sylvan *will* go on," she said affectionately. "Ignore him. It's just attention seeking."

Tom had already picked up the office rumour that Marcie McKenna and Sylvan Ross were… well, more than just friends. He decided that they had both had too much to drink and, concerned about the trend of the discussion, was grateful for his fairy godmother's intervention.

From then on Sylvan Ross ("Call me Sylvan, dear boy; can't stand all this formality. As for the Yanks: they claim to lack starchiness, yet they are the most formal people in the world") became Tom's mentor. He piloted him around, saw that he met people, and invited him to join the tennis club.

Everyone in the embassy and throughout diplomatic Washington, Tom discovered, admired Sylvan. In this new world of clever and important-sounding people, he seemed to dominate effortlessly. After graduating from Cambridge with a first in modern languages, he had moved easily into the Foreign Service and was soon earmarked as a potential high-flyer. The sun shone on him and Tom basked in its reflection.

When Tom joined the embassy staff, Sylvan Ross was a First Secretary with a finger in a lot of pies. His office was the Clapham Junction of the communications network: downwards, transmitting the instructions of 'HE', His Excellency the Ambassador Sir Geoffrey Leeds, and the ceaseless flow of telegraphic messages from London; upwards, co-ordinating desk views on all subjects into briefs for HE, aides-memoire for the State Department or a counter blast of telegrams to London.

In spite of all these demands, Sylvan's office ran smoothly and his in-tray was never as cluttered as Tom's soon came to be.

"How do you manage to keep your desk so clear?" Tom once asked.

Sylvan smiled beatifically.

"Anything that has been there more than a week I simply throw away, dear boy. Whatever it was, it can't have been that important."

Chapter Four

The work in Archie Struthers' office proved to be easy and largely routine. Charlie Weaver of the US Navy Department became a good friend, and they would sometimes meet for a drink after work. Tom found his circle of acquaintances rapidly expanding, along with his social life: receptions at Embassies and parties with Georgetown hostesses filled his diary. There was precious little wartime austerity here, and 'showing the flag' at these and more public occasions was all part of the job. Juniors gave their own parties, exhausting their allowances of duty-free Scotch or gin, stabilised only by packets of nuts and crisps. After one such party in April, eleven months since he had joined the Embassy, he met Sylvan on the way in to a committee meeting they were both to attend.

"Dear boy, you look disgusting! Where were you last night?"

"I'm not sure," said Tom. "I think it was in Georgetown. A stag party, you know. God, I need a cup of coffee."

Ross laid a comforting hand on his shoulder. "We all get blotto at times, but watch it, young man: it's easy to rot away here. You're under-employed, that's your trouble, shifting paperwork about corned beef and cooking oil transports. We'll have to do something about it; you have quite a good brain, actually."

Well, thanks a bunch! Tom thought in his newly-acquired American idiom. But his pleasure in Sylvan's concern vanquished the insult.

"Catch up at lunchtime in the canteen? Let's hope you're looking a bit more like a British naval officer by then." Before Tom could retort that Sylvan couldn't know many British naval officers he had gone.

* * *

The next morning, Tom was crossing the Navy Department car park after a routine meeting, carefully skirting the puddles left by the overnight showers, when he heard his name being called.

"Lieutenant Davis!"

He turned and saw the Russian Assistant Naval Attaché, a man he knew well enough to say hello to, approaching him. Grigori Potemkin was clearly upset.

"Lieutenant, I wish to tell you that I and my country have been insulted by the Americans."

Not wanting to get caught up in a diplomatic incident, Tom said discreetly, "I'm sorry to hear that. What happened?"

"OK. I arrive here just after you. The Marine who guards the entrance… you know?"

Tom nodded.

"Well, he waves *you* through, says '*havvaniceday*' as they do, very, how do you say… casual? Me, I am taken to the guardroom and have to wait for an escort to take me to my appointment. Meanwhile I am treated like a prisoner! How you can explain this?"

Luckily, thought Tom, I *don't have to. Our American chums overstepping the mark again.*

"It does look as if the guard behaved poorly. I think your best bet is to inform Captain Sodkin and get him to take up the cudgels on your behalf."

"Yes," said Potemkin grimly. "I will do that."

That afternoon Captain Sodkin, the Russian Naval Attaché, phoned Tom, inviting him to the Soviet Embassy the next day for a chat.

Slightly alarmed at the apparent escalation of the incident and even more at his seeming involvement in it, Tom thought the best thing was to agree, but decided not to mention it to Archie Struthers. Not yet anyway.

To his relief, Captain Sodkin greeted him in a very friendly manner, thanked him for coming, and insisted they sit down together to the vodka and caviar set out on a low table.

"It is the best vodka!" he said, laughing. "We have our suppliers. The caviar could be better, but – you know – there's a war on!"

After Sodkin had demonstrated how vodka should be drunk the Russian way and Tom was beginning to feel quite relaxed, he said, "Lieutenant Davis, I did not ask you here to complain about the way the American Marine treated Lieutenant Potemkin. It is nothing to do with you, but as you understood at the time, I believe, Potemkin was justifiably angry."

Back on the alert, Tom nodded rather than say anything.

"I have spoken with the – what do you call them – the '*top brass*' Americans, and they have apologised. No, I just wanted to take this opportunity of saying, as one sailor to another, what excellent work the British Royal Navy has been doing, especially on the convoys. I believe you were involved, were you not?"

It seemed that Sodkin had been on the Murmansk run as well. They were soon exchanging reminiscences and Tom said how much he regretted having to give up active service in the Navy for a desk job.

"No, no, you are doing fine work here. Let me tell you it is my dearest hope that our two navies will work together always, as good friends and allies." He poured another shot of vodka and raised his glass. "Shall we drink to that?"

Two days later Sylvan called Tom into his office. Without preamble he said: "Tom, you went to the Soviet Embassy yesterday at eleven a.m. You stayed there till twelve-thirty. Was there any good reason for this?"

Feeling as if he were being spied on, Tom said defiantly, "Captain Sodkin invited me in for a chat and to compliment the British Navy for its great work. Seems a good enough reason."

"And what triggered this invitation? A bit out of the blue, isn't it, for Sodkin to invite the – if you don't mind my saying it – lowly British *Assistant* Naval Attaché for a" – sarcastically – "*chat?*"

Tom realised that Ross had a point. He described the incident in the car park, and then added, "You know what? Thinking it over, I can see that Sodkin was suggesting to me pretty clearly – although not in so many words – that the Americans are becoming a bit careless about their allies. I think he wanted me to feel that they treated *both* of us – Russians *and* Brits – as tiresome relatives, not partners in the coming victory. He wants us on side."

"Did you agree?"

"Well, I do agree. But I didn't say so. I didn't have to respond. Captain Sodkin didn't make the point directly." Sylvan remained silent, tapping his teeth with a pencil.

Encouraged by the silence Tom ventured: "Well, come on, Sylvan, we all get a bit fed up when the Yanks, the army people especially, seem to think that they and they alone are fighting this damn war. The French hardly make a secret of how *they* feel about it and look how our information people have to nudge the press to remind them that we are still in there. Pentagon briefings would have the press report nothing but the heroics of GI Joe. Now the Russians…"

Sylvan cut him off with a gesture. "It's better if you don't go there again, Tom. Don't get mixed up with them. If they ask you round say you are busy."

He put down the pencil, leant back in his chair, seeming to relax, and put his hands behind his head.

"Anyway, if you aren't busy now, you soon will be. Remember I suggested you needed an upgrade? Well, I've arranged your transfer, at least in principle. Archie won't want to lose you and won't let you go until he is promised a new slave." He pulled a file towards him dismissively. "He'll fill you in on what's involved."

Somewhat chastened, Tom returned to his office. He considered any criticism should have come from his immediate superior, Archie Struthers. He was annoyed at being spied on and that Sylvan hadn't let him finish what he had had to say. Indeed, Tom still thought it rather a good thing to have been invited to call. The Russians played hard-to-get in Washington and generally kept very much to themselves; if he was invited again, he would ask Struthers. He didn't need Ross's permission.

* * *

"I'll be sorry to lose you, Tom," said Archie Struthers, filling his pipe, "you've done well during your year in this office, but there we go. Greater things, eh? Right, now this is the job. You are to go over to the Chancery to help Meredith Hobson, the Economics Minister. London say they have no one to spare at the moment. You've got a degree in economics. Cap fits. Used to be an Oxford Don, Hobson, now a Treasury wallah; expect you've met him? Poor chap, he has all these post-war plans dumped on his plate, including the solvency of our own dear country. He tells me, by the way, that we are already broke three times over. Encouraging, what?"

Struthers' pipe was proving difficult to light and he broke off until he had it drawing to his satisfaction. "But there's more to it. As you know, a lot of us are involved in this atomic business. I've kept you out of it so far, but Hobson is in charge of negotiations over long-term development; so as well as learning something about the science you will be deep into the politics of the bloody thing. Oh, and by the way – where did I… ah, here we are," and he passed Tom a copy of the last Admiralty signal on the matter: "Officer to retain use of his rank," it concluded.

"Meaning?"

"What it says, I suppose. You can still wear your uniform with the wavy stripes when it suits, and I assume you are still subject to naval discipline; King's Regulations and Admiralty Instructions and all that. Well, good luck."

Tom's degree in economics certainly helped, though he found himself grappling with facts and theories way beyond the old textbooks. Of much greater importance was what he learnt about 'this atomic business', not to mention finding himself *deep into the politics of the bloody thing*, just as Archie Struthers had predicted.

He learned about the fission process and then about the bomb. The UK had pooled all its resources with those of the US and Canada, and British scientists were helping develop the monstrous thing in secret places in the Western deserts. Like Hobson, Tom had to have some knowledge of the technical developments in order to carry out his commission. Britain had impressive scientific capability but was seen by some as a wild card in the inevitable struggle for nuclear supremacy. Even as they were still battling Nazi Germany together, in Washington the transatlantic relationship was becoming darkened by shadows of mistrust.

In a high-level committee, the UK met with US and Canadian opposites to ease problems and review progress. And Sylvan Ross was the British secretary.

"It's a relief to find you here, Sylvan," said Tom after the first of these meetings. "Not really surprised, of course," he added, laughing. "I know you have a hand in just about everything around here."

"Nonsense, dear boy; I know nothing about it all. But a good secretary does not need to know about the subject in hand. The art for which Whitehall is famous is pen-pushing and using the King's English correctly. All I have to do is to write up the minutes; the sort of minutes that make Permanent Secretaries purr! But why the relief?"

Tom was silent for a moment as he tried to find the words. "It's lonely. This job, I mean. It's the secrecy that does it. I sort of have to lock up everything I learn and throw away the key. But sometimes I feel I need to talk to someone."

"Well," said Sylvan, "I really am an ignoramus in these matters, but since we are on the same team, I guess you can let your hair down with me from time to time."

Chapter Five

It was the custom at the Georgetown house for the first one up to make the coffee and turn on the radio. On the sixth of June, 1944, it had been Tom. He stood listening open-mouthed for a few minutes then yelled from the kitchen, "Miles! Miles, get in here! Listen to this!"

Together they stood in their pyjamas, the water in the saucepan boiling over on the stove, while the invasion of Normandy was announced. Miles was the first to come to: he lunged for the pan and saved it just before it boiled dry.

"You bugger, Davis! You knew about that, didn't you? All this secret stuff you're mixed up with!"

"Good God, no, absolutely no idea. What about you?"

"No, honestly. Scout's honour!" and he grinned, making the Scout salute.

"There must have been people in the Embassy working on the Washington end night and day but I haven't heard a whisper. Quite something to keep secret."

"*Night and day,*" yowled Miles, "*Night and day, you are the one, only you beneath the moon…*"

"Shut up for heaven's sake, the neighbours will think you're being murdered!"

"We're in!" yelled Miles, waving the saucepan! "We're in! Watch out, *mein Führer*, here we come!"

Like Tom, Miles Hansen had been on active service earlier in the war, flying in the Battle of Britain. His grandparents still lived in

Norway. He had survived a horrendous plane crash, which had put paid to his career as a flyer. After the coffee was made they calmed down and sat in silence, both visualising the approach to those beaches, the dread of air attack on cargoes of khaki-clad soldiers, the barrage of fire as they waded ashore. Tom tried to imagine the days of build-up, the troop and truck movements through the wooded lanes of Hampshire and Sussex he had loved as a boy when he stayed with his grandmother near Portsmouth. He wondered if Miles wished he could have been there, but he didn't ask. And he wondered the same about himself, but couldn't answer.

Throughout that day each news flash was seized on. Later in the afternoon word was passed that everyone was to go to the Residence, where a staff officer 'put everyone in the picture' to the point of assuring them that everything had 'gone remarkably well' so far. The ambassador said a few words, and all were invited to partake of a rather meagre offering considering the circumstances: a glass of sherry or tomato juice. There was little encouragement to linger. As they left, Sylvan joined Tom, and said, "Thank Heavens it did!"

"Did what?"

"Go remarkably well."

Wondering if Sylvan might have been one of those involved at the Washington end, and hoping in that case for some inside information, Tom asked, "Did you think it might not?"

"Not at all. I just can't help thinking what it would have meant for us if it hadn't."

"Christ, utter disaster! I can't imagine we could ever mount the same effort again."

Sylvan waved an airy hand. "Oh Lord, I've no idea of the *military* implications. I just mean, think of the fuss if the Germans had been tipped off! Think of the witch-hunts! Every Department of State, every embassy would have been ransacked for the traitor. It was that sort of little administrative problem I had in mind. You service chaps haven't a *clue* to the problems we administrators face!"

Tom wasn't entirely sure if Sylvan was being serious or cynical.

It was sometimes hard to tell. Everyone knew there were German agents in Washington. There were embassies of countries not involved in the war at all, whose diplomats were nearer to the fascist and Nazi doctrines than to the way of the democracies. All the staff had been put on their guard against 'maggots at the core of the Corps Diplomatique' as Boots put it.

As they walked back to the office together, Sylvan said, "You'd think, from that briefing, that Britain again stands alone, this time on the edge of victory. But it's an American show, of course: they're in the saddle now."

His patriotism hurt, Tom retorted, "That may be so, but honestly, you'd think from the news flashes we've had all day on the radio that the Yanks are in there all on their own! But we were an essential part of this operation. We all love the Americans, but really, sometimes…"

"Come round to supper tonight, we can talk a bit more."

After supper they stayed for a while on the deck, a wooden terrace built out over the garden from the house and comfortably furnished with a rocker and cane chairs. Mauve sunset light filtered through the dark, looming trees; fireflies danced and crickets kept up their endless busy noise.

Eventually Sylvan said, "Let's go in. We need another bottle."

Once he had refilled their glasses, he said, "Tom, you must try and understand, it's not just us that the Yanks will trample on, it's the whole world! With their trusts, combines and international companies, now backed by unmatched military power, they can take over everything. Let me tell you, I fear the Americans more than I fear the Russians." He picked up his glass, twisted it in his hands, set it down. "God," he said with shocking vehemence, "I hate America!"

Startled, Tom countered, "But, why? The Americans…"

"No, not all Americans, of course not, but the corruption of the American ideal by capitalism, the ultimate symbol of greed." He picked up the glass again and drank. "The USA will come out of this war unchallengeable, wealthier than when it came in, able to buy up the world, and if anyone doesn't like it, there is the atom bomb. Only one country can stand up to America: the Soviet Union. And only one philosophy can stand up to unbridled capitalism: communism."

"But that would mean that Uncle Joe Stalin would have to match the US nuclear arsenal: bomb for bomb. Now that *would* be a terrifying prospect."

"Not really. All the options are pretty grim, but the best hope may be a balance of power; of terror, if you like, so that neither side dare use the bloody thing!"

"So what about this United Nations project we are going to launch? And I know that President Roosevelt has authorised a plan to hand over the whole nuclear setup to an international agency. That's a brilliant, selfless and imaginative bit of thinking. And it makes a lot more sense than your gruesome scenario."

"Oh, yes, sense to the *Americans*, yes: for who but the *Americans* will have the plant, the technology and the boffins to run it? In one move they get to control the world!"

"Steady on," Tom said. "That depends on the structure of the agency; as you know we are working on it right now. We, the French, and in due course the Russians – and just about everybody – will be protected by built-in safeguards."

Sylvan all but spat. "You make me laugh. If the Russians join this United Nations thing at all, they will fight your atomic agency plan to the death. They want their own nuclear industry and they want the bomb. They are well on their way, and a front – a flimsy front of international bureaucrats won't stop them!"

"What about us? The UK? Are you telling me that our involvement is just a waste of time?"

"Oh, come on. Look at Hobson: what's his job? Come on, what's his job? I'll tell you! It's this: to make damn sure we get our own bomb! When it comes to so-called 'international control' we will be in the same boat with the Russians, determined to do our own developments, hell-bent on preventing an American monopoly."

Tom was well aware of this, but there were powerful voices at home and around the world calling for international control of this new and unpredictable force, so there was hope that sense would prevail.

"Fortunately," Sylvan went on, "British foreign policy is constant in one respect: it requires that you never mean what you say. Our Ministers will say 'Hurrah for international control!' while quietly working to undermine it. So much smoother than the policy of the poor old Russians, which is to block every proposal by just saying '*Nyet!*' over and over again."

In the pause that followed Tom mentally reviewed the discussions he had had recently, with the Americans, yes, but also the French, the Dutch and other 'exiled' Europeans with missions in Washington, and even with the Chinese,: Chang Kai Shek's people.

"You mean I'm just a part of this front? A fall-guy?"

"You said it. I didn't."

Another pause. Then:

"Tom, American-style capitalism doesn't have to be the answer. But nor does Russian-style communism. Think of our past. England has a long and proud history of the working man telling truth to power: from the peasants' revolt, through the Levellers and Diggers in the seventeenth century, the Chartists, right through to the Labour party. It's our own version of communism, and a better one. We should build on their struggles and cut out all the deadwood – the Clivedens, the big money men and their international deals – and the working class would come to its fulfilment. But it would need a revolution."

"So where would you and I end up come the revolution, with our well-known 'solid working class' backgrounds?"

"A good question. Probably in front of a firing squad. I've got a friend in England, Guy, who says…" Sylvan's voice trailed off.

"What? What does Guy say?"

"Oh, sorry, dear boy, can't remember… not relevant, anyway."

He stretched and laughed. "Got a bit carried away. Sorry. But it's good to be able to talk about these things. Here's a resumé." He frowned and drained his glass. "Mr Ross observed that keeping the ship afloat, however rotten it might be, was the prior requirement for all, but for some was the additional responsibility for designing a safer ship and a sure haven for it. There were difficulties here; for, as Mr T.S. Eliot had noted in another context, 'Between the idea and the reality, Between the motion and the act, Falls the Shadow.' Ah well. Thanks for indulging me. Are you off? Goodnight, then, see you in the morning."

Tom found it hard to sleep that night. Was the bomb the huge looming shadow of *The Waste Land*, of *The Hollow Men*? What *would* follow the eventual end of the war? Crushing retribution, economic bankruptcy, unemployment for the returning heroes – all as 'last time'? Why should anyone think otherwise?

And over it all, the Shadow.

Now that the war had entered its final phase, the tempo of the office sped up and Tom had his work cut out to keep pace. Meredith Hobson had a host of problems in his charge, and Tom became his trusted adjutant, with particular responsibility for 'this atomic business'. Less than a year after he had joined Hobson's team, on the twelfth of April, 1945, to the shock and grief of the nation, President Franklin D. Roosevelt died. Along with thousands, Tom stood hatless in the National Mall as the gun carriage draped in the Stars and Stripes passed by. He felt it as an almost personal blow to his idealism. But then a month later came VE Day, Victory in Europe, and finally the end of the long war seemed to be in sight. In the first week of August, the light at the end of a six-year long tunnel arrived with a blinding atomic flash over the Japanese city of Hiroshima.

On September 2, General George MacArthur, Supreme Commander of the US Pacific Fleet, formally accepted Japan's surrender on board the *USS Missouri* in Tokyo Bay.

As the challenges of peace replaced the challenges of war and relationships between erstwhile allies continued to cool, there had been plenty to keep the embassy staff occupied that autumn and winter and into the spring of 1946.

In October, fifty-one countries met in San Francisco and signed the Charter that created the United Nations. Such an entity had long been a dream of President Roosevelt: an international organization committed to maintaining international peace and security, developing friendly relations among nations and promoting social progress, better living standards and human rights. Indeed, the name itself had been dreamt up by Roosevelt. Regular visits to New York to advise the British delegation to the fledging UN became part of Tom's job. How sad, though, he reflected, as the northbound train rattled towards New York, that FDR had not lived to see his dream come to fruition.

Chapter Six

Tom woke with a start. He was still sitting on the bench in the Mall, but the sun was lower in the sky and the crowds had dispersed. He stood, stretched and made his way back to the car.

The Georgetown house, when he got home, was empty. Miles had not returned from a tryst with his girlfriend, one of the secretaries from the typing pool. Tom poured himself a stiff bourbon and settled on the verandah. He couldn't get over some things that had been niggling him all day. From what the doctor had told him, Marsden must have died on Saturday night, maybe at ten or eleven o'clock. Why, if he had been intending to shoot himself, had he bothered to change into his pyjamas and make a cup of tea? And that note on the desk – the handwriting was much more careful than might have been expected from someone in an extremely agitated state of mind. In his mind's-eye Tom saw the piece of paper, blood soaking through the words: *This has to end. I can't go on t*

Suddenly a light switched in his head – it wasn't a tick at the end, as it had seemed at first glance, but the letter 't'! The sentence was incomplete. Marsden had been writing something when he either stopped, or was interrupted. He remembered what Sir John had told him about Marsden being a Russian agent; had it really been a suicide note… or a confession? *I can't go on telling lies*, perhaps? *I can't go on taking…*

There was more to this Marsden affair than met the eye. Tom had a sneaking suspicion that he was being used somehow, taken for a ride; not by the police but by his own people. The haste to put it all behind them smacked of a cover-up. And when he'd signed the forms attesting to Marsden's suicide, he had become a part of it.

On arrival at his office the next morning Tom found a note on his desk from Sir John, asking him to arrange Patrick Marsden's funeral.

For God's sake, why me again? he thought with some annoyance. But there was no point arguing; he would just have to finish the job and then, with luck, he could forget the whole wretched episode.

He returned once more to Marsden's apartment, hoping to find a clue to the dead man's religious affiliations, if any. On the bookshelves were a couple of paperback novels and a physics textbook, as well as the bound copy of the Manhattan Report and the Left Book Club titles he had first noticed: they covered pacifism, imperialism, and the prescriptions for social reform to be found in many households in pre-war Britain; ideas that the war had quickened and might yet help re-shape the battered but purged country. But they weren't exactly helpful in the present circumstances. Then he found a Bible, lightly thumbed, with a plate pasted in the frontispiece indicating Patrick Marsden as the recipient – 'for diligent study', from the undersigned, the superintendent of his Wesleyan-Methodist Sunday school.

Tom made enquiries and discovered that there was a Methodist Church in a new development on Connecticut Avenue. To Tom's relief the minister turned out to be sympathetic and helpful. He proposed the service should be at the crematorium rather than at the church and offered to officiate.

"I thought no hymns?" Tom suggested.

"Oh, but my organist, wonderful lady volunteer, she's always glad to play. In fact she'd be quite offended if she wasn't asked! Same for the choir ladies. We will find one of Wesley's hymns everyone will know." He grasped Tom's hand and pumped it warmly. "We're only too pleased to be asked. Let me tell you, son, America can never do enough for England. Not only did she give the world the great John Wesley, she upheld the torch of freedom throughout the recent terrible war almost single-handed."

The service took place the following Monday morning. Quite a sprinkling of embassy staff attended, not only the expected but many others, known and unknown to Tom, for the news of the suicide was now public and there was curiosity as well as sorrow in the eyes turning towards the casket as it was carried in. Of the senior Chancery personnel there was no-one but Marcie McKenna until, almost at the last minute, Sir John slipped in and sat at the back.

When everyone had left, and a few words exchanged with the pastor and his kind friends, someone took Tom's arm. It was Marcie. She was wearing a black, bias-cut dress and simple pearl earrings.

"Drinks, please, darling," she said.

She told him to follow her Packard convertible to the Chevy Chase Club a mile or two back along the road.

"You did that very nicely, Tom," she said, as a waiter took her coat and another hurried up to take their order. "I'm sure you could do with a stiffener. How about a Horse's Neck? Yes? Two, please, Charles, very strong, lots of ice." She excused herself for a moment, "to tart myself up," she said, improbably.

Tom lay back in the deep armchair before the low table at which they had been seated. Through the open windows came sounds of tennis and of an elderly foursome readying themselves for golf. The club was not busy on a mid-week morning. He wondered how long Marcie had been a member, reflecting with some cynicism that one probably needed a handle to get in. Tom had been there before, but only with the richest Americans he knew. The atmosphere was restful and tastefully elegant, and Tom had a delightful sense of guilt as he thought of his empty desk — a bit like bunking off school.

Marcie returned. The waiter brought their drinks and Tom raised his brimming, ice-cooled glass. "Cheers! And thank you for this. I've hardly earned it."

Marcie lit a cigarette and offered him one. He was close enough to notice her large, grey eyes and dark lashes. Some goddess, he remembered from his school Ancient Greek, some goddess was always being referred to as being grey-eyed. Well, there was something in it. Marcia McKenna had the most amazing eyes.

She interrupted his reflections.

"You have, you know: arranging the cremation and all that, and writing to the poor boy's family. I told John he'd have to find someone else besides me; I simply couldn't have coped. We shipped their Excellencies off to Montana last night. That will be their forty-third state; the ambassador is determined to visit them all before he retires in July. That kept me busy – telephone calls from the Governor, train schedules altered, and what shall poor Gertie wear? Can't you just see it! So yes, I am really very grateful for all your help this week."

Hugely content with the moment, the setting, the company, but not believing that the momentary high could be sustained, and the empty desk nagging at the corner of his enjoyment – this was, after all, a Monday, not some dreamy weekend – Tom set down his empty glass.

"Well, I suppose I'd better be going; but thanks again. It's been a wonderful break in what I expected to be a depressing day."

"Nonsense. I'm going to treat you to lunch. But first: Charles! Same again, please. Now, let's see what they've got on the menu today."

She led the way to the plant-filled conservatory where a buffet was laid out with platters of cold meats and a huge variety of salads and dressings. Most exotic of all, to Tom's eyes, were the ice-packed bowls filled with sliced avocados piled with shrimp and crabmeat.

As he devoured a large plateful and she picked at a small one she volunteered, "I'm only a member of this club because of my father, you know. He was Minister here, in the thirties. Everyone here loved him very much and he was made an honorary member, and all the family too. But it was a bit too much for him, poor man; he became a dipso."

"Your father, the *Duke*?"

She laughed, pushed away her plate and lit another cigarette.

"Oh, no! *He* died when I was very small. Don't really remember him. But Mother married again, later on, and it was this Foreign Office chap, my stepfather George, whom I called Daddy. He and John were at Eton together," she added.

"You refer, I presume, to the good Sir John Portent, our present Minister here?"

"That's the one. Why I got the job with the ambassador, I suppose."

Although he had never been an especially militant class warrior, all Tom's liberal instincts resurfaced at this reminder of the pernicious old-boy network, something he had had brought home to him when at Oxford. Indeed, it was partly this which had driven his decision to join the Navy as an ordinary seaman instead of applying for the officer's commission for which his university education would have made him eligible. Coming from a grammar school, he had been astonished by the effortless sense of privilege of the public school entrants who dominated the university student body. He had also bumped up against Marxism. Perhaps his early Presbyterian upbringing had helped to keep him grounded, and he had never swung as far to the left as many of his fellow undergraduates; but he maintained a strong dislike of the English upper classes in general, along with an equally strong desire for social justice.

Suddenly annoyed by this beautiful, titled woman with her absurd aristocratic lineage, her elegant clothes and expensive car, whom the waiters made such a ridiculous fuss over – the ambassador's wife's social secretary for heavens' sake – he more or less told her as much.

She was silent for a while, then she said, "You sound just like Sylvan when he gets started."

"I do?"

"You do. Down with the rich, fair shares for all. Sylvan believes there's a possibility of a new and better world being born out of the ashes of the old, even if we do all end swinging on the lamp posts."

"French revolution, then? Aristocrats to the lanterns?"

"Not to mention the guillotine. Did you know that French aristocratic women wore red ribbons tied round their necks?"

"Why? Wouldn't that be asking for trouble?" He was visualising a narrow, blood-red ribbon around Marcie's white throat.

"I don't know why. But I'm very poorly educated, you'll find. Unlike you and Sylvan. Oxford, wasn't it?"

"Yes. How do you know?"

"You'd be surprised what I know. The thing about Sylvan is he has a vision. But…" she paused, as if reluctant to continue, then appeared to come to a decision. "Sometimes I'm afraid for him. He is so impatient and he can't afford to be. He should just work to get to the top: Foreign Office first, he could do it easily, then he could go into politics. As I expect you've found out, Sylvan has the knack of charming everyone he meets. He could speak out, act, change the world…" Her smile returned. "Well, Britain, anyway, and that would be a good start."

Tom began to warm to her again. He was growing interested in his companion. Her evident sympathy for Sylvan and her choosing Tom as her confidant dispelled his sudden surge of progressive self-righteousness. He tapped tentatively on her well-armoured exterior with a question of his own.

"What do *you* believe in, Marcie?

"Me?" She gave a short laugh. "I believed in the war. I hate the Nazis. My cousin fell for some beastly Nazi baron; he was high up in the SS. God knows what happened. We think she shot herself in the end."

She stopped and looked out of the window.

He was quite shocked. He hadn't intended such a level of intimate revelation. After a moment she turned back to face him and said, "Then, yes, I believe in people. I believe in people who believe in something, something good and commit themselves to achieving it. Like Sylvan."

Bloody Sylvan again, thought Tom. The funeral had revived his earlier unease about the aftermath of Marsden's death and his unwilling part in it. Well, maybe Marcie might have some answers. "Marcie, do you believe that Patrick Marsden committed suicide? You're friends with Sylvan, did he say anything to you about it?"

She looked at him for so long he began to feel he had overstepped the mark and killed off any blossoming friendship. "I'm sorry," he attempted, "none of my business. Anyway, I should be getting back to the office…"

And then to his immense relief she smiled.

"It's already three in the afternoon. You can write today off. You couldn't do any work, anyway, the state you're in, darling. I'll order coffee. Oh, and while I'm thinking of it, do you know Lewis Grearson?"

"The columnist from the *Washington Mail*?"

"Yes, that's him. I've been invited to a party at his house on Saturday and don't have an escort. How about it?"

An entrée to the circle of the famous and controversial journalist was very tempting. Also he was becoming more and more intrigued by Marcie.

"I'd be honoured."

"Excellent. I'll pick you up around half six."

Chapter Seven

Marcie drove a big green Packard drop-head, which was open to the pleasant spring evening when she picked Tom up. She was a confident driver and it wasn't long before they arrived at a bluff overlooking the Potomac, where she turned onto a rough path and parked.

"Lewis lives just down there," she pointed. "We're a bit early. Tell you what, I'll put you in the picture about Lew and his pals while you admire the view."

Tom was already admiring it. Only a tram ride from the city centre, but another world. Below was a cataract where the river foamed over its rocky bed; the steep bank opposite, above the dark shadow of the gorge, was bright with the snowy white blooms of flowering dogwood.

"Lewis likes what he calls 'intellectuals'," said Marcie. "All you need in America is a university degree and lo and behold, you're an intellectual!"

"Does he consider you to be an intellectual?"

"Good Lord, no! Never went to a university myself. You, however, will go down in a big way. Of course you know that Lew Grearson is probably the most influential journalist in the country," she continued, "but be warned: you are about to enter the snake-pit, so I suggest you keep your thoughts to yourself. Lew *is* a liberal and he hates these witch-hunters as much as you or I do, but he is something of a witch-hunter himself. Can't help it – it's patholog-ical – that's why his column is syndicated through every scandal sheet in the USA. And why he is so rich! And he is feared. If he fingers you, you've had it. Mainly he exposes the real baddies, but if he smells scandal anywhere, he and his sleuths are on to it. He keeps a stable of jackals and they don't all share Lew's nicer instincts." She switched the engine back on. "Let's go then, but watch your tongue, sweetie."

Their host, a man in his late forties with a pencil moustache and receding hairline, was on the porch with some of his guests. "Marcie!" he exclaimed, throwing an arm around her shoulders. "Good to see you! You look wonderful as usual. I was afraid you might not come after all this unpleasantness."

"Unpleasantness, Lew?"

"This young fella of yours being killed."

Marcie blinked, as though not fully comprehending.

"Oh! The suicide? It was rather ghastly, I believe. I don't know much about it. I never met the young man."

"But *was* it suicide, Marcie? Was it?"

She just shrugged and said, "Lew, this is Tom Davis, Assistant Naval Attaché."

They shook hands and Tom said, "Thanks for having me."

"Any friend of Marcie's is a friend of mine, Tom. Good to meet you." Grearson leant closer. 'So, Tom, can *you* tell me anything about it?"

"Don't tell him anything, Tom!" cried Marcie in mock alarm, "he's a journalist!" She gave Grearson a friendly pat on the arm and said, "I'm going in to find myself a drink." She turned away with a warning glance at Tom. Seeing a chance of making himself useful to Marcie, Tom explained that it had been his job to see the body, the police and the doctor; and that there had been absolutely no suggestion that this was anything other than suicide.

Someone else was listening, a short, sharp-looking man; one of the jackals, perhaps. Lew Grearson turned to him.

"You heard all that, Carlo? Knocks your story out of the ballpark, eh? Tell it to this man. I'd better go inside to see that everybody's happy." He followed Marcie inside.

"So, what's your story, Mr, er… Carlo?"

Carlo shifted eagerly on his feet.

"I work for Lew: stringer, know what I mean? Collect material for the column. But for the FBI, too. They give me assignments. A buddy of mine there told me that J. Edgar Hoover himself is convinced that the Russians have a man in your embassy."

Careful, thought Tom. Putting on a look of injured dignity he exclaimed, "Ridiculous!"

"My reaction exactly, sir. But then this" – he paused for a second – "suicide last weekend; the FBI are said to believe he was a Russian agent."

"So are you suggesting the Russians killed him, before he could be exposed?"

"Why!" exclaimed Carlo brightly, "that's a possibility! I was just following the lead in the FBI story."

"Which was?"

"That the Brits killed him, before he could be made to sing and expose the big shot behind him."

To give himself time to think, Tom fished out a cigarette and lit it. His heart was beginning to race. He drew heavily on the cigarette.

"Seems to me there are a couple of flaws here. All this is hearsay, you said so yourself. Not surprising Lew was cool about the whole thing: the secret of his success is that no one can challenge the so-called evidence set out in his columns. Oh, sorry." He offered his cigarette case to Carlo. "Apologies. And second; the Brits – the embassy, that is – couldn't have thought that Marsden was working for the Russkis, or they would have been on to him one hell of a lot sooner."

He stamped out the remains of his cigarette and made to go inside.

"Point taken, sir. Anyway, Lew, you know, is real soft on you Limeys and I know when he don't want to follow up a story that might not reflect well on you guys." He grinned, in quite a jackal-like way, Tom thought uneasily. "But it will stay on file. We've lots of unfinished symphonies at the back of the store. You never know, years later, maybe they're dusted off and the coda can be written. Nice meeting with you."

Disagreeing privately with the sentiment, Tom went inside, where he found a table set out with drinks. He helped himself, then looked around for Marcie. He couldn't see her, but then spotted Sylvan weaving his way slightly unsteadily through the crowd and waved.

"Lew always throws a great party, *great* party," enthused Sylvan as he joined the younger man. He thrust his empty glass into Tom's hand. "'Scuse me, got to go and turn the horse around. Rather a lot to drink, don't you know. *Great* party!"

Abandoned, Tom wandered through an open door towards the sound of conversation.

Seated in a capacious leather chair beside a big fireplace was an elderly, grey-haired man wearing glasses. Not only did he look like an intellectual, Tom happened to know he *was* an intellectual: the Oxford professor and world-renowned philosopher, Ezra Bern. Standing and seated around him were half-a-dozen or so eager listeners. For a second Tom was back at a seminar in Oxford. A tall, thin man sporting a bow-tie moved to the fireplace to knock the ashes from his pipe.

"So, Ezra, to put it in a nutshell, you are saying that freedom is simple to measure — it lies in the absence of restraint; that there is no ideal government that will guarantee freedom?"

Marcie was suddenly at Tom's shoulder.

"That's Jerry Khon," she whispered, "from the Justice Department."

"So put, my dear Khon," Ezra responded in his thin, high voice, "it sounds a small shell and a very small nut!" He smiled beatifically. "But allow me to sum up." He put his fingers together under his chin, and Tom prepared for the lecture.

"If, as the scientific materialists argue, human-kind is — are, that is — just another lot of machinery, responsive only to the environment and external stimuli, what is left of choice? Judgement? Concepts of right and wrong? Dulled by the opiates of materialism we become fatalists, and worse, prey to the great manipulators, the ideologies of fascism and communism, strange sects and cults. 'Freedom for the Masses' we are conditioned to cry out, and suchlike slogans, but we've lost the hallmark of our humanity: freedom to choose and judge for ourselves." He coughed delicately and re-crossed his knees. "Happily for you in thrice-blessed America…"

There was a disturbance behind them. It was Sylvan Ross, blind drunk. He stumbled as he missed the short steps down into the room from the main hallway and his glass fell to the floor. Everyone was staring at him. Marcie froze.

"Still churning out that crap, are you Ezra?" Sylvan griped. "You're right on one point though; what was it you were going to say about the great Manipulator? Blessed America! Bugger America! Freedom? Freedom to exploit the world!"

Marcie recovered, moved swiftly to turn Sylvan around and propel him back up into the hall. Lewis broke the stunned silence.

"I never cease to wonder at the freedom of the British public servant to speak his own mind while unflagging in his duties. Refreshing, isn't it, after some of the zombies we meet in this swollen bureaucracy of ours. Now, everybody, an interval; there's food next door."

Tom's apologies were accepted coolly and without protest, and he hurried outside to find Marcie bundling Sylvan into her Packard.

"Here's the keys to Sylvan's car, Tom. Would you drive it back to his house, please? I'll see you there."

Some party, thought Tom bitterly as he followed the Packard to Tilden Street. He got out and offered to help Marcie get Sylvan inside, but she told him to wait in her car. *She's done this before*, he realised. Bloody *Sylvan*.

When she finally emerged, she came and sat in the driver's seat, staring ahead, not looking at Tom.

"Is he OK?" he asked after a while.

She turned to him and in the street-lights he could see she was clearly upset.

"Yes, he's OK. He'll sober up and forget it happened." She made an effort to pull herself together. "Wretched man – made us miss supper! I'm starving. What say we go and find an all-American diner and grab a hamburger?"

"What say we do," he responded with a grin of relief.

Chapter Eight

The diner was long and narrow, resembling the old-fashioned railway carriages that had been converted into the original diners in the previous century. Behind a counter that stretched the length of the small building a cook flipped meat patties and hot-dogs on a large grill, while another man tended the noisy soda machine. A dozen mono-pedal stools formed a row like flat-topped mushrooms in front of the counter, where a quartet of chattering youngsters, whom Tom took for college students, sat enjoying milkshakes while waiting for their hamburgers. On the street side were six small booths with rather hard-looking bench seats. The first of these was occupied by a young couple who were clearly oblivious to everything but each other; the others were empty.

Marcie led the way to the furthest booth, where a middle-aged waitress with a faded smile and dark circles under her eyes came to take their order.

"Two cups of coffee, please, and hamburgers for both of us, no pickle with mine, ketchup on the side, one order of French fries – that's for you, Tom, growing lad. I have to watch my waistline."

Impressed by his companion's take-charge attitude and her arcane knowledge of American not-so-fine dining, Tom just nodded. Marcie waited until the waitress had brought the meal before saying, "I suggested we come here, not because I am enamoured of the cuisine, but because it's an excellent place to talk without anyone listening."

Hopeful for a few seconds that she might be about to declare herself enamoured of *him*, Tom resigned himself to the more likely probability that, in view of the previous fiasco, she was preparing to talk about Sylvan's role in the fate of Patrick Marsden.

"You remember back in February, when the *Mail* published Lew Grearson's exposé of a Soviet spy ring in Canada?"

"Of course," he said. "Everyone accused him of making it up to sell more papers, until the Canadian Prime Minister himself confirmed the story. There was the most almighty flap that perhaps there were Russian spies lurking in our own embassy."

"Well, I know John Portent has already told you… Patrick Marsden has been passing information to them."

Carlo's words and weasel face came back to him: *Hoover is convinced that the Russians have a man in your embassy… the Brits killed him before he could sing and expose the big shot behind him.*

"Marcie, you don't think that *our* team, that is… Marsden. They wouldn't have killed him? It's not possible, is it?"

"No, I wouldn't suggest that at all; it could have been the Russians or even the Americans. It's a murky world, espionage."

"But it wasn't suicide?"

"No. Look, Tom". She seemed surprisingly nervous, as she glanced around and whispered, "There's something Sylvan and I have agreed to tell you."

"Sorry, what did you say?"

"I said, I have something to tell you. Are you *deaf?*"

"As a matter of fact I am a bit, but only in my right ear."

Marcie looked horrified.

"Oh, good Lord, what a *faux pas* – I'm *so* sorry…"

"That's all right, you weren't to know. I sometimes have to strain a bit to hear when people talk very quietly, but it's not really a problem for me. I was born like this so I don't know what so-called 'normal' hearing is supposed to be like. It was a problem for the Navy, though, that's why they withdrew me from active service when I got my promotion. Let's try again… what were you saying?"

Marcie had regained her normal poise.

"Sylvan and I, we meet a lot of people – in our positions we can glean useful information for HMG. We… well, we both work for MI6."

Tom stared at her, hamburger halfway to his mouth. Eventually he said in a cautious whisper, "MI6?"

"Oh Tom, you know who I mean, for God's sake. Foreign intelligence service. To put it bluntly, MI6 is *our* spies, MI5 catches *theirs*."

"Yes, of course I know what you mean, Marcie. It's just – it's just – well, I'm surprised."

Come to think of it, he reflected, *I'm not. Not about Sylvan at least. I've always felt he's been holding something back. Some secret. But Marcie? Well, her job does give her perfect cover; she mingles freely with Washington's elite, and nobody's likely to suspect Lady Gertrude's social secretary of being in British intelligence.*

Tom glanced around cautiously but Marcie was right: nobody was interested in them and the booth was eavesdropper-proof. *Oh God*, he thought, *I'm behaving as if I were in a film. But that's what it feels like.* He tried to get a grip on the situation; to crush the renewal of the feeling that he had experienced in the aftermath of Marsden's death: that he was somehow being made use of.

"Marcie, why are you telling me this?"

"Because Sylvan wants your help in a secret operation he is hoping to get off the ground pretty soon."

"*My* help?" He was uncertain whether to be flattered or alarmed.

"Your sea-faring experience."

"My sea-faring experience?"

Some of her old sharpness returned.

"Oh, Tom, do stop repeating everything I say!"

"Sorry. It's just that… it all sounds so… cloak and dagger." He pulled himself together. "An operation? What does that mean?"

"I can't tell you much, the whole thing is just starting to take shape. It's a very small team. Sylvan wants you on it, but I thought I'd make my own recce first." She leant across and touched his hand. Fire ran through his fingers, though whether it was her touch or the childish, dangerous thrill of being chosen for a 'secret operation', he couldn't tell.

"And by the way, you've been thoroughly vetted. We even know you have read your Marx." She smiled again. "You'll do, Tom."

Caution took over. "Marcie, I don't know…"

She leant closer still and whispered, "Yes, you do. You want to change things some day, and in the right direction. You're a bit like him."

"Tell me a bit more, for God's sake."

"No. I can't. That's enough for now. Sylvan will fill you in when necessary."

"But…"

"Are we going to eat this or not?"

They drove back to Tom's apartment in silence, then sat in the car for a while. Then Marcie leant over and kissed him on the cheek. When he moved to put his arm around her she turned away and said, "Good night, Tom. Sleep well."

But he didn't. The initial excitement had worn off, and a certain disappointment had taken its place; in spite of Marcie's farewell kiss, it seemed she had only wanted his company in order to help Sylvan.

Then there was Marsden. He had not taken his own life; Tom was convinced of this. Yet it was Tom's signature that had certified his suicide at that strange, hurried inquest at the embassy – a cover-up if ever there was one. Cover-up for whom? Although the Americans were promoting international control, Tom had seen from the inside something of Britain's fight to develop an independent nuclear deterrent. The stakes were high. The British had need of ruthlessness too; so there had to be some hard men behind the bland front put up by the embassy staff. The meeting with Sir John Portent and Lord Zender had shown that these amiable establishment figures could be tough and swift to act when they had to be. Boots, the Security Officer, also, with his earlier wartime career in the Military Police. And Sylvan Ross – Marcie had said he was an agent of MI6 – a spy; could he be ruthless too?

Tom kept telling himself that he did not have to accept the FBI's theory that the British had killed the pathetic Marsden; *not a principal, just a cog in the machine,* Sir John had labelled him. It must have been Russian or American agents, as Marcie had suggested. They did that sort of thing. Most likely the Russians. Supposing that he was their agent and that American sleuths were on to him, they might well have decided to eliminate him. This seemed as good an explanation as any.

But Marcie's revelation about Sylvan and MI6 changed things. What was Sylvan's involvement in Patrick Marsden's death? It was he, after all, who had arranged for Tom to be sent to Marsden's flat that morning, to sign the documents that concealed what he now believed to be the truth. Tom dreaded what would happen when they next met. Worse, perhaps nothing would be said. He was being drawn into a conspiracy of silence. It had been the same with the bomb, talking about it to no-one but Sylvan.

He finally slept, but only after deciding that he would definitely not become involved in whatever mad escapade was being planned.

Chapter Nine

The phone buzzed. "Tom! Roger here. Fancy a spot of sailing this weekend? Weather forecast looks good."

Roger Devereux had joined the Embassy the previous May, shortly after VE-Day. He was about Tom's age, but his background could not have been more different. His father was English and was a scion of one of England's oldest families; but his mother was American. He had spent several of his earlier years in the States and he had numerous friends and relatives around the country. This heritage had given him his easy manner and assured self-confidence – surely the basis of his promise as a career diplomat – yet in spite of this, as well as the fact that he had a private fortune of his own, he was a delightful companion and, Tom's egalitarian principles notwithstanding, the two of them got on surprisingly well. Roger had also hit it off with Sylvan, and they were often to be seen lunching together in the canteen. During the war, Roger had served in some liaison capacity between the British and American High Commands, but he almost never mentioned his experiences. Tall and athletic, he kept himself fit, and was a keen outdoors-man. He owned a small dinghy at a private marina on Chesapeake Bay, and finding that Tom shared his enthusiasm for sailing, the two of them had on several occasions gone out on the water together last summer.

"My friend Hank – remember him? – has invited both of us to go out with him on his schooner, the *Dulcibelle Adams*. He's got a shack where we can spend the night."

Tom decided that a spot of sailing was just the antidote he needed against the unsettling happenings of the past couple of weeks.

"Yes, that would be excellent. I'm free for the whole weekend."

"Splendid. I'll pick you up Saturday morning at eight – catch the tide. Bring a sleeping bag. By supreme serendipity I just happen to have a bottle of fine single malt that I'll bring; the Pater sent it over in the diplomatic bag that arrived yesterday."

"Roger, Roger."

They both loved this joke.

On Saturday Roger arrived in the MG TA sports car he had imported from Britain before the war. Roger was also a vintage car buff, and, when he wasn't polishing the MG's British Racing Green paintwork and her chrome fittings to a dazzling brightness, liked nothing better than to join the chauffeur under the bonnet of the ambassadorial Rolls, which was just old enough to be interesting. In Tom's opinion Roger drove too fast, but at least he drove well.

The *Dulcibelle Adams* lay at anchor about fifty feet offshore. She was one of the last of the classic Chesapeake Bay schooners, and Tom was immediately enchanted by her graceful lines and her fine sheer, her overhanging counter. Somehow, she had survived into this century, perhaps because of the gentle climate and the loving attention of generations of owners whose source of income was the business of the bay.

Hank was waiting for them on the jetty. Half Portuguese, half Cherokee, and a hundred per cent American, he looked, Tom decided, every inch the pirate with his swarthy skin, black eyes and long hair worn in a plait. His family owned a number of trawlers and an acclaimed seafood restaurant in Annapolis where, the year before, he had treated them both to a memorable meal to celebrate the surrender of Japan.

They shook hands, climbed down the jetty steps and settled themselves in the dory. Hank started the outboard and in a couple of minutes they were alongside the schooner and climbing aboard.

"Welcome on board the *Dulcibelle Adams*, gentlemen," said Hank with a big grin, "and let me relieve you of that bottle of excellent

Scotch you're carryin'." He waved an expansive hand. "She's quite a bit smaller than most of these old boats. But in fair weather two men can handle her under sail with no difficulty, and with three it's a piece of cake. And I can manage her by myself with just the engine."

Tom looked around with pleasure, taking in the well-raked masts, the bowsprit, the tidily coiled ropes. Most of the timber had taken on its own colouring, a soft silver grey, stained here and there with rust from bolts and ironwork. The deck planks lay wide open, uncaulked, and shrunk from each other.

"She needs a good tidy-up, poor old lady," said Hank. "I'll get her spruced up again this summer."

They followed Hank down the hatch, to stow their belongings in the compact, square cabin. It was painted white, and here the varnished beams on the deck-head, the wainscoting around the single bunk and built-in settees, and on the fiddled mahogany table, shone freshly, as did the brass lamp swinging in its gimbals. When the little iron stove was going, it would be cosy. There was just enough headroom for Tom, at a shade under six feet, to stand upright.

When they were well clear of the dock, Hank got Tom and Roger to haul up the big mainsail and the two foresails. With the tide just turned to the ebb and a light breeze from the north-east filling her sails, the *Dulcibelle* settled into a comfortable broad reach across the wide, glittering waters of the bay, Hank keeping her well clear of the shipping lanes. There were only a few smaller leisure craft out on the water on this fine spring day, and they passed a couple of skipjacks, the shallow-drafted sailing boats that were traditionally used by the local fishermen to dredge for oysters. Although it was still early in the season, it was warm enough that Tom needed only his light windcheater. He revelled in the feel of the wind in his hair, the sun on his face and the movement of the boat; it was indeed just what he needed to blow away the cobwebs of disquiet from his mind.

Although Tom had sailed in the bay last summer in Roger's dinghy, it was only now, as the *Dulcibelle* coasted along, whispering over the water, her great mainsail murmuring to itself and her spars creaking gently, that he fully appreciated the extent of this magnificent stretch of water. From his place at the tiller, Hank grinned at him and said, "Enjoying yourself?"

"Am I just!" He shaded his eyes from the sun with his hand and gazed out at the receding shore. "Hank, do you know how big Chesapeake Bay is? It seems to go on for ever."

"Sure," said Hank with the pride of a local aficionado. "Over two hundred miles north to south as the crow flies; more'n thirty miles wide at its widest point. It's not really a bay, it's the estuary of the Susquehanna River. Largest estuary in the US of A. Bay's sheltered, waters are shallow. Something to do with the glaciers melting, I was told. My ancestors lived here for generations fishing for oysters and eels, bass, crabs. Still make a livelihood out of it today. Want to take over?"

He stood up and relinquished the tiller to Tom, who slid across and grasped the varnished sycamore.

"You'll find she carries a bit of weather helm. Watch the wind; it's gone round some more on the starboard quarter." And he moved quickly and easily forward to adjust the sheets.

There was enough wind for Tom to sense the tiller under his arm nosing up-wind and he gripped it firmly, countering its mildly insistent pressure. The sensuous enjoyment of making this beautiful schooner do as he wanted took over and he forgot everything else except the way ahead and the direction of the wind as it caressed his cheek.

The marshy fringes of the bay were dotted with islets and indented with innumerable coves and inlets frequented by a great variety of waterfowl. Hank anchored in one of these at midday; they sat on deck in the spring sun eating ham rolls and peaches, watching ocean-going ships from Baltimore follow the dredged shipping channel south almost two hundred nautical miles to Hampton Roads and out into the Atlantic Ocean. They spotted herons, pelicans and ospreys and, best of all, a bald eagle. It soared effortlessly high above them until it disappeared into the azure distance. To Tom it somehow symbolised not only America but the vastness of America; the generosity of its ever-changing landscape. As often he thought of Britain by contrast: so small and contained and bounded by the sea.

It was late afternoon when they dropped anchor at the mouth of one of the smaller inlets on the west side of the bay. After stowing the sails, they climbed into the little dory, Hank started up the outboard, and they soon came alongside a rather rickety-looking jetty in front of a low wooden building. The water here was no more than three or four feet deep and quite clear; Tom could see the underwater grass swaying gently in the current and small fish meandering among the fronds. An oystercatcher stalked along a tiny beach just a short distance away, paying the intruders no attention as it probed for crustaceans with its red bill.

What Roger had described as Hank's 'shack' was actually a sturdy and comfortable cabin situated at the end of an unpaved track that led back to the main road. It had a central room with a large fireplace, and two bedrooms equipped with bunk beds. There was a galley kitchen, a shower room, and a chemical toilet out the back. It even had a telephone and electricity, though Hank advised them to keep the lights off if they could when the windows were open.

"The lights just attract the bugs, and there are so many of them, those flyin' critters will get through the screens and drive you crazy. Myself, I just prefer a kerosene lantern."

"A telephone? Out here in the wilderness?" Roger asked sceptically.

Hank was almost apologetic.

"My folks come here sometimes in the summer. Dad's got a weak heart, and I got the phone installed so's Mom can keep in touch. Keeps the old lady happy."

After sunset they built a camp fire in the fire-pit close to the water. Hank had brought local oysters, sweet and succulent, Tom thought he had never tasted anything so delicious. The water was still as glass, the gentle on-shore breeze barely touching its surface;

the only sounds were the croaking of frogs, the rustling of leaves, and the nocturnal chorus of a myriad of insects. A few distant lights showed along the shore of the bay, too far away for their dancing reflections to reach the three men lying contentedly on the grass gazing up at the night sky brimming with stars. Roger sat up and pushed back a lock of the recalcitrant blond hair that had flopped over his tanned forehead. He pulled out his cigarette case and passed it to his companions before lighting one for himself and carefully blowing a perfect smoke ring.

"D'you know, I passed up a chance to see the Red Sox play the Senators at Griffith Stadium to come sailing with you fellows this weekend."

Hank snorted derisively.

"Those Senators are about as useless as their namesakes in Congress. I reckon the Detroit Tigers are gonna take the Pennant this year."

"Not a hope," said Roger, "it'll be the Sox, mark my words."

"Red or White?" asked Tom, trying but failing to emulate Roger's feat with the cigarette, "there's a pair of Sox, remember."

"Boston for sure."

"But you know the trouble with baseball?"

"What?"

"*It's just not cricket!*"

He and Roger banged each other on the shoulders, snorting with laughter. Eventually Roger managed to say, "Hey, Hank, is there any of that Scotch left?"

Hank sat up and turned the bottle upside down, then shook it. "S'all gone," he said sadly. "Pity. Damn fine whisky."

"Susan – Admiral Somerstown's Wren," said Tom, "thinks the Yankees have a good chance this year now they've got DiMaggio back. Susan's the only girl I know who's genuinely keen on baseball."

Although he sometimes suspected she was keener on a certain baseball player than on him.

"Is she the elegant young lady with whom I saw you at the pictures last week with?"

"Good thing there's no whisky left, old son; your words are tripping over themselves." Remembering that Roger didn't seem to have a steady girl-friend, and deciding to be helpful, Tom added, "By the way, d'you know Melanie in the typing pool?"

"The blonde with the magnificent knockers?"

"If you say so, Roger. Miles is going out with one of her friends – she says Melanie has the hots for you. You should ask her out some time."

"Not my type, I'm afraid. Nice girl, but thick as a plank."

Tom chortled. "And nobody likes their Bird's thick!"

There was a pause. Then Roger started laughing uncontrollably. "Thick Bird's! Nice one!" he crowed when he had recovered his breath.

Hank stared at them both, puzzled.

"Birds – girls – Bird's Custard, supposed to be runny," Roger tried to explain.

Seeing that Hank still looked mystified, Tom added, "It's a British thing." He tapped the side of his nose confidentially, then he and Roger collapsed into sobs of laughter.

Hank shook his head. "You two jokers," he said fondly, "you just crazy."

They were all contentedly quiet for a while, then Hank said, "Tom, I know you were in the Navy, but where'd you learn to sail small craft?"

Tom rolled over onto his front.

"My brother and I used to spend part of the school summer holidays with our grandmother in a little village called Bosham, in West Sussex on the edge of Chichester harbour. I loved small boat sailing; always hanging around to crew if anyone needed an extra hand. Richard – my brother – didn't care for sailing – he took flying lessons at Goodwood."

"Newport in the summer with my cousins," said Roger. "Jolly useful having relatives in places like that. Imagine how you might have ended up if your Granny lived in Watford."

"I'll have you know that some of my best friends live in Watford!" retorted Tom, pulling out a clod of grass and throwing it at Roger who yelped and threw it back, then collapsed again, staring at the stars.

"You know what, though, Roger," said Tom," you have a bloody good point."

"Wassat?"

"That how much of what shapes us is just luck, good or bad."

"Yeah," said Hank, "suppose I'd been born in Düsseldorf instead of Des Moines, I'd probably be dead on the Russian Front by now instead of shooting the breeze with you guys." They all considered this, then Hank went on, "I volunteered for the Navy, of course, right after Pearl Harbour, but they wouldn't have me – said my work managing our fishing fleet was too important, a 'reserved occupation' they called it. I don't think that's right. If a guy wants to fight for his country, they should let him. Must be plenty of slackers who could take his place on the home front. I sure know plenty."

"You Yanks," said Roger in the tone of one who has just discovered a great truth, "just fight for your *country*. We Brits fight for *King* and country. Rule Britannia. I mean God save our gracious…"

He hiccupped.

"So, what's the difference?" said Hank. "We're still patriots, just as much as you Limeys."

"Ah, patriotism, the last refuge of a scoundrel."

"Whaddya mean? I'm a true-blue patriot! Whaddya mean a scoundrel?"

"He didn't mean anything, Hank," Tom intervened, "it's just a quotation."

"What ass-hole said it then?"

"No idea. Some scoundrel, probably."

"Your guy Churchill: he was a patriot if I ever saw one. What possessed y'all to get rid of him?"

"Well, I didn't personally get rid of him." Tom thought about it. "I suppose the electorate was weary of six years of blood, toil, tears and sweat. But it was sad for him, so close to the finish line. Talking about quotations," he added, "did you hear what Churchill said in Fulton when he was over here in March? It really hit me hard." He frowned. "How did it go? 'From', from, can't remember, never heard of it, somewhere in the Baltic," he continued, "'to Trieste in the Adriatic, an iron curtain has descended across the continent.'"

Hank said: "That speech must have gone down well with a lot of folks here. There's plenty of anti-communist feeling, whipped up by that son-of-a-bitch J. Edgar Hoover."

"And yet," Tom observed, "socialism ought to be the way to go, ideally." He recalled an evening with Sylvan. "A hundred years ago there were some amazing socialists in Britain. And now we've got the labour party. Social justice, that's what it's all about."

"Right," said Roger. "Some of these socialist ends are fearfully jolly. Chicken in every garage. Car in every pot. Or something. If capitalists were smart, just such would be their pro… pro… pro*claimed* ends. They alone have the means – the capital, the dough – to get there. The poor old Bolshies haven't got the means, so they can't achieve the ends. Anyway, it's all ideological. Jus' like, jus' like the bloody Nazis and look where that ended up."

Tom remembered that when he was growing up, Churchill, then just a back-bencher, had been accused of overstating the threat posed by the Nazis. But of course he had been right then, and he wondered if the old warhorse was being equally prescient now about the Soviets.

"My old dad   he's a clergyman   said something to me when the Spanish civil war was on about the difference between ideology and idealism. I've never forgotten it. He said that ideology is the assertion of a doctrine that has to be served at whatever cost to one's self or to others. But idealism is the search   never ending   for the Ideal: the right, the true and the good."

Roger snored.

Hank laughed. "Hey, you put Roger to sleep!"

"God, sorry to be so boring!"

Hank stood up and nudged the supine body gently with his foot.

"Hey, Roger, wake up! We ain't carryin' you inside."

Chapter Ten

The inevitable moment arrived, however, when on Tuesday Sylvan Ross put his head around the door of Tom's office.

"Tom! Happy coincidence. You are going to New York tomorrow. Well, so am I. We'll go together on the Pennsylvania Railroad. Jean will book us both in at the Barbizon. And, by the way, I've wangled an invitation to come to your show too."

Tom's 'show' was a party on the British aircraft carrier *HMS Ferocious*, then in New York on a goodwill mission. With some recollection of his having been in the Navy and a former Assistant Naval Attaché, he had been asked to represent the ambassador, who was away again, while other senior members of his staff appeared to be otherwise engaged.

They boarded the train at the Union Station and found their seats in the club car where an ebullient Sylvan ordered highballs for them both.

They chatted for a while on harmless topics but Tom's new-found knowledge of his companion's's involvement with the intelligence services weighed him down and he found it hard to respond. After a while Ross fell silent, fishing a paperback out of his pocket. It was noisy in the old coach and silence was mutually acceptable. As they chugged through Baltimore Tom stared moodily out of the window, taking in the distant masts, funnels and cranes of the busy port, its waters sheltered by the Delmarva Peninsula that acted as a buffer between the Atlantic Ocean and Chesapeake Bay. Here ships of both the British and American navies rubbed shoulders with commercial vessels of many nations, although the main American naval base at Norfolk, Virginia, lay many miles to the south, at the mouth of the bay. In his previous position as Assistant Naval Attaché Tom had become quite familiar with the dry docks in both facilities where ships of the Royal Navy came for repairs.

They passed the busy scenes at the Baldwins Locomotive works adjoining the tracks. Amid lines of dead-looking old locos were shining new ones, and the flash from an opened firebox fanned the clouds of steam to puff-balls of orange.

They arrived at Grand Central Terminal, whose vast, soaring, cathedral-like interior well deserved the accompanying adjective, and took a Yellow Cab to the Barbizon. Much used by the embassy people, it was not the smartest place on offer in New York, but with its view over Central Park it set the visitor on New York's wavelength. As, indeed, did the rest of that evening with friends of Sylvan's who owned a penthouse on Fifth Avenue, also overlooking the Park.

The party ended up in the early morning at the Blue Angel supper club, *the* place to be seen in New York. Tom was surprised at how small the place was: the well-dressed (and doubtless well-heeled) patrons sat cheek by jowl at tiny tables and the little stage had room for only a performer, a piano and a handful of musicians. The musicians were all black and there were several non-white faces in the audience. Coming from racially segregated Washington where the only coloured people one encountered were almost always in menial positions, Tom found this extraordinarily liberating and encouraging, and his initial discomfort at finding himself in a venue so obviously catering to the rich was somewhat mollified. The jazz, which until now he had only heard on recordings, was astonishing: seemingly free from restraint it soared and swung, crooned and pealed in joyful celebration. Of what, though, he wondered? What have these people got to celebrate? Perhaps it's just the sheer joy of music itself. Let's hope their time will come.

Turning to his host to express his pleasure, he saw the man was being greeted by a woman who, had it not been for the dim light, he could have sworn was the celebrated singer Billie Holiday. He looked more closely. It *was* Billie Holiday. He pocketed a small match-book with a rococo cherub on the cover as a souvenir of this adventure.

Mingling with the elegant upper-crust New York clientèle were others, more outlandishly dressed and behaved. As their group left the club they brushed past two young men in tight white t-shirts holding hands and he thought he saw one of them wink at him. Perhaps it was just a trick of the light. Still, he hurried after his companions, hoping they hadn't noticed.

Next day Tom and Sylvan went their separate ways to their different contacts. Tom's appointment with the head of the British delegation at the United Nations was not until eleven a.m., so he was able to sleep off the effects of the previous night. They met up in the afternoon and took a cab down to the pier where *HMS Ferocious* was docked.

"How did you like the Blue Angel?" asked Sylvan, as with much honking of the horn the cab threaded its way through the heavy traffic.

"It was wonderful. The music was amazing, but I have to admit, some of the clientele seemed a bit… decadent?"

Sylvan laughed.

"You've obviously lived a sheltered life, dear boy, you need to get out a bit more."

"You're probably right…"

"Hey, you two must be Limeys," the cab driver called out over his shoulder.

"We're *British*," Sylvan corrected him in an exaggerated British accent.

"Yeah, I knew you was Limeys, I can tell by the way youse talk. I was stationed in England during the war: Norfolk, d'ya know it? Real friendly folk in Norr-foke, especially the Norfolk Broads… dames, geddit?"

They laughed politely with the driver as he guffawed at his own humour.

"But, jeez, I dunno how they can drink that warm beer, and the food – would'ya believe they eat frogs an' stuff? I ain't kiddin', I saw it on the menu – 'toad-in-the hole'! Jeez!"

Sylvan rolled his eyes. "You're mistaking us for the French, my good fellow. They're beyond redemption. But no worse, surely, than eating dogs, as they do here in America."

"Whaddya mean? Oh, hot dogs, I guess. No, those ain't *real* dogs, just sausages."

The two passengers winced as the cabbie squeezed his vehicle between a double-parked van and an oncoming bus, almost knocking over a cyclist as he did so. "Yeah, nice country youse got. Pity you've put a commie in charge."

"Prime Minister Attlee?" queried Tom. "He's not a communist, he's a socialist!"

"Socialist, shmocialist. He's still red, ain't he? The reds, they're everywhere you know, and Hoover says most of 'em are homos. The universities are full of 'em. What we need's a test for anyone who gets money from the government, make sure they're loyal to our country."

"Like walking on red-hot coals? Ducking stools?" Sylvan muttered *sotto voce.*

"You can drop us here, driver," said Tom, "the pier's right over there."

They handed over the fare and escaped from the cab as quickly as they could, Tom still chuckling, Sylvan stony-faced.

At the pier head, the aircraft carrier's raking stem seemed to reach out over them and the steady trickle of fellow guests making for the gangway, yet *Ferocious* herself was dwarfed by the eighty thousand tons of the *Queen Mary* in the adjoining berth: her three enormous smoke-stacks gleaming in the late afternoon sunshine. Whenever he came to New York, Tom had always tried to make time to go down to the Hudson River piers to see the great liners. He'd never actually sailed on one, though on convoy duty early in the war he used to watch for hours as some of their smaller sisters ploughed alongside the tankers loaded with petrol and the smaller cargo steamers zigzagging their way home. The 'Greyhounds', the *Queen Elizabeth* and *Queen Mary*, in their uniform of battleship-grey paint and relying on their speed, had survived without recourse to convoy escort.

Abandoning his reminiscing, Tom followed Sylvan on board. Handshakes with a reception committee of senior officers were followed by attachment to one of several parties being conducted around the ship. Apart from some of the New York-based staff, neither Tom nor Sylvan knew any of the other attendees, so feeling he had done his duty, Tom suggested they leave. Sylvan said: "Tom, I want to tell you something. Let's get out on top again."

From the cavernous hangar where the party was taking place they found a lift that took them to the flight deck. They strolled aft along the length of it to the great White Ensign trailing lazily from its staff astern. By now the sun was almost set and the Hudson River ran away from them in streaks of bronze. Across the river, lights were coming up like pinpricks in the black silhouette of the New Jersey shore, black against the red glow of the setting sun. The temperature dropped quickly as night approached and Tom shivered, partly at the sudden chill in the air, but also in anticipation of what Sylvan was going to say.

"Was your ship as big as this, Tom?" asked Sylvan.

It was not the question he had expected, but he patiently explained, as he had certainly done before, that his sea service had been confined to convoy duties on a small and very elderly destroyer. He had come to understand that people don't take in what you say about your world – they are too fully occupied with their own – until or unless they find themselves with some powerful reason to enter it as Sylvan seemed to have at that moment. His eyes ranged over the carrier and the great liner nearby, now aglow with lights and with wisps of smoke rising from her funnels.

"I envy you all the same," he said almost wistfully. He threw out an arm to embrace the Queen Mary. "And with our lovely ships here I am suffused with an intense glow of patriotism."

It was quiet and Tom could hear the rattle of the street-cars far below.

"I never doubted your patriotism, Sylvan."

"I'm glad of it." He took out his cigarette case and offered it to Tom. "I gather Marcie has been putting you in the picture?"

"To some extent, yes."

"And?"

"And what?" said Tom, annoyed. "I have no idea what all this is about and I'm not sure I want to."

"Perhaps you will when you know more. There's this…"

A group of naval officers and their female partners emerged noisily onto the flight deck, chatting and laughing loudly as they attempted to fill their glasses from the bottles of champagne they were carrying.

"Not now," said Sylvan. "I'll fill you in on the train."

They took the late train back to Washington. The coach was almost empty and Sylvan said, "We can talk here. Even at the Barbizon it's not safe."

"Safe from whom?"

"The CIG," whispered Sylvan.

"The what?" asked Tom, who hadn't quite caught the acronym.

"You know, the Central Intelligence Group. The Americans are still trying to figure out how to organize their espionage operations. It was all under the military in the war, but President Truman wanted civilian control, so they set up the National Intelligence Authority and the CIG, and now it's becoming the Central Intelligence Agency."

"Sort of an American MI6," said Tom, remembering what Marcie had told him about Britain's own national security services.

"Something like that. I do business with the CIG, and the CIG don't trust anyone they do business with, so I expect to be bugged. In this game you've got to watch your back all the time. Now, shall I tell you what's up?"

In spite of his late-night decision not to allow himself to be sucked in, Tom was curious to learn more. "All right."

"Then, if you still don't want to come on board you must forget everything you've heard."

Tom almost felt like adding sarcastically, "What, on pain of death?" but he remembered Patrick Marsden's head and just nodded.

Although the carriage was empty and there was a considerable background rattle and clanking of the train, Sylvan lowered his voice. "You know a good deal, of course, about Los Alamos, the atomic weapons centre in New Mexico. Quite a few of our best boffins are working there. One of them is called Viktor Bronski. Heard the name?"

"Of course. I haven't met him personally, but he's a leading theorist in the thermonuclear field. Comes from Budapest originally, I think? Worked with Ernest Rutherford at the Cavendish Labs in Cambridge in the early thirties, then went back to Eastern Europe but became a refugee in some purge or other."

"Spot on. Anyway, a few months ago the FBI suspected a leak of secret information from Los Alamos. Sir John arranged for me to visit the laboratories as the escorting officer when a party of British VIPs were visiting. I met and talked extensively to Bronski on that occasion; entirely openly and above-board while going around the plant, but also very privately, at a sort of guest house outside the laboratory reservation. It's one of the few off-limits resorts where the senior staff can escape from the shop talk. Also, I expect they must find their own close-knit company somewhat tedious and oppressive on occasion, so they are responsive to a sympathetic ear. Anyway, it seemed to me that Bronski himself was the problem."

"What made you think that?" asked Tom, genuinely curious now.

"He was frightened. One of the party was an old acquaintance from Cambridge. It upset him."

"Was that all?" he asked somewhat dismissively.

Sylvan shook his head. "There's no doubt. Bronski is in touch with the Russians."

Tom thought again of Patrick Marsden. Bronski was presumably a good deal more than a small cog in the machine.

Sylvan leant forward. "They have their claws well into him and if the Americans find out there will be all hell to pay. He's in breach of their security laws, as well as ours. In the present atmosphere there would be no mercy for him. You know the Yanks are nervous as cats with all these foreigners working over here. They suspect everyone, not least the British, and as far as they are concerned he's as good as British. At the moment we are beggars at the Americans' table. If they come to distrust us, the present nuclear co-operation will end, but, probably worse, pop goes that 'special relationship' that keeps the pound sterling afloat and the British economy just ticking over."

Somehow, it always seemed to come back to this.

"Well, yes, I can see it's a tricky situation, but what if anything can be done about it?"

"Get him away before the FBI or the CIG or whoever gets on to his tail."

"Have him recalled?"

"No, if he is playing traitor the establishment can no more use him at home than could the Yanks. And it's worse. He's not actually given the Russians much: he doesn't exactly hand out blueprints of bombs or anything like that. As you know, he's a particle physicist, whatever that is. Dammed if I understand any of it. All he does is exchange figures, formulae, ideas in this arcane field with an old contemporary of his who lives in Leningrad. A Soviet scientist, colleague from pre-war days. But what the Russkis want is not secret drawings and plans; what they want is Bronski himself."

Considering that Sylvan was secretary of the US/UK/Canadian committee overseeing their joint nuclear development, Tom found his assertion that he was ignorant of the science oddly disingenuous. But in spite of himself his interest quickened. "Sylvan, how on earth do you know all this?"

Sylvan slumped back in his seat. He looked suddenly exhausted.

"It's my business to know."

"But why are you telling me all this? What can I – or any of us – *do* about it?"

"I am going to do something about it – *we* are going to do something about it. We have a little time. As of now no one knows he is playing footsie with the Russians."

Except you, apparently, thought Tom.

"We've got to lift him, as they say. Tom, I'm telling you all this because I trust you and I need someone else on board. You can still walk away. You've only heard the idea, not the details. That's because there aren't any yet. But if we don't lift him, they will. Then we must get him to England. That will be up to you. You know all about ships. There are lots of our Navy ships repairing in the US Navy yards; with all your Navy connections you could fix up that end of things. Think about it."

Tom could only laugh out loud. "Sylvan, you're mad! Forget it!"

Sylvan stayed silent. Minutes passed before he spoke again.

"I'm meeting with John Portent tomorrow – that's almost this morning – at ten-thirty. Please clear your decks and attend. Perhaps he will convince you."

Chapter Eleven

"So Sylvan has brought you in on Operation Roadrunner," Sir John said to Tom. He turned to Sylvan and, with an air of mild irritation, added, "By the way, Sylvan, why Roadrunner?"

"It's a rather delightful bird, native to the south-west, you know, Arizona, New Mexico, likes to kill rattlesnakes and run like the blazes." He smiled happily. "Frequently along roads."

Sir John harrumphed.

"The whole thing is most unfortunate, but thanks to Sylvan we are in a position to save the day. The embassy will do it. No one else will be involved. Completely hush-hush. Very important you remember that, as nobody will have your back if any of this comes out. We will deny it; talk about rogue actors, that sort of stuff. The world will never know, but we will have saved this man from his folly, saved our country's reputation, and, I hope, retained the services of a top scientist we undoubtedly need. It's gone right to the top for approval, I may tell you, Davis. I flew to London last week, saw Sir Gaspard Jebb – Permanent Secretary at the Foreign Office – and he took it to the PM."

Sir John stood up, sighed, and went to the drinks cabinet.

"Sherry? Or something stronger under the circumstances? Scotch? Godammit, Sylvan, couldn't you have chosen one of those *verdammt* Germans disguised as Americans as your prime suspect? There are dozens of them to choose from wherever test tubes fizz and magic formulae are, ah, formulated. Ah well. Here's to Operation Roadrunner. Cheers."

Tom knocked back his whisky in one. He was finding it harder by the minute to back away. The fact that Sylvan's plan had approval from on high made the whole thing seem more realistic and feasible, and there was also the implied assurance that a defection by Bronski would have been as damaging as he had suggested. Tom's sense of adventure and his patriotism were both stirred. *I've been sitting behind a desk for too long*, he thought.

"When the operation is ready to go, Davis, I suggest you take some leave. I'm sure you're due some, but I'll fix it with Hobson if necessary. Then you can follow Sylvan's instructions without exciting suspicion. Think that's about it. Oh, of course, you chaps were in New York last night. How did it go?"

Tom said the party on board *Ferocious* had been a great success and done much, he was sure, to help cement the Special Relationship, thinking at the same time that if the Americans discovered what Sylvan was up to, that would put a large bomb under said relationship.

"Jolly good, jolly good," said Sir John setting down his glass. "Shame you missed the Air Marshall's showing of that RAF recruiting film last night. Excellent. Well, jolly good luck." He smirked slightly. "Bombs Away, what!"

Sylvan said nothing until they were out of the door and going down the stairs. "Thank God you invited me to your navy do, Tom. Can't imagine anything worse than having to sit through some ghastly propaganda piece full of squadron leaders with moustaches covering their stiff upper lips."

"I didn't invite you, Sylvan. You invited yourself!"

They had reached Tom's office. Sylvan stopped.

"So you're in."

It was a statement, not a question.

"Yes."

Sylvan grasped Tom's hand. There was a look of relief on his face.

"Good man. You won't regret it, I promise. Drinks at mine on Wednesday, six-ish? I'll fill you in then."

* * *

Sylvan lived alone in a rented house below the unfinished cathedral where the streets traversed the little ravines running down to Rock Creek. There was still a pleasant sense of tamed wilderness about the area. The house was comfortably if sparsely furnished, with, rather unexpectedly, very few personal touches. On his first visit Tom had scanned the bookshelves with some disappointment: they hosted little more than a complete *Encyclopaedia Britannica,* a set of Charles Dickens' novels and a few pulp paperbacks. On the walls some anodyne Impressionist prints. The only striking thing was a small painting of calla lilies.

"Like it?" Sylvan had asked. "It's by Georgia O'Keefe. Cost me an arm and a leg," he added, "but well worth it."

Tom had never heard of the artist and wasn't sure if he did like the picture. His mother, he knew, would certainly not like it. The only word he could think of to describe it was 'rude'.

It had been a warm day, and the evening was mild. They opted to sit out on the deck, sharing a bottle of Californian cabernet sauvignon.

"Apologies for it not being French, but the Yanks are beginning to produce some passably drinkable wines, believe it or not." Sylvan sniffed his glass, then took a tentative sip. "Hmm. Quaffable, at least. Now to Roadrunner. Marcie, of course, is in."

Of course, Tom wondered. Why *of course?*

Sylvan continued, "And our fourth musketeer is Roger."

"*Roger?* Good God!"

It was clear from the expression on Sylvan's face that he was enjoying Tom's surprise.

"Oh, but absolutely Roger. He knows the south-west pretty well and that's where all the action is going to take place. He worked on a dude ranch in Colorado before the war, remember? Anyway, Roger has come up with an absolutely brilliant plan for bringing our parcel back east. Do you know Jay Firbaker, senior Senator for Colorado – oil tycoon, rich as Croesus?

"Know *of* him. Wouldn't say I know him."

"Ah, but our Roger does. Well, that is to say, Roger's mother does. Did. Jay Firbaker is, as it happens, a former boyfriend of Roger's mother. No, me neither. Fortuitously, Jay is going out to Colorado Springs for a family wedding in late June in his private plane, and Roger has hitched a ride, so to speak. He's told Jay he's been invited to spend some time with friends out there: the people who own that dude ranch where Roger worked. Not strictly true, as they won't actually be there then, but apparently he's always welcome to stay. Roger also knows all about cars." He waved an airy hand. "You know me. *Hopeless* mechanically. Just turn the key and pray the wretched thing will start."

Tom rather doubted this, but just looked enquiringly at Sylvan. "Roger's plan is that when he gets there he'll buy a second-hand car, then drive down to the ranch. It's about three or four hours south of Colorado Springs, just north of the state border. He'll hole up there until you and Marcie join him with your passenger."

"*Me* and *Marcie?*"

"You're forgetting your grammar in your excitement, dear boy. Marcie and *I*. Or, from my point of view, Marcie and you."

"Sylvan, stop being pedantic and *explain*, for God's sake."

"You and Marcie are going to collect the package and bring him – it – back to DC in Roger's car."

"*What?* I thought I was brought into this escapade for my sea-faring experience! Why doesn't Roger do it? Seems obvious."

"Because," said Sylvan flatly.

There was a long silence while Tom took this in. Then he said, "But Los Alamos is in New Mexico, not Colorado."

"Indeed. Clever lad. Have another glass of this surprisingly decent wine."

Tom picked up the refilled glass and the scent of blackberries rose from it, bringing back memories of an English autumn.

Sylvan was watching him.

"And now you will appreciate my true genius in choosing Roger for this caper. What we need is a base: somewhere handy to the Los Alamos laboratories where we can lie up and wait for as long as might be necessary. Sort of command post for the operation. Well, Roger has an elderly aunt, lives in New York, but also keeps a house, *Piñones*, near Santa Fé, not more than twenty or thirty miles away, I understand. She intends to spend half each year there, but never does. Her man, Pedro, and his wife live on the property, keep it ticking over, maintain the grounds and so on. Well, Roger has Aunt Sissie's blessing for his friends to stay at Piñones for their holiday – that's the story he gave her. The friends," he said with a sly grin, "are you and Marcie."

Tom considered the many attractions of spending an indefinite time with Marcie at Aunt Sissie's. After all, he had agreed to this. But he was also beginning to appreciate that New Mexico was a very long way from Washington DC.

"Right," he said slowly. "But how will Marcie and I get there? We're not going to drive all the way in her Packard, are we?"

"Good Lord, no! You'll go by train, and there's a vehicle on the property, so you'll have wheels. When you get to the dude ranch with your passenger you'll switch vehicles with Roger, and he'll drive the Piñones car back there while you three make your way sedately to Washington. You should be safe by then; the proverbial will hit the fan when the Feds find out that Bronski's gone missing, but they will want to keep a tight lid on all this, so I very much doubt there'll be anything on the radio, and they won't put out a country-wide APB. Any pursuers won't know which direction you've gone, and they'll be looking for a car with New Mexico plates, not Colorado ones. Nobody is likely to suspect a respectable brother and sister taking their Aged Uncle back east. Just be careful, don't draw attention to yourselves."

"It is the Wild West, after all," said Tom, trying to make light of what was becoming an increasingly serious situation, "I suppose we could always gallop around on horses, like Tom Mix."

Sylvan gave a small sniff of disapproval.

"I believe there are horses at Pinoñes. Nasty brutes: can't trust either end. They either bite you or kick you. Roger, on the other hand, adores them. He and Marcie have already been down there – they travelled separately, of course, we don't want to arouse suspicion – on a little recce. Spent the whole time out riding, I gather. Naturally, Marcie is very good on a horse."

They both sat in silence, and Tom assumed that Sylvan, like himself, was visualising Lady Marcia Mckenna in boots and breeches, her dark hair in a bun and covered by a hat with a veil, riding crop in hand...

Tom was puzzled by the relationship between Sylvan and Marcie, who obviously enjoyed an easy and enviable familiarity. Had they been lovers, as rumour had it? He rejected that idea, perhaps from wishful thinking on his part. No, it must be that they were just particularly close friends He realised that he knew almost nothing about Sylvan's friends, male or female; although Sylvan had introduced him to many people, especially in Tom's first year in Washington, apart from Marcie there seemed to be no one to whom he was especially close.

Sylvan's voice interrupted his reverie.

"And *you* are very good in a boat, according to Roger. Not me. Seasick. So, going back to our original discussion, what do you think of my suggestion of getting our *parcel* to England with the help of our own magnificent matelots?"

Tom laughed again. "If that's going to be an option, I think you'll need higher authority than mine!"

"That can be arranged," said Sylvan. "But I need you to do the legwork. I want you to complete a timetable of sailing dates for both naval and merchant shipping to British ports for the whole Atlantic seaboard for the next three months. Can you do that?"

Oh well, thought Tom, *in for a penny, in for a pound.*

"Of course. Tell you what – why don't I get in touch with my American buddy, Charlie Weaver, and get him to take me round the dry docks in Baltimore, and maybe Norfolk. It would give me a feel for what's happening, and I could chat to people – perhaps get some intel," he added slightly self-consciously.

Sylvan nodded gravely and said, "Excellent idea. Don't give Charlie any hints of what we are up to, though. We don't want the Minute Men pouncing before we do."

"The who?"

"The Minute Men? I'm sure you can work it out. We're using code. Sounds frightfully spy story and all that, but believe me, it's essential. I'm Mr Woods. Obviously. The other side are the ballerinas. Marcie's idea, don't you just love it? Bolshoi Ballet. She says it sounds plausible, as if they're planning a goodwill tour."

"Sylvan…"

"Yes, dear boy?"

"I only have a hazy idea of how you intend this to work, apart from using Aunt Sissie's house as a base and getting the parcel from there to here and then to England. What about the crucial – kidnap? Lift? Rescue? How is that going to work?"

Sylvan smiled and got up to fetch the wine bottle.

"Best if you don't know at this stage, old chap; safer that way."

"Probably just as well. I don't see myself charging about New Mexico on horseback defying the Russians – or the FBI – with a gun in my hand. Marcie, on the other hand…"

"Ah yes, Marcie. What a woman. You know, if she had dropped in by accident on Churchill's secret headquarters in the darkest days, she would have sat at his right hand. Had she boarded Lenin's armoured train, carrying the fuse to light the Bolshevik revolution, the comrades would soon have been confiding their secrets to her and seeking her advice. That's why she's my first lieutenant. No offence meant."

"None taken." Tom raised his glass. "To Lady Marcia McKenna."

Chapter Twelve

One week after his conversation with Sylvan, Hobson called Tom into his office.

"Our esteemed Foreign Secretary, Ernest Bevin," he said, with what Tom registered as distaste, "will be in the country next week, and he wants to be briefed on this Atomic Energy Commission thing before he meets with his American counterpart. He'll be staying at the Waldorf Astoria in New York. You can meet with our UN chaps while you're there. Kill two birds with one stone."

"But surely he would expect to be briefed by someone more senior, like yourself?"

"No, no," replied Hobson, peering at Tom over his horn-rimmed glasses, "you know as much about it as anybody. And I believe you've requested a few days to go to Baltimore and Norfolk for a visit to the naval yards with our chum Charlie Weaver? That's approved. Still the old sea-dog at heart, eh?"

The trip to the navy yards proved informative, as did a subsequent conversation with Tom's former boss, Archie Struthers. The Naval Attaché was pessimistic about the valiant attempts by the Americans to help refit the British fleet.

"The lot we've got over here are total write-offs in my view. Scrap them, I say. But the Americans are so keen; they love mucking about with our old *Temeraires*. And generous! And since they are more than happy to pay for it all, the Admiralty gives them a free hand. The Treasury love it."

Nor were there any naval ships due to sail for England in the immediate future. Tom reported this back to Sylvan, who asked him to focus on merchant shipping.

The following Monday, Tom took the train to New York and a cab to the Waldorf Astoria. Once inside he stood still for a moment, almost overwhelmed by the Art Deco magnificence of the lobby. The epitome of luxury, the Waldorf Astoria seemed a curious place for the British Foreign Secretary, a socialist, labour activist and lifelong trade unionist, to stay. But Ernest Bevin was not a well man, and perhaps he had earned such cosseting. Tom admitted to himself that he wouldn't mind staying here too, as long as someone else was paying, even if in this case it was the British taxpayer. And it wouldn't do for the Americans to think that the British Government was so broke that it couldn't afford the best for its most senior officials. Even if it was.

He took the elevator to the thirtieth floor and knocked on the door of Bevin's suite.

"Lieutenant Davis?" asked the man who opened the door. He appeared to be about the same age as Sylvan, good-looking, his dark hair swept back above a high forehead. "I'm Guy Bowman, the Minister's Private Secretary." He didn't offer a handshake. "Come in."

Bowman led Tom into the reception room of the suite. Seated at a card table in the middle of the room was a corpulent, barrel-chested man with a head that seemed too large for his body. Tom had heard that the Foreign Secretary weighed eighteen stone, and seeing him in person, he could believe it. On one side of the room was a portable bar holding nothing but a jug of iced water. On the other side, totally unexpectedly, sat a large, grey-haired, middle-aged woman, knitting. Somewhat bemused, Tom assumed her to be Mrs Bevin and nodded towards her rather uncertainly. She smiled sweetly, gave him a friendly nod, then lowered her gaze back to her needles.

"Lieutenant Davis, sir," said Bowman.

"Thank you for coming, Lieutenant, please sit down."

Tom leant over the table to shake Bevin's proffered hand, then sat down opposite. Bowman took the seat at the end of the small table. Clearly Mrs Bevin was to be ignored. Perhaps she was there to listen in and offer her opinion to her husband later?

As succinctly as he could, Tom outlined the American plan for a world development and control centre for atomic energy, and explained why he supported it.

"Under whose instructions? Has anyone in London told you to do this?" asked Bowman quietly. He was sitting on Tom's right-hand side, the one with limited hearing, and Tom had to strain to hear what he was saying.

"Well, no, not as such, but it's the only way to go."

Guy Bowman raised a supercilious eyebrow, and Tom felt his hackles rise. The Private Secretary exuded arrogance. There was something rather louche about him.

He turned his attention back to the Foreign Secretary who appeared to be swelling as if he were about to explode.

"You mean you are trying to put us under this control organisation? What is it but an American scheme to corner the world atomic market! No, we British are going to have our own nuclear power plants, lad, and our own bomb!"

It was just what Sylvan had warned him about so many months ago, over a year before the first atom bomb had even fallen, when an international atomic agency was still mostly just a plan in the mind of the former President. So much for eliminating, or even controlling, nuclear weapons.

"It's as though nobody in the British government is taking this scheme seriously," complained Tom as he reported back to Hobson on Wednesday. "I suspect they just want us to play along with the Americans until the thing peters out. Do they *really* want the uncontrolled proliferation of nuclear arms? How is this attitude different from the Russians, who would happily eliminate all the world's atom bombs – which, of course, are exclusively American at the moment – as long as they are free to then develop their own?"

Hobson shook his head sadly.

"The nuclear genie is well and truly out of the bottle, alas, and is not going to go back in. Well, there's nothing that you or I can do about it, so don't let it get you down."

By June the vacation season had begun. Washington was already hot and sticky and unusually quiet; it had the feel of a city taking a collective siesta. People had, of course, taken vacations during the war years, but this year was different. Now whole families, reunited with husbands, fathers, brothers and sons released from the armed forces, and freed from the wartime constraints, took to the road en masse to enjoy their first full summer of the peace.

Tom had heard nothing more about Operation Roadrunner, and he was even beginning to hope it was just a figment of Sylvan's over-active imagination, when Sylvan breezed into his office quite as he used to do.

"Lunch, dear boy?"

They took their trays to a quiet corner of the canteen where they couldn't be overheard.

"I looked for you last week; they said you were in New York."

"Yes, Hobson sent me to meet the Foreign Secretary. He told me we are going to develop our own bomb, so I'm sure he will be happy to have you-know-who, his own nuclear scientist."

"You met with Bevin?"

"Just briefly. I don't think he was impressed."

Sylvan snorted.

"The man's out of his depth in the Foreign Office. Should have stayed with the trade unions."

Gingerly Tom broached the subject that was on his mind:

"Sylvan, when are we going to be needed? I'll have to tell my boss if I'm going to be away."

"Patience, dear boy, patience. Hobson has been told that you are going on a trip to those parts of the states you have not yet explored. Which is true. However, may I suggest you don't accept any invitations for July Fourth and the two weeks either side."

"The reason being?"

"Think about it. National holiday! Everyone somewhere else. Don't notice if people not where they should be. Also, it's a Thursday, which means very many people will be taking the Friday to make it a long weekend."

"Meaning it would be a good time for the ballerinas to try and lift him?"

"Or us," said Sylvan.

Chapter Thirteen

On the twenty-first of June, Sylvan suggested to Tom that they abandon their hot and airless offices and take an amble round the Chancery garden.

"Ready to go on your hols, Tom?"

"Whenever you say, Mr Woods."

Tom used the code name jokingly, but Sylvan was serious.

"Right." With the air of a magician doing a conjuring trick he whipped out an envelope and presented it to Tom. "Here's a train ticket to Chicago on Tuesday and a ticket on the Super Chief to Albuquerque for the twenty-sixth. Take a good book to read – you'll have a night on the train from Washington and another on the Super Chief, but I think you'll enjoy it. You like trains. The ancient aunt's faithful retainer will pick you up at the station and take you to base camp."

"And then?"

Sylvan smiled enigmatically.

"You'll see. I have arranged with Marcie to touch base by telephone every evening at nine o'clock for any necessary communication, and I will meet up with you at some point before the actual receipt of the parcel."

"Sylvan?"

"Yes, dear boy?"

"Are you expecting me to go charging off into the blue without a clue as to what I am supposed to be doing?"

"Absolutely, dear boy." His tone changed and he took Tom's arm. "All will be well, and all manner of things shall be well. Trust me."

"No horses?"

"No horses. But I can't promise no guns. By the way, you can use a gun, can't you? Naval officer and all that?"

"Yes, of course; I've had small arms training. But look, Sylvan, I do need to know: what happens to the parcel when we get back here?"

"Before your naval expertise comes into play?"

"Yes."

"That's Marcie's department. She'll tell you all about it on the train if you ask her nicely. Enjoy the ride."

The great locomotive, with its distinctive red-and-gold livery, pulled smoothly out of Chicago's Dearborn Station, the four powerful diesel engines making light work of hauling nine gleaming stainless-steel cars in its wake. For all his recurring misgivings, Tom's heart lifted. This was the famous Super Chief, flagship of the Atchison, Topeka & Santa Fé line, one of the country's premier train journeys. There were no draughty carriages with hard benches here; each passenger had their own private sleeping compartment in one of the Pullman cars, complete with washstand and toilet and an attentive porter to set up the bed at night and tidy up in the morning. Truly a hotel on wheels.

He settled into a comfortable seat in the large, air-conditioned observation lounge and a waiter brought him coffee. As the train gathered speed, Tom gazed out of the window at the American heartland flashing by at over sixty miles an hour and felt a huge sense of excitement and freedom, as if he were really going on holiday. Georgetown already seemed light-years away. He wondered idly if his house-mate Miles would remember to water the potted plants.

"Well, he*llo*. Fancy meeting you here. What a coincidence."

It was Marcie.

"Well, yes, quite a coincidence…"

She slid into the seat beside him. "Don't be silly, darling, of course it's not a coincidence. Sylvan told you I'd be on the train with you."

"Yes, but when I didn't see you on the train from Washington…"

"Sylvan didn't want us to be seen leaving together. He's being very careful. I came a day before you and took advantage of some free time in Chicago yesterday to spend a few happy hours pottering around the Art Institute. Fabulous place. They have a huge collection of Impressionist and Post-Impressionist works."

"I didn't realise you were an art-lover."

"I told you before I have a few surprises up my sleeve. Now I suggest we settle back and have a pleasant journey. We've got at least twenty-four hours together."

He wasn't quite sure whether to be thrilled or terrified by the prospect.

"Marcie, sorry, but Sylvan said you would tell me what is happening to the… parcel when we get back to DC."

"Well, you know our much-loved Ambassador Sir Geoffrey's term is up and he's going home. But he wants to complete his tally of all forty-eight states, so he and Gertie are off to – guess where – Alaska!"

"But Alaska's not a state, it's officially a territory," Tom pointed out.

"A mere technicality, darling. It will be a state one day, and H.E. desperately wants to see it – spectacular, apparently – and he's mad keen to shoot a grizzly bear. They won't be back until the end of July, and the new chap won't be installed till September, so there will only be a skeleton staff in the embassy. I asked Gertie if it would be all right for my not-very-well elderly uncle to stay in the residence for a short time while they are away. I explained that the relative who normally looks after him had to go into hospital." She clapped her hands like a little girl admiring herself. "Clever or what?"

"Brilliant," said Tom with enthusiasm.

"That's what I thought." She turned to the waiter who hovered nearby. "Coffee, black, no sugar, please." Then she indicated the well-worn volume that Tom had laid on the small table beside his seat. "What's the book?"

"*Riddle of the Sands*. Do you know it?"

"I told you I was uneducated."

"Doesn't matter. It's a spy story set before the Great War. I must have read it several times already and keep coming back to it. It's all set on an old yacht in the Frisian islands."

Her face suggested that it really wasn't her sort of book.

"Oh," he added suddenly, "why didn't I spot that before?"

"What?"

"The yacht – she's called the *Dulcibella*!"

"And?"

"It's the name of Hank's yacht – the *Dulcibelle Adams*."

"Hank? Is that Roger's sailing friend?"

He nodded.

"Well, there *is* a coincidence."

Marcie pulled out a *New Yorker* magazine from her bag and opened it.

Well, you managed to kill that *conversation*, he thought, picking up his book again. But then she turned to him with that captivating smile and showed him the page she was perusing.

"Do look at this great cartoon by Carl Rose."

"Carl Rose… spinach?"

"Yes, best cartoon the *New Yorker* ever ran. Mother to daughter: 'It's broccoli, dear.' Daughter to mother: 'I say it's spinach'…"

"… 'and I say the hell with it'!" they chimed in unison, then burst out laughing.

"I wanted to be a cartoonist when I was a boy," said Tom, "well, an animator, to tell the truth. I wanted to draw the pictures for *Steamboat Willie*. Only one problem: I was no good at drawing, so I decided I'd be a train driver instead. Then I ended up in the Navy. What about you? What did you want to do when you grew up?"

"Well, when I was a very little girl I wanted to run off and be Queen of the Gypsies. My mother was from Kerry, and she used to tell me the most wonderful Irish stories. My father was Anglo-Irish, and after he died I was packed off to a convent school – I was only seven – and decided that one day I would be Mother Superior."

"I'm glad you didn't become a nun."

"Me too," she said with a laugh. "I dropped that idea when I went to Godolphin Ladies College in Salisbury for my school cert. I loved Godolphin. I really blossomed there, learned to ride, captain of lacrosse for the school…"

"Head girl, at least."

"Oh, absolutely! That's how I got to be so bossy. Finishing school in Switzerland, then I came out as a debutante and did the season, Queen Charlotte's Ball and all of that. Didn't enjoy it much. Best thing about it was meeting the Queen. George – my stepfather – and Mother moved to Washington in 1934. I didn't really know what I wanted to do after I left school. I got a job in London, which I hated, so after… well, later I came over to join them. Usual story – did a secretarial course, got a job at the British Embassy – the family connection helped, of course, but I worked hard and actually I'm damn good at what I do."

"Do your parents still live in Washington?"

"No, George died in 1939. Cirrhosis of the liver – I may have mentioned that he was an alcoholic – and Mother went back to Ireland. So, now you know my whole life story. What about you?"

"Not much to tell, I'm afraid." *And not at all glamorous*, he thought. "My mother was the daughter of the bank manager in Bala, in North Wales. Dad was from Cardiff, though his mother was English. He was a Presbyterian minister in a rather dull suburb in South London; I went to the local grammar school, scholarship to Oxford, then the Navy as soon as the war broke out. I'll be twenty-eight years old next month and I'm still trying to figure out what I want to do when I grow up."

"You're funny!" To Tom's ears, her laugh sparkled like champagne.

"May I buy you lunch?" he asked.

Like Sylvan said, he intended to enjoy the ride.

When they met in the dining room the next morning, America looked very different. After polite inquiries as to how each had slept, they settled down to a large, leisurely breakfast, content just to enjoy the awe-inspiring views of the stupendous Rocky Mountains marching away to the horizon, as the train followed the route of the old Santa Fé Trail across the south-east corner of Colorado and into the heart of New Mexico.

"Makes Snowdon look a molehill," Tom commented.

It seemed too short a time before they reached Lamy, the nearest station to Santa Fé, where they alighted from the train. Pedro, Aunt Sissie's faithful retainer, a small, wiry, leathery man wearing a large straw hat, collected them in a beat-up station wagon and drove them to Piñoñes, some thirty miles to the north. Pedro knew Marcie from her previous visit with Roger and had clearly fallen in love with her. *As who doesn't*, thought Tom. At the house they were greeted by Pedro's wife, Rosa, also obviously Marcie's devoted servant. Jack Sprat and his wife, Tom decided, looking at the latter's ample figure.

"Señor Roger not come with you?" Rosa asked, glancing at the strange man who had arrived with their adored one.

"Not this time," Marcie replied, "but he's going to meet us in Albuquerque some time next week or the week after; we'll leave then and he'll come here. I'm afraid he was rather vague about the details, said he'd let us know."

Rosa smiled indulgently; she had known Roger for a long time and was used to his whims.

As Rosa fussed around Marcie, and Pedro unloaded their suitcases, Tom took a good look at Piñones. A one-storey, flat-roofed, adobe-style house, the structure fitted perfectly into its environment. It lay, he thought fancifully, like a lioness in the desert scrub: sagebrush and juniper and the little piñon pines that gave the house its name. Around it, like the lion's cubs, were outbuildings – stables and work-shops – while Pedro's house lay a little further distant. Tom shaded his eyes with his hands; at almost 6,000 feet above sea level, the sun here was intense, but although it was as hot as Washington, the crisp dry air was far more comfortable than the enervating humidity of the capital. He could see the far peaks to west and east, appearing only as thicker pencil lines framing the picture of the desert. The

Rio Grande meandered through a gorge cut across the vast bowl of the desert. It was hard to judge distances for eyes unused to such space. There was not another building to be seen.

They followed Rosa through a small porch that shaded the front door, and into a spacious dining-living room. There was a big picture-window looking out towards the mountains on the eastern wall and sliding glass doors on the west side. Tom was surprised and pleased at the coolness of the interior, which was decorated in soft earth tones. The floors were of pinkish-brown Spanish tiles, strewn with rugs patterned with Native American designs.

"Your meal is ready at half past six," said Rosa. "I hope the Señor likes tamales?"

"We both *adore* tamales," said Marcie firmly. "Don't we, Tom?"

"Oh, absolutely. Adore them."

"*Bueno*. Follow me, please."

While Pedro brought up the rear with their cases, she led them down a corridor and opened a door on the left.

"This is your room, Señor. The bathroom is next door."

Tom looked around the large and pleasant room: a double bed with a white cotton bedspread, a wooden dresser, and a small writing desk against one wall, on which hung a watercolour painting of the same mountains that he could see through the window. *Well, this is a bonus*, he thought. *Thanks, Aunt Sissie.*

"You are in the same room you had before, Señora Marcie. You have your own bathroom, and you can step right outside through the sliding doors if you wish."

"I remember, It's lovely; I'll be very comfortable."

"Be sure all the doors are firmly closed at night, Señor, there are snakes and tarantulas here in the desert and you don't want them coming inside."

He hadn't reckoned on snakes and tarantulas, and he could feel Marcie close beside him suppressing laughter.

"No, don't worry," he said. "I'll make sure everything is secure."

Showered, changed and ready to face the tamales, whatever they might be (if not the tarantulas), Tom stepped out into the corridor and found his way to the huge, cool, dim living room.

"Ah, there you are! Here, try this!"

Marcie, looking stunning in silk trousers and a white embroidered shirt, handed him a chilled glass with a wedge of lime positioned on the edge. He sniffed it cautiously.

"Smells interesting. Looks amazing." He sipped gingerly. "My God! What is it?"

"Margarita. It's what you drink here. Like it?"

"I could certainly get used to it," he said happily, and raised the glass towards her. "Cheers. Here's to Aunt Sissie."

"Cheers. C'mon. Let's sit outside and listen to the cicadas."

She led the way through the big glass sliding doors onto an extensive paved patio softened with planters filled with native shrubs; a low brick wall demarcated it from the desert outside the perimeter. In the centre the rounded canopy of a Navajo willow provided shade. Marcie settled into one of the comfortable wicker chairs, putting her glass down on a tile-topped table. "Just thought I'd mention it, but it's not only tarantulas and rattlers you need to watch out for."

"For heavens' sake, there's more?"

"Oh yes: cougars. Mountain lions," she added helpfully.

"Well, thanks." He looked around. "I'm probably safe, the mountains are a long way away. What are they called, by the way?"

She followed his glance. "Those to the east are the Sangre de Cristo range and those are the Jemez Sierras to the west. Sorry," she said, looking remorseful, "I was just winding you up – couldn't resist it. Your face when Rosa mentioned tarantulas… No, mountain lions are hardly common. But Pedro did shoot one a few years ago. He'll show you the skin if you ask him."

The late afternoon sun caught and held some glinting silvery structure far away across the wilderness of arid scrubland.

"Los Alamos," said Marcie. "Twenty miles west."

"Marcie?"

"Tom."

"Shouldn't we discuss Roadrunner?"

"Tomorrow," she said firmly.

The tamales, which Tom had never even heard of, let alone tasted, were indeed delicious, although after observing his sneezing fit with some amusement, Marcie suggested to Rosa that she put a little less chilli in tomorrow's supper. After Pedro and Rosa had cleared away dinner and gone back to their own house, Tom and Marcie sat on the patio enjoying tequila shots while they waited for Sylvan to touch base. As darkness crept over the valley, the rays of the westering sun broke through to touch the pencil line of the Sangre de Cristos that formed the eastern horizon, burnishing the peaks with red for a few minutes only. "The blood of Christ," murmured Marcie. Then the scarf of night, studded with stars so bright and close Tom felt he could reach out and touch them, enfolded everything. Across the darkness of the valley to the west a single light showed, a tiny, hard, unwinking pinpoint of light set on some tower or chimney in Los Alamos.

Greatly daring, Tom stretched out a hand and touched Marcie's wrist. He kept it there for a moment.

"You thinking what I'm thinking? I bet they are looking at us."

"Bet they are! Better put out that cigarette!"

They laughed together, but somehow he knew that Marcie, too, felt that they were on the edge of dark events.

Chapter Fourteen

Sylvan had confirmed that there was no immediate urgency, so
Marcie had told Tom that they would go on a recce today to famil-
iarise him with the area, and that he should be up early. But when he
entered the kitchen there was only Rosa making coffee at the stove.

"Señora Marcie is not feeling well," she said, tragedy etched on
her leathery face. "She has, what you say, a migraine?"

"Oh no. I'm sorry," said Tom, slightly alarmed at the feeling
he was now de facto in charge of Operation Roadrunner. "I don't
suppose – but is there anything I can do?"

"No, no," said Rosa, dismissive of eternal masculine incompe-
tence. "We jus' leave her alone in the dark, poor lady. I take her
plenty of water. She will be better this afternoon. Happen last time
she was here. Here, Señor, your coffee." She set it in front of him
and placed a basket of warm bread rolls beside it.

After he had eaten, Tom poured a second cup of coffee and went
out to sit on the patio with the unread copy of *Time* magazine that
he had brought with him. But he couldn't concentrate. Even the
sight of a hummingbird at the nectar-filled feeder Rosa had placed
under the Navajo willow, its iridescent wings coruscating in the
sunlight, couldn't hold his attention.

With Sylvan's assurance that everything was under control, he
had been carried along on a wave of confidence and excitement: in
the build-up to his departure; during the long, immensely enjoyable
train journey in the company of a relaxed and out-going Marcie;
and the novelty of their arrival, the landscape of the south-west

and this house. Now his earlier doubts resurfaced. How did Sylvan know about the proposed abduction of Bronski by the Russians in the first place? Was it just a hunch he had got when he had visited Los Alamos and Bronski had seemed – Tom tried to remember the word Sylvan had used – *frightened?*

He recalled quite vividly other snippets of that conversation: *if the Americans find out there will be all hell to pay… they suspect everyone, not least the British.*

Great, he thought. *And what happens to us if we're caught rescuing the guy from under the noses of both the Yanks and the Russkis. The latter would probably shoot us, no questions asked, and the Yanks would incarcerate us in Alcatraz.* Neither prospect was appealing.

As of now no-one knows he is playing footsie with the Russians.
But Sylvan did.

He got up abruptly and went back through the glass doors into the living room, still cool and dark in spite of the growing light and heat outside. He stood for a moment letting his eyes get used to the dim light, taking in the details which, still keyed up from the journey, he hadn't considered yesterday evening.

The furnishings were old and well-worn but of good quality: a wooden dining table with high-backed Mexican chairs, a deeply-cushioned sofa and armchairs, a coffee table made from a polished slice of an intricately whorled tree. Bright throw cushions added splashes of colour.

He crossed to the end of the room where the massive fireplace was flanked on both sides by floor-to-ceiling bookshelves. Browsing their contents he discovered an eclectic collection, from popular and classic novels to poetry, history, science and philosophy. There was an entire section devoted to volumes of anthropology and the natural history, geology and Native American culture of the South-West. Looking around, he decided that this must be a passion of Aunt Sissie's as he began to identify the Indian arts and crafts – pottery, baskets, woven hangings, bone flutes – displayed everywhere. A small painting caught his attention: at first he wasn't sure whether it was pure abstraction but, looking closely, concluded that it was a landscape of hills in the same colours as the woven rugs: soft pinks and dun, with a sliver of ultramarine sky.

Deciding it would be interesting to find out more about this alien and beautiful land, and also to take his mind off the reason he was there, he selected *Flora and Fauna of the Desert South-West* from the shelves and settled down in one of the huge armchairs, sinking back into the tobacco-coloured leather upholstery.

As he had hoped, the book was absorbing and his concerns started to recede. Also, the chair was incredibly comfortable. More fatigued from the tension of the past week than he had appreciated, he soon dozed.

Rosa woke him at midday with quesadillas, and he asked guiltily after Marcie.

"Ah, she is still asleep, Señor. That is good."

He wandered after her into the kitchen, fished a beer out of the fridge, and took it back into the living room.

For the rest of the afternoon he read and dozed and dozed and read. By four he decided that he should go and take a look at the local flora and fauna instead of just reading about it. Besides, he needed some fresh air; he would take a walk around the property. He crossed the patio and opened the little gate that opened to the outside. From the corner of his eye he glimpsed a jackrabbit darting for cover. A covey of small birds pecked busily in search of ants and other insects in the sandy soil, the comma-shaped plumes on their heads bobbing up and down. Gambel's quail, thought Tom, pleased with himself, identifying their distinctive markings – black head, russet crown, russet wing-tips with white stripes. Just like the picture. So much for the fauna. He decided to have a go at the flora, spotting the aptly named barrel cactus, and the prickly pear with its flat spiny leaves, though nervous about encountering the vicious jumping cholla – fauna or flora? – which, according to the book, was definitely to be avoided.

He strolled over to the workshops and peered into two of them.

One was equipped for woodworking, the other was evidently where Pedro carried out minor repairs and maintenance. In the stable block there were four empty stalls. Two bay horses grazed placidly in the adjacent paddock. As Tom leant against the fence, one of them wandered over to investigate. He patted the animal's neck; it turned its head and rubbed its muzzle against his hand as if seeking food. Finding none, it softly snorted a puff of warm air at him and resumed grazing. *Next time I must bring some carrots*, thought Tom. He remembered Sylvan's comments about horses: they either bite you or kick you. These friendly, docile animals seemed capable of neither.

He found Pedro in the carport beside the house, diligently polishing the headlamps on the big Ford Woodie station wagon in which he had fetched them from the station.

"Nice car," said Tom.

"She belong to Señora Shaw," said Pedro, straightening up and patting the hood of the vehicle. "She is old and not so pretty maybe, but I take good care of her." *I hope he's referring to the station wagon, and not Aunt Sissie*, thought Tom irreverently, as Pedro opened the driver's side door so that Tom could look inside. Although the metal fenders were dented and scratched, and the wooden side panels faded from years of exposure, it was clear that Pedro meant what he said. The wood on the dashboard was polished until it shone and there were new floor mats in the front. Clean canvas covers had been stretched over the original upholstery of the two sets of bench seats.

"You and Señora Marcie can use her while you stay here. I give her new spark plugs and a big drink of oil."

"Thanks, Pedro, but don't you and Rosa need the car?"

"Is OK, we have our own pickup."

Returning to the house, Tom found it deserted; Rosa was not yet back on duty and Marcie was still nowhere to be seen. Worried about her long absence, he hesitated for a moment, then padded barefoot down the corridor towards her bedroom. The door was open and he looked around it cautiously. She was sprawled on the bed, eyes closed, wearing a silk kimono that had ridden up her long legs, her dark hair loose on the pillow. Hardly daring to breathe, he stood and looked at her, guilty in one way at seeing her so disarmed and somehow vulnerable, while, at the same time, cherishing the precious moment.

She opened her eyes.

"Oh God!" he said, "Marcie, I'm so sorry, I just came to see how you were. I was worried about you."

He had thought she would be coldly angry at discovering him to be a peeping Tom (there's ironic, he thought in self-disgust) but to his relief she showed no surprise and made no attempt to sit up or adjust her kimono. Instead she smiled slowly and said, "That was very sweet of you."

"How are you feeling?" he asked anxiously. "Is there anything I can do?"

"Much better, but exhausted. Yes; you could make me a lovely cup of good old British tea if you can find any."

He returned to the kitchen and put a saucepan of water on to boil, wondering if the Americans would ever have the sense to take to kettles. He found a tin of loose tea however, Lapsang Souchong, presumably Aunt Sissie's preferred brew.

He carried the mug back to Marcie's room and again peered cautiously around the door. She was sitting up on the bed, her kimono now decorously covering her knees with the pillows stacked behind her.

"Your tea, Madam."

"Well, thank-you, Jeeves. You can put it down there."

He set the mug down and reluctantly turned to the door, but she patted the bed.

"Don't go. Have you made some for yourself? Bring it in here and let's be sociable."

He hurried from the room before she could change her mind and before she could see what he knew was a silly smile on his face. When he got back she was cradling the mug between her hands.

"This is just what I needed. Who called it the cup that cheers but doesn't make you drunk or something?"

He sat down carefully beside her but not too close.

"Pass. Reminds me though: my parents sent me an article about tea from one of the English papers by George Orwell – heard of him?"

She nodded. "Rabid socialist."

"*Socialist schmocialist!*" quipped Tom happily, remembering his New York encounter with the cab driver, and she actually giggled.

"Tea is one of the mainstays of civilisation, according to Orwell," he went on. "He claimed there are ten, no, *eleven* rules for making a cup of tea."

"Surely one just boils the kettle and pours it on the tea-leaves!"

"Surely one just lets the butler do it!"

She laughed and slapped his arm gently.

"Tom, do stop."

"And he wouldn't approve of Lapsang. He said – and I remember because I thought it so funny – that you don't feel wiser, braver or more optimistic after drinking China tea. Only Indian will do."

Marcie was holding her mug in both hands and looking down into it. Her hair fell forward and hid her face. She murmured, "That's a shame. Perhaps we need to feel wiser, braver and more optimistic."

"Marcie!" said Tom in genuine alarm. He had never heard her talk like this before.

She raised her head and looked at him.

"Marcie, please don't tell me you've got cold feet about Roadrunner! I rely on you to keep me going along with it. I was always a bit sceptical, but somehow Sylvan convinced me… I spent the morning worrying about it. Please, please don't say *you* are losing confidence!"

"No," she said, "no, I haven't got cold feet. We're going to do it and we're going to bloody well make a success of it. Just sometimes though, in general, I find everything very hard, very hard to… bear. Sorry."

"Oh Marcie," he said and reached out his arms. She let him hug her, murmuring with a smile, "Mind my tea…" then after a moment, more briskly, "Well, can't stay here all day."

He stroked her thin shoulders under the silk, thinking *why not*, but she moved sideways to set the mug down on the bedside table and swung her legs onto the floor.

"Girl's gotta get dressed, honey," she said. "See you at six."

He stood up and picked up her mug, noticing as he did so a book lying face down beside it. George Orwell's *Homage to Catalonia*, his memoir of the Spanish Civil War, wasn't quite the sort of reading he would have associated with Marcie.

"Well, there's another coincidence," he said.

"What? Oh yes, Orwell. Yes, isn't it? Go on, see you later. Thanks for the tea."

She appeared for supper looking washed out, but smiled when Rosa asked anxiously how she was feeling.

"Much better, thank you."

Rosa hovered. Marcie looked at her inquiringly.

"Señora, is it OK if me and Pedro go on Monday to Alberquerque for our grand-daughter's *quinceañera*?"

"I'm sure that'll be fine. What is a *quinceañera*?"

"Is a special occasion for a girl when she turns fifteen and becomes a young woman and there will be a big party. We will leave here about midday. We will stay the night and be back on Tuesday in the afternoon."

"Sounds lovely. What's tomorrow? I've lost track. Oh, Saturday. Then on Sunday… shouldn't you have time off?"

Clearly used to servants, reflected Tom a little unkindly.

"Oh, is OK, Señora, we are happy looking after you."

"No, I tell you what, why don't you leave after lunch on Sunday? Then you won't have to rush."

You'd think Madam had handed over a hundred dollars rather than half a day off, he thought, as Rosa thanked Marcie profusely.

"I will make chilli con carne for you and leave it in the refrigerator with a salad."

"That would be splendid."

When Rosa had left, Marcie said to Tom, "A *quinceañera* sounds a great deal nicer than coming out as a deb. Remember I told you? God, it was awful. Total marriage market. Ghastly spotty young men with sweaty hands. We had an unofficial list of those who were known to be 'not safe in taxis.'"

"But you clearly escaped."

"You bet I did, pardner."

After supper, Marcie opened one of the drawers in the massive carved sideboard in the living room and produced a large-scale sketch map.

"Roger and I made this when we were here on our recce. We'll drive over this area tomorrow so that you get to know the country. I'd planned to do this yesterday, but in fact Saturday's a good day to be nosing around because there will be tourists out and about."

She spread it out on the table and pointed.

"We are here – see: Pinoñes. Now according to Sylvan our – client – meets his contacts from the Bolshoi Ballet *here* when he hands over stuff to the ballerinas." She indicated. "See: Moose Lodge, on the road north to Taos. Next time he does the trip Sylvan is sure they will try to lift him, so we'll have to pick him up first somehow."

"Unless the Minute Men get there before us."

"Sylvan's antennae seem to extend in that direction too, and he thinks we are still at least one step ahead of them."

"Marcie, how the devil does Sylvan…"

She ignored this.

"So tomorrow we'll drive there over the mountains, check out Moose Lodge without looking conspicuous, do some touristy stuff in Taos, trickle back. It'll take us all day."

"Are you sure you're up to it?"

"Oh yes. These things only last a day, thank the Lord. Right as rain the next morning. But I'm pretty tired still. I'm going to bed, which means you will have to wait up for Sylvan's call. Wake me if it's urgent."

She came round the table and dropped a kiss on his forehead.

"Nighty-night, sweetie. Thanks for caring. Sleep well."

Chapter Fifteen

"I have fixed for you a picnic lunch," said Rosa. "There's fresh tortillas, cold chicken, tomatoes, and some brownies left over from last night. And two bottles of water. You must drink plenty in this climate!" she added scoldingly as she handed over the large picnic basket. "Would you and the Señor like pot roast or chillies rellenos for dinner this evening?"

"Oh, chillies rellenos, definitely," said Marcie. "We can have pot roast any time in Washington. I want Tom to try some of these wonderful local dishes you made when I was here with Roger. I know he'll love them."

Well, probably, thought Tom somewhat wistfully, picturing a heaped plateful of succulent slow-cooked beef, smothered in onions.

The Ford's V8 engine started up first time, and the floor-mounted stick shift slid smoothly into gear as Marcie backed the station wagon out of the carport, then turned and headed down the long driveway towards the main road. A short way north lay the pueblo of Pojoque, where a sign pointing to the right directed them to *The High Road to Taos*.

"Where's the Low Road, then?" asked Tom.

"In the other direction, of course, silly."

He glanced at her with a grin and sang "*Och, you'll tak' the high road —*"

"*And you'll tak' the low road,*" she joined in.

"*And I'll be in Scotland afore ye!*" they sang, Tom finishing the chorus.

"You have a very good voice," she commented, watching the road.

"That'll be the Welsh in my soul, look you."

"Silly," she said, laughing.

For the next few miles she concentrated on the road, which was narrow and had obviously not been resurfaced for years. After a little while she said, "But don't you think there's something in the Celtic myth?"

"I don't know. The Welsh thing was all invented in the last century anyway – bards and eisteddfods and the like."

"But even so… Tom, do you realise we are all Celts?"

"We are? Who's we?"

"You and me and Sylvan."

"So we are. Well, all I can say is perhaps it explains why we all ended up in this absurd situation. Hopeless romantics, the lot of us. Look you," he added, just to hear her laugh again.

The road wound up and up through forests of twisted piñon pines, oak and aspen. Here the country seemed quite lush and intimate by contrast with the great plain below, which was studded with stunted, scrubby bushes almost as far as the eye could see. Tom spotted infrequent homesteads scattered through the steep woodland,

As Marcie navigated the bends, Tom saw that they were driving parallel to a vertiginous drop on the near side of the road. She slowed right down on one particularly sharp left-hand curve, where a small stream burbled across the road and tumbled into the ravine. Tom found himself staring down into it.

"Dear God," he exclaimed. "If you approached that bend just a little bit too fast you'd go straight over the edge!"

A short way off the road, in the U-shaped peninsula of land tucked into the lee of the sharp bend, stood a small building, its rusted tin roof crowned with a wooden cross. The rivulet they had driven across ran down from the slope behind and around the south side of the structure. Marcie pulled off to park in a small lay-by on the opposite side.

"Roger and I thought we could meet up with Sylvan here," said Marcie, getting out of the car. "Come."

She led the way to the little chapel and pushed open the ramshackle wooden door with its peeling paint. The interior was dark after the bright sunlight and it took a while for Tom's eyes to adjust. Gradually he made out an altar at the far end with unlit lamps hanging above it. A few of the votive candles in the rack nearby were lit and reflected gleams of light from the tinsel and tin decorations. Among them perched brightly painted Holy Families and a bevy of saints.

He peered into some of the deeper recesses and found rows of grotesque figurines in pottery, shelf upon shelf. Few could be called pretty; many must have been specifically designed to be hideous.

"Look at these, Marcie. Spooky, don't you think?" He turned and saw her lighting a candle, which she placed in the rack; he remembered the convent education.

"Those," she said, joining him, "are the souls of the damned. But here they are about to find peace with the Holy Family here and these rather jolly looking old saints."

"What's a place like this doing way up here?"

"It was probably a sacred Indian site before the Spaniards invaded, then the newcomers built a chapel on top of it. They did that a lot, to try and exterminate the indigenous religions. There's probably been a shrine of some sort here for hundreds of years, and the two traditions have become quite intertwined. The figurines are Indian in origin, but these…"

She indicated some curious little items lying on the altar. Made of pottery, tin or wood, they were shaped like miniature body parts; arms, legs, feet, hands, even a tiny carved heart.

"…these are Hispanic, they're called *milagros*, little miracles; they're charms people leave here when they need healing. So if you've broken your leg you leave a leg charm, and so on. The little heart could be for a heart attack or love-sickness."

"Marcie, you must have an encyclopaedia in your head. How do you know all this stuff?"

She gave him what could only be called a cheeky grin.

"I'm just showing off. I got it all out of the books at Piñones when I came here with Roger."

"Well, I'm still impressed."

"Come on, we'd better get going, it's still quite a long way to Taos. You can drive now and get used to the road. We may have to do it fast in the dark."

It took them fifteen minutes to reach Moose Lodge. Built for the tourist trade but sadly decrepit after the war years, it stood on a small eminence on the west side of the road. The rusting Coca-Cola sign across the front porch and the rotting picnic tables in the front yard were uninviting. Before the war it must have been used by tourists on the way up to the Indian centre of Taos; now it appeared to be a place for a drink or a game of pool for local farmers and their families. A couple of pickup trucks, an ancient Ford and a red Chevrolet convertible were parked outside and Tom pulled in beside the Chevy. They entered through swing doors into a large bar room with bare wooden floors and a scatter of deal tables. At one of these, three men were seated with mugs of beer in front of them: two Indians and an old, bent, thin-faced man wearing a tattered deerskin jacket over a torn check shirt. He had a wispy beard and sucked, seemingly out of habit rather than smoking pleasure, on an ancient but empty corn cob. He looked like some trapper who might have come west with Davy Crockett. A couple of farmers, in well-worn jeans and scruffy Mexican riding boots, were propped easily against the bar, smoking, chatting and sipping their beers. The two groups looked up briefly at Tom and Marcie, then returned their attention to their companions and their drinks. At the far end of the room a tall, skinny youth and a young woman in a faded gingham sundress were shooting pool at the long table and ignored the newcomers.

"What can I get for you folks?" asked the bartender.

"Oh, hi there. Two Dr Peppers, please," said Marcie.

Once again Tom marvelled at her ability to fit in; listening to her speak, no one would have guessed she was not American born and bred. Tom didn't much care for Dr Pepper, but he was reluctant to risk their tentative but, he hoped, growing rapport by asking for a Budweiser instead.

They carried their drinks over to a table by the somewhat grubby window, then lit cigarettes and sat quietly, surveying the room while pretending not to. After about ten minutes, Marcie caught Tom's eye and almost imperceptibly moved her head and looked towards the door. Picking up her unspoken message, Tom set down his glass, hoping she wouldn't notice he'd only drunk half; they got up unhurriedly and sauntered out.

"Curious choice of location for our foreign friends to meet," he commented as they drove away.

"Well, I guess they have their reasons. They would need a place where they could be sure there was no one else from Los Alamos, and this almost certainly fits the bill."

"And we were obviously strangers, but the locals paid almost no attention to us, which would also suit the ballerinas."

As they approached Taos there was a noticeable increase in traffic.

"Taos is quite a tourist attraction," Marcie told him. "And it's an absolute Mecca for artists: the scenery, the clean air, the light."

They parked the car and strolled slowly through the town. The pinkish-brown adobe buildings seemed gilded by the sunlight and contrasted with the verdant green of the many shade trees and the brilliant purple of bougainvillea. Wooden planters were filled with brightly-coloured portulaca and spiky, silvery agave, and the air smelled faintly of sage and lavender. And over all arched an almost cloudless azure sky.

In the centre of the main plaza was a small, paved park, with wrought iron benches, a large cottonwood tree, some smaller shade trees and a gazebo. The buildings surrounding the plaza were mostly adobe, no more than two storeys high; wooden pillars supported a wooden ceiling above the side-walk. The shop windows were filled with tooled leather belts and boots, cowboy hats, fringed buckskin jackets; camping and mountaineering gear; Indian pottery, moccasins and carved wooden animals; and a miscellany of souvenirs.

Marcie paused by a shop window to inspect a display of silver jewellery set with turquoise, topaz and malachite.

"Do you know, I think I'll treat myself to a pair of those divine earrings." She turned towards the door. "Coming?"

Impulsively he said, "Let me buy them for you… O Queen of the Gypsies," he added, to take away any perception of his being presumptuous.

"Oh, *très galant*, kind sir, but I couldn't possibly allow it!"

"Indulge a humble sailor, your graciousness."

"Well, just this once," she said and positively dimpled.

They wandered on past the shops, Tom's eye caught by one selling leather-work and hunting knives. Marcie nudged his arm and said, "Do you know, it's almost one o'clock. Let's eat lunch here: we can sit over there, look, in the little park. I'm jolly peckish."

"Me too – I'll fetch the picnic basket. Stay there and don't go away!"

"Promise."

When he got back she was sitting on one of the benches in the shade of the cottonwood tree. She offered him a package wrapped in brown paper. Inside was a leather belt, intricately worked, with a silver buckle.

"Marcie, you shouldn't –"

She held up an admonitory finger.

"Hush. I know it's your birthday soon. And it was either that or a hunting knife, and I don't think you'd have much need for one of those back in DC."

"Thank you. I'll treasure it."

They ate slices of cold chicken wrapped in Rosa's tortillas, with small ripe tomatoes. When they had finished Marcie said, "We've still got plenty of time. Shame to go straight back. Why don't we go and see the pueblo? We'll have to drive there, though."

The pueblo – one of the oldest continuously inhabited

communities in the United States, according to the signage – was certainly impressive: a sprawling complex of multi-level adobe buildings, which in places rose to five storeys. Wooden beam ends poked out just below the flat roofs, and the wooden door and window- frames were painted bright blue. Behind rose the lofty peaks of the Sangre de Cristo mountains.

"We can't go inside, people live there," said Marcie, indicating a gaggle of laughing children playing with a circular disk on a string, whirling it round then pulling and releasing to make a buzzing sound. She took his arm. "Let's take a look at the church."

The church of San Geronimo was built of the same adobe as the pueblo, its matching bell towers flanking the facade and crowned with three white crosses. In the plaza in front, Indian women in their traditional dress of colourful skirts, a dark bodice over a white blouse, a woven sash and calfskin boots, sold their handicrafts from half-a-dozen little stalls clustered around a mesquite tree. The interior was small, but, unlike the mountain shrine they had visited that morning, filled with light; Tom much preferred it. Statues of saints stood in blue-painted niches cut into the thick, whitewashed walls and a Madonna smiled benevolently down on them from her own niche above the altar.

As they walked back to the station wagon Marcie said, "I don't think we need to retrace our steps from this morning, do we, Tom? Let's take the low road back."

The road south, wider and better paved than the mountain road, crossed a high plateau then squeezed into the narrow corridor between the mountains and the Rio Grande gorge. When they reached the junction at Pojoque, Marcie turned to the right.

"Piñones is in the other direction. I just want to go as far as the river."

In less than fifteen minutes she pulled off and parked in an open area to the side of the road. The gorge was not as deep here as further north, with flat banks on either side wide enough and at a suitable height to support a single-lane suspension bridge, with sides and roadbed of wood, over which the road continued. It looked hardly strong enough to take an automobile, let alone a lorry. There was no traffic coming, and Marcie led Tom a little way onto the bridge so that they could see down to the river below, its quiet flow belying the turbulence upstream. The water was a muddy brown from the suspended sand and silt washed down from the mountains.

"I love this old bridge," said Marcie, "I hope they never replace it with some ugly modern monstrosity."

She turned and looked to the west. "That's the way to Los Alamos," she said.

Tom said nothing, but also looked in the direction of her gaze. The air was so clear that he could see all the way to the wooded slopes of the Jemez range fifteen miles away; the community of Los Alamos, the headquarters of the American nuclear programme, nestled at their base. *Viktor Bronski could be looking at the same mountains right now*, he mused, *with no idea of what is in store for him. How do we know that we are doing the right thing?*

In the distance a lone vehicle was speeding towards the bridge. Marcie touched his arm lightly: "Come on, time to go back to Piñones."

They had almost reached the car when Tom stopped and pointed towards a very curious bird poking at something that was trying to hide in the dusty bushes on the other side of the road; it looked like a prehistoric chicken, with long brown tail feathers and a spiky crest on its head.

"What on earth's that?"

"Roadrunner," she breathed in awe.

The object of the bird's attention reared up, flicking its long, pink forked tongue rapidly in and out at its tormentor; Tom could clearly hear the distinctive sound of the rattle at the end of its tail. The roadrunner raised its tail feathers, spread out its wings and stabbed at the snake with its wickedly sharp bill. The rattler ducked, the bird stabbed again, the snake's head darted forward as it tried to strike, and for a few seconds the two creatures circled each other in a deadly dance, stabbing and striking, before the snake had evidently decided that enough was enough and tried to make a dash for the safety of the bushes. Its body undulated with surprising speed, but the powerful legs of the roadrunner were faster. Its bill caught the snake just behind the head and lifted it up, smashing its victim against the hard ground again and again until the flailing body went limp.

"Bloody hell!" exclaimed Tom with a deep exhalation. "Roadrunner triumphs over rattlesnake. Let's hope it's a good omen."

They arrived back at Pinoñes as the evening sun was lighting up the mountains, and went their separate ways to shower and change, before meeting on the patio for margaritas, followed by the promised chilli rellenos.

After supper they sat at the table, waiting for Sylvan's phone call. They went over the day, rehearsing the probable scenario for the actual collection of Bronski. They were trying to avoid the obvious words – kidnap, lift, heist – until Tom suggested the word he had used in his discussion with Sylvan: *rescue*.

"Oh, that's absolutely it," said Marcie. "That's exactly what we are doing. We're rescuing him; from the Russians, the Americans, and himself."

Tom was reviewing the layout of Moose Lodge in his head.

"I can't think the Russians will try and snatch him inside, in the bar, do you? They'd be more likely to bundle him into their vehicle in the car park. Or entice him," he added.

"So realistically we will need to get him before he arrives at Moose Lodge. How are we going to do that?"

They were silent for a while. Then Tom said slowly, "You remember that dangerous bend just before the chapel? Well, we know he's driving, and he will have to slow right down into second, probably first. Suppose we put up some sort of fake 'Road Closed' sign so he has to stop. Then we persuade him – God knows how, I suppose Sylvan knows what he's doing – to come quietly with us in the station wagon. We drive sedately on past Moose Lodge, our passenger lying doggo in the back seat with a blanket over him and then drive hell for leather for the Colorado state border."

"What about his car? We can't just leave it can we?"

Tom saw again the sharp left-hand bend, the ravine below with the thundering river, a couple of rickety trestles of unsawn larch the only thing that stood between safety and certain death. Hardly believing what he was saying, he murmured, "We could push it over the edge… it would look like an accident. Or suicide?"

At nine the phone rang and Marcie took it. Tom listened as she outlined their idea to Sylvan. Putting the phone down she said, "He agrees. Says it's a good plan. He's somewhere in the area and is going to check it out himself tomorrow."

"Is he coming here?"

"No. Says it's better if we're not seen together. He says he will provide some road lamps for the fake closure, and you can spend tomorrow making the sign."

"Oh great. Just how I'd planned on spending tomorrow."

She yawned and stretched her slim arms above her head in a gesture almost of abandonment.

"But didn't we have a lovely day? God, I'm dog-tired. I'm off for some shut-eye. Goodnight, sweetie."

"Marcie…"

She looked at him. "Sweetie?"

"Nothing. I…"

She came around the table and kissed him. He didn't dare move.

"Goodnight," she murmured, and turned to leave the room. He watched her go.

Chapter Sixteen

At breakfast the next morning Marcie said, "I thought I'd take out one of the quarter horses with Pedro before he goes to Alberquerque this afternoon. They need exercising. You don't ride, do you?"

All of her upper-class background came out in that last question and Tom was suddenly smarting. And he was getting fed up with the way she seemed to be leading him on and then backing off. Just like Susan after all. Stupid to presume that Lady Marcia would be interested enough in him to even think about… about…

"No, I don't," he said, getting up abruptly and taking his coffee cup outside onto the patio. It was still pleasantly cool, but the sun was starting to creep across the desert, which already shimmered in the light. After a short time he heard her come through the glass doors. She sat down beside him on the wooden bench. He didn't look at her.

"Tom, dear, what's the matter? Have I upset you?"

He had determined to act as if he couldn't care less about anything Marcie did or said.

"No, of course not," he snapped.

She waited.

It was no good. He put his cup on the table and sighed. "Well yes, OK, it's just… I don't know, it's nothing really. Well just now, you came over all Lady Marcia speaking to the oik, and I thought we, I thought… I don't know what I thought, to be honest."

In a small voice she said, "I'm *so* sorry. I wouldn't want to upset you for the world. I'm very… I'm very fond of you Tom."

He looked up hopefully. "Really?"

"Really. Don't let's argue. We've got a couple of days still to relax and… and enjoy ourselves in this lovely place. It's like being out of the real world. Let's make the most of it."

She stroked his arm and his irritation vanished as quickly as it had come and he felt ashamed at his absurd prickliness.

"I won't stay out long. It gets too hot and I haven't ridden for a while so I'll end up stiff as a board if I overdo it."

"Anyway," he said, suddenly happy, "I've got a 'Road Closed' sign to construct."

"Come over to the stables with me and Pedro can show you where to find stuff."

Tom watched enviously as Pedro led out the horses and swung Marcie up into the big western saddle. His initial vision of her in hunting habit with bowler and veil had been overtaken by the real-life woman in jeans, checked shirt and Stetson. She slid her feet in their cowboy boots into the heavily ornate iron stirrups and gathered up the reins, holding them high in one hand, American-style. Looking down at him she smiled wickedly and said in an exaggerated British accent, "Absolutely *not* what one is used to when one rides to hounds with the Quorn, darling!"

He had to laugh as he watched the horses lope slowly and rather reluctantly towards the band of shady mesquite trees that showed the course of the now dry river. Then he picked up the hammer and nails Pedro had produced and, whistling "Loch Lomond" loudly and tunelessly, went to find some old pieces of wood.

After a light lunch they waved goodbye to Pedro and Rosa as the couple set off to Albuquerque in their truck, then went gratefully back into the cool interior of the house.

"I'm going to nap," said Marcie. "Probably did stay out a bit too long this morning, but old Blue is just such a lovely willing horse – he'd go all day. See you later. Cuppa at four?"

"Of course. We're British. Must keep up the standards among the natives."

Left alone, Tom took *Riddle of the Sands* into the living room, determined to finish it. The excitement and tension of the final chapters gripped him yet again, and he read through to the very last page where the double agent steps over the side of the yacht and disappears, rather than face disgrace in England. Satisfied, he was about to close the book when he noticed that the title of the last chapter was *We Achieve our Double Aim*. Hope that's another good omen, he thought. He flopped on the sofa, kicked off his shoes, let his eyes close and abandoned himself to sleep.

"Wake up, Sleeping Beauty, I've brought you a cup of tea."

Tom opened his eyes and sat up. "Four o'clock already? I only meant to doze for fifteen minutes."

"It's this place," said Marcie, setting down the tea tray, "very conducive to relaxing. I've only just got up from my nap myself – won't sleep a wink tonight."

She poured out the tea and handed a cup to Tom.

"Do I see chocolate cake?" he asked.

"Yes, Rosa made it for us. Devil's Food cake. Fabulous name,"

"Brilliant," he said, biting into a large slice. When he could speak properly he said, "I've been meaning to ask you: that little painting, it's very odd, but I like it."

"The landscape? I love it. It's by Georgia O'Keefe. She lives near here somewhere."

"Doesn't Sylvan have one of hers? Those lilies?"

"Yes, he got that a while ago. A very good investment."

When he had finished a second slice of cake she asked, "Do you play chess?"

"Well, I know the moves, but I'm not exactly a Grand Master. Used to play sometimes with my dad, but haven't touched a board in years."

"Did you see this?" She indicated a small carved table under the east window with a chessboard incorporated into the top. "Fancy a game? Loser makes the drinks."

They found the matching chess pieces in a box on one of the shelves by the fireplace, which was stacked with sets of cards, jigsaws and board games.

Marcie played decisively and with undivided attention. *Just as you might expect,* Tom mused as he watched her, a slight frown creasing her forehead as she concentrated on calculating her next move. It took all of Tom's skill to keep up with her, but eventually she declared triumphantly, "Checkmate!"

"Told you I was rusty."

"No, actually you play well, that was a challenge. But I won, so you can make the drinks – I'll have a margarita, please."

He stood in the kitchen making the margaritas while Marcie took the chilli con carne from the fridge and put it in the oven.

"There," she said. "That's about the limit of my cooking skills. They did try and teach us some basics at the convent, but I was never interested."

"What were you interested in?" he asked cutting and squeezing limes.

"Not much. I liked French literature. I'm quite good at French. And lacrosse."

"Captain of the school team. Here, what do you think of this?"

Marcie took a sip and gasped.

"Tom, however much tequila have you put in it?"

"Quite a lot, actually."

"Well, you need to balance it out with some more triple sec. Here, give me the bottle."

They took the drinks out on the patio and sat side by side on one of the wooden benches, shoulders occasionally touching, staring out into the desert night. Tom sipped his drink contentedly. *If nothing else,* he thought, *I will never forget this moment, sitting here, in this extraordinary, beautiful place, with this extraordinary, beautiful woman beside me, watching the stars appear and listening to the ghostly trilling of the owls.* He could tell that Marcie was as reluctant as he to break the mood but eventually she said, "I'd better go and retrieve Rosa's chilli. It would be a shame for it to dry up in the oven. And we'd be hungry."

She patted his thigh gently and left.

Sylvan phoned at nine to check in and to tell them to definitely stand by for the third in three days' time.

Tom was exploring the large collection of neatly catalogued records which covered just about every mood and taste.

"What do you fancy?" he asked.

"You choose. I have no taste in music."

A friend at Oxford had introduced him to the Elgar cello concerto, and he found it now. He set the record on the turntable, lowering the needle carefully and the gorgeous sound filled the air. The wrought-iron lamps with their parchment shades cast a warm glow around the room.

They sat in silence until it had nearly finished and he realised she was crying.

"Marcie…"

He put his arm around her and she laid her head on his shoulder and they stayed like that until the last chords died away.

"Sorry. Bit weepy at the moment. Must be the music. It's so – so – I don't know how to describe it. It's… it's heartbreaking."

He hugged her.

"It's fine. It's fine. Weep as much as you want."

He was hoping against hope that she wouldn't retreat back behind her everyday sharp and witty persona.

She pulled away and fumbled for a handkerchief.

"Not just the music – it's what it brings back."

He waited.

"It was Gareth's favourite piece."

He hardly dared speak but wanted her to go on. "Gareth…?"

"My fiancé."

"Your…?"

To his horror, it seemed the mask was back in place.

"You're doing it again Tom! Yes, my fiancé! Or did you think I was a dedicated spinster?"

"No. No, I didn't. Someone as beautiful, as, as amazing as you – how could anyone not love you? He is, was," – he struggled – "a very lucky man."

To his joy and relief, she leant back against him.

"Gareth was killed in the Spanish war. In thirty-eight. He was an artist. An artist! Of course my parents thought the whole thing quite appalling. Artist… Marxist… you can imagine."

"*Homage to Catalonia*," he murmured.

"Yes. I take it with me most places."

She sniffed like a child, and said defensively, "I think he would have been a very good artist had he… had he…"

They were quiet. Through the open door they could hear the chirruping sound of cicadas and the distant howl of a coyote.

She turned her head to look at him. "He was Welsh, like you. Perhaps that's why… no, it's not. It's just you."

She put her hands to his face and kissed him passionately. Then she drew back a little and said fiercely, "I'm not being unfaithful to Gareth. I loved him, but he's gone, he's *gone*."

She put her head back on his shoulder and he laid his cheek on her sleek hair, wondering at its softness. They sat there peacefully for some time, then she stood, took his hand and led him to her bedroom.

Chapter Seventeen

They stayed in bed late the next morning, then they made coffee and sat at the table in bath robes swapping stories about their pasts and learning more about each other. Though she had not gone to university, Marcie was not uneducated as she had self-deprecatingly claimed. Tom discovered that she was something of an autodidact; she was well-read, and had an impressive knowledge of history, art and literature.

"You know that I'm three years older than you, don't you?" she asked.

"No, I didn't know that, and what's that got to do with anything anyway?"

"I thought most men liked younger women…"

"Well, I'm not most men. I like *you, ergo* I like older women."

She looked intently at his face.

"You have very blue eyes – that's unusual."

"All the men in my family – Dad, my brother and me – have the same colouring, blue eyes and mousy hair."

"It's not mousy," she replied, leaning across the table to run a hand through its slightly wavy thickness. "Hmm… I'd call it honey-coloured, somewhere between dark blond and light brown. Very fetching."

Eventually she stood up, sighed, stretched and said, "Suppose we'd better get dressed…"

"Why?" said Tom and pulled her onto his knee. She snuggled against him and said, "There's a bottle of white wine in the fridge. Why don't we take it back to bed with us for lunch?"

"Why don't we?"

So they did.

The sun was already dipping below the western mountain range when Tom went to take his shower. From his bedroom window facing east, he could see the peaks of the Sangre de Cristo bathed in shadow. Feeling refreshed and reinvigorated, he wandered into the kitchen, to find Marcie standing by the open refrigerator, staring inside.

"What are we going to eat for dinner?" she asked, sounding worried. "We finished the chilli, and Rosa doesn't seem to have made us anything for today."

"Fear not," replied Tom, "I know you have admitted to being a hopeless cook, but though I say it myself, I am a dab hand around the kitchen. Miles has an amazing old book called *Fannie Farmer's Boston Cookbook* – something like that, anyway – and we two always-hungry bachelors have taught ourselves to whip up the most amazing meals. Are there any eggs?"

"Yes, lots."

"Cheese? An onion? Tomatoes?"

She got the ingredients out of the fridge and set them on the counter. "There's a bunch of spinach in here too, can you use that?"

"Spinach! And I say –"

"– the hell with it!"

"Perfect!" declared Tom, when they had stopped laughing. "Prepare for your taste buds to be dazzled, dear lady, by my world-famous *omelette de jour*."

Marcie pushed back her plate and patted her stomach.

"Mmm, that was perfectly scrummy. I'll need to digest for a little while. Anyway, we can't go to bed yet, dammit, we've got to wait until nine for Sylvan."

This reminder of the reason for their being here was unwelcome, but Tom felt he would be grateful for one more blissful night, one 'gaudy night' in the words of the Bard. He hadn't had a clue what Shakespeare had meant when he had first been made to study *Antony and Cleopatra* at school, but had found himself unexpectedly enchanted by the gorgeous language and the high romance. *Well, we're more Antony and Cleopatra than Romeo and Juliet*, he thought, *and now I know what a gaudy night is: one full of velvet skies and stars and fireworks exploding and deep wells of nothingness… one more gaudy night, then, and after that, who knows? Perhaps Marcie… perhaps he and Marcie…*

Determinedly, he put these fantasies to one side. To distract his mind from the rather sober recollection that none of the aforesaid lovers ended well, he went to explore the games on the living room shelf. "Oh look," he said, "Monopoly. Want to play?"

She wrinkled up her nose and rolled her eyes.

"Boring. And takes far too long."

"Anyway," he said, putting it back, "it extols and encourages capitalism. Dammed if I'm going to participate!"

She laughed. "Oh Tom, you're in your Sylvan mood again."

"No. I'm not. I'm in my own mood, and it's a very good one." He sat beside her on the sofa and kissed her ear. "I remember a story going around during the war that the British Secret Service hid things like compasses and maps and money in Monopoly sets and then distributed them through fake charities to POW's in Germany. To help them if they escaped. Not sure if it was true, though. What about checkers? Or racing demon?"

They settled on backgammon and played contentedly until the phone rang. Marcie took the call.

"It's definitely on for the third," she said slowly, as she put the phone down. "He's going to let us know the final details tomorrow." She came over and sat beside him on the sofa and stroked his hand. "Tom, are you all right with it?"

"Yes, of course. I'm not backing out now! But…"

"But what?"

He shook his head.

"I still can't work out how Sylvan gets all this information. I know you said he works for MI6 but…"

He looked at her.

"He has contacts…"

"What do you mean? What sort of contacts?"

"Russian," she said.

"Russian? Meaning what? Because he works for MI6? Do they give him information?"

"It's more than that."

"Marcie, what do you mean?"

A long sigh.

"The Russians have some sort of hold on Sylvan; something that happened a long time ago. They've been blackmailing him for years."

The gaudy night fireworks crashed and burned. He stared at her and saw Patrick Marsden's shattered head.

Chapter Eighteen

"Sylvan… are you saying… is he… *Marcie*!" Tom almost shouted, angrily.

She held up her hands as though to defend herself, and he was instantly contrite.

"Sorry! Sorry. It's just… I find it hard to believe."

"Of course you do. Me too. But I've known him long enough and well enough to know it's true."

Again, unpleasant suspicions about the relationship between her and Sylvan forced themselves into his head. "Do you and Sylvan… have you and Sylvan, please Marcie, you have to tell me."

She smiled. "No," she said, "believe me, we don't have that sort of relationship. There's been no one since Gareth died that I've cared for. Except you."

"I should never have asked, oh God, I'm so sorry. It's the shock. Forgive me."

Marcie reached out and gently placed her hands over his.

"I had other affairs after Gareth, but none of them lasted, none of them meant anything. I've been sleepwalking all these years. You've woken me up."

She stood up and went to the drinks cabinet, opened it and took out a bottle of Jim Beam.

"Double?" she asked. "You look as if you need it."

She came back with the glasses and he took a grateful swig.

"Better?"

"I suppose. But why are you telling me this?"

She hunched her shoulders and hugged her glass to her.

"To be honest, I don't really know. Because of last night? Today? It just came out. But I think we should all be honest with each other."

"Well, bloody Sylvan's not been honest with me, or anyone else for that matter, has he!"

"No. But it's why he's been instrumental in setting up Operation Roadrunner."

Tom shook his head. "I don't see…"

Marcie took two cigarettes from the silver box on the coffee table and put them between her lips. She lit them both and handed one to Tom, who took a deep drag to calm himself; he found her simple gesture almost painfully intimate.

She drew deeply on her own cigarette and let out a long swirl of smoke.

"It's a – what would you call it – an act of redemption. By rescuing Bronski from a fairly ghastly fate with either the Russians or the Americans, and by handing him over to the Brits, Sylvan will have made up for any sins he has been forced to commit, any betrayals of his country."

"Is that what he told you?"

"More or less."

"He's mad!"

"A holy fool?" she murmured. "The essence of the Catholic faith is the promise of salvation for all who truly repent."

"Is that why we're here? To make Sylvan feel better about himself? I always had my doubts about his plan. But now I'm convinced it's crazy."

"Or," said Marcie, "an act of great patriotism? He can't do all those bonkers things that won Victoria crosses; you know, capturing a machine gun post single-handed or, or… oh, driving a torpedo boat into a German battleship, so it's something he can do. To make up for the past."

"A grand gesture. Well, let me tell you, grand gestures can get you killed," said Tom bitterly. "My brother Richard, he led the German planes away from the inexperienced boys under his command, and where did that get him? The bottom of the bloody English Channel, that's where. Oh, they gave him a posthumous medal, but I'd rather have a live brother than a dead hero."

"Oh Tom, I'm so sorry," she said quietly.

"Well, I suppose it's too late to back out now." He put his head in his hands. "And it was all so wonderful, magical, being here, and now…"

"Now what?" she asked, and he felt her arm come around his bowed shoulders. "Why should it come between us? Why spoil it? Tom, you have made me so happy. I've not felt like this for a very long time."

She put her fingers under his chin and lifted his head so he had to look at her. She kissed him.

"Come to bed."

Pedro and Rosa arrived back at lunch time on Tuesday to find Tom and Marcie sitting decorously on separate sofas in the living room reading magazines.

"Did you have a wonderful time, Rosa?"

"Si, Señora. It was lovely. And you? You have managed all right without us?"

"Oh yes, *gracias*. Just about got by," she said, completely straight-faced. Tom didn't dare catch her eye.

"By the way, Rosa," she added, "Roger phoned while you were away. Remember I said when we arrived that we were going to pick him up in Albuquerque and drive down to El Paso together?"

This was the cover story they'd agreed on, to explain their sudden departure and to misdirect anyone who might come looking for them; but without knowing the exact timing of what they were now referring to as 'the rescue', Marcie had deliberately skimmed over the details. Now she improvised.

"Well, he wants us to come tomorrow afternoon to have dinner and stay the night with his friends in Albuquerque, then we'll go to El Paso the next day for the holiday weekend."

"So soon, Señora Marcie? I thought you would be here a few more days."

She sounded genuinely regretful.

"Yes, it's a little sooner than I'd expected, but, well… you know Roger!"

"He'll be back here soon," Tom added. "Marcie and I will go back east directly from El Paso, and Roger will come back in the station wagon."

"Me and Pedro, we will miss you very much, Señora, you are like family."

"And I'll miss you," said Marcie, standing up and giving the other woman an affectionate hug. "You've been so kind to us, and the food has been divine. I'm a hopeless cook, but if my own grandmother had cooked as well as your *abuela,* maybe I would do better."

"I make mole for your supper, is OK?"

"Certainly is. Isn't it Tom?" He could only nod.

As soon as Rosa had left the room, Tom asked, "So, what is moh-lay? Will I like it?"

"Of course you will. It's spelled m-o-l-e, like Ratty and Badger's friend," explained Marcie, "but pronounced moh-lay. It's very special, has lots of ingredients and takes a long time to make, I believe. Rosa's doing it as a farewell gift. Trust me, you will love it."

In the afternoon they walked together out into the surrounding desert, and Tom proudly pointed out the various plants that he had read about. Some of the cacti were in bloom, with flowers like brightly-coloured jewels. It was hot, but the air was dry and the sun felt good against their skin. *This will probably the last time we will ever come here*, he thought.

When they returned, Rosa brought them tea in the living room.

"Pedro asks if you like to go for a ride before dinner, Señora Marcie, when is a bit cooler?"

She hesitated for a moment and then said, "Yes. Yes, I think I will. Would you tell Pedro, please?"

Tom just about waited until Rosa was out of the door before lunging at Marcie and whispering in her ear, "Lucky old Blue!"

"Don't! I won't be able to stop laughing and Pedro will think there's something wrong."

"There's nothing wrong," he said, kissing her, "Everything is just A1."

For a moment a shadow of doubt seemed to show on her face. "Are you sure?"

"I am completely sure."

Rosa brought the serving dish to the table and stood by watching as they tasted the food.

"It's absolutely delicious," Tom told her.

"Is mole poblano, Señor, from my *abuela's* own recipe. Can you guess what is in it?"

He played along with the guessing game.

"Tomatoes, onions… a little bit spicy, so chilli peppers, I suppose, a bit sweet? What gives it that deep brown colour? Prunes? I give up… ground-up moles?"

Marcie laughed, Rosa looked puzzled.

"What are moles?"

"Small furry animals."

Rosa was shocked and alarmed. "Oh no, no Señor Tom, you must not think that! It is chocolate, Señor, chocolate! The finest dark, unsweetened, Mexican cacao." She added huffily, "It was my country that gave chocolate to the world."

Trying to make up for his mistimed joke, he said, "Rosa, I would never have guessed, and it's quite the best thing I have ever eaten. Please let me assure you that the world is eternally gratefully to your country for the gift."

Mollified, she left; Marcie kicked Tom's ankle and giggled.

The call came promptly at nine. Marcie said very little in response to Sylvan beyond "Yes, OK. Will do," then came and sat beside Tom and took his hand. "We're on. Our passenger will be at the pick-up point at seven-thirty tomorrow. The ballerinas will be waiting for him there, so we have to get the road works into place further down the road at the bend shortly before he's due. Mr Woods wants us at the rendezvous by five-thirty, so to be on the safe side we'll have to leave here by four at the latest. I timed it. He says our passenger won't be followed, but if the Minute Men have got wind of this they could be up there somewhere."

Her use of the absurd code they had devised half-jokingly brought him back to the seriousness of what they were taking on.

She continued, "The car is a Hillman Minx, so easy to spot."

"A *Hillman Minx*?"

He was pleased to see her smile at the absurdity.

"Apparently he loves British cars. Oh God, we mustn't forget the road sign! Mr Woods will meet us there with the rest of the equipment. And we need to take water and something to eat. There's plenty of fruit in the kitchen, and tortillas, I don't think Rosa will notice if we take some of them."

"I could sneak an extra sandwich at lunch…"

"There's a couple of horse blankets in the back of the station wagon – we'll need those, it'll be a long night."

He kissed her. "I hope this one is too. It's our last here."

"I know," she said. "Let's make the most of it."

Chapter Nineteen

At three forty-five the following afternoon, Tom and Marcie waved goodbye to Pedro and Rosa and headed the station wagon down the driveway. The turn-off at the main road was a long way from the house, so there was no chance of the hospitable couple seeing that they turned north instead of south towards Albuquerque. Tom felt a pang as they drove away from Pinoñes. It had become for him a magical place, their own Shangri La. These days here with Marcie – *God, was it really only five?* – had been some of the happiest in his life. He turned his head and caught a last glimpse of the house in the distance as the car crested a small rise, and then it was gone from sight. Marcie had seen it in the rear-view mirror; briefly she took her hand off the steering wheel and lightly touched his arm.

At four-thirty they pulled into the lay-by outside the old chapel.

"Stay here for a minute," said Tom, "I'll check and see if there's somewhere to park round the back, out of sight of the road – just in case."

As he walked up the slope towards the building, he spotted a large motorcycle parked outside the back door and stopped in his tracks. After a tense moment he cautiously approached the front. With a loud creak that made him jump, the door opened a fraction. He stood completely still, nerves tingling. Suddenly the door opened wide and a familiar figure emerged.

"Sylvan!" Tom grabbed the other's outstretched hand. "Good Lord, you nearly gave me heart failure. I thought the ballerinas were waiting for us."

"Sorry, dear boy, had to be sure it was you and *not* a ballerina. You're here in good time," replied Sylvan, patting Tom on the shoulder with his other hand. He called out to Marcie, "Pull your car in behind the chapel, Marcie, and park under the trees. There's room to turn it around so you're heading in the right direction when you leave."

Having parked as Sylvan specified, Marcie joined her fellow conspirators. She and Sylvan hugged and kissed each other on the cheek and whatever assurances Marcie had given him Tom could not smother a tiny pang of jealousy.

"Let's run through the plan," said Sylvan. He led them across the road to the cusp of the sharp bend. The drop into the ravine must have been close to three hundred feet, and there was nothing that could check the fall, except for a low bank along the shoulder of the road, surmounted by the pair of wooden trestles.

"Bronski will be driving up this hill." Sylvan pointed to the south. "His car will be easy to identify; probably the only Hillman Minx in the whole of New Mexico. It's a nice little machine, though to most people they are a heap of trouble. We had a clear entry to the US market after the war, this car was our spearhead. But as usual there were no spares, no service. Another British last."

There was a bitter edge to his voice.

"Get off your soapbox, Sylvan," said Tom, "we've got a job to do."

"He'll have to change down to first for the bend," Sylvan continued, ignoring Tom's reproof. "We set out the fake roadblock using your sign; I've got the lights, and we can use those trestles to make it more convincing. I hope he'll remember me, and when we tell him what's waiting at Moose Lodge, he'll cooperate. I know he's frightened of the Russians."

Back in the chapel, Sylvan showed them the two battery-operated hurricane lanterns, covered with red paper, that he had brought, then opened up the large Gladstone bag that was on the floor beside the altar.

"Hopefully we won't need these, but better safe than sorry," he said, pulling out a pair of small handguns and offering them. "Here's yours, Marcie, Tom."

Marcie took the weapon without hesitation, briefly weighed it in her hand for balance with a seemingly practised ease that Tom found somewhat disconcerting, and put it into her shoulder bag. Tom kept his hands at his side.

"Guns? Why do we need guns? I certainly don't intend to shoot anyone."

"You might have to if you come face to face with a Russian agent who was about to shoot *you*," said Sylvan grimly. "Don't look so peeved. Remember, I told you I couldn't promise no guns. I've got one too."

Gingerly, Tom took the proffered weapon and its cold, heavy deadliness brought flashbacks of the war. He checked the safety catch, then tucked it carefully into the pocket of his windcheater. Up to this point he had regarded Operation Roadrunner as a rather exciting escapade; suddenly he admitted to himself something he had been avoiding for too long: that it was both serious and dangerous, possibly deadly.

"Now, you go and find the location for our roadblock – I'm going to check out Moose Lodge – won't be a jiffy."

With a roar of the engine, the motorcycle took off quickly along the road to the north. Tom watched it go, recalling Sylvan's earlier denial of all mechanical knowledge. And where had he acquired the bike anyway? He was swiftly coming to realise that there was a great deal more to Sylvan than he had realised.

He was about to join Marcie on the other side of the road when she called urgently, "Something's coming!"

They sprinted back into the chapel, leaving the door open just a crack so that they could see the road. The vehicle passed slowly and continued on down the hill.

"Just a farm truck going home," said Marcie. "That's the only thing we've seen on the road since we got here; let's hope there won't be many more. We need to find a place to wait where we can spot Bronskl's car coming."

Tom looked back along the road. About one hundred yards south it sloped down and curved to the left, affording a long view down the hill.

"This is good; we can see all along the ridge from here. Should be able to identify the Hillman well before it reaches us."

"You take the first watch, Tom," said Marcie, "no point both of us hanging around out here. I'm going to go back to the chapel and get a few minutes' rest."

Tom positioned himself so that he could see any car coming up the hill. He looked at his watch: six thirty-five; Bronski was supposed to meet the ballerinas at Moose Lodge at seven-thirty, so would likely be here within the next half hour.

The barrier of the western mountains cut off the rays of the dying sun, which cast deep shadows beneath the trees. A little way beyond where he was waiting, Tom saw a deer leap from a thicket and dart across the road. He watched it disappear into a dense stand of aspens on the other side.

He lit a cigarette as once again doubts assailed him. *What are we really doing here?* He had so many questions for Sylvan, but knew Sylvan was not about to share his secrets. He pondered last night's revelations. If Sylvan really was, or had been, in cahoots with the Russians, as Marcie had suggested, then sooner or later the truth would inevitably come out and he would be in serious jeopardy, branded as a traitor. Didn't they hang traitors? And if he had also killed Patrick Marsden… no, Tom didn't even want to consider that.

He paced back and forth across the road trying to remember what Marcie had said about an act of redemption. Did he believe this?

One of the tenets of his Christian upbringing, which had stayed with him because of its moral and ethical sense, was that absolution can follow a contrite act. Sylvan, at great personal risk, had defied his Russian masters, if such they were, and had broken whatever hold they may have had on him. By snatching Bronski from both the Russians and the Americans, depriving these opposing powers of the scientist's potentially apocalyptic knowledge and turning it over to his own country, Sylvan was atoning for his sins of perfidy and deception. And maybe worse. He stubbed out his cigarette and absent-mindedly lit another.

"Penny for your thoughts, sweetie."

Marcie's voice interrupted his reverie.

"Oh, sorry, just daydreaming. Cigarette?"

"Please. I haven't got any with me."

He lit one for her and said, "Marcie…"

She drew on her cigarette and raised her eyebrows.

"I've been thinking about what you told me last night. About Sylvan."

"Mmm?"

"I think I understand. What he is trying to do. You know, an act of redemption. He's performed his penance and done so rather more effectively than by reciting a string of Hail Marys, in my opinion."

She let out a long breath and whispered, "I'm so pleased."

At that moment they heard the roar of the motorcycle and Sylvan came careening down the road, pulling up abruptly beside them.

"That was quick," said Tom, "you've only been gone about half an hour."

"I asked if I could use their bathroom. That was a mistake. Primitive beyond belief. And in America! But it gave me a plausible excuse for just popping in and out quickly. No sign of the Minute Men," he reported. "But there was a trio of toughs inside who were definitely not locals. Have to say they didn't look much like ballerinas either!" He chortled at his own joke. "Right, chaps, time to take up battle stations."

In his adrenalin-heightened state of awareness, Tom had a sudden flash of insight: Sylvan was actually enjoying this, revelling in the adventure – and the danger.

Tom and Marcie lifted the larch trestles from the verge and placed them squarely across the road, while Sylvan hurried back into the chapel to fetch the lanterns and Tom's *Road Closed* sign.

Within a few minutes they had constructed a makeshift roadblock. The barrier was more a psychological one than physical: it wouldn't stop a driver determined to push through, but it would do for the task at hand. Sylvan nodded with approval.

"Jolly good, that'll work. Now we just have to wait for our client to show up. Shouldn't be long."

And it wasn't.

"Look! There's something coming now."

A flash of light blinked and disappeared then blinked again as the last rays of the sun caught the metal trim of a car that was slowly driving up the winding, tree-covered escarpment towards them. Tom hurried back to his vantage point and stared intently at the approaching vehicle.

"Yes, that's his car," he called, and ran to join the others in front of the flimsy barrier.

They switched on the hurricane lanterns; Sylvan waved one at the oncoming vehicle as it cautiously approached the sharp bend. The Hillman slowed to a complete stop and an anxious-looking Bronski stuck his head out of the window.

"What's the problem," he asked in a querulous voice. "Why have you stopped me?"

Sylvan stepped forward to the driver's side.

"Road hazard ahead," he said firmly. "Step out of the car please, sir."

Responding instinctively to the authority in Sylvan's voice, Bronski picked up a small briefcase that was lying on the passenger seat and did as he was told. His face wrinkled into a frown as he stared intently at Sylvan.

"I know you, don't I? Ah, yes, Mr Ross, we talked at Los Alamos."

"Good evening, Professor Bronski, it's good to see you again."

"Why are *you* here? What is going on?"

"I'm sorry if we frightened you, but it was imperative that we get you to stop. The people you are going to meet this evening are planning to kidnap you and take you back to the Soviet Union. We're going to make sure that doesn't happen."

"No, they wouldn't… I don't believe you."

"Believe me, Professor; you know they are ruthless people. You will be their prisoner, you will never come back to America. Is that what you want?"

Tom was astonished at the change in Sylvan's demeanour: authoritative, to the point, almost threatening. It was obviously working on Bronski. His shoulders slumped and he groaned, "No, no, I don't want that."

In a softer tone Sylvan said, "We are British agents. Come with us, we'll take you back to Washington and then to England. You'll be safe there."

"How do I know I can trust you?"

Sylvan indicated Tom.

"This man is a British Royal Navy officer. Very high up. He has also worked on the atomic programme on behalf of the British. He will guarantee your safe conduct to England."

Tom swore under his breath in choice British Royal Navy language. Was this the real reason Sylvan had wanted him along?

Sylvan continued, "And this is Lady Marcia McKenna, a senior member of our embassy. You'll have to take a chance on trusting us, but I give you my word as a gentleman that what I am saying is true."

"England," muttered the scientist, "yes, I was happy in England. I worked there with Rutherford, you know. I could go back to Cambridge perhaps…" He looked at Tom, who tried to smile encouragingly. It seemed to work, for Bronski stood up straight and said, "Very well, Mr Ross, I will come with you."

Sylvan breathed out slowly.

"A wise decision. You won't regret it. Please give me your wallet, and your jacket. It's all right, we aren't going to do any harm. Thank you. Marcie, take Professor Bronski into the chapel. Tom and I will join you in a few minutes."

He waited until the pair were inside.

"Right, Tom, we'll have to ditch the Hillman."

He opened the driver's side door, put the car into neutral and released the handbrake.

"OK, put your back into it. A good hard shove and it's over the edge."

A rumble of falling rocks reverberated through the ravine as the little car crashed against the walls and came to rest on its back at the bottom.

"Pity about that," said Sylvan with a sigh. From the side of the road he picked up a rock the size of a large grapefruit. He put Bronski's wallet into the pocket of the scientist's jacket, wrapped the jacket around the rock and hurled the weighted bundle as far as he could out over the edge of the ravine.

"They'll find the car eventually," he said, "but of course it will be empty. If they find the jacket and the wallet let's hope they conclude that the body was thrown out in the fall and the eagles and mountain lions and coyotes and whatever other ghastly creatures roam these parts have taken care of it."

They went back into the chapel, where Bronski was sitting on the wooden bench at the side, looking quite bewildered by this sudden and unexpected turn of events. *Hardly surprising*, reflected Tom: the man had thought he was only leaving some papers for collection. He had had no clue that he was bound for the Soviet Union, still less that the indicator board had changed, and that he was now on his way to Britain.

Sylvan beckoned Tom and Marcie into a corner.

"Bronski was early," he said, "it's only just after seven. It'll be close to eight before the watchers at the Lodge realise that he's not coming. If you go right now you'll have a good head start, and they'll probably expect you to head south, which will buy you more time. The Russians won't be able to chase you once you're out of the mountains, too conspicuous."

"What about the FBI?" asked Tom.

"Tomorrow's a holiday, remember, and nobody will be at work on Friday. It'll be Monday or even Tuesday before anyone realizes that Bronski is missing. You'll be OK for a few days, but once you get back to Washington we'll have to keep him well hidden till we can get him out of the country."

Tom took the gun from his pocket and offered it to Sylvan.

"Good thing we didn't need these."

"You never know, you still have to get out of New Mexico. Hang onto them until you get to the dude ranch, then you can hand them over to Roger."

Tom didn't argue. With great reluctance, he replaced the weapon.

They helped Bronski into the back of the station wagon.

"Lie down, please, Professor," Sylvan instructed firmly, "and stay as still and as quiet as you can till you're well past Moose Lodge. If you're spotted by anyone there we could all be for the high jump."

"Are you not coming with us, Mr Ross?"

"No, I have things to do" – and exactly what were those *things*, Tom wanted to ask – "but don't worry, Lieutenant Davis and Lady Marcia will take good care of you."

Bronski nodded in acquiescence and curled up in a foetal position on the floor of the car, clutching his briefcase to his chest much as a child might its teddy bear. Tom covered him with one of the blankets and arranged their bags as well as he could to disguise the man's shape before climbing into the front passenger seat. Marcie was already behind the wheel and had switched on the ignition. As Sylvan leant through the window to say goodbye, she touched his arm.

"Sylvan…"

"Yes, I know, I'll be careful. You too. Now get going, my little chickadees. Last one back to Washington's a sissy!"

Marcie gunned the engine and pulled out from under the trees, heading north on the High Road to Taos. She slowed to a more sedate pace as they passed the Lodge. When they were well clear and there appeared to be no sign of pursuit, she pulled over at a wide spot by the side of the road.

"OK, Professor, you can come out now."

Tom opened the tailgate and helped the older man to his feet. Bronski briefly stretched his cramped limbs, then rather awkwardly indicated the trees that fringed the road.

"May I...?"

"I guess if you have to," said Tom unhappily. Just suppose they lost him now. He tried to keep an eye on Bronski's figure among the dark trees, but to his relief the little man was soon back and clambered into the back seat with the blanket draped around his shoulders. They were on their way again within minutes.

There were few people on the streets of Taos this evening; the Native American residents here had little reason to celebrate July Fourth. Before they reached the pueblo, the fugitives turned off onto a back road that cut across the Sangre de Cristos Mountains.

It was dark now, and a thin crescent moon was rising. It was slow going on these narrow, twisting mountain roads, with steep drop-offs and hairpin bends and only the car's headlights to illuminate the way. It wasn't just the road that was dangerous: a collision with one of the many deer that inhabited the pine forests that cloaked the slopes would be disastrous. They could sense rather than see the great peaks rising over twelve thousand feet on either side, blotting out the stars.

It took almost four hours to cover the hundred miles from Taos to where they rejoined the main road to Denver, and from there it was just half an hour to the Colorado state border.

Roger had given them detailed directions to the dude ranch near the town of Trinidad. It was after one o'clock in the morning when Tom turned off the road, drove under the hanging sign and bumped up the dirt track. A flashing torch waved them down.

It was Roger.

"God, am I glad to see you, old son," said Tom, climbing stiffly out of the car and pumping Roger's hand.

"Sylvan telephoned," Roger said, hugging Marcie. "Told me you were on your way. Well done. Pretty hairy drive, I expect."

"Not the most fun in the world, though Marcie did a lot of it.

Bronski managed to snooze a bit at the end." He opened the side door. "Wake up, Professor, we're here."

Roger led the way into one of several wooden block buildings clustered around the main ranch house.

"You can get your heads down here for a few hours. You'll need to be on your way early in the morning, you've got a long way to go. Marcie, this'll be your room, and you two chaps can bunk in here. The bathroom's just down the hall."

The simple room had two sets of bunk beds. Tom took off his shoes and lay down on one of the bottom bunks; Bronski was already lying on the other, snoring gently. Tom was so keyed up from the tensions of the day that he was sure he wouldn't be able to fall asleep, but it seemed he had hardly closed his eyes when Roger was shaking him awake.

Chapter Twenty

"Time to get up, Tom. Marcie's already in the kitchen and I've rustled up a spot of breakfast for you."

It was almost seven o'clock, and the sun had already risen well above the eastern horizon, lighting the mountain ranges to the west in a wash of pink and gold. He'd had barely five hours' sleep, but he'd often managed with far less during his time at sea.

There were thick slices of fried ham with fried eggs, beans, piles of toast and coffee.

"There you are," said Roger, beaming. "Cowboys' breakfast. Just what you need."

"Too true," said Tom, filling his plate. Beside him, Bronski, although still looking somewhat bemused, was tucking into the food with gusto. Tom finished his first helping, then took a third slice of ham and more coffee.

"Well done, Roger, I'm starving, we missed supper yesterday. Had some tortillas and fruit to keep us going but it wasn't what you'd call a square meal."

"You gave Pedro and Rosa the story we agreed on?"

"We did," said Marcie, "told them we were going to El Paso with you and that you'd bring back the station wagon."

"Excellent. It's a long drive from there all the way down to El Paso, so to appear plausible I'll keep the station wagon tucked away here for a few days then head on down to Piñones. If there is any hue and cry, it should have died down by then, at least in the local area."

They gave their guns to Roger, and Tom felt as if a weight had been lifted from his shoulders. They had done the hard part; they should have no trouble getting Bronski back to Washington, and then his involvement was over.

"No problem finding a second-hand car for you," said Roger, "now that they've started making civilian cars again, everyone wants to unload their pre-war vehicles and get the latest model." He led them into a cavernous garage, and proudly pointed out the large dark-green vehicle inside. "Got a real bargain on this baby: a 1941 Buick Roadmaster, twin double-barrel carburettors, 165 horsepower, column-mounted shift. I've fixed her up under the bonnet, and she's got a full tank of gas – petrol – so she's ready to roll. Takes six passengers easily, there'll be plenty of room for the three of you to stretch out on the journey. She's even got a radio so you can have entertainment as you travel. Hope you like it in green."

"What shall we do with it when we get to Washington?" asked Tom.

"I'll pick it up from your place, after you get back. Got a friend in Virginia who is looking to buy exactly this model."

They headed north-west across the corner of Colorado and into the flat plains of Kansas. Marcie and Tom shared the driving, and they made good time on these straight, lightly-travelled roads.

Roger had provided a bag with clothes and a few necessities, and Bronski was now kitted out in light-weight slacks and a bright, short-sleeved shirt. With a baseball cap on his balding head, he could easily pass for just another tourist. He had emerged from his daze and become wholly cooperative, apparently reconciled to whatever was going to happen.

"Lady Marcia..."

"You know," she interrupted, "I'm probably being over-cautious but I don't think we should use our real names. You can't go on calling me Lady Marcia, Professor. I'm supposed to be American; nobody in America is called Lady something..."

"Ladybird?" suggested Tom, but they ignored him.

"...and we can't call you 'Professor', you're supposed to be our uncle. How about Mr... oh, I know, Mr Mann!"

"And my father was Pyotr, so I will be Peter. Uncle Peter."

"Excellent! Something simple and forgettable is what we need. No need to change yours, Tom, it already matches the criteria."

Bronski chuckled: "Thomas Mann, just like the writer."

"Should we have something beginning with M-a-r for you," Tom asked Marcie, "in case we slip up? How about Marlene?"

"No."

"Marigold?"

"Don't be ridiculous."

"Marjorie? Margot? Marnie?"

"No, no and NO."

"I know – Margarita!"

"That isn't even worthy of comment."

"Martha is a good name for a Catholic," Bronski chipped in.

"Martha. Yes, I can live with that – I always had a soft spot for Martha. She seems like a free spirit compared to her sister Mary." She smiled. "So we are Thomas Mann, his sister Martha Mann, and Uncle Peter Mann."

"You could say we're the family of Mann."

"Honestly, Tom, I don't think you're taking this seriously enough," said Marcie sternly, though the corners of her mouth were twitching in a smile that she was trying hard to suppress. Well, she was right, he thought; now that the dangerous part was behind them, it was becoming a *Boys' Own* adventure again.

In the small towns through which they passed, patriotic red, white and blue bunting festooned the main street, and the parks were filled with families enjoying the Independence Day holiday. Most establishments were closed on July Fourth, but they stopped at a drive-in restaurant and ordered hamburgers and milk shakes for lunch.

Seemingly endless fields of wheat stretched for miles on each side of the highway, and trucks, tractors and combine harvesters were busy bringing in the crop. By five p.m. they were still only halfway through Kansas. In an anonymous town west of Wichita, Marcie pulled into the front of the Shady Palms Motor Court.

"Let's stop here for the night," she said, "I guess we're all pretty tired."

She swanned into the little office, and with a dazzling smile and her best American accent, she asked for two twin rooms, "one for me, one for mah brother and mah uncle."

The goggle-eyed desk clerk handed her two keys.

"Down the end, away from the road, it's real quiet, Miss… Mann," he said, glancing at what she had written in the register.

From Kansas they rolled on into Missouri, crossing the Mississippi River at St Louis, and then through Kentucky and into West Virginia, where the green-clad Appalachian Mountains were a smaller, gentler version of the rugged mountains they had driven through in New Mexico and Colorado. Each night they stopped at an unpretentious motel, and Marcie went through her 'Miss Mann' routine. Each day as they travelled they listened to whatever local radio stations they could tune into, fearful there might be a news flash about a missing nuclear scientist, relieved that there never was. They told stories, played I Spy and other games Tom and Marcie had enjoyed on car trips as children, and sang songs. Bronski was particularly taken with the simple, repetitive "One Man Went to Mow", singing the last line in a ringing baritone: "One man AND HIS DOG, went to mow a meadow!"

They had finished eating dinner one night at a nondescript restaurant in a nondescript mid-western town when Bronski said, "Tom, Martha, my dear friends, I would like to tell you something about my real family, if you would care to know."

Tom suspected the story was not going to have a happy ending but he said, "Of course we would, wouldn't we, Marc – Martha?"

Bronski looked at them with affection from under shaggy grey eyebrows. He lit one of the strong black cigarettes he favoured.

"You understand we are a Jewish family. When we escaped from the persecutions of the Jews in Hungary in 1937 we went through Germany. We didn't realise it was even worse there. We stayed in Munich with friends, but we were caught in a Jewish putsch; the Nazis, you know. The house was raided. I escaped only because I had gone out to buy some cigarettes – and some wine, yes – for our hosts. I came back just in time to see the dear Katzes bundled into a van. My loved ones were already inside it." He dragged on the cigarette and exhaled. "I managed to make my way to England. As I had been at Cambridge earlier with Rutherford, my English friends had already arranged for me to work there again. I was so grateful."

"And your family – do you know what happened to them?" asked Marcie.

"I heard nothing about them for many years. When I came to Los Alamos in 1943 Russian agents traced me. They told me that my family – my wife and two sons – had been taken from a Nazi concentration camp in Poland when it was overrun by the Red Army, that they were now in Siberia. They said they would allow them to join me in America if I would work for the Soviets. A terrible choice."

"The bastards," muttered Tom.

"I temporised, tried to put them off, to keep the option open. I passed them harmless, but, I hope, stimulating papers written for my old associate Mikov in Leningrad. As for my dear ones, I confess that I have given up hope of ever seeing them again; I don't even know if they are still alive. I've been given nothing to prove that they are. It is nearly ten years since we are parted. Imagine what they have been through! I think and think! I can see only a black pit. That they had survived the Nazi camps would be a miracle; to have survived in some labour camp in Siberia would be another miracle."

He wiped his eyes and took a drink of water before continuing.

"It was… it is agony. Probably the NKVD lied to me, but I just don't know."

He picked up the leather briefcase that was all he had brought with him from Los Alamos and passed it across the table.

"In here are my most important papers. I was taking them to the meeting. I thought that if I gave those Russian devils something of real value, they would finally tell me the truth about my wife and children. But even as I have talked to you about this, I realise that I have been deluded, that they will never let me off their hook, that I will never be reunited with my family. You must take these papers and send them to Lord Zender in your embassy's diplomatic bag, in case anything should happen to me."

"Nothing's going to happen to you," said Tom firmly, "but we will take custody of your papers if you wish."

"You have to look forward now, Uncle Peter," said Marcie, her voice gentle and reassuring. "You still have much to contribute, and you will be safe in England."

Chapter Twenty-One

Six days after leaving New Mexico, they stopped for the night at a motel in West Virginia. Tom and Marcie had had no opportunity for intimacy on their trip, but for Tom it was enough to enjoy her company. Bronski had seemed tired that day and had dozed frequently on the back seat, complaining of a backache. This evening he had retired early, and Tom and Marcie sat together on the stoop, with a cigarette and a beer.

"Feels like we've been in a cocoon in the Roadster for the past week," said Tom.

"Mmm." She leant against his shoulder. "It's actually been lovely. As though the three of us have just been enjoying a holiday together."

"But tomorrow we'll be back in the real world. What happens then?

"Well, we're not out of the woods quite yet."

"Marcie…"

She laid a finger gently on his lips. "But there's no reason why we can't continue the holiday for a few hours longer. Uncle Peter's sound asleep, he won't notice if you sneak in late, and there's a double bed in my room… "

Tom raised his eyebrows: "*Martha*, what are you suggesting?

"Well, it's hardly incest, is it?"

The story broke the next morning, Wednesday. As they crossed the Virginia state line a brief news bulletin came over the radio. The car of missing scientist Viktor Bronski had been found at the bottom of a ravine in the mountains of north-eastern New Mexico. Bronski had not turned up for work at his office in Los Alamos on Monday, and now it had been discovered that no one had actually seen him since before the July Fourth holiday the previous week. An official statement said that Bronski had met a tragic accident on a dangerous bend as he drove to Taos to do some sightseeing.

"Do you think anyone's going to buy that story?" asked Tom.

"Wouldn't think so for a minute," Marcie said morosely. "Someone's bound to point out that, for starters, there was no body in the car. But fingers crossed."

They drove into the Washington suburbs in the mid-afternoon, growing quieter and more tense as they approached the embassy. Tom breathed a sigh of relief as he parked around the back of the house at the tradesman's entrance.

They sat in silence for a while until he said, "Well, that's it then."

"No it's not," said Marcie, sounding irritated. "I've got to keep Uncle Peter under cover until we get the signal to leave. I think that's your department."

"Sorry. I think I meant, I meant…" What did he mean? He tried again. "What I was trying to say was that the past fortnight has been like a dream… just doesn't seem real; and now we're back to reality."

"Yes," she said – wistfully, he hoped – "so we are."

She went ahead to check that no one was about while Bronski peered anxiously out of the window.

"This is the British Embassy?"

"Yes, it is."

"Then I am safe. Thank you, Thomas."

Then Marcie was back.

"All clear," she said, "come on, Uncle Peter. Tom, you take his briefcase, you're likely to see John Portent before I do. I'll call you tomorrow."

And she and Bronski disappeared inside.

Tom drove the Buick back to Georgetown; Roger would pick it up later. He arrived at the house just before Miles got back from work. Tom had dreaded this moment, knowing Miles would be full of friendly enquiries about the trip, and he hated having to deceive a good friend. But the story he had concocted, leaving out Pinoñes and Bronski and based on their return journey, was largely true. As it turned out, Miles had various adventures of his own to recount, and by the time they had shared a couple of Old Fashioneds and Miles had put together a passable spaghetti bolognese, Tom thought he was in the clear.

Then Miles asked, "Heard about this guy who's disappeared from Los Alamos?"

"Just caught a short news bulletin," Tom replied warily. "What about him?"

"It's all over the papers today. Some big-shot scientist with a Russian-sounding name just disappeared. They say it was a car accident, but there's a lot of speculation that he's defected to the Soviet Union, taking all his secrets with him. Thought you might know something about him, as you've been working on the edges of all that atomic stuff."

"Only on the edges," said Tom. "Listen, Miles, I'm whacked after all that driving. I think I'll turn in. See you in the morning."

Tom reported into the office first thing on Thursday morning.

"Good trip?" enquired Meredith Hobson.

"Yes, sir, thank you," Tom said, thinking, *that must be the biggest understatement ever.*

"Well, you've certainly been to parts of the US I haven't. You've heard about Viktor Bronski's disappearance of course?"

"Yes, picked it up on the way back."

"You weren't in New Mexico, were you?"

"No," he lied, "only got as far as Colorado."

Sylvan was not in his office, neither was Sir John. Tom telephoned some of his contacts in the British Intelligence community to find out what they had heard. There were lots of them in Washington: naval, military and less identifiable civil agencies. In the Pentagon and in the Navy Department there were doors marked *British Intelligence Dept: Keep out* or *No Unauthorised Persons Beyond this Point*. And to establish their bona fides the agents would wear conspicuous identity badges to show that they were something rather special.

No-one had anything concrete to tell him beyond the official explanation, but they did say that, as expected, the FBI and the American intelligence services were furious that the man had apparently been missing for nearly a week before anyone noticed. Tom tried to catch up with his paperwork, but was too restless to concentrate. When the phone went he jumped, then grabbed it.

"Tom?"

"Marcie! How's it going?"

"Not very good news, I'm afraid. Uncle Peter has had a bit of a bad turn. It was quite frightening: pains in his chest and down his arms, pale and breathless. So I called Sir Geoffrey's personal doctor – I couldn't think what else to do – and he came and confirmed a heart attack. No, don't panic, fortunately a mild one. The doctor says he will be all right, given him some sort of medicine – pills – but he will keep an eye on him."

"Oh God, talk about bad timing! You told the doc he was an elderly relative?"

"Yes, but I had to explain that I had Hungarian ancestry as well as Anglo-Irish." And she chuckled, to Tom's relief.

"Marcie, when can we meet?"

"Not tonight, darling." He reminded himself that she called everyone darling. "Sylvan's going to look in later to catch up. He's going to phone you about a debriefing, but better if we don't all get together."

Tom felt stupidly jealous. Stop it, he chided himself, she's already told you there's nothing going on between them. Trust her.

"Look, how about tomorrow evening?" she asked. "You can let me know progress on Act Two."

"We're making it sound like an am-dram production."

"Not a bad idea. Keep people guessing. And my *uncle* wants to talk to you. You know where the garden entrance is? I'll meet you there at six." *An amateur dramatics production,* he thought. *That about summed it up. Am-dram with guns.*

The minute he put the phone down it rang again. It was Charlie Weaver.

"Hi, Tom, you're back. Good trip? Great. Say, Gracie and I were wondering if you'd like to stop by for drinks this evening, seeing as we missed you at Cape Cod. Got a few friends coming over."

"Thanks, I'd love to," he replied, knowing guiltily that he would rather be with Marcie, but that drinks with Charlie would keep his mind off the current amateur dramatics.

"Great. See you later then."

The next caller was Sir John's secretary.

"Lieutenant Davis? Sir John asks if you would go round to the house this afternoon. Two o'clock suit you? Good."

Then Roger looked in.

"Glad you're back safely. People have been asking after you."

"Yes, the phone's been running red hot."

"I've been in touch with Marcie. Tells me it all went tickety-boo."

"Oh yes," said Tom, quelling a rising desire to laugh wildly and inappropriately, "completely tickety-boo. And your end went off successfully?"

"Sure. Motored down to the old homestead, squared the faithful retainers, caught the Atchison Topeka back, grateful thank-you call to Aunt Sissie."

"More grateful than she'll ever know," said Tom, thinking, or you either, Roger.

"Well," said Roger, seemingly at a loss, "see you around. Tell you what, shall I fix up another weekend sailing with Hank?"

"That would be excellent," said Tom. Right now, apart from Marcie in his arms, there was nothing he could think of that he would like better than another day on the shimmering waters of the bay, far from the skulduggery of the past few weeks.

After lunch he went over to Sir John's house, holding tightly on to the document case containing Bronski's papers and trying to appear nonchalant. The same white-jacketed manservant as before showed him to the study. Sir John was seated at his desk and in a nearby chair was Tom's old boss, the Naval Attaché, Archie Struthers.

"Ah, Lieutenant Davis – Tom," said Sir John. "Good to see you. Sit down. Thought we'd better meet here rather than in the office. More secure, what? I'm afraid Sylvan has got me quite obsessive about secrecy, he thinks everywhere is bugged. Marcie rang up last night – gather you had a successful trip?"

"Yes, thank you, sir."

"And you have something for me, I believe?

Tom handed over the packet and immediately felt better.

"Seen today's newspaper?" Sir John pushed a copy of the *Washington Mail* across his desk.

"'Missing Scientist Feared Dead'," Tom read. He'd heard on the radio report yesterday that the wrecked Hillman had been found, and now apparently there had been a new discovery. Some miles down the fast-flowing creek at the foot of the drop, just before it joined the Pecos River, they had recovered Bronski's jacket. Inside was his wallet, intact, with money and his identification papers.

"Another newspaper you won't have seen," added Sir John, "is *Pravda*. Now *they* are taking an interesting line. They've been surprisingly prompt and no pussy-footing around, saying he has definitely *not* defected to Russia. There's been a great deal of speculation about this, as you are probably aware. *Pravda* says it's all nonsense. Their line is that he took his own life rather than be further involved in the scheming of imperialist circles – that's us and the Yanks – to develop the bomb. They paid tribute to his achievements and mentioned his known distaste for weapons development. Anyway, you will doubtless be pleased to know, that's the line most of the press here and at home are taking."

Tom was still remembering the Hillman going over the edge. It had been so easy. It would have been just as easy for Bronski.

"My sources tell me that the Americans had figured out that

Bronski was passing information to the Soviets, and were planning to pick him up themselves," Sir John continued, "so as you can imagine, the FBI are spitting nails that they were pipped at the post. Officially they are still saying it was an accident, but I suspect they are casting their eyes around for whoever else might be involved. And it won't just be the Russians, even if they take their denial with a pinch of salt. So, mum's the word."

"You can rely on my total discretion, sir," Tom replied.

"Good man. Knew I could count on you. I don't need debriefing." said Sir John, "Sylvan has brought me up to date. And the less I know the better. So now we are in Act Two, I gather."

"Looks like it, sir."

"Well, Archie here will be in charge, so I'll hand over to him." And he busied himself with his pipe.

"Like Sir John," said Archie, frowning, "I don't want to know any more than I have to. Anyway, even with all this evidence of, ah, suicide, this doesn't mean that the US security people are satisfied. Not a bit of it. It's not plain sailing yet, let me tell you. We know that all the ports are being watched for a possible abduction of Bronski. We can't get your passenger on a naval ship, nothing due out for a while – I think that's what you anticipated and I can confirm. But, thanks to your research, we've picked on a freighter, due out of Baltimore next Tuesday night – that's the sixteenth. We've given orders to the Master – he's a senior Royal Naval Reserve captain, name of Evans – to be prepared to receive a passenger to be conveyed in greatest secrecy to Liverpool."

"Why Liverpool? Won't London be expecting him?"

"It's the ship's home port. Not very convenient, admittedly, but best we can do under the circumstances. Now the question is, how do we get this cargo on board without arousing the suspicion of our American friends and allies? Because," he added lugubriously, "because sadly, as Sir John implied, we are not above suspicion ourselves nowadays."

"So the freighter is going to be in Baltimore..." Tom was

visualising Chesapeake Bay and the promised weekend's sailing with Hank. "If we can get to her from the water, not the land, just before she was due to depart, that would be safe. I presume she will be anchored in the Baltimore approaches?"

Archie's bloodhound gloom was suddenly transformed into a smile.

"Good thinking, young man. Knew I could depend on a sailor. Got a vessel in mind?"

"Yes I have. She's an old Chesapeake Bay schooner."

"Well, assuming that works, we have to think about transferring your passenger. I don't think we could transfer from a schooner onto a cargo ship very easily, and it would look odd to any possible watchers. Tell you what, here's an idea. Old friend of mine, Henry Watts of the *Dido:* light cruiser, got badly knocked around in the war, she's laid up in Baltimore, waiting for her turn at the Norfolk dry dock. *Dido*'s duty boat could pick up your passenger from the schooner after dark and take him to the freighter. She's the *Orme Head,* by the way. Think that's water-tight? You need to get on to your chap, make sure he's on board with it, and then I suggest you communicate directly with Watts."

Do sailors always talk in sailing metaphors? Tom wondered.

"I'll give him a ring now," Archie went on, "tell him the plan, then best thing probably is for you to pop over to Baltimore tomorrow and speak to him in person about the details. What's she called, by the way?"

"Who? Oh, the schooner. The *Dulcibelle Adams.*"

Archie sighed wistfully.

"Ah, those old bay schooners. Beautiful. Y'know, I just fancy myself retiring to a little cottage on the shores of the bay and pottering around in one of those lovely things for my final years. None of all this nonsense."

And he waved his hand around vaguely.

Tom was beginning to feel the same way, but preferably starting this afternoon. However, the play still had to go on.

"Oh well," said Archie. "Steady as she goes, what?"

Tom found Roger in his office.

"You know we were talking about a sailing weekend? Well, do you think Hank would be up for helping us out with, you know, our passenger?"

"Why? What would you want him to do?"

"Just pick up said passenger at his place on the bay and transfer him onto a ship anchored in the Baltimore approaches."

Roger drummed the desk with his fingers for a while.

"What's the story?"

"Umm… he's helping a top-secret British naval operation?" suggested Tom.

Roger grinned.

"I'm sure I can sell that to him. He's a great admirer of the British Navy. When? Tuesday? I'll give him a ring now, see if I can get hold of him."

He soon confirmed that Hank was very happy to join in, and Tom reported back to Archie, who had arranged for him to meet with Watts the next morning at eleven.

Pleased that the grown-ups now appeared to be in charge, Tom set off for the Weavers' house, looking forward to being able to forget about Operation Roadrunner for the duration of the evening. Charlie and Gracie's teenage son Elliot, a tow-headed boy with oversize feet and a grin to match, let him in.

"Hey, guess what, Lieutenant, I made the school basket-ball team!"

"That's great news, pal, well done. Where's the party?"

"They're all out in the back yard," said Elliot, "I just came in to get a bottle of pop from the fridge. Dad won't let me drink beer till I'm eighteen."

The 'back yard' was a large garden, filled with shade trees and flowering shrubs. Many of the guests' faces were familiar to Tom from previous get-togethers at the Weavers', though some of the names escaped him. He accepted a beer, exchanged pleasantries with a couple of women, and soon found himself engaged in an enthusiastic discussion about the America's Cup J-class yachts with one of Charlie's Navy Department colleagues. "Hey, Tom" called Charlie, "come over for a minute, willya?"

Exchanging hopes for the revival of the classic sailing race, they parted, and Tom joined Charlie and three other men sitting around one of the wooden tables.

"You remember Mac, don't you Tom?" Tom nodded, though he wasn't entirely sure he did. Something to do with the State Department? "Well, Mac's been telling us that some top boffin's disappeared from Los Alamos, guy named Bronski."

"With a name like that he sounds Russian," commented one of the other men, "but nowadays I suppose he may just as well be American."

Tom groaned inwardly; he'd really hoped that Charlie's friends would not be interested in the subject. "You've been involved in all this kind of business, Tom, know anything about him?" asked Charlie.

All Charlie knew was that Tom had been assisting, in some quite junior position, it was implied, in the planning of an international control organisation. But he decided it was probably better not to feign ignorance.

"Actually, he's British."

"You don't say!"

"Yes, he worked with Rutherford at the Cavendish Laboratories on the historic first splitting of the atom. We lent him to you to work at Los Alamos."

"I also heard that he was one of those against the bomb," said Mac. "Maybe it wasn't an accident. Maybe he killed himself rather than go through with it."

"Not goddamn likely," said a burly man who had two empty beer bottles in front of him already and was halfway through a third, "betcha he's sold out to the Russkis and faked it."

"Simplest explanation's usually right, Wes," said Charlie. "He was driving too fast, went over the edge. They said it was a dangerous bend."

"Then how come they didn't find no body?"

"Thrown out of the car when it went over. Those mountains are full of predators, mountain lions, bears, eagles, coyotes. And what they didn't eat, the vultures polished off. I'm not surprised they didn't find anything after a week."

"I agree with Wes," added the man who had commented on Bronski's name. "Russian by name, Russian by nature. He's gone over to Uncle Joe."

"Didn't you see this morning's paper, Steve?" asked Gracie Weaver, leaning over her husband to refill the bowl of potato chips on the table. "Said they'd found his wallet and ID. Wouldn't he have taken those with him if he'd defected?"

Wes tapped the side of his nose in a knowing gesture.

"Just goes to show how clever these Russians are. They did that deliberately to fool everyone."

Tom shifted uncomfortably in his chair; this was getting a bit too close to the truth. Time to change the subject.

"Anyone been following tonight's ball game?" he asked cheerily. "What's the score."

"Postponed," complained Elliot, who lay stretched out on the grass sipping a bottle of grape Nehi through a straw. "Pouring with rain in Cincinnati."

Undeterred by the attempted diversion, Wes drained his beer and continued to expand on his theory. Anything suspect was always attributed to Soviet malfeasance. The national witch-hunts for 'reds' had never let up, and many otherwise sensible Americans shared this anti-communist paranoia.

"Don't trust any of these foreigners," he grumbled, "least of all you Limeys. Have the skin off our back yet. How many billions did we lend you in this lousy war? And you never paid your last war debts either."

"Not everything can be reduced to monetary value," said Tom. "I suggest there are at least three things of high significance Britain has contributed to the American technology of today and her war-winning potential: radar, the jet engine, and the brains of Viktor Bronski!"

So often had the dollar sign drifted back in as the measure of national sacrifice. Tom decided it was not worth fighting the point. He said a grateful goodnight to Gracie and melted out onto the porch.

Charlie followed him out.

"Sorry about Wes. He's a good guy really but get a coupla drinks inside him and he says things he'll deeply regret tomorrow."

"No offence taken. I can appreciate his frustration. Thanks for the invite, Charlie, really enjoyed it."

Chapter Twenty-Two

It's Friday already, Tom thought, as he left the District of Columbia and drove to Baltimore, where Archie Struthers had arranged for him to meet with Captain Watts. There were only three full days left before the *Orme Head* sailed, and it would take most of Tuesday to get to her from Hank's place, where they would board the schooner.

Captain Watts was a spare, angular man with a square jaw and a handshake like a vice grip.

"Let's go for a walk, shall we?" he suggested, "fewer people about, and it's a splendid day."

Tom was pleased that Watts evidently understood the need to keep their conversation confidential and their meeting away from potentially prying eyes. They walked along the edge of the harbour, and the captain proudly pointed out his ship, HMS *Dido*, riding at anchor.

"Archie Struthers gave me the gen about your operation; glad to help."

Tom outlined his plan to bring his VIP (who had not been named; if Watts guessed at his true identity, he kept the knowledge to himself) to Baltimore aboard the *Dulcibelle Adams*.

"Our boat will meet your vessel off the Baltimore Harbour Light," said Watts, "you'll see it on the port side as you come up from the south."

The *Orme Head* was due to sail on the tide at 21:30 hours on Tuesday. They discussed the details of how the transfer would be carried out.

"I'll give the duty officer some supposedly urgent papers to be handed over to Captain Evans," Watts added, "that should explain why we are going alongside. And Archie suggested I might send one of my men to accompany the passenger. I've got just the chap – young lad called Marks, medical orderly. Cheeky beggar, sometimes, but competent and entirely trustworthy – he'll make a fine petty officer one day. It'll be good for him to be doing something useful. He's due some leave anyway, so he'll be jolly glad to get to England."

Confident that he had done all he could to ensure that the plan worked smoothly, Tom thanked Captain Watts and left the old sailor gazing out at the constant comings and goings of the many vessels that plied these waters. Tom checked his watch; it was already twelve-thirty and he was feeling hungry. There was a coffee shop opposite the dockyard; might as well stop here for a quick lunch before driving back.

As Tom entered, a man called out to him from one of the booths by the window.

"Lieutenant Davis, isn't it?"

"Captain Sodkin! What an unexpected and pleasant surprise!"

"Where there is Naval business there will be Naval Attachés. Please, do come and join me."

They had participated in some of the same meetings over the past couple of years, but had not sat down alone together since the time Tom had been invited to the Soviet Embassy during the war. He recalled Sylvan's advice, but decided he was long past caring. He liked Captain Sodkin.

They shook hands, Tom sat down and ordered coffee and a ham sandwich on rye bread. "I hope you have not forgotten how to drink vodka the way I taught you," said Sodkin with a smile.

"I haven't! Perhaps I can call on you again some time. I'll bring a bottle with me and teach you how to drink Scotch whisky."

Sodkin laughed ruefully.

"That would be delightful, Lieutenant, but alas, will not be possible. You may know that I will be leaving Washington very soon. Passage has already been booked for me to England. I have been promoted to be head of our Information Division in London."

"No, I haven't heard; I've been away for a while. Congratulations, sir, I'm sure you deserve it – oh, thank you," he said to the waitress who brought his order to the table.

"I'm not entirely sure that it *is* a promotion, but I think I will like living in your country better than here. I find the United States very… disturbing at present. Relations between our two governments are not good. When we have a change in leadership, perhaps…" he looked around to make sure that no one else was listening.

Tom found that he was also lowering his voice.

"Is that likely anytime soon?"

Sodkin shrugged his shoulders expressively.

"It is hard to tell. He is not a well man…"

There had been little speculation about what would happen after Stalin. What there was concerned which of those grim, over-coated figures lined up beside him on the Kremlin wall in photographs of the May Day parades would take the dictator's place. Keen Kremlin watchers noted who stood nearest to Stalin, or who might be absent. The Molotovs, the Vyshinskis, one or two like that had made their own marks on the page of history, but mostly they were unknown, grey faces, one of whom perhaps had been ordained to maintain control of this monstrous monolith of the USSR, others who might be liquidated if they stepped out of line.

"Are you aware that there are fifteen separate republics, perhaps 250 or 300 million people in the Soviet Union? Ukranians, Georgians, Uzbeks, Tartars – and all have their own histories, languages, ethnic and religious customs."

"No, I didn't know that," Tom admitted. "The central government must have a hell of time keeping all of those disparate elements under control, even with all the instruments of terror they've got." He thought he could risk a subversive remark. "If history's anything to go by, there'll be loads of people – nationalists, idealists, religious bigots, whatever, and probably a few complete nutters – secretly working for the day of liberation.”

Sodkin nodded. “Indeed, it is so. Sadly,” he continued, “the usual pattern of revolution is for its pioneers to be consumed in its flames. Now the tinder is not yet dry enough for the critical conflagration. Many will perish, but not before they put their crowbars into the clefts in the great rock, and sooner or later it will crack apart.”

Tom was surprised to hear the captain talk in this way, against the system of which he was an officer. Perhaps it was because he would soon be leaving the country, perhaps he was in the mood to unburden himself to a relative stranger, but one he liked and trusted.“And what happens then?”

“Then, then, God knows! Can *you* see what will replace the USSR? Frankly, I can’t. But that will be for others to worry about.”

“Capitalism?”

Sodkin gave a bitter laugh.

“Heaven knows what your capitalists will do when there is no communist bogey. Hegel, you know: thesis, anti-thesis, and synthesis. A synthesis will emerge.”

He pushed aside his empty coffee cup and stood up.

“And now, if you will excuse me, I must return to my duties. I have, as you English say, bent your ear enough; perhaps you will be kind enough not to mention this conversation to anyone.”

Tom held out his hand and Sodkin took it in both of his.

“*Dosvidaniya*, my friend. I doubt if we shall meet again.”

After the Russian had left Tom sat quietly and finished his sandwich, though he found he had little appetite.

“May I have my check, please?” he asked the waitress as she came to take away his plate.

“That’s OK,” she told him, “the other gentleman already took care of it.”

Marcie was waiting for him when he got to the Embassy at six. He wanted to grab her and kiss her passionately but under the circumstances he didn't dare even offer a polite peck on the cheek. She looked into his eyes and he was sure she felt the same.

"Oh, Marcie," he said, "It's so good to see you. I've missed you."

"It's only two days," she said tartly, then whispered, "but I've missed you too."

He followed her through the little wicket gate into the garden where the famous roses were in full magnificent bloom, and he remembered the garden party where he had first met her. A table held a bottle of white wine and two glasses. They sat in wicker chairs and Marcie gave him the bottle and a corkscrew.

"It's a man's job," she said.

The air was warm and sultry and mountains of pearl-grey clouds filled the evening sky, hinting of rain later. Pigeons cooed and fidgeted in the branches of the cherry trees as they settled down for the night.

Tom handed Marcie a glass of wine, then took hold of her hand, which was trailing lazily over the arm of her chair. They sat contentedly for a while enjoying the wine.

"Smells like gooseberries," he said. "Reminds me of Mum's gooseberry crumble."

"Don't be so prosaic! Reminds *me* of Pinoñes. We had a bottle of this Sauvignon Blanc there, if you remember."

Stricken, he said, "Oh God, I don't. Not specifically, I mean. But Pinoñes…"

"I forgive you."

After a minute's happy reminiscing he suddenly remembered why he was here and asked anxiously, "How's the patient?"

"Seems to be getting along well. I told you Doctor Masudi said he would keep an eye on him, and he's been really good, pops in every day after work." She glanced at her watch. "In fact you might catch him this evening."

"Masudi? That's an unusual name." Where had he heard it before?

"Yes, he's Egyptian. He's been in Washington about three years now. The ambassador's brother is a cardiologist at Barts, trained with this Dr Masudi and recommended him to H.E. Sir Geoffrey swears by him, won't see anyone else." She frowned. "There's only one problem. Uncle Peter doesn't trust him."

"Doesn't trust him? What, his medical skills?"

"No, it's not that. Personally, I just think it's this old Jewish-Arab antagonism. Sylvan doesn't think there's the smallest smidgeon of suspicion that Masudi is working for the Bolshoi."

Tom sighed.

"Well, I don't see that it's up to us to do anything about it. That's the security people's job, and they must have given him top level clearance if he has access to Sir Geoffrey. Let's just concentrate on getting the patient out of here."

She moved her hand from his, sat up and refilled their glasses.

"That's what you're here to tell me about."

He outlined the plan he, Archie Struthers and Captain Watts had concocted and she listened and nodded.

"So how do we get the patient onto Hank's boat?" she asked.

"Roger suggests you could drive him down to Hank's little shack on the morning of the sixteenth. That's Tuesday. Roger will come along as well as back up; means there will be two vehicles in case sod's law kicks in and you get a puncture or something. And you can just follow him rather than trying to find it yourself. We need to leave there about mid-morning for the tide."

"Will do. And then it's all over?"

"Christ, I hope so. And by the way, where is bloody Sylvan? The whole thing was his baby, and now he's disappeared off the face of the earth."

"No he hasn't. We're in touch. He'll contact you at the weekend."

"Well, about bloody time, excuse my French."

"And he suggests we all stayed glued to a telephone for the next three days, in case of developments." She put down her glass and stood up. "I'll go and fetch the patient." She smiled and touched his lips with a forefinger. "Don't go away."

He grabbed her hand before she could withdraw and kissed it.

She appeared about five minutes later with Bronski, who was walking with the aid of a stick. His face was pale and pinched.

"Hello, Uncle Peter, good to see you. How's it going?" he said, rather too heartily, as he pulled out a chair.

Bronski sighed and waved his hand.

"Oh, you know, so so. I have not been well. It was a shock, you know. And I fear it may happen again. But I am most pleased to see you again, Thomas."

Tom settled Bronski in the chair and sat down himself.

"Well, I'm here to let you know that we've worked out a way to get you secretly to England."

"To England? As you promised? Thank God, then I will be safe."

"We've arranged for you to go on board a ship leaving Baltimore on Tuesday night."

Bronski's face fell.

"But not until Tuesday? Then that is another three, four days!"

"I'm sorry, we just can't do it any sooner."

At that moment they heard a car coming up the drive and stopping outside the front entrance.

"I'll go and check," said Marcie, "probably Doctor Masudi."

"Thomas," said Bronski urgently as she left, "this doctor, this Arab, Doctor Masudi, I don't trust him."

"Anything specific? I believe he's a very good doctor," said Tom, trying to sound encouraging, "and surely if the ambassador trusts him, that should be a good enough guarantee?"

The other man shook his head mutely, and at that moment, Marcie returned.

"Doctor Masudi, this is Lieutenant Davis. A personal friend," she added to explain his presence. Dr Masudi was almost bald now, but Tom remembered where he had seen him before: the embassy garden party, soon after he had come to Washington.

"How do you do, Lieutenant?"

It was apparent that the doctor had no recollection of their previous encounter, so Tom said nothing about it.

"Do you mind waiting here for a little while, Tom?" asked Marcie. "I'll take Uncle Peter back inside so that Dr Masudi can examine him."

"Of course, if you don't mind me finishing the Sauvignon."

She was back about twenty minutes later. Tom thought she looked tired.

"I saved you some of the wine after all," said Tom, "you look like you need it."

"Thanks," she said gratefully, as he emptied the bottle into her glass. "The doctor's left and Uncle Peter has gone to bed. I'm a bit worried about him, he doesn't seem at all well today."

"I expect you both need a good night's sleep. I'm sure you'll feel better in the morning."

"Hope so. Dr Masudi kindly said I could call him at any time if I needed him. And you're right, it's getting late. Time you left, Tom, or people will be talking."

"I don't care," he said. "Marcie, when can we…"

"Let's get Roadrunner wrapped up first and then…" She stopped, and added, smiling, "Careless talk costs lives, remember, as we all used to tell each other."

The house was quiet and dark when Tom arrived back and he remembered that Miles was had left earlier that afternoon for a weekend with friends in the Hamptons.

The phone was ringing as he went in the door.

"Ah, dear boy, there you are," said the familiar voice. "I've been trying to get you for at least an hour."

"About time you did, Sylvan!"

"I know. I am utterly contrite. Been lying low. Thought it better. Come round tomorrow for what the Americans call brunch. Frightful word, but rather a good concept. Make it about ten."

Putting the receiver down, Tom realised that this would be his first proper meeting with Sylvan since Marcie's revelations about his connection to the Russians. While he'd been waiting and reflecting outside the chapel, he had come to accept Marcie's 'redemption' story, and then, when Sylvan arrived and the rescue swung into action, there had been no chance to consider the implications. But now he would be seeing his old mentor in an entirely new way, and he wasn't sure about it at all.

Chapter Twenty-Three

Sitting on Sylvan's deck the next morning, Tom hoped that his host's idea of brunch would consist of more than the large Bloody Mary with which he had been greeted. He was relieved to find that his new knowledge seemed not to be affecting his feelings about Sylvan, and he held the idea of expiation firmly at the forefront of his mind; but he was wary nonetheless and conscious of distancing himself to some extent.

"I've talked to Archie and Sir John," said Sylvan, "so I know the plan. Several bits to slot together, but should work. I suggest we run over it now and see if we can spot any gaps or weaknesses."

They went through it and Tom filled him in on his meeting with Captain Watts. Though they both agreed it was not totally foolproof, it was probably the best answer.

"Well, let's get some food to settle our stomachs," said Sylvan eventually. "Come inside and amuse me with small talk while I cook."

So Tom regaled him with the journey back while Sylvan put bacon on to fry and mixed up a bowl of batter, which he poured by spoonfuls onto a hot griddle. "Oh damn, telephone. Flip those pancakes, will you, and keep an eye on the bacon?"

From his position at the stove, Tom could see through into the hall. Sylvan wasn't saying much apart from "Yes. When? I see." Then he added, "Tom's here. I'll talk to him."

Marcie?

"That was Marcie," said Sylvan. "I'll make the coffee, then let's take this outside and talk."

He unloaded the tray onto the table on the deck and sat down.

"Seems our patient wasn't too good during the night, so Marcie got the doc in again – he's very obliging – not sure who's going to pay for his services. Foreign Office, I suppose. She suggested the patient might have to leave the embassy soon – deliberately vague, of course – and the doc was quite worried, wanted to know what sort of medical care he would get? Well, I suppose the ship has a sawbones, but God knows what standard."

Tom was beginning to feel defeated. To have gone through all the past month only for Bronski to ungratefully drop dead on them before they had even got him on board.

"How serious is it?" he asked.

"I have no idea," Sylvan replied. "Perhaps I ought to go and see the doc?" He poured the coffee. "We can't abort at this stage. Can you find out via Archie if there is a medic on board the *Orme Head*?"

"If I can track him down. It's the weekend."

"Oh, you know Archie never goes away at the weekend. That would be much too exciting. He stays home with Nora and does the garden and whatnot."

This Tom knew to be true.

"Can I use your phone? We haven't got much time."

Archie said he would phone back and did so within half an hour.

"No, not a proper sawbones," he told Tom. "Should have ideally, but since the war it's been difficult. The officers have a certain amount of medical knowledge and there's a sick bay attendant. That's where your patient will go, safer to keep him away from the rest of the passengers."

"Passengers? I thought she was a freighter?"

"Oh, she is. But she's fitted out to carry passengers as well – not many, around thirty, I believe? Mostly service or ministry people on official business, it seems."

Tom reported back and Sylvan murmured, "Hmm. Well, maybe there's a doctor among the passengers? I suppose we must just pray our patient gets through the voyage without succumbing. Don't see any way round it. Do you pray much, Tom?"

He was thrown by the question, uncertain as to whether Sylvan was serious or not.

"I used to. My Presbyterian upbringing, you know. Sure I told you my old man was a clergyman before he retired due to ill health? It was church twice a day on Sunday for us. But I gave it all up with no regrets when I went to university."

Sylvan sipped his coffee.

"I do," he said. Then, "How about another Bloody Mary? You know, I think I might talk to Doctor Masudi. Stay by a phone and I'll be in touch."

Sylvan phoned late in the afternoon. "Well, I've seen the doc. He's quite adamant the patient could have another heart attack and needs ongoing medical care of a high standard. So how about this? We had a long chat and the doc says he would be happy to accompany the patient on his voyage to the old country."

"You told him that Br – Mr Mann – was going to England? On a ship?"

"Well, there was no way round it. He doesn't know who he's dealing with, just an elderly relative of Marcie's who, I suggested, is something of a miser, but stinking rich, and the family will happily pay for the doc to accompany him."

"Sylvan, are you sure… it's, well, for one thing, Marcie probably told you that the patient doesn't trust Masudi, and also we seem to be bringing more and more people into the business. Not to mention spinning more and more unlikely yarns."

"Yes, I know. A tangled web indeed. But when you think what the Jews have been through in the past few years I'm amazed they trust anybody. And I can tell you categorically, that the doc has absolutely *nothing* to do with the ballerinas."

"If you say so, Sylvan."

"I do, old son, I do. I've got on to Archie and he's getting a passage fixed up for our medic."

"Does the patient know?"

"Not yet. Tell him tomorrow when everything is in place. Don't want him to get over-excited."

When he had put the phone down, Tom contemplated the prospect of how to get through the rest of the evening and the long Sunday that stretched ahead tomorrow. He groped for distractions. A game of tennis or softball, perhaps. A film? He was loath to go alone; he could have got in touch with various acquaintances, but he didn't know how he could talk to them just now. Anyway, he couldn't go out, Sylvan had told him to stay close to a phone. At least he could go into the office on Monday, and then it would be Tuesday and for the Musketeers the final act would be over. Then it would be Wednesday and Marcie… and perhaps Marcie…

He picked up Conrad's *Lord Jim* but the sentences wouldn't hold together. He started a letter to his parents, but the platitudes and the deceit were too much to cope with. He put a Duke Ellington record on the turntable and hummed along while rooting around in the fridge to see if Miles had left anything edible for supper. The phrase Sylvan had used kept intruding into his thoughts: *A tangled web.* Spinning yarns, a tangled web. Then he got it. It was one of those irritating little homilies his mother used to ply him with as a child:

Oh what a tangled web we weave
When first we practise to deceive.

There was no need to get up early on Sunday morning. Miles wasn't there, and Tom had nothing planned for the day. He took a shower, made a pot of coffee and spent some time clearing the decks, to use another of Archie's favourite nautical expressions. He checked his bank statement and, having ascertained that there were sufficient funds in his account, he wrote cheques for the bills that had accumulated while he was away. He sewed a loose button onto his uniform jacket, then walked down to the corner store to buy a pack of cigarettes and the Sunday *Washington Mail.*

Back home, he opened a Budweiser and took a plate of cold frankfurters out of the fridge. That would have to do for lunch.

There wasn't much else, he'd eaten all the left-over macaroni-cheese last night. He took a swig of beer and unfolded the newspaper.

An article at the bottom of the front page with Lewis Grearson's by-line caught his eye. As he read, it became apparent that Grearson did not believe Bronski had gone over the edge with his car, either accidentally or intentionally. Bronski, he claimed, had been snatched by an unnamed 'foreign power'. Further, despite the official story, the Americans clearly didn't believe it either and were thinking along the same lines as the journalist. Grearson reported that the police were watching the seaports, airports and train stations for any sign of the missing scientist.

Well, Operation Roadrunner seems to have stirred up quite a hornets' nest, Tom reflected. Sylvan was right to take all possible precautions. And it wasn't over yet, not until the day after tomorrow. He opened the newspaper to the crossword and was about to start on the frankfurters when the telephone rang.

"Tom – it's me. Can you come over, please? Now?"

She sounded upset. Tom abandoned his lunch, got in the car and drove over to the embassy. Marcie met him at the back entrance.

"Is he OK? He hasn't…"

"No," she said, leading him up the stairs, "he's well. But Sylvan came this morning and told him he's arranged for Doctor Masudi to travel with him on the ship. Uncle Peter nearly broke down. Said he wouldn't go if the doctor is going as well. I don't understand. Sylvan is adamant there is no Russian connection."

"And he ought to know," said Tom, sourly.

"Anyway, he insisted on talking to you."

"So what am I supposed to do?"

"I have absolutely no idea," she snapped as she knocked on a door and ushered him into a small bedroom.

Bronski was sitting in a chair by a window, Sylvan standing staring out of it. Tom remembered briefly that they had decided that they shouldn't all be found together, *but here we all are after all,* he thought angrily. *Except Roger.*

As they came in, Bronski struggled to stand and Marcie went quickly to his side.

"Tom's here, Uncle Peter. Why don't you sit down and make yourself comfortable? Don't get upset."

She indicated a second chair, which Tom took, while she went to stand next to Sylvan.

"Thomas," said Bronski, "you must stop this. They want to put this Arab doctor, Masudi, on the ship to look after me. But I don't trust him."

In the most sympathetic voice he could muster, Tom said, "Yes, I understand. You told me yesterday. But can you tell us why you don't trust him?"

"It is difficult to say. Something's not right."

Sylvan said, "I've told him that Masudi has had highest level security clearance – I checked it out – and he is absolutely, categorically, *not* working for the ballerinas."

Almost petulantly Bronski said, "But I don't want him to come! I don't need him! I will be all right without him."

Tom leant forward and put a gentle hand on the other's knee. "But it seems you *do* need medical care, Uncle Peter. He's really worried you could have another heart attack, there's no qualified doctor on board, and we wouldn't want to be responsible for your not having the best attention on the ship. Not after all we've gone through together!" He hoped an appeal to their happy 'vacation' week would prove helpful.

And Bronski did seem to relax a little.

"Yes," he murmured, "yes, we have been through much together." He looked vague and seemed to retire into himself, and nobody said anything for a while. Then he suddenly perked up and, clutching Tom's arm, said. "Yes! I have it! You must come too. If you are with me, I am safe."

Chapter Twenty-Four

"What? I can't come to England with you!" Tom protested.

"Why not? If Mr Ross can arrange for this Arab gentleman to take passage at such short notice then he can do the same for you!"

"No, he can't – it's not like that – he can't do that, can you Sylvan?"

There was a pause. Then Sylvan said, "Don't see why not."

"Well, of course I can't come. I've got a job to do, in case you hadn't noticed. I can't just walk away from it at a couple of days' notice!"

"John Portent could square it with Hobson. After all, it wouldn't be for long. It's what, eight days sailing time, have a week back in jolly Old England, see your beloved family. It's a long time since you did that, isn't it? Sure you're due some overseas leave. Then, if you came back by sea that only makes it a tad over three weeks, and you never know, they might even be persuaded to fly you back."

"It's ridiculous!"

"No, it's not," said Sylvan. "It might be the only way. Don't forget, this operation has been authorised at the very highest level, and we have got to see it through. There won't be any trouble from your superiors."

"Marcie?"

She just shrugged.

"I have to agree with Sylvan. Why not?"

Because, thought Tom, *I was hoping that on Wednesday night you and I would be in bed together. Weren't you?*

"I'll get on to Sir John, said Sylvan, "he's at home today. May I use the phone in your room, Marcie?"

Tom wanted to shout, *how the hell do you know there's a phone in her room?*

She came back by herself. "Sylvan says John agrees, and he will square Hobson and get on to Archie about arrangements. You've got tomorrow to tidy your desk. Have you had lunch?"

"Not what you would call lunch."

"I'll take you to the club."

She went to Bronski's side and crouched beside him.

"That's all arranged, Uncle Peter. Tom will come on the ship with you and take care of everything. I'll go and fetch your lunch up – Linda left it in the kitchen – then you can have a good nap this afternoon."

"For God's sake, Marcie," said Tom laying waste to his first Horse's Neck. "Sylvan just thinks he can take over our lives."

He had sulked all the way in the car, refusing to speak.

She put her hand over his and for a second he felt like pulling it sharply away, but didn't.

"I know. But he is so desperate to see this through to the end. And he trusts you. As does the Prof."

They sat there quietly, until he muttered, "And I was hoping that we, you know – you said when all this was over, and now it won't be over for me for another month at the earliest as far as I can see."

"I'll still be here," she said simply.

He sighed and said, "Well, I'll have to change things a bit. No point me driving my car to the cabin, I won't be able to get it back to Washington."

"You can go with Roger. I'll bring Uncle Peter, I'm quite capable of finding my way."

By the time he had polished off a large lunch he had made up his mind to make the most of the situation. He would, as Sylvan pointed out, be able to visit his family. This was something he had put off doing for some time. He could have got overseas leave earlier, but had used the excuse that since the war had ended, everybody was anxious to visit the families in England whom they hadn't seen through all those long six years and someone had to stay in the office. It wasn't a prospect that filled him with joy, but he had had nagging feelings of guilt for far too long, and now there was a chance to do his duty and feel better for it.

"What am I going to tell Miles?"

"I don't want to tempt fate but what about saying one of your parents is gravely ill?"

"'Oh what a tangled web we weave'…"

"…'When first we practise to deceive'," she finished. "I know. But it's not for much longer. And I will be here when you get back. I promise."

"Oh Marcie."

"Don't get all maudlin on me, Tom. How about pecan pie for dessert?"

Miles got home just before eight. "Great weekend," he enthused, taking a couple of bottles of beer from the fridge. "What have you been up to?"

"Bad news from home, I'm afraid," said Tom. He waved an air-letter vaguely in front of him, hoping that Miles wouldn't notice that it was actually one he had received some weeks earlier, then shoved it quickly into his pocket. "Got a letter from Ma yesterday. Seems the old man's in a bad way."

"Good Lord, what rotten luck!" said Miles in some alarm. "What are you going to do?"

He opened his beer and handed the other bottle to Tom.

"They've been jolly nice about it at work, given me some immediate leave to go over there. I'm off on Tuesday, Archie's got something fixed up."

He hated having to lie to Miles and Marcie's comment about tempting fate nagged at the back of his mind. He tried to be vague about the details of his trip, and possibly his reluctance made it seem more genuine.

"And you just got back. Oh well, needs must when the devil drives. Anything I can do to help?"

"Just hold the fort until I get back. And don't forget to water the plants."

"I hope your father is going to be all right," Miles said sympathetically, making Tom feel even worse about his deceit.

"I'd rather not talk about it. See what transpires when I get there. I'd better go and sort some things before I leave, throw a few togs in a bag…"

As he took some socks from the drawer, he noticed the leather belt with the silver buckle. He tucked it into his duffel-bag. It would remind him of Marcie.

He spent the rest of the morning clearing his desk and after lunch went round to the embassy garden to finalise plans for the next day with Marcie.

They were both nervous and on edge, and when they had finished the discussion they sat in silence while Marcie chain-smoked. After a while she reached out her hand.

"Why must you be so grumpy, Tom? You're going away and I'll miss you. Don't be like this."

"Well," he said, squeezing her hand gratefully, "if I'm grumpy, you're Snow White."

To his delight she giggled and stubbed out her cigarette.

"No, you're not Grumpy. You're the Prince who comes to wake me out of my long sleep. And you did, you know."

Happiness suffused him.

"So who *is* Grumpy?"

They spent an enjoyable few minutes assigning the names and characters of the seven dwarfs to various high-placed members of the British diplomatic corps, then Marcie asked, "Is there a wicked Queen?"

"The wicked queen is made up of all the political evils that we're trying to combat."

"And the Huntsman?"

He pondered this, not wanting to get it wrong.

"The Huntsman is Sylvan, who betrays the evil queen to save Snow White."

"That makes Bronski Snow White, not me."

"No, Bronski is Prof, the dwarf who didn't make it to the final cut."

Eventually he said reluctantly, "Well I'd better be going, I suppose. Can we say goodbye now? There won't be a chance tomorrow."

"Not here. Come upstairs with me. Uncle Peter is probably asleep."

Tom threw his duffel-bag and small haversack into the boot of the MG and climbed in. Roger accelerated quickly along O Street and slung the sports car to the right onto Wisconsin Avenue, heading south. It was too noisy in the open car for conversation, so Tom sat back and let himself enjoy the throaty hum of the souped-up engine and the tug of the wind as they sped towards Chesapeake Bay.

Roger turned off the paved road and drove down the track that led to Hank's place.

"We're far too early," he said as he pulled up outside the cabin. "Plenty of time for some coffee before the others get here."

He extracted a key from a lobster-pot tucked under the step, unlocked, and went inside. Tom took his things out of the car and set them on the stoop, then he sat down in one of the pair of wooden rocking chairs and looked out over the inlet. Under a hazy sky the water was still, and a few faint wisps of the morning's mist drifted across the surface. Among the rushes along the edge of the creek Tom could see a great blue heron standing motionless, its long neck outstretched, poised to snatch the first unwary frog that came too close. As yet, the *Dulcibelle Adams* was nowhere in sight.

I guess this is Act Three, he mused. *Wonder if there will be Acts Four and Five like a Shakespearean play? But are we in a tragedy or a comedy?* Whichever, he thought, *better pray for a happy ending.*

"Here we are," said Roger, emerging from the cabin with two mugs. "Hope you don't mind it black."

He handed a mug to Tom and took the other chair.

They sat quietly for a few minutes, sipping their coffee and watching a pelican skim across the water and scoop up his breakfast fish. Then Roger said rather tentatively, "Tom, can I ask you a personal question?"

"Don't guarantee I'll answer, but fire away."

"Well, it's about Marcie... in Colorado, I saw how you two looked at each other... just wondering...?"

Up to this point, Tom had not dared to put it into words, but now he said: "Yes, I'm in love with her."

After a pause Roger said, "Gossip has it that she and Sylvan... well I can tell you categorically, not true, not at all."

"I know."

"What about Susan?"

"Oh, that was never going anywhere. She dumped me a while ago – just after our sailing weekend with Hank, as it happens – went off with some baseball player."

"Tough luck. Cigarette?"

"Thanks, don't mind if I do."

He drew on the cigarette and sipped some more coffee as Roger pursed his lips and blew out a circle of smoke.

"How do you *do* that? Mine always just fall apart."

"Years of practice, dear boy. It's all in the lips and the tongue."

Even a month ago, Tom might have made a wisecrack about the innuendo, but now he just said, "How about you, Roger? Have you never wanted to settle down, get married?"

"Not really an option. The Mater used to try fixing me up with the daughters of her friends, but I think she's finally given up, thank God."

Roger stood up and picked up their empty mugs. "You're a lucky sod, you know," he said. There was a wistful tone in his voice. "You've got a chance at a future with the person you love. Don't screw it up."

Tom was about to reply, but at that moment Marcie's Packard came bouncing down the track.

"Speak of the devil," murmured Roger.

She parked next to the MG, and Tom hurried down to open her door, hugging her as she stepped out.

"Hey, you," she said affectionately, returning his embrace. "We're a bit early; it's only half-past-ten, but I thought we'd better get here in good time. Is that coffee – is there any left?"

"Probably squeeze out another cup," said Roger. "I'll heat it up for you."

She followed Roger inside while Tom helped Bronski get out of the car and settled him in one of the rockers. Marcie soon joined them on the stoop, holding her mug of coffee.

"Hank not here yet?"

"On his way," said Tom thankfully, pointing out to the bay where now they could see the *Dulcibelle Adams* making her slow, majestic way towards them.

The phone rang in the cabin and they glanced at each other in surprise. Then they heard Roger's terse reply: "Yes, everyone's here – right – will do."

Then he was on the stoop, his usual cheerful expression replaced by a look of alarm.

"That was Sylvan. The Russians have got wind of us and are heading this way like a bat out of hell. You've got to get out of here PDQ!"

Chapter Twenty-Five

The schooner had not yet reached the anchorage. Marcie ran to the jetty and jumped up and down, frantically waving her arms above her head to attract Hank's attention. He was still quite far out but spotted her and raised a hand in a casual greeting.

"No, no, you idiot!" she yelled, stamping in frustration, "hurry *up!*"

"He can't get here any faster," said Tom, trying to suppress his own impatience. "He's got to anchor first." He looked at his watch and at the schooner's progress, mentally calculating the time and distance. "I don't think he can get here in less than fifteen, more likely twenty, minutes."

Marcie glanced anxiously up the access road.

"What if the Russians get here first?"

"Fear not!" said Roger, "I will delay these pestilent pursuers. Set up a road block or something, like you did in New Mexico." He grasped Tom's shoulder, suddenly serious. "Get the professor away safely, Tom, old man. For Sylvan."

He sprinted towards the MG. "*Vaya con Dios, amigos!*" he cried as he jumped into the car. And with a squeal of tyres he was gone.

Tom quickly moved their bags onto the jetty, trying to keep calm as he watched the *Dulcibelle Adams* approach the anchorage at a snail's pace. It seemed for ever before Hank finally stepped into the dory and started the outboard.

"He's coming," he called to Marcie, who had returned to the shade of the stoop. She held out her hand to help the Professor get up from the rocking chair. He stood and kissed her outstretched hand with old-world gallantry.

"Dear lady, how can I ever thank you…" He choked up, unable to continue.

"Goodbye, Uncle Peter," she said, her voice a little shaky. "*Bon chance.*"

They were all on the jetty when Hank drew up alongside and threw them the ropes, which Tom quickly secured to the bollards.

"Sorry, Hank, no time for you to come ashore," called Tom, "we've got to leave pronto."

"You're the boss."

They settled Bronski on the centre thwart and Tom handed down their bags for Hank to stow. He turned to Marcie: "I'll be back soon. I promise!"

"You'd better be," she said, kissing him fiercely on the lips. "Now get out of here: go, go!"

Tom scrambled into the forward seat as Hank fired up the outboard and Marcie let loose the ropes. As they scudded over the water, Tom watched her go back into the cabin, then emerge a few minutes later, lock the door, and replace the key in the lobster pot. She ran back to the jetty and waved; he waved back and watched her standing there till they drew close to the *Dulcibelle Adams*. There was still no sign of the Russians.

"We're sure in luck with the weather today," observed Hank as they approached the schooner, "get a lot of summer storms in the bay, but I guess someone up there is smiling down on us. Grab that painter and make us fast, Tom, willya?"

Helping Bronski on board was harder work than getting him into the dory, but they managed it and Tom took him down below and settled him on a bunk. When he came back on deck, Hank told him to take the tiller while he winched up the anchor, and minutes later they turned from the shore, heading towards the fork in the bay, beyond which the river would take them up to Baltimore. Tom glanced back at the fast-receding jetty, but it was empty.

We did it!

They chugged across the glassy surface of the bay, the inboard engine thumping gently and reassuringly. Here and there the last streamers of morning mist reached up to the sun and evaporated in its warmth. It was going to be a hot day again. Hank came aft to where Tom was leaning on the huge tiller.

"There'll be a bit of wind coming in from the south-east, I guess. We'll get up the sail. Meantime, a little something, huh? Are you OK with her while I go below?"

When he returned he brought up coffee and a plate of rolls, cold boiled beef and gherkins.

"Your Mr Mann says he'll stay below."

They ate in comfortable silence, and Tom began to relax for the first time since they had returned to Washington.

And then the breeze sprang up. Hank left Tom at the tiller while he sweated up the great mainsail and gathered in the sheets as the heavy boom swung out to take the zephyr wind, just enough to help the boat along nicely. Hank throttled the diesel back to the softest 'plop-plop'. They were on a broad reach that could well last to Baltimore. The wind backed more to the east. It was now abeam, so Hank set one of his two foresails, and the schooner responded, thrumming against the wind, the tiller tugging against Tom's restraining hand. He imagined Marcie, sitting at his shoulder in the stern-sheets, sharing the joy of the wind. *One day*, he told himself, *one day*. He listened contentedly to the gentle complaining creaks of the deck planking, the sibilation of wind through the rigging, the murmuration of canvas and the purl and plash of the little waves at bow and stern. The old familiar magic of controlling and yet working with the elements wove its spell as that beautiful old lady, the *Dulcibelle Adams,* forged her way north.

Before the hot copper sun came low, the wind died away and they resumed chugging. The water grew darker. There were oil slicks, and garbage floated past. The evening light now showed the masts and funnels of Baltimore, its towers and steeples, and the hills rising behind the more discrete, richer suburbs, where lay the Peabody Conservatory and other monuments to both its merchant and intellectual past.

There was still traffic moving on the river including tugs, dredgers and smaller craft, and Tom began to be concerned that among them might be some coastguard or harbour police patrol. They had slowed enough only to keep way on the schooner. In the distance Tom saw the lighthouse at the entrance to the harbour, then he spotted *Dido*'s boat.

The little vessel made straight past them, downstream, and so proceeded for a quarter of a mile or so before turning about and coming alongside the schooner. It was now quite suddenly dark. The coxswain had done well to hide his intentions from any watchers there may have been in the last of the daylight.

A quick, warm goodbye to Hank, then Bronski and Tom were transferred to the Navy boat. Only a few minutes and they were nuzzling up against the black hull of the *Orme Head*. There was an open door in the ship's side with a rope ladder let down from it. Tom helped bundle Bronski up the ladder, then followed him up and through the port into a dimly lit corridor. Their bags were thrown up after them, and behind them the door clanged shut.

"Good evening," said the ship's officer. "I'm Mr Benson, the purser. You, I take it, are Lieutenant Davis, with your patient. Please follow me."

The purser took them to the sick bay, which lay well forward, and introduced them to the sick bay attendant, Williams. A small adjoining cabin had been prepared for Bronski, who by now was stumbling with exhaustion. Williams introduced them to Able Seaman Fred Marks, a young man built like a rugby forward.

"Captain Watts of *Dido* has released him from naval duties while the ship's laid up so he can look after your patient. Only kicking his heels around on shore and getting into trouble."

Not at all abashed, Marks at once took control of Bronski.

"Don't worry, sir," he said, "I'll see he's settled in comfortably."

"Captain Evans sends his compliments and would like to see you as soon as possible once we are under way. All our passenger accommodation is fully booked so you are to sleep in the captain's spare cabin," continued the purser stiffly as they returned along the corridor. He clearly was not happy about the last-minute disruption to his passenger list.

The assigned quarters adjoined the captain's own room where Tom was greeted by the captain's steward, Dixon.

"Captain's on the bridge, sir, while we weigh anchor. If you want anything, sir, just ask."

Exhausted himself, Tom settled for a large Scotch, a sandwich and a bath. By the time he had completed all three, his naval uniform had been unpacked, pressed and laid out on his bunk. Not only that, but Dixon had taken it on himself to renew his glass of Scotch. *Good chap, Dixon*, he decided. *Should go far.*

Now he could feel the movement of the ship and the steady throb of the engines under his feet. Through the porthole he saw that the big ship was moving smoothly down the length of Chesapeake Bay before making the easterly swing that would take her out of these sheltered waters. He could still – just – make out the low shoreline he had left that morning. It seemed an aeon ago. Another age, another world.

Captain Evans was a small, strongly-built man with bright blue eyes in a wrinkled, weathered face. A Welshman, as was clear from his first few words, a business-like greeting. Then, "Probably best if you don't mingle with the passengers too much, avoid any awkward questions. Consider yourself my guest, and you can take your meals in my state room, if you so wish."

"Thank you, Captain Evans, that's most thoughtful of you."

"There is quite a flap on, it seems. The Americans appear to have lost something valuable, and they have been quite *sniffy* about it. It is as well we sailed out when we did, or we might not have got away without search parties all over the woodwork. Of course, we know nothing about it, do we? Anyhow, we are clear and away now, I think I can say." He went over to a porthole. "Norfolk Roads ahead. You'll feel the good old Atlantic quite soon."

He peered at Tom closely.

"Look, boy," he said, turning to the door, "you appear to be pretty pooped, if I may say so. Just ask my steward for some more Scotch, or whatever you like. Then go to bed and get a good night's sleep. I'd better get up top and make sure we don't hit some last lingering chunk of America."

Tom stumbled to a first slight dip as the ship faced into the Atlantic. He soon fell onto his bunk and slept until Dixon called him the next morning.

Chapter Twenty-Six

Tom had had the forethought to pack his sailing gear: cords and his old seaman's jersey. This morning he pulled them on, aiming for a nondescript appearance. Passengers might conclude he was part of the ship's company; the crew, who knew he was no such thing, might assume that here was a passenger who liked to look as though he belonged to the sea-going fraternity.

Captain Evans invited him to share a light lunch in his cabin. He was very proud of his ship.

"How do you like the *Orme Head?* Laid down before the end of the war, she was, and finished to peacetime standards as a passenger/cargo ship. We carry thirty-five passengers and, let me tell you, they get a better deal in many ways than those on the Blue Riband liners. Cabins are larger, our service more personal, and only one class. Very socialist!" He gave a sly grin and Tom, already at ease in his company, warmed to him even more. "But," continued the captain, sounding regretful, "It's an eight-day crossing, see, nearly twice the time taken by the Cunarders."

Eight days, thought Tom. *Nothing can happen in eight days on a self-contained floating castle. Just relax and enjoy the ride.*

In the afternoon he went forward to the sick bay. This far forward, away from the constant throb of the engines and the churn of the propellers, it was comparatively quiet. Ships, he was reminded, are full of noises: creaking carpentry in cabins, the roar of ventilators, the whip of lashings where the wind slashed at them, wind in the rigging that even a modern ship like this one carried.

"Mr Mann! How are you? Glad to see you sitting up."

Bronski was indeed sitting up, dressed in trousers and sweater over an open-necked shirt. He looked much better than when they had come aboard. He didn't respond to Tom's courtesies, but said urgently, "Shut the door. Now, listen please. You know I have had this heart attack. I know about these things, enough to know that the next could carry me off. This does not worry me. It would be worse to have a stroke, to be paralysed, unable to talk or write. That is terrifying. I have much work yet to do."

He pulled Tom down to sit on the bunk with him. In hardly more than a harsh whisper, he added, "There is something else. Let me tell you – let me warn you – these Russian devils are not finished with me yet. You see, I have never given them what they wanted, what they know I have to give. Credit them with that. Your dear countrymen at Cambridge never really got the measure of my work. Do I boast? Yes, maybe I boast. But it is true. I have told you how Russian agents traced me to Los Alamos, how I passed them some innocuous information. They were not satisfied, of course. I understand now, that is why they were about to kidnap me. It is nothing on paper, Thomas. It is my mind" – he tapped his forehead – "it is this that they want. They may even be on board this ship."

Uncertain how to reassure him, Tom brought out a few platitudes about relying on the British, the high-security clearance and approval of the whole operation, the unlikelihood that foreign agents could have discovered the plan to join the *Orme Head*. Whether Bronski was happy with this or not, Tom wasn't sure, but when he changed the subject, the professor responded willingly enough.

"So, how are they treating you?"

"I must say, very well. The food is a little strange but there is plenty of it. Not that I have much appetite. This young man, the orderly, Marks, he is a good person, I think. Nothing for him is too much trouble. And," said Bronski, his face quite suddenly creasing into an unexpected smile, "the sick bay attendant, Williams, do you know what his name is? His given, Christian name?"

"No," said Tom, "what is it?"

"It is William! William Williams!" He almost choked laughing, and Tom worried for a moment that he might have to summon the young man under discussion. When Bronski had calmed down, though still chuckling to himself, Tom said. "How very Welsh."

That evening he dined with the captain in the latter's cabin. Doctor Masudi was invited for drinks beforehand, although he refused anything alcoholic, opting for a glass of tonic water with a slice of lemon. He gave an encouraging report on the patient but said he should rest as much as possible. The heart attack in Washington had not crippled him, but another before long was a possibility. Lieutenant Davis could visit him of course, but should try not to upset him; Mr Mann had been a little worked up after the visit that afternoon. The doctor apologised for his wife's absence and explained that, while he himself was enjoying the voyage so far, she was still in her bunk suffering from seasickness.

"Seems a decent enough chap for an Arab," observed Evans after the doctor had left. "Good of him to come aboard at such short notice."

"He says he's always wanted to visit London and his wife's ambition is to shop at Selfridges."

"Well, truth to tell, I'm quite pleased to have a proper medic on board, just in case. Now, *you* don't object to gin with your tonic. Care for a top-up?"

Dixon served them with soup, followed by pork chops, and during the course of the meal the captain told Tom that he came from Amlwch, in Anglesey, where generations of pilots had awaited the shipping at the Mersey Bar, and from whence generations had gone to sea.

"It was Welsh captains," he said proudly, "who were the backbone of the square-rigger trade round the Horn and up the western coasts of Latin America. By the way, that was a splendid little schooner you came alongside in. Just caught a glimpse of her through my binoculars in the last of the light."

"Ready for pudding, sir?" asked Dixon, looking around the door.

"Thank you, Dixon. What is it?"

"Spotted dick, sir."

"Splendid! Sorry there's no cheese to have with the port," he added, turning to Tom, "but as you know, I am sure, the Americans are useless at making cheese."

It was easy enough for Tom to avoid conversation with the other passengers; his nondescript disguise was apparently working well. People passed the time of day, commented on the weather when taking the air and exercise on deck. If he was unable to avoid further conversation without appearing so anti-social as to invite comment, a naval officer going home for a spot of leave was not that unusual. He selected a steamer chair and dragged it into a secluded corner and here he spent most of the next day, letting himself be mesmer-ised by the endless rise and fall of the white-caps while the cobwebs and worries that cluttered his head were blown away in the light south-westerly breeze. He had stuffed *Lord Jim* into his bag at the last minute, but had decided it wasn't good for his morale, so had abandoned it in the cabin.

They were now on the rhumb line for Liverpool. They had passed the low coastline of New England, invisible to the west, and were heading for the Newfoundland banks. The sea heaved and scurried by, but the big ship hardly deigned to notice and Tom gave himself up to the pleasure of her steady motion, the wind and sun on his face and memories of Marcie. He might be confronted with some keen questioning on the whole Bronski operation when he got to London, but he wasn't going to fret about that just yet.

It was an odd feeling as a Naval officer to be on board a ship with no duties to perform. He felt listless and bored. Before lunch the next day, Tom went forward to visit Bronski, who was delighted to see him.

"Come and join us, Thomas. Mr Marks has been telling me about his experiences during the war. You have things in common, I think."

HMS *Dido*, it turned out, had also been on the Murmansk run in one of the last actions of the war.

"We had a pretty bad time," Marks said. "Our convoy had been decimated already by a hunting pack of Jerry U-boats. We was somewhere off the North Cape?" – Tom nodded that he knew the area – "so then we received orders to move off so as to divert a surface squadron. If we couldn't do that, engage with it. Never expected that," he said, shaking his head, "the German fleet usually stayed hunkered down in the Norwegian fjords, the cowardly bastards. Just our luck. She's only a light cruiser, you know, the *Dido*. Well, we was forced to engage and we fought 'em off till nightfall." He paused and Tom offered him a cigarette. "Thank you, sir. Anyway, they broke off eventually and left us to it. Seems they picked up a signal that a larger British group was approaching, so they cut and run."

He took a long drag on his cigarette.

"I don't mind telling you, sir, it was hell down there in the sick bay. Incoming shells from the Jerries was one thing, but our own five-inch turrets were right overhead. And cor blimey, they don't half shake you up! You don't forget the sight of them bodies either. Smashed to bits, some of 'em, but still alive, poor bastards."

Tom caught his eye and glanced at Bronski, who had been nodding along as he followed Marks' tale but was now shaking his head and frowning. *Yes*, thought Tom, *the abiding folly of man's inhumanity to man never ceases to appal.*

Dido had survived, but badly injured. She had managed to limp back to the sanctuary of Scapa Flow and thence to Glasgow where she had been patched up temporarily and taken out of service for several months. Britain, however, did not currently have the capacity to do more major, permanent repairs, so earlier in the year she had made her way with a skeleton crew to the US for what promised to be either a virtual rebuild or, failing that, consignment to the scrap-yard. Hence Marks kicking his heels in Baltimore.

"And you, Thomas?" enquired Bronski.

Tom felt almost embarrassed when he compared the young man's experiences with his own; much of the time their patrols had been routine, and on those occasions when they had been in action, his ship had never taken a direct hit and he been spared such up-close encounters, despite the death and destruction all around him.

"Nothing like as exciting as yours, I'm afraid. We got through all right. I was in *Athene,* an old destroyer. We guarded all kinds of vessels, you know, merchant ships like this, petrol tankers, shipping of all sorts. We'd pick them up off Iceland and escort them to the Western Approaches, towards Glasgow, Liverpool, sometimes further south to Avonmouth. Pretty routine. Oh," he added, remembering, "I met someone in Washington who was also on the Murmansk run. Chap called Sodkin. The Russian Naval Attaché, actually. It was fascinating to hear his version."

"The Russkis were our allies in the war," said Marks, "and now they seem to be our enemies! How did that happen?"

Tom changed the subject hurriedly before Bronski could intervene, and luckily Williams, the sick bay attendant, stuck his head around the door.

"Sorry to break this up, gentlemen, it's time for Mr Mann to have his medications and his lunch."

Tom found himself a small table for one in a dark and unpopular part of the dining saloon and ordered a pint of pale ale to have with his own lunch. He had just contentedly taken the first sip when he realised.

Sodkin.

Russian.

What had Bronski said? *They may even be on board this ship.* No, impossible. Or was it? Sodkin had contacts. He'd told Tom he had a passage booked 'very soon'. Had he already left? Could he even be on board the *Orme Head*? Whose side was he on anyway? In this looking-glass world of shifting allegiances how could you tell who or what was actually the enemy? Had Tom let slip any information about Operation Roadrunner when they'd met? The Russians had known of the getaway from Chesapeake Bay; they might know also the plan for shipping Bronski out. And anyway, what the hell could he do about it?

He spent much of the afternoon pacing the deck, furtively glancing at the faces of the regular passengers, while at the same time trying to avoid being drawn into conversation. Eventually he told himself not to be so stupid and went back below. After a rather anxious supper in his cabin, he decided he needed fresh air, and went up on deck again. He walked to the stern where he leant on the rail, lingering to watch the way the low sun flecked with gold the straight white carpet of the ship's wake, and breathed in the old familiar smell of salty wet iron. He stayed there long after it had got dark, thinking of Marcie and wondering how the final act of Operation Roadrunner would end.

Chapter Twenty-Seven

"There she blows!"

The passengers on deck rushed to the rails and saw, far off, the waterspouts pluming above the gentle heave and swell of the mid-Atlantic. Several of them had binoculars, including a middle-aged man standing next to Tom. As he lowered them, he asked, "Would you care for a look?"

Tom thanked him and raised the glasses. He was just able to make out the long, low grey backs, rising from the waves like sandbanks. In his years at sea he had never seen a whale, and felt an overwhelming sense of awe.

"Amazing, what?" said the man.

"Aren't they, though! Never seen one before, but I suppose that's not surprising."

"Saw them when we came over to the US last year," said the other. He looked curiously at Tom. "Visiting the old country, are we? Spot of leave?"

"That's right," said Tom, smiling and handing back the binoculars. "Thanks for the loan."

And he left, deciding to go and see Bronski.

But the latter was not interested in cetaceans. He took hold of Tom's arm and gripped it.

"I have something to give you. You must guard it with your life."

"Isn't that a bit melodramatic?"

"No, no! You must take this seriously, Thomas! Who else can I trust?"

Feeling compassion for the elderly scientist, who had good reason to mistrust everyone, Tom said cautiously, "But what is it? I thought you had given all your papers to Sir John to go to London in the diplomatic bag?"

"Yes, but this is something more. I have kept this with me, but I am not a well man, and also… something may happen to me."

Although he and Tom were the only two in his little cubicle, he glanced around nervously, then rummaged under his pillow.

"Here. I trust you, Thomas."

He pressed a small, much-creased envelope into Tom's reluctant hand.

"You must, if I cannot, give this with my compliments to Lord Zender."

"Can you tell me what it is?"

"You know a little, I believe, about thermonuclear energy?"

"Very little, really. Only what was needed for my job."

"*This* is why they want me." Bronski tapped his forehead. "I have here the secret of the power of the sun and the power to explode the oceans!"

For a moment Tom wondered if Bronski was beginning to lose his reason under the strain, but the professor went on in a less excited manner, "I have contributed much at Los Alamos, but I have also learned. You will find in this envelope little sachets; they are microfilm about current bomb construction, which I think your masters in Great Britain do not know about. And I think they should. But, Thomas, don't leave anything in your cabin. Has the captain a safe, or the purser? Get it locked there as soon as you can. They will search your cabin, ransack it…"

"They? Here on board?"

"There is someone coming. Hide those!" And, as Tom slipped the envelope in his trouser pocket, "You must go!"

But it was only Williams. Tom waited in the corridor, and when Williams emerged he asked him quietly what he thought of Bronski's frame of mind.

"Oh, he's up and down. One day cheerful, next sees dangers in every shadow, But physically he's improving. Plenty of rest and good food."

Tom decided not to repeat the patient's comments on the food, but asked, "And any other visitors?"

"No, sir, none. I'll let you know if anyone comes poking around."

In the late afternoon Captain Evans invited Tom up onto the bridge. Apart from the fact that he was as delighted as a schoolboy to be asked, the envelope containing the microfilm was burning a hole in his pocket. Still not sure if Bronski was making all this up in the grip of well-justified paranoia, he had cautiously opened the envelope in the security of his own cabin and slid a string of little bags onto the bunk. He checked one. It contained microfilm. He would ask the captain to place the envelope in his own private safe.

Tom spent a happy hour or so on the bridge, and finally decided reluctantly that he should not outstay his welcome.

"Thank you so much for inviting me up. Could I have a quick word in private before I go?"

They were out on the wing of the bridge where they had to shout to converse, so Captain Evans led Tom to the lea of the wheelhouse, out of earshot of the quartermaster at the wheel and the officer of the watch.

"I've received a top-secret package that I would be very grateful if you could keep in your or the purser's safe. I'd like to get it there ASAP."

"Certainly. Drop in this evening and we'll have a quick drink before I have to go and do my duty at the captain's table."

Dixon poured them both gin and tonics, and when he had gone Tom handed over the envelope and watched Evans lock it in the safe.

"Thank you," he said, "that feels better. Look, I know it sounds melodramatic, but if anything happens to Mr Mann or, well, or to me, and we can't get it to the Foreign Office, can I ask you to see that it's taken there by hand and given to the Permanent Secretary, Sir Gaspard Jebb?"

Evans looked at him for a while.

"Of course. Whatever the customer wants is right. That's the principle on which this line operates."

"Thanks again. Maybe I'm making a mountain out of a mole-hill, but…"

"Better be safe than sorry, mind," said Evans reassuringly. "Did you see the whales this afternoon?"

"I did. Amazing sight."

"What a joy it is to look through your binoculars and see whales spouting and not periscopes. Those bloody U-boats decimated our merchant fleet. You were on the Russian convoys, weren't you? We owe you a great debt of gratitude. Troubled much by the bastards?"

"Could have been worse. We rather hoped that we depth-charged one once, but it was never confirmed. Awful though. To die like that."

"There aren't so many good ways to die at sea."

Tom had thought he might go up to the main saloon that evening, but after his encounter with the friendly man at the rail that morning, had opted to eat in his cabin where Dixon brought him his supper. The mention of U-boats had reminded him of an incident early in his time in Washington when he had still been working as Assistant Naval Attaché under Archie Struthers. When he had finished eating he asked Dixon for a glass of port and tried to remember the details.

He and Sylvan had been lunching in the canteen when Sylvan mentioned that he had been reading about the development of submarine-based missiles.

"Funnily enough," Tom had said, "I saw some scribbles on Archie's desk that looked exactly like what they're talking about."

"Whole business sounds absolutely fascinating, don't you think? I'd be interested to hear more about it."

Archie Struthers was often away at the big American naval HQ in Norfolk, Virginia. In his absence Tom had rooted around in the office until he found the drawings, no more than sketches torn from a foolscap writing pad, and, pleased with himself, had taken them round to Sylvan's house the next evening.

Sylvan turned the sheets of paper this way and that, looking puzzled.

"It looks to me as though Archie has been doodling. He's an old submariner, isn't he? *Twenty Thousand Leagues Under the Sea* and all that. Still, Verne was writing all that in the 1860s as I recall; I don't suppose there were any real submarines, were there, before the turn of the century?"

"The Americans had some kind of submarine facility during the Civil War," said Tom, pleased that he could impart interesting knowledge that Sylvan wasn't aware of. "It was the Confederates, actually. They did some damage but the subs kept sinking and drowning the crews. Yet they were never short of volunteers."

The conversation had taken another turn, and at one point Sylvan had left the room to fetch another bottle of wine. He had been gone a while, and when he returned commented, "Couldn't find the corkscrew." When Tom got up to go, Sylvan said, "Oh, and you'd better take Archie's scribbles back with you. Never know, he might turn out to be the Picasso *de nos jours.*"

Tom had returned the papers to the office, replacing them carefully exactly where he had found them. He had felt it was trivial enough, but had to admit to himself that it had been wrong to take papers out of the office – any papers – let alone someone else's. And such a pathetic motive – to show off before Sylvan.

Now he recollected that evening not only with a sense of shame but almost horror. Could those rough sketches have been important or useful to an enemy? Had Sylvan deliberately encouraged him to 'borrow' them? And what had he been doing when he allegedly *couldn't find the corkscrew?* Tom groaned, then told himself firmly he was indeed making a mountain out of a molehill and that what he needed was a good night's sleep.

He felt better the next morning, with the microfilm safely stowed in Evans' safe, and Williams' reassurances about the lack of suspicious visitors.

It was Sunday, and he decided, partly out of politeness, to attend the service that the captain led. It also reminded him of some of those still, small moments of calm during his war service, when attendance was expected, assuming your ship was not being shelled, torpedoed or bombed at the time. Afterwards Evans came over and said, "We have only three more full days at sea. I thought I would invite Dr Masudi and his wife to dine at my table tomorrow – I understand she is back on her feet now. Would you care to join us?"

Why not? Nearly home and dry.

"Thank you, sir. I'd like that."

He went down to the sick bay where he found Bronski in a calmer mood. Still no suspicious visitors. "But he's taken to getting up and wandering around in the night," Marks confided outside the room. "Not sleep-walking – he knows what he's doing. When I found him and asked what he thought he was up to, he gave me a cheeky grin like, and said 'looking after Thomas'. That's you, sir."

Tom had to smile.

"That's thoughtful of him, but *I'm* supposed to be looking after *him*!"

"Yes, I know, sir. But don't you worry, I'll keep a weather eye out for him."

Chapter Twenty-Eight

The next day the weather, which up to now had been generally bright and sunny with a following south-westerly, had changed. The brisk force four had died away, and sullen cloud reflected a grey sea.

"Wouldn't you know it," said the friendly man, as they passed each other on their morning circuit of the deck. "Approaching good old Blighty, that's what it is. Might have known it."

Tom smiled and agreed, wondering if he could be a Russian agent, out to kidnap his charge.

He took *Lord Jim* to the saloon, managed a few more chapters, and went to visit Bronski.

"Mr Mann went walkabout again last night, didn't you?" said Fred Marks reprovingly and Bronski positively grinned. "Yes indeed. But as you see, our Thomas is safe."

"I'd rather you didn't all the same, Uncle Peter," said Tom. "I'm very grateful, but you really must stay put here, you know. Anything could happen."

"My point exactly," said Bronski looking very pleased with himself.

Reassured, Tom felt safe enough to join in a game of deck quoits in the afternoon.

As he got dressed for dinner that evening, he began to wonder about their arrival in Liverpool. Sylvan had assured him that Sir John had put arrangements in hand for the professor's reception, and Captain Evans had informed him earlier in the day that he had learnt that they would receive a radio signal nearer the time telling them what the procedure would be. He was not sure, however, what he was supposed to do. Get himself to London, presumably, for a debriefing. He was not looking forward to it.

He went to the dining room and joined the company at the captain's table. Apart from the Masudis and him, there was a pleasant American couple going to see their daughter in Scotland for the first time since the start of the war.

"And we have a new granddaughter we've never even seen, can you believe?" said Mrs Desmond. "Oh, she's just the cutest thing! Let me show you her picture. Wilbur, do you have that picture of Dolly in your wallet, you know, the one Norma sent to us just recently? Oh, you haven't? Oh what a shame. Listen, hun, can I show it to you some other time?"

Tom was pretty sure they weren't Russian agents or, if they were, they were making a damn good fist of being an All-American couple. But perhaps that was exactly the point? *Oh, for God's sake*, he told himself, and settled in to enjoy the steak-and-kidney pie, which Wilbur was pushing suspiciously around his own plate.

Mrs Masudi was seated on his right and he turned to talk to her. The captain had introduced them when he came in, but she had said nothing beyond "Good evening." It was only when she said, "I hope you have tried Coca-Cola in the last three years, Lieutenant," that he realised that she remembered when they had met before.

"You have a good memory, Mrs Masudi," he said. "I am afraid mine is not so good – I have forgotten where you told me you came from – Libya, is it?"

"No, not Libya – we lived there during the war, but I am from Beirut, Lebanon," she said in that charming, deep husky voice. "I am a Maronite Christian."

"Of course – Lebanon's in the Bible, isn't it? All I know about is that cedars grow there."

"Yes, it is true. They are very beautiful. It is a very beautiful country. You should go there some time now this terrible war is over. But my people have suffered a long time at the hands of the Muslims." She took a sip from her glass of white wine and leant towards him so that Tom could smell her spicy perfume. "But my husband, you know, he is a Muslim."

"Yes, I assumed so. Um, that must be a bit difficult on occasions?"

Don't get involved in this one, he thought.

She nodded sadly.

"Yes, I must follow him where he goes and he tells me very little. Like now, you see. I enjoyed so much being in Washington, I love the Americans. But now off we must go at the drop of the hat to England. But I am looking forward to Selfridges, and all the other beautiful and famous places in London."

"I'm sure you'll enjoy it."

"Perhaps we will go to France," she said hopefully. "I love the French also."

Tom was reluctant to disillusion her about the devastation inflicted on both Britain and Europe in the war years, but fortunately at this point the steward intervened, and then she turned to ask Captain Evans, "But where are we, right now, please, Captain?"

"We're off the south-western coast of Ireland, Ma'am, if I have calculated correctly which, I hope for all our sakes I have." There was some nervous laughter and he went on to regale his guests with a strongly nautical conversation about the size, speed and seaworthiness of the *Orme Head*, of storms experienced and records broken across the Atlantic. While feeling a little sorry for Mrs Masudi, who was clearly bored, Tom couldn't help admire the enthusiasm with which Evans talked, considering he had to produce the same spiel every night for a week. Pudding came – trifle – and then coffee. Mrs Masudi made her apologies and left, followed shortly by the Desmonds.

"Captain Evans," said the doctor, putting down his napkin, "may I buy you a drink at the bar as a small thank-you for your hospitality tonight, not to mention keeping us all safe on this wonderful ship? And you too, of course, Lieutenant Davis."

He ordered tonic water for himself while Tom and the captain settled for whisky and soda, and they chatted about what they planned to do on arrival.

"See my parents," said Tom. "It's been a while."

Doctor Masudi said how much they were looking forward to visiting London: "Westminster Abbey, Hyde Park, Buckingham Palace. And of course," he added with a grin, "Selfridges."

The other two laughed, and at that moment the steward delivered a message from the bridge.

"I must apologise," said Evans, "I'm needed up top. We're proceeding through the southern approaches, through the St George's Channel – you'll know where I mean, Lieutenant? Seems some mines have broken from their moorings and been reported in the north-western approaches. All shipping has been advised to take the southerly route, and there's thick fog. So if you'll excuse me." He beckoned to the steward. "If you would care for another drink, please have it on me. And I'm glad the ladies left us before I was called away. Don't want to upset them, do we?" He stood up and settled his cap firmly on his head. "Thank you for your company, gentlemen. Goodnight."

"Another one?" Masudi asked.

"No thanks, I've still got a way to go on this one."

Masudi asked for another tonic water, then said, "So, you are looking forward to returning to not-so-great Britain?"

Tom's patriotism was pricked. "Not-so-great Britain? What do you mean?"

"Well, what are you without the great Churchill? Your country is now little more than a socialist satellite, pandering to the might of the Russians."

"Oh, the Americans will keep the Russians in check."

"The Americans! In my opinion Roosevelt betrayed us all at Yalta. He played footsie with Uncle Joe and let the Russians run over half Europe. The freedom all those young men died for was sold to the Reds before the War was over."

"Come on, the Russians fought bravely. They had enormous losses."

Masudi shrugged.

"But this is what has always happened in Russia. Think of the armies of the Tsar. Cannon fodder, ignorant masses driven forward by the revolvers of their officers."

"Doesn't sound as if you have a lot of time for the Russians."

"I don't. But nor for the Americans. The Americans are decadent." He shrugged. "Yes, decadent. They care only about money, and all the new toys that money brings them."

Sounds like Sylvan when he's had a few, thought Tom. *But the doc doesn't drink, of course.* He tried: "So what about the United Nations, the Atlantic Charter?"

"United Nations? Wishy-washy sentimentalism."

By now the bar was empty, partly due to the increasingly uncomfortable motion of the ship, and Tom decided the conversation had gone far enough. "Well, it's getting late, I'd better go. Not that I have to get up in the morning or anything."

Masudi put down his glass.

"Do you fancy a turn on deck? Fresh air is probably good for us."

They went up on the deck whose darkness was lit by a few bulkhead lights, dim and gloomy in the swirling fog. "Not too long, I think," said Masudi, "it's not so pleasant. Let us take one turn before we turn in, as you English say."

There was a big swell running and Tom noticed that the doctor had no sea-legs, stumbling awkwardly as the ship pitched and rolled, while he himself settled comfortably into its rhythm. As they made their way aft, Masudi said conversationally, "I expect you have heard of Friedrich Nietsche? He is the western fount of our thinking. He saw that to release the future, the present with all its sickness must be destroyed. This is just what we are going to do."

"And who is *we*?"

"Islam. What you call the Middle East, but also many other nations. Islam is waiting for new leadership. This we will provide."

He's the one who's mad, thought Tom, *not the poor old Prof.* They had arrived at the stern, just about over the propeller on the port side. Through the openings of the hawse-pipes the foam and spume of the wash seemed near and full of sound. Two great ventilators roared nearby. Tom suddenly felt the doctor push him against the rail and at the same time stick something hard against his ribs. He knew instantly what it was. Masudi spoke close to his ear.

"Yes, it is a gun, I advise you not to struggle. And don't call out, though no one will hear you with all this noise. Or see you in this gloom. We need Bronski – oh yes, I saw his photograph in the newspaper, I know who he is – and you are in the way."

Tom's mouth was dry but he managed to choke out, "Bronski?"

"He will make our bomb and then we will destroy this decadent civilization of yours."

Tom's head had cleared after the initial shock and he thought desperately, *just keep him talking, then there might be a chance. And he's awkward on his feet.*

"But, but how…"

Masudi sounded proud of his plan.

"Oh, he will be taken very ill when he is ready to leave the ship. There will be a private ambulance at the pier, which I shall commandeer for my patient, who will soon be on his way by air to our citadel in Africa."

"Your citadel?"

With extraordinary clarity and total inappropriateness he heard Marcie say impatiently, *Oh Tom, stop repeating everything I say,* and thought, *if I'm going to die, which it looks as if am, at least I'll go thinking of her.* Masudi was still speaking against the continuing roar of the ventilators.

"The great Rommel built it. It was to be a key point in holding up Montgomery in the desert war. All we need to destroy you is perhaps just two of the professor's remarkable bombs dropped on the heart of the high altars of this debased cult of modernity, of this filth: Paris, Rome, New York. Terror will do the rest."

At that moment the enormous foghorn above their heads bull-roared into the night and, taken aback by the unearthly, ear-splitting sound, Masudi looked up and his grip wavered. Tom hurled himself sideways and kicked out at the other's ankles. He had calculated correctly. Unable to regain his balance Masudi fell hard on the deck, the gun skittering from his hand and towards the scuppers. Tom leapt for it and grabbed it, then scrambled to his feet and turned. A small figure was standing over Masudi and hacking at him with an axe.

"For Christ's sake," Tom yelled, "What are you doing?" He hurled himself forward and dragged Bronski off. "Put that bloody thing down!"

And then Fred Marks was there.

"Fuck's sake," he said. "What in God's name happened?"

He bent over the bloodied and mutilated body, then knelt and felt at the neck. "Well, he's a gonner," he said.

He looked from Tom to Bronski who was now sitting on the deck panting.

"He tried to kill me," said Tom, finding it difficult to frame the unbelievable words. "I mean him, Doctor Masudi. He's mad – *was* mad." He held out the gun, feeling it was almost too heavy to hold. "With this."

"So that's what it was all about, was it, Mr Mann?" said Marks. "Looking after the Lieutenant? Well, I apologise." He looked at the body again. "We got to do something about this ASAP. Anyone could come along and spot it and then all fucking hell will break loose."

Tom could feel his pulse racing madly as the enormity of what had just happened struck home. He drew a deep breath and tried to get a grip on the appalling situation.

"Cover him up with something?"

"With what? There's nothing here, and by the time I get below and find something it could be too late. There's only one thing for it, mate. Chuck him overboard."

Even in this awful predicament Tom noted how difference of rank had disappeared, they were both in this together. Moreover, Marks seemed to be the one making the decisions.

"We can't…"

"Bloody can. If you know a better 'ole for 'im, go to it. Think up a story later. Come along, grab his legs, I'll take the top half."

With difficulty they got the heavy body onto the rail, and it was gone. Williams took one look at his white jacket, now fouled with blood, stripped it off and threw it overboard too.

"And the gun," he added, "and the flipping axe. Where'd he get that from, the old bugger?"

"It's a fireman's axe. In emergency break glass. That's what he did."

Marks tossed it over the rail. "That broken glass will take a bit of explaining. Never mind that now, we have to get this mess cleaned up."

He located a hydrant and ran out a length of hose. "You take this and get this deck hosed down." Even in the dark Tom could see his quick smile. "You know how to do, that, sir?"

"Yes, I do. Give me the hose. You'd better get Mr Mann back below. He looks bad."

When he was sure the scuppers and deck were completely clean, he followed them down. Marks appeared in a clean white jacket.

"Mr Mann's asleep; I've given him a pretty strong sedative. So the old boy was right about you being in danger. Told you he'd been wandering around, didn't I? Well, like I said, I bin keeping an eye on him, so when I found he was off on his travels again tonight, I lit out after him. Come on deck and saw movement aft and came *tout de suite*. The rest is history, I guess." He fished out a cigarette, lit it and offered one to Tom. "Any chance you can tell me what all this is about?"

"Not really. Sorry."

"Thought not. Anyway, I'll go along with whatever you want to tell the captain. Never liked the cut of that doctor's jib."

Tom looked at his watch. It was less than an hour since the captain had left his table. It was difficult to believe.

"We'd better get on with it. But he's probably still on the bridge."

"I'll get a message to him that you want to see him urgently in his cabin when he comes off duty. By the way, sir," and Tom saw their relationship begin to return to everyday normality, "there's some blood on your jacket. Not a lot, but you should change it, have a wash and scrub up."

Tom told Captain Evans pretty well the whole story. His face remained impassive and he said nothing until Tom had finished.

"And can you confirm this story, Marks?"

"Yes, sir. Like he said, Mr Mann was worried that some harm could come to the Lieutenant, and he was right, sir."

"Very strange, very strange," murmured the captain. "Who would ever have thought of such a thing. A citadel in the desert, eh? Well, I expect our MI5 fellows will want to hear about that. Probably be quite grateful. And we should inform them of the fake ambulance – they can sort that out. I will send a radio signal. Odd, these sort of fellows: they always have to boast about their crimes. Their fatal flaw – certainly in this instance. So you... disposed of the body overboard. I suppose it was the best thing in the circumstances, but I will tell them that as far as I know Masudi threatened you at gunpoint and he fell overboard in the struggle – not a hope of picking him up in those seas at night. No need to say anything about Mr Mann." He stopped and drummed his fingers on the table. "But now it seems we are missing a passenger from our manifest. Any suggestions?"

Tom remembered Bronski's car sliding over the edge of the road into the gorge.

"Suicide? Or just on deck for air, leaning on the rail, ship was pitching and rolling badly and I saw he didn't have sea legs, that's why I was able to..." he tried to recollect exactly what had happened, but it was no good. He was shuddering, and he clasped his hands tightly together.

Captain Evans seemed to have made up his mind.

"We will have to make the best of a very bad job. Presumably when Mrs M wakes up in the morning and discovers her husband is not there she will raise the hue and cry. We search the ship but nothing turns up. I will suggest to her that we will hold a memorial service on deck – can't do a burial at sea as no actual remains. Not much likelihood of said remains turning up in an identifiable state: certainly not so as to be able to assess the cause of death. Very well. Now, I certainly need a large snifter of brandy and I'm sure you do as well, Lieutenant. Mr Marks?"

"Oh, I don't know, sir…"

"For heaven's sake, Marks, this is no time to stand on ceremony."

"No, sir. Thank you, sir, yes, I'd be grateful."

When Evans handed him his glass, he risked a joke.

"Saves breaking out the sick bay brandy, for medicinal use only, sir."

They raised their glasses.

"Chin up," said the captain. "And let's hope we have no more alarms and excursions before we dock. By the way, Lieutenant: Mrs Masudi. Do you think she will kick up a stink? I had the impression that they were not a very devoted couple, did you?"

"No, I don't think they were."

"That's a relief. Well, we have all seen some pretty funny business in the last few years. Nothing surprises me much any more, but this takes some beating. And now, gentlemen, I'm sure we all need our sleep – I know I do – so I will wish you both good night."

She didn't kick up a stink, far from it. Shocked but under control, she acquiesced to the memorial service. Toward noon the next day the engines were slowed in an oily calm; the *Orme Head* was now away from the Atlantic swell, somewhere near the Fastnet, with the southern Irish coast on the horizon. Captain Evans was at his Welsh best as he intoned the words from Psalm 130, *De Profundis*:

Out of the depths have I cried unto Thee, O Lord,

Lord, hear my voice:

Let thine ears be attentive to the voice of my supplications.

If thou, O Lord, shouldest mark iniquities, O Lord, who shall stand?

But there is forgiveness with thee....

For with the Lord there is mercy, and with him is plenteous redemption.

And he shall rescue Israel from all his iniquities.

Chapter Twenty-Nine

Tom woke to a grey, still morning to find the *Orme Head* anchored in the river. He had turned in early the night before and, with the help of some sedatives Marks had given him, had slept right through the ship's passage up the Mersey.

Dixon brought him tea and toast and he dressed in his uniform. It seemed the best choice.

The evening before, Evans had confirmed that he had received a signal that detailed the arrangements for the transfer of Mr Mann into the care of His Majesty's Government. A genuine ambulance would be waiting on the dock and the Professor would leave the ship after all of the passengers had disembarked. Marks had volunteered to accompany him to wherever he would end up. In view of Masudi's story, whether true or not, of the fake ambulance, Evans suggested they use a password and asked Tom to suggest one.

"Rattlesnake," he said.

The Verandah Bar smelt of last night's parties: the stale, morning-after smell of beer, spirits and loaded ash-trays. Tom slumped in one of its leather-style club armchairs and watched the passengers leave. It really did feel like the morning after but far, far worse. Details of the nightmare kept skittering before his eyes: Masudi's bloody corpse, the gun he had grabbed from the scuppers burning his hand, Bronski, like a maddened dwarf, swinging the axe, *oh God, what had Marks done about the broken glass?* But it wasn't a nightmare. It had actually, unbelievably happened. And there were only four people in the whole world who knew, and it was unlikely he would ever see any of them again after today. He ached to be back in DC. At least he could tell Marcie and Sylvan. And Sir John of course.

That deep contralto voice behind him. "Lieutenant Davis?"

He jumped and turned quickly, standing as he did so. "Mrs Masudi! Good morning. I'm so…" he broke off, unable to continue.

She laid a white-gloved hand on his arm and again he smelt that strong flowery, spicy perfume.

"Please. Do not upset yourself. I haven't. I am a strong woman, you know; I come from generations of strong women." She smiled. "You know, I am quite looking forward to visiting London by myself, the freedom to do what I choose, and also to the future. I will be very comfortably off. I will confess to you, there was not much love in our marriage, so please don't feel sorry for me. I hope you have a pleasant stay in England. Goodbye."

He watched her stately progress to the door.

A vacuum cleaner began to hum; stewards were collecting the empty glasses.

"Sorry to disturb you, sir, we got to clear this lot away."

"Sorry, steward, yes of course."

There were few passengers left and he decided to go out on deck for some fresh air, walking to the stern of the vessel and leaning on the after rail, from where he watched the pinnaces transferring passengers to the dock. With the tide on the flood, the stern faced up river; the tired and battered lower quarters of the city were still shrouded in mist. Higher, the sun was breaking through. The taller towers and spires of Liverpool glinted; the faded gilt on the great Liver birds turned to gold.

In another age there had been a floating landing stage here, with pavilions where bands had played to greet or to send off the legendary Cunard and White Star liners. *It must be twenty years*, he thought, *since I stood on the same landing stage with Dad to watch the Samaria move out.* As a boy, Tom had read all there was to read about these magnificent ships and had made clumsy models of them, some of which still survived in his parents' attic along with his clockwork Hornby Dublo engine. He ran through the comforting litany of names in his head: *Mauretania*, *Aquitania*, *Majestic*. And before them, *Lusitania* and *Titanic*, and their smaller sisters *Franconia*, *Carinthia* and *Samaria*.

"Ah, found you, sir." It was Dixon. "Sorry to interrupt your reverie, but Captain's compliments, and will you join him as soon as possible please. This way, sir."

Evans was seated at his small desk in his cabin.

"Morning. Sleep well? Good. Good to be back? Right, I've received your marching orders. You're to accompany the patient ashore with Able Seaman Marks and hand him over to the waiting escort. We've double-checked on this one, and any opposition has apparently been dealt with. If there ever was any opposition. They were a bit cagey on that. When that's completed you're to report to the Naval Officer-in-Charge. He will kit you out, advance you some cash and give you a ration book and a rail warrant for, let me see, the three thirty-five to Euston. A room is booked for you at the St. Kilda Hotel."

"Where's that?"

"I don't know exactly. Just ask a copper – that's what they're there for. But I believe it's very convenient for Whitehall. You are to present yourself for some sort of debriefing meeting at the Cabinet offices at eleven hundred hours tomorrow. Well, I think that's all…"

"Hell, I nearly forgot – the envelope!"

"Oh, my word, yes." Captain Evans swivelled his chair and unlocked the safe. "Here you are. Hope it's useful to somebody."

"It will be. Thank you for keeping it safe."

"My duty and my pleasure." He stood up as Tom did and they shook hands.

"Good luck, my boy. You've been through a lot. Don't let the bastards grind you down." He grinned. "And watch out for mad mullahs in St James Park. You never know. But I expect our own spooks are even worse. I'll be at the gangway in fifteen minutes to see you safely off my ship."

* * *

"Goodbye, Thomas," said Bronski, "Thank you for everything, my young friend – *shalom aleichem.*"

He embraced Tom warmly, kissing him on both cheeks.

Tom watched the ambulance bearing the professor and Marks leave. He had been to see the young seaman earlier and thanked him for his watchfulness and cool-headedness on that terrible night.

"Comes of being under fire, sir. No time for flapping in those conditions."

"Did you ever think of trying for petty officer?"

"No, sir, not really, sir. Not officer material, me. Not like you, sir. A natural officer. And a gentleman, of course."

It was difficult to tell if this compliment was genuine, but Tom gave Marks his Washington address and told him that should he ever want a job reference in civvy street, he would provide one.

"Thank you very much, sir. Much appreciated."

Sylvan is right about our rotten class system, he thought now. *Marks is better officer material than I will ever be. And there was a moment when we could have been friends.*

England looked as tired as Tom felt. He could see it already in the train, in the hard, dirty, moquette-covered seat he collapsed onto after stowing his haversack and duffel-bag in the rack. He could taste it in the godawful food they served him later in the dining car: the tinned grapefruit, the grey, close-grained meat that he assumed was beef, served with overdone cabbage and underdone potatoes floating in thin gravy.

All right, he thought, *they've had a rough time, to put it mildly.* Five years of bombs, shortages, black-outs, rationing. His parents had lived without a window in the house for three years. It put his nervousness about the next day's meeting in Whitehall in some sort of perspective. All the same he wasn't looking forward to it, and dreading even more the reunion with his family and their inevitable banal questions: "Did you have a good trip?" (*not really*). "How's Washington?" (*Wonderful. God, I wish I were back there.*)

"Are you seeing anyone nice?" which meant, when are you going to get married, settle down and give us grandchildren? (*Yes, Marcie. But I'm not sure 'nice' is the word I would use to describe her.*) Then the oppressive, narrow norms of English suburban life. His visits home had been far and few between after he'd joined the Navy, and there had been none since he went to Washington.

Washington.

He thought of it with longing: the little house in Georgetown, evenings with Miles and other friends drinking cold beer from the fridge, barbecues, sailing in the bay with Roger and Hank.

Marcie.

How soon can I get back?

Chapter Thirty

There was a note waiting for Tom at the hotel confirming his eleven o'clock appointment at the cabinet offices, with instructions on how to get there. In the morning he had time for a large and surprisingly good breakfast of bacon and eggs, toast and marmalade (America didn't do proper marmalade) and a pot of tea. *The Times'* lead story that morning was about America's successful test of an atom bomb at Bikini Atoll in the South Pacific, the world's fourth nuclear explosion and the first one underwater. *Hobson was right,* he thought gloomily, *the nuclear genie is definitely out of the bottle.* All the more urgency for international controls before it all got out of hand.

He found himself in St. Anne's Gate with time to spare. Above him, a shattered wall bore the bizarre imprint of a bus wheel blown into it at the height of the Blitz. "Gawd knows what 'appened to the rest of the bleedin' bus; excuse my French," one of the hotel porters had told him that morning. He had gone on to say how not a house, office, church, water main or sewage pipe had been undamaged, how bombs had fallen the length of Whitehall and on Parliament. "Much worse in the East End, though. I'm from Whitechapel. It were terrible. Terrible." Tom walked down the steps into St. James Park. He stopped at the lake to check that the pelicans were still there and went on to the war memorial opposite Horse Guards Parade. It was chipped all over from bomb blast, as were most of the frontages he had passed. It helped to calm him down, to think what the people here in London had been through. He remembered air raids on Portsmouth before he ever went to America; they had turned his stomach to water. These people, hotel porters and cabinet ministers alike, had been through years of it.

Thinking of others did the trick; he straightened his back and took a deep breath. Time to go in.

Tom's instructions were to walk along the back of the garden wall of No. 10 Downing Street and look for a tunnel-like entrance into and under the adjacent offices. These, he realised, were the Cabinet offices, with access to No. 10 at an upper floor level and to the Old Treasury Building, which fronts onto Whitehall. The stone facings, blackened with a century of London soot and fog, were now doubly forbidding with their sandbags and bricked-in basements. The whole was a warren of offices and it was here that Prime Minister Churchill had had his underground war-room. Of all the world citadels of power, only the Kremlin had a greater reputation for secrecy than Whitehall.

Through a glass-paned door Tom could see the gate-keeper sitting in a booth inside, sucking his pipe and reading a newspaper. He took Tom's particulars and summoned a porter to escort him.

This was going to be very different from Washington, Tom thought ruefully, where he had attended meetings in several departments of state and, indeed, at the White House; as different as taking tea with the house master and his family after the school cricket match was from waiting outside the headmaster's study for a wigging. A porter ushered Tom upstairs and along corridors into a high-ceilinged conference room where a dozen or so men were seated at a long table and whose deliberations were not in the least interrupted by his arrival. Left standing by the door, he glanced around the table and, to his surprise and relief, saw Sir John Portent. Whatever was he doing here? Tom thanked a kindly deity for facilitating it. Sir John caught his eye and gave the slightest nod. After a few further exchanges there was some sort of break and with a gentle pressure on his elbow the escort pushed him forward.

"Ah, come in. It's Lieutenant Davis, right?" said the man at the top of the table, presumably the chairman. He was tall, with fading reddish hair and a clipped moustache; he exuded authority.

"Yes, sir."

"Good morning, and thanks for coming. I'm Sir Walter Bridger. Sit down, please," said the chairman, indicating a vacant seat close to Sir John. "Now we've heard about the American end of Operation, er…" – he glanced at his notes – "Roadrunner. Hmm. We'd be grateful if you would fill in some of the blanks."

From halfway down the table a sharp-faced man addressed Tom, explaining that he represented the Attorney General.

"Young man," he said, "it seems to me that two unfortunate incidents in one operation could be construed as carelessness. I understand you lost the ambassador's doctor."

"I didn't *lose* him," Tom protested, alarmed at this opening shot, "it wasn't *my* fault he fell overboard."

"At ease, my dear fellow, nobody is casting aspersions on your conduct," Sir Walter interrupted, glancing reprovingly at the man who had been casting the said aspersions. "Captain Evans has reported the death of Doctor Masudi; dreadful thing, tragic accident, but you are not to blame. You did well bringing the subject safely to these shores. His expertise will be of inestimable value to the British nuclear programme. He's been given a new identity and moved to a secure location, details known only a select few, including Lord Zender, of course."

He shifted in his seat, leant back and twiddled a pencil in his fingers.

"Whatever our friends across the pond may think, your operation was quite a success. Professor Bronski was not lifted by the Russians, nor, in the nick of time, was he exposed by the FBI, or whoever, as yet another British-sponsored traitor. Sir John?"

Portent had raised his hand.

"Thank you, Mr Chairman. As you all know, I believe, our American friends are not at all happy about Operation Roadrunner, to put it mildly. They suspect that we are involved in some way, but have no proof. I have told all of you that the whole plan was hatched in my office at the Embassy but wish to confirm that it was endorsed, you remember, by Sir Walter here, your chairman and Secretary to the Cabinet, and by Sir Gaspard Jebb who runs the Foreign Office."

Sir John indicated the rotund, bespectacled man sitting on the opposite side of the table.

Tom suspected that Sir John had intervened to reassure him that he was not alone.

"Jolly important stuff!" enthused Sir Gaspard Jebb, who, in spite of the summer warmth, wore a three-piece tweed suit with a gold watch chain across his ample stomach. "Great success! I gather you played an important part, Lieutenant. Well done!"

"Let me remind you, gentlemen," said the chairman, somewhat reprovingly, "that Professor Bronski's disappearance has been the subject of some speculation in the American press; accident, suicide and abduction have all been suggested. However, there is nothing to connect us with his… repossession."

"Interestingly enough," said someone else, "*Pravda* issued another strong statement denying any knowledge of the British professor, while other Soviet sources are declaring that American capitalist circles had done him in for obscure reasons of their own."

"You remember at Yalta," said Sir Walter looking around the table, "how Stalin's people were always seeking to drive a wedge between the Brits and the Yanks? They're still at it. That's all. No story, no press! A hope rather than an edict, but so far, the press in this sceptred isle are not as sharp as that in America. We will probably get away with it. However, there is a further issue. Sir Gaspard?"

"Mr Chairman, thank you. Yes. The operation was masterminded on the spot by our man Sylvan Ross. Sir Walter's endorsement was needed because frankly, it is unusual – very unusual – for the Foreign Office to involve itself in… er… practical work of this sort."

"The dirty work," someone suggested.

Sir Gaspard ignored the interruption.

"There is, as you know, the Secret Service." He glanced over to a rather insignificant-looking man sitting in the far corner, who had contributed nothing to the discussion so far. "What were the intelligence services up to, Symes? Were they not in the act?"

The man in the corner retorted sourly: "It was most irregular. The Director was – still is – furious. Not all of you may know that Ross works for British Intelligence." Several startled faces looked up. "His task is to watch this proposed new Central Intelligence Agency set-up and to keep close to certain individuals in the US scientific community. We were not consulted about this… this operation, if it can be dignified with that title. Why? We would still like to know!"

"If you must know," said Sir Gaspard tartly, "it is all to do with our historic relationship with the United States. Your people have built up an intimate relationship with the American security service. I don't know just how close your lot is to that little plant of British spooks holed up in New York, but I gather they work closely with and even for American intelligence."

"You mean that they were hardly qualified to take the pants off the FBI and the NIA or the CIG or whatever they call themselves now?" remarked Sir Walter.

"Yes, just that."

The man from MI5, as though to retrieve attention, stood up.

"To cut the story short, Mr Chairman, we have reason to have some doubts about this Mr Ross from the Foreign Office. We have put in a request that he should be recalled, now, as soon as possible."

"It's in hand," Sir John said brusquely.

Before Symes could retort, Sir Walter said firmly, "That's all for today, gentlemen. Sir John, Lieutenant Davis – thank you for being here, there is no need to detain you further." He banged his gavel on the table. "The meeting stands adjourned."

So that was all. Tom realized that his apprehensions had been unfounded; his presence here was merely a formality. The attendees hurried out of the room, leaving the MI5 man talking to Sir John, who signalled Tom to join them.

"Tom, I want you to come and have lunch with me at the Travellers. First though, Symes here wants a word."

Tom had only the vaguest idea of what a secret service man did but Symes certainly didn't look the part. Not at all sinister, in fact a typical civil servant: pin-striped trousers, vaguely regimental tie, black jacket.

Tom's proffered hand was met by a brief nod and Symes went on speaking to Sir John as though Tom were not there: "– so we want Lieutenant Davis to report to Leconfield House tomorrow morning. A car will pick him up at his hotel at eleven o'clock."

Chapter Thirty-One

As they emerged into the sunshine of Horse Guards Parade and walked through St. James Park, Tom felt the tension in his body dissipate. He would have liked to thank Sir John for his tacit support during the meeting but wasn't sure where to start.

"Tragic what happened to the doctor," said Sir John. "An accident, was it? Or suicide? The ambassador will be most distressed. His Excellency thought very highly of him."

"Well, it's a little more complicated than it appears, sir."

As succinctly as he could, he told Sir John the whole story, grateful to unburden himself.

"Good Lord," was all Sir John could say in response.

"Bronski didn't trust him," Tom explained, "but I would never have suspected Masudi. I was focussed on the Russians. All that Rommel and middle-eastern citadel stuff came completely out of the blue."

"There have been rumours – but a lot of people think that's all they are – MI5 have been alerted, then. Probably as well. I suppose that's what they want to talk to you about. Who else knows about all this?"

"Captain Evans, of course, and the medical orderly, as well as Professor Bronski – I mean, Mr Mann."

"Good Lord," said Sir John again, "hard to believe that that old man… awful business." He shook his head as if trying to dispel an image in his head. "Well, no need for this to get out, so we'll say no more about it. Captain Evans has reported the doctor's death as an unfortunate accident, and I'm sure he and the others understand the necessity to be discreet. Let's hope it stays under wraps, like *l'affaire Bronski*. I have been thirty-five years in the Foreign Office, and I don't need anything jeopardising my long-standing hope to retire soon with a decent ambassadorship."

At the Travellers, they ate soup then sole, followed by mutton chops with the inevitable cabbage and potatoes. They had made good headway through a flask of Club claret when Tom remembered something.

"That chap at the meeting mentioned two unfortunate incidents. I suppose Masudi was one, but what was the other?"

Sir John put down his knife and fork and sighed.

"I'm afraid I have some bad news. Thought I'd wait till after you'd had your lunch before breaking it." As Tom looked up in alarm, he continued, "I am so sorry to have to tell you this, Tom, but while you were escaping with Bronski in the schooner, Roger Devereux ran his MG into a car with a pair of Russians heading in the opposite direction, presumably to stop you. Freak accident, obviously, probably speeding, you know how fast he drives – drove – lost control of the car taking a bend too fast, or skidded on the road trying to avoid them. There were no survivors. The Assistant Naval Attaché, Grigori Potemkin, and another chap from the Soviet Embassy, were also killed in the crash. All quite horrible."

"Roger… *died?*"

Sir John nodded.

"Oh God… *Marcie.* She wasn't far behind."

"No, don't worry, she wasn't involved in the accident. But she was first on the scene, went to the nearest house and called the police. Very shaken, naturally, but she'll be fine. Marcie's very strong, you know. A remarkable woman."

All Tom could do was say lamely, "Will you tell her… I… I hope she's all right."

"Of course. I'll make sure she gets your message." After a sympathetic moment he continued, "The Russians kept quiet about it as long as they could, but eventually their embassy put out a statement saying that Roger had been drag-racing with Potemkin and their cars collided. Rather feeble story, but they could hardly say what they were really up to."

Tom shook his head. "No, I suppose they couldn't." He was still trying to come to grips with what he had been told.

"And more bad news, I'm afraid. That same night Sylvan Ross went berserk. Smashed up his office in the Chancery, got thoroughly drunk, smashed things at home. He'd been under enormous stress, and it's my belief that Roger's death tipped him over the edge. I understand they were good friends. We got him into a private nursing home and they diagnosed a serious mental breakdown. Now he's on his way home – on the *Queen Mary* – left New York this morning, in fact. Frankly we needed no advice from MI5 on this. Here, let me fill your glass."

The horrific news – *Roger* – was still swirling around in his head. But Sylvan. He remembered Marcie's revelations. Had it all become too much for him? He wanted to tell Sir John what she had said, but she had told him in confidence, and he would not break her trust even to this man, who was firmly on their side.

He gulped the remains of his wine – he needed it.

"That MI5 man, Symes, said that they had doubts about Sylvan?"

Sir John looked carefully around the by now almost deserted dining room before confiding *sotto voce*, "The spooks think he is a spy."

Tom forced himself to say it: "A double agent?"

"'Fraid so. They have built up quite a dossier on him. They are sure there is a traitor in their own outfit; indeed, they believe there is more than one."

Tom winced at the word. Traitors were hanged, like William Joyce, better known as Lord Haw-Haw, who had broadcast Nazi propaganda and had been executed in January that year.

"These intelligence agencies just don't trust each other," Sir John continued. "I knew Sylvan was working for MI6. Several pretty bright Foreign Office people have been enlisted on secret assignments, and even their own bosses aren't privy to these. But I truly did not know Sylvan's particular task until that unpleasant chap Symes spilled it out this morning. They think Sylvan may be a great catch for MI5; they think exposing him as a Russian agent will get both MI6 and the politicians off their necks because, as the world knows, there have been scandals enough."

"So Sylvan was spying on the Americans for the British and at the same time feeding stuff to the Russians? No wonder he went off the rails. It must have torn him apart." Tom emptied his glass. "Well, suppose it's true, and then he had this idea of, of, well, of making amends with some kind of counter-plot, counter espionage, you might say. And that explains Operation Roadrunner."

Sir John pondered this. "And then as it were, seeking to redeem himself by shooting down both his task-masters in flames?"

"Something like that."

They sat in silence for a while.

"I've got to meet these MI5 people tomorrow," Tom said. "What if they ask me about Sylvan? What am I going to say?"

"Nothing. We all learn to say nothing to them, even if it goes on all night. They may be tough but remember they are not a court. Just keep them guessing"

"And after that? How do I get back to Washington?"

"Well, we think you should stay here and lie low for a little while. As you can imagine, recriminations are flying in Washington over the Bronski affair. Although it's not generally known that you were involved, best you're out of the way till the heat dies down."

"But Hobson… my job…"

"Don't worry, old chap, Hobson is looking after the atomic business, and they've sent out a new man from the Treasury to deal with the financial side of things. We've fixed up a temporary assignment for you with the Foreign Office – they'll get in touch tomorrow. By the way, you are still officially in uniform. If you want to join us for the long term, you will need to resign your commission and sit one of these FO exams. I'll see what they can arrange."

With a sinking heart, Tom said, "That's very kind of you… oh Lord, nearly forgot." Feeling in his breast pocket, he found and fished out the envelope containing the microfilm.

"I know you brought his papers over in the diplomatic bag, but Professor Bronski gave me these on the ship for safe-keeping. Just as well. It's important. I promised him that I would deliver them to Lord Zender. Sorry, bit overwhelmed with all the bad news."

"I'll give them to him personally. It's been good to have this chat with you, but again, so very sorry about young Devereux. What a waste."

"Will you… that is, are you allowed to let me know how Sylvan gets on?"

"I'll see. Don't know why not. Now, I need a full report on Operation Roadrunner from the inside, from start to finish – confidential of course, for the record, and obviously Sylvan can't do it. You have people in London, I understand?"

"Close by; my parents live near Cheam."

"Jolly good. Go there for a couple of days and write up the report, and the Personnel Department will be in touch with you in due course. Now off you go, I need that report by Monday. I'll stay on a bit. Certainly don't want to waste the rest of this excellent claret."

Tom left the Travellers, his brain still surging uncontrollably with thoughts of Sylvan and Roger. Thank *God* Marcie… but Roger and Sylvan… *I'll deal with it all later*, he told himself firmly; first he had a task that couldn't be put off.

There was a telephone box on the corner. He put some coins in the slot, dialled his parents' number and pushed the button as soon as he heard his mother answer.

"Ma? It's me, Tom – I'm in London."

"Tom! How lovely to hear from you! Will you have time to come and see us?"

"Of course. Is it convenient if I come tomorrow evening and stay for a few days?" He could hardly credit how calm he sounded.

"Of course it's convenient, Tom *bach*. You don't have to ask, this is your home."

Except it wasn't really, he reflected.

Chapter Thirty-Two

The car from MI5 arrived at St Kilda's Hotel promptly at ten the following morning. Tom had already checked out and had his two small bags with him. Symes was waiting for him in the back seat.

"Leconfield House, Jimbo," Symes said to the driver, who wore dark glasses and a shirt unbuttoned at the neck, so his loosely-knotted tie served no purpose unless it was to advertise his preference for busty girls such as the one screen-printed down its length. Symes said nothing more. Like the train from Liverpool, the car smelt of sweat and cigarette smoke. Tom pushed away his mental fastidiousness: petrol, clothing and many food items were still rationed in this country, and even basics like soap were scarce. He recalled his mother mentioning proudly in a letter that the King had led the nation in water economy by drawing a line in the Royal bath five inches deep above which, presumably by Royal Decree, the hot water might not rise.

The car had made its way through the narrow streets of Mayfair and now drew up at what appeared to be the back entrance of a largish brick building that might have been a private residence in grander days. As they waited for the door to open, Tom asked Symes if he too was from the Foreign Office. Symes seemed to relent a bit.

"No, King's Messenger. Carried the Diplomatic bags all over the place, all over the world."

There was a hatch in the door, like they had in the old American films about speakeasies in prohibition days. A panel slid back and they were admitted to a small foyer giving directly on to the open cage of one of those lifts with sliding lattice-work doors. It does not move if the doors are not properly engaged, a sensible enough safety device, but one which reduced Jimbo, the driver, to fury, and to language Tom had not heard since he had first joined up as a seaman. Symes took over.

"Not very mechanically minded are we, Jimbo! Here, let me do it!" Symes was clearly the dog-handler; in this small instance he handled the other man as he might a fierce guard dog. As the lift clanked upward, Jimbo was panting heavily and Tom assigned him a rather nasty role in this company of spooks, as Sir John had dubbed them.

The room they entered, leaving Jimbo outside (to guard the door, presumably) was more of a sitting room than an office, with several armchairs, mostly occupied. Symes introduced Tom to the Director, and then the rest of the group, instantly forgettable except for one: "And this is Mr Kimball from the FO and also in Intelligence." Kimball had an easy smile and a firm handshake, lined features in a young-old face, restless eyes. "Philip Kimball," he said pleasantly. "Good to meet you, Lieutenant."

"Haven't got for ever; let's get on," said the Director, moving across the room to sit at a small desk. His large frame, exaggerated by a loose-fitting double-breasted suit, seemed to bulge out and overflow it. He took time to relight his pipe, then said to Symes: "Good work, Jack. I should have got to that meeting yesterday, but you did all right. Thanks for phoning in your report; I've put everyone in the picture. And now you have brought us Lieutenant Davis." He turned to Tom. "I think you may be able to tell us something about Sylvan Ross. We're going to ask you a few questions."

There was a shifting of chairs; the soft afternoon sun had filtered through the Venetian blinds, but these were now closed and a light switched on. Tom was ushered to a seat on the other side of the desk.

"Now, Mr Davis, what do you really know about Sylvan Ross?"

What a stupid opener, Tom thought. *I can hit that for six.*

"Well, sir," (he decided a 'sir' was in order here) "you must know more than I do since he was working for British intelligence."

"What? Who told you that?"

"Mr Symes told the meeting so yesterday. It caused quite a sensation."

The Director frowned.

"Jack, is this true? Well, never mind now. We're in the last act, so you may as well know, Mr Davis, that our American friends have some leads on Ross and they have concluded that he is a Russian agent. Yes. He *has* worked for us, actually told us more about the Americans than the Russians." He made a noise deep in his chest that sounded like a chuckle. "We can't confirm the American evidence yet, but we have had our own suspicions. But the Foreign Office," and here he turned to Kimball, "have protected him like a baby. Our enquiries there end in a ball of cotton wool."

He looked over to another of the men in the background.

"Mr Bright, you started this in-depth enquiry business. What do you want to ask our young friend?"

Bright, who sported bushy eyebrows and a beaked nose, coughed, cleared his throat and said, "Well, Director, we didn't need the American experience to conclude that we had plenty of reds under our beds. Martin Dies' congressional committee may have done harm by going too far, and now the House Committee on Un-American Activities has been made a permanent fixture, but they had the right idea. With your permission, Director, we need to cut through the old-boy crust. Mr Davis: about Mr Ross – we know now that at Cambridge he was already a Marxist. Were you aware of that?"

Tom wasn't, but he leapt upon its irrelevance.

"He may have been," he said, "but so what? Marxism is, to this day, a perfectly respectable interpretation of history."

"You mean then, that you too are a communist?"

"No I don't. But the communist system under Stalin, which admittedly sounds pretty terrible, doesn't invalidate Marxism as a philosophy of world history. After all, do we think the terrors of the Inquisition totally discredit Christianity?"

His interrogator was not to be diverted.

"While still at Cambridge, Ross came under the influence of dedicated communists – of Stalin's people – please note."

Tom shrugged.

"A lot of us did; Oxford as well. There was plenty we wanted to change in our benighted, class-ridden society before the war, and plenty who survived still do, as a matter of fact. Many of them went out and died for King and Country."

"You appear to take the Foreign Office view. Have you talked to anyone in the Foreign Office?"

"I only landed in Liverpool the day before yesterday. I've not yet even seen the inside of the Foreign Office."

"We will be looking into your history, Davis: what vetting you had, who placed you in the embassy in Washington. How was it that you came to be involved in this atomic work?"

Tom sensed danger here. He glanced at Philip Kimball who nodded encouragingly.

"The embassy was short-handed. It was a local arrangement. With the war running down and Washington still full of British missions – and admirals – the Naval Attaché Office was a bit surplus. I was released to assist Professor Hobson. He was our channel for discussing with the Americans our post-war collaboration on – and indeed world control of – atomic energy."

"And this was quite unauthorised?"

"Well, there were signals to and from the Admiralty who released me temporarily for these duties, at the ambassador's request. I've never been discharged."

"But you might be anybody! Here were you, with access to the most secret work in the embassy and, as we now know, an intimate friend of Ross. Good grief!" He turned on Kimball. "Mr Kimball, is this arrangement possible in the Foreign Office?"

Kimball had so far not joined in the discussion, though he had clearly been following it intently. He now spoke for the first time.

"As Mr Davis – that is, Lieutenant Davis – says, it was a local arrangement. I understand that you were given the rank of a third Secretary – locally engaged?"

"Correct."

"So he's not really on the Foreign Office books as yet, but we often take on people locally in this way. Have to take 'em where you find them. Sorry Lieutenant Davis," he said with a charming smile, "nothing personal, but you know what I mean."

"Director," said Bright quite angrily, "we have waited too long for a response to our paper on the need for positive vetting throughout Whitehall. We *must* get that authority soon from the Prime Minister and starting with the Foreign Office!" He glared at Kimball.

The Director interrupted.

"We're getting nowhere. This is about Ross. Get on with it, Bright."

"All right, I'll come to the point." He addressed Tom again. "First: you liked Ross?"

"Well, yes, of course. Everyone likes him. He's a first-class administrator, popular too. He helped me a lot when I turned up in Washington as a greenhorn."

"A what? Never mind. So I suppose that is why you assisted him in this mad Bronski scheme? Had you thought that he might have been, how should I put it – *softening* you up?" He glanced down at his notes. "We have a copy of the embassy's preliminary report, unfortunately rather sketchy. It seems from what Sir John Portent– the Minister – wrote, that you were one of the very few people involved. You saw Ross in action. Did you not guess he was working for the Russians?"

"No, I didn't," he countered angrily. "And can you imagine a more patriotic act than snatching Bronski from both the Russians *and* the Americans?"

"How did you come to know that the Americans were closing in on Professor Bronski?"

"Ross told me. He found out about it – probably because he was working for your lot – and then he pulled a fast one on the

Americans, knowing what a stink it would cause HMG if they exposed Bronski."

"But odd, isn't it, that he did not tell this office? But now, let me ask you this. How did you conspirators know that the *Russians* intended to lift him, and the exact hour?"

"I haven't really thought about it."

"On the morning you left to go on board the *Orme Head,* who phoned to tell you the Russians had wind of you all and were coming? It was Ross, of course, through his Russian contacts. He was at the centre of the web. A double traitor."

That word again.

"No one else could have known," he continued, "unless of course *you* have some explaining to do about your part in all this, Lieutenant?"

Tom began to speak, but stopped. *Don't incriminate yourself any further.*

"You were going to say?"

"No, nothing."

Bright sat back in exasperation. The Director relit his pipe. Two matches were needed before a satisfactory smoke signal emerged from the bowl.

"So, no answer," he said finally. "Well, I think that is enough for the present. Now look, we aren't out to extract some confession from you, Lieutenant, nothing like that. The case against Ross is not yet complete. We are just trying to build up a clearer picture of the man. But there is another thing: Doctor Masudi. We had a brief radio signal from Captain Evans, but we obviously want to hear your story."

Tom repeated the approved version, enlarging on the details of the alleged citadel somewhere in the African desert. When he'd finished, the Director said. "Certainly interesting. Yes, I can tell you we've heard rumours about this before, but there's nothing we can actually pin down. We suspect it's the fantasy of a small fanatical group, but dangerous all the same. So it's valuable information. We'll check out what's known of Masudi and trace his contacts."

The meeting broke up. Kimball even offered Tom a lift to Victoria Station, but he said he preferred to walk. It gave him an opportunity to think. They hadn't been very interested in him – or in Dr Masudi – it was Sylvan they were after. Recalling John Portent's remarks, he also assumed they were more worried about traitors in their own ranks. He'd not been really surprised when he'd had confirmation that Sylvan had been in cahoots with the Russians; just sad and somehow disappointed. There had been clues: his interest in Archie Struthers' drawings of the nuclear-powered submarine; his anti-American rants; his seemingly preternatural knowledge of the Soviets' intentions with regards to Viktor Bronski. But Sylvan was his friend; he had chosen Tom to be a partner in his act of penitence, and Tom was determined to defend his good name. The spooks might suspect Sylvan Ross of being a traitor, but he was damned if he was going to help them prove it.

Chapter Thirty-Three

Had he known he would be making this journey, he would of course have purchased presents in America for his parents; as it was he would have to make do with whatever war-shocked Britain could offer. His knowledge of London shops was minimal and by name only: Fortnum & Mason? Bourne and Hollingsworth? He thought of Mrs Masudi, and hoped she was having a good time in Selfridges. She probably deserved it. He had enquired of the hotel desk porter after breakfast.

"May I suggest Jermyn Street, sir? It's not far and has a good choice of purchases."

It wasn't and it did. But first, on a whim, Tom walked the short distance to Piccadilly and stepped into the Aladdin's cave of Fortnum & Mason's. Frock-coated gentlemen walked the floor and attended counters loaded with exotic foods, delicacies from all over the world. Even in New York he had seen nothing more extravagant. Here, in still-rationed London, it was almost repulsive. His curiosity about this fabled place satisfied, he walked out through the side door and down the hill to Jermyn Street.

It was difficult to know what his parents would want or like but eventually he decided on a pipe for his father – safe; and then, because that was possibly rather dull, he added a large red silk handkerchief with polka dots. As he left the shop, he spotted Paxon & Whitfield, Cheesemakers. Going closer he saw that it proudly stated the fact that it operated *by appointment to His Majesty King George VI*. If it's good enough for the king, he decided, it's good enough for my old Ma.

The shop was dark inside and there didn't seem to be a lot of cheese on display. A shop assistant inquired what he was after.

"I'm not sure, exactly, but I'd like to buy some cheese – something a bit unusual?"

"Not one of our regular customers, are you, sir? I have some very passable Stilton, even some Wensleydale. Makes a nice change. During the war, of course, we couldn't get *proper* cheese – milk all went into the production of Government Cheddar." He shuddered dramatically.

"I was hoping for something a bit more exotic."

"Well, we do have this, sir."

He indicated a couple of round boxes on the counter with a sign saying: *Camembert from Normandy, 2/6 a box.*

"I'll take one."

Tom agreed with Evans' judgement on American cheese, and while he certainly wouldn't have brought that to England as an exotic gift, he still wanted to find something that related to that indescribable world across the Atlantic that they would all want to hear about. The best answer seemed to be a bottle of bourbon and the ingredients for an Old Fashioned, and also for a Manhattan cocktail, including the cherries. They probably wouldn't like it, but he would, and he might need a few stiffeners. There wouldn't be any wine, of course, so he bought a couple of bottles of an inexpensive red as well.

A light drizzle had passed and it was quite warm. In the garden of St. James, Piccadilly, he paused to look at the ruin of the eponymous church. In every town and hamlet in England, churches like this one had stood for centuries, giving form and foundation to the faith of their builders. This historic church, built by Sir Christopher Wren something like three hundred years ago, would probably be rebuilt. But would new stone, bricks and mortar, new carving and gilding, revive the message it had been dedicated to carry? And were a thousand churches up and down the country, untouched by bombs, any less dead than this one?

Still, there they are, he thought as he continued across the park. *And I expect I will be visiting one this Sunday.*

He passed Buckingham Palace and soon reached Victoria Station, gateway to the southern suburbs he knew so well. He bought a ticket for St Andrew's Halt. It was well before the rush hour and there were few passengers. As the train chuntered fussily towards Clapham Junction, he watched the moving townscape slide past the window: close-packed acres of streets and terraced housing, now criss-crossed with the trail of bombs and sticks of incendiaries, the gaping sites softened with the blowsy purple of willow herb, the roofless little homes. Nor had the bombers followed the line of the streets: the whole area was sliced this way and that. The target must have been the ganglion of railway tracks converging on the Junction itself, the nerve centre of the Southern Railway. He glanced down at his *Evening Standard*, angry with himself for succumbing to the same morbid curiosity that compels passing motorists to slow down at the scene of a car crash… he tried hard not to think of Roger and went back to staring out of the window.

It was drizzling again and the slate, tiled, and tarpaulin-covered roofs glittered like the surface of a wave-tossed sea. Among them rose the grey roof of another church, a Victorian monstrosity, riding the waves like a whale. And now he had seen whales. It had been a life-enhancing moment, and thinking back on it, he found that, oddly enough, it seemed to calm his agitation and distress.

He turned his mind to the impending family reunion. For the past forty-eight hours, propelled into the grey yet somehow exotic world of Whitehall, he had been in unfamiliar territory in every respect. But this was familiar ground; as the train sighed to a halt at each station, huffing and hissing, he knew where he was without even looking out of the windows. A strange fear grew of the familiar and yet not familiar suburban round – mundane as he now thought it: tennis parties, cinema outings, Sunday church, Sunday lunch. And the eager questions. He could no more tell them of the good life in Georgetown than of the horror of that terrible night on board the *Orme Head*.

His parents had been given to understand that the reason for his spending critical years of the war across the Atlantic was highly secret work, so it would not be difficult to play his recent past as very hush-hush. His regular letters to them would have done nothing to alter that impression. War-time censorship of letters from serving members of the armed forces had greatly extended the art of sounding interesting while saying absolutely nothing, and that, he thought sadly, was but an extension of their usual pattern of family intercourse. The strength of the English bourgeois family, he decided, lay in not probing the deeper questions, in confining conversation to the weather, the big match results, or the morning's news… dull, yes, but people got by; arguments were avoided. He could recall no conversation with his own relatives, in the years of growing-up before the war, that had had any lasting significance; he had never discussed anything with his parents more serious than a railway timetable. So if the family convention of non-communication had persisted until now, a veil could be drawn over the past, and perhaps over his unresolved prospects for the future too.

The little train, almost empty now, hummed and rocked along as it sped towards St Andrew's, the last station before the end of the line at Cheam. As his parents had told him in their letters, this too had been bombed; a temporary shed still served as a booking office and shelter. There was not much other damage round about, but they had said there had been doodlebugs, the puttering little V1 rockets, in the neighbourhood. One had fallen on open ground not a hundred yards from their house.

Chapter Thirty-Four

'Home' was less than ten minutes' walk from the station. As he approached the house, he noticed that the hedge and the grass were uncut, and the front garden was littered with soggy, decaying petals washed from the overblown roses by last night's rain. The house looked neglected, unpainted for years, with patches of plastering fallen away. One window was still boarded up. A sinking feeling made him hesitate before ringing the bell, but the door was thrown open anyway.

"Well!" said Mrs Davis, "here you are at last." And she held out her arms.

For a second Tom hesitated. They had never hugged or kissed since he was a toddler. The warmth of her embrace was not the stuff of their pre-war relationship, of that leave from Portsmouth in early blitzkrieg days, when they had sat through an air-raid, each in their own chair, unable to reach out and touch each other or in any way give comfort or share their fear, trying not to cringe when bombs whistled down. As Tom hugged her he could feel her shoulder bones and was shocked at how thin she had become. His eyes prickled with tears.

They went inside arm in arm and Tom's mother called out, "He's here, Ted!"

Tom's father rose from his chair in front of the sitting-room fire, where he spent much of his time since illness had forced his early retirement. He reached out both hands and took Tom's in his.

"Oh, my boy," he said. "I can't tell you how good it is to see you."

"Sit down there, by your father, *bach*," said his mother, reverting to the Welsh endearments of his childhood, "and I'll bring in the tea. No, no, you sit down, *cariad*, I can manage."

They sat with their cups of strong brown tea ("No, really, Ma, no sugar thanks"), and Tom answered all the immediate questions which he had been anticipating.

The tea things barely cleared away, Mr Davis turned on the huge old wireless set at his elbow for the five o'clock news.

"He has his routine," said his wife, with a fond smile. "Now, dear, you must be tired. Go and have a wash and brush up. You'll find your room just as it was, you can sort out some of your old things."

Throughout their childhood he and his brother Richard had shared this room with its dormer window looking towards the North Downs. Tom opened his old chest of drawers. There were his shirts, handkerchiefs, his school rugby jersey all neatly folded. He opened his brother's. It was the same. Ma had washed, ironed and tidied everything away.

For all that strange coolness that had marked their years into manhood, this motherliness had been there all the time. The tidy room, the carefully folded clothes were the signature of her love. He touched the medals that had been carefully laid on a sheet of tissue paper on top of his brother's shirts. His eyes began to sting.

At some sacrifice to their parents, Tom and his brother had been sent to a bleak prep school, and then to the grammar school in Cheam, whose headmaster, a strict disciplinarian, prided himself on frequent enforcement of the school rules with a cane. Reluctant to confide his unhappiness to his parents ("big boys don't blub" was the general principle), he had buried himself in academic work and sport, in both of which he excelled. During his school holidays with his grandmother in Sussex his greatest joy was to be alone on the water. As an unhappy teenager, John Masefield's poem "I must go down to the sea again" had seemed to sum up everything he yearned for. Only his elder brother Richard had understood, but when Tom was sixteen Richard had left home to train as a pilot with the RAF.

Tom had gained a scholarship to Oxford, to his parents' joy, but the war had postponed any need for professional career decisions. Ending up in Washington had been the purest fluke. He wondered now if he had almost welcomed the prospect of war, of joining up so that decisions about a career could be postponed. His parents had begged him not to go and it was only now, in this familiar house, that he began to understand how they must have felt.

Tom's ship HMS *Athene* had been stationed at Scapa Flow when he had been told of Richard's death. He could remember vividly the tidal wave of despair that had engulfed him. He had curled up on his bunk in a foetal ball; he couldn't breathe, he couldn't speak, he couldn't think, conscious only of the pain inside. He was given a week's compassionate leave. Even then, he could not connect with his parents. In the face of overwhelming grief, his mother still struggled to maintain the stoicism that she felt was expected of her as a minister's wife. Each had remained cocooned in their own grief; there would be no unseemly outpouring of emotion in this house. Only their sister Gwyneth was seen to shed tears. His father seemed to have aged overnight – Tom was sure his physical deterioration dated from that day, September 4th, 1940 – a year and a day since the start of the war.

He flopped onto his old bed and dozed for half an hour. Then he went to the bathroom and splashed cold water on his face, before having a proper wash. Back in his bedroom he started to unpack and pulled out the belt Marcie had bought for him in Taos. He ran it through his hands, admiring the leather work and the ornate silver buckle. *Ridiculous thing!* he thought. *I could never wear it here. But thank-you, beloved Marcie. It's all I have of you.*

From the chest of drawers he selected the most comfortable and comforting clothes he could find: an old cricket shirt, loose grey-worsted flannels and a sweater, then went downstairs, carrying his presents.

In spite of having a pipe rack already full of pipes, Mr Davis showed great enthusiasm and appreciation at being presented with yet another one.

"Camembert?" said his mother, "French cheese? Well, that will make a lovely change, I'm sure! You can get tired of cheddar. We will have it on Sunday – Gwen and Brian are coming for lunch."

A decanter of sherry, with accompanying tiny glasses, had been placed on the sideboard. Tom thought longingly of the bourbon still sitting on his chest of drawers, but decided now was not the right occasion. Sunday lunch, in the presence of his bossy elder sister and her dreary husband, was the time when the bourbon would be needed. He would have a swig later to strengthen his resolve, if necessary.

"Of course we wouldn't normally have sherry at this time of day and on a Friday," said his mother, "but we wanted to celebrate your arrival somehow."

They raised their glasses.

"To the sailor home from the sea!" said his mother.

"Well, from DC!" added his father with a big smile.

Tom couldn't recall his father ever making a joke, even one as mild as this, and he laughed in sheer pleasure.

There were plates laid out for high tea with wafer-thin slices of brawn and salad from the garden, bread and butter, home-made blackberry jam and the inevitable large pot of tea. There was also a heap of the spicy little Welsh cakes that had been Tom's favourite as a child; he knew his mother had made them especially for him.

"You must be accustomed to such a variety of food in America, Tom; I'm sorry, it all has to be very plain cooking here, with the rationing. I do hope it doesn't go on too much longer," and Tom saw on her face the toll those hard years had taken. He drank two cups of stewed tea, polished off the Welsh cakes, ate the last slice of bread and butter over-loaded with jam, and genuinely enjoyed it.

His offer to help his mother with the drying up was accepted, while his father settled down again with his pipe and the crossword. Tom was hoping that, having got through the simpler questions earlier, they could move on. Mrs Davis had already asked anxiously how long he was likely to stay and he had been non-committal. But back in the sitting room, with his mother knitting contentedly, his father took his pipe from his mouth and asked, "I know your work in Washington is very hush-hush – quite understand if you can't say much about it – but where do you see yourself going in the future, now the war is over?"

If only I knew, thought Tom. He was still struggling with Sir John's suggestion – no, order – that he stay in England for a while and consider taking exams for the Foreign Office. Was a desk job what he really wanted?

"Well, everything is up in the air at the moment, as you can imagine. I'm thinking about the Foreign Office. Not sure. Perhaps now I'm here, I'll have a chance to decide."

His father grunted. "You need to settle down to something soon. Any chance of your returning to England?"

"Again – at this stage, I just don't know." He hardly dared look at his mother's face.

"Ah well. Always hoped, you know, that you might have had a calling."

"A calling?"

His father looked irritated.

"You know what I mean, son. For the church. Something we never really talked about. But when you went up I discussed it with your Dean. The college had quite a name for its clerical output, including bishops, and, yes, one archbishop. Pity we didn't go into it more fully."

Tom had had some idea of his father's wishes, and it had added to his determination to escape and join up at the start of the war.

"Oh," he said, "no, I would never have made a priest. Needs a special sort of person," and he smiled with genuine admiration at his father.

Mr Davis seemed to appreciate that he wasn't going to make any progress on this particular subject so, after relighting his pipe, he said, "Got a surprise for you. Remember I told you we let the old Humber go to war? I believe she served with distinction as an ambulance."

"Well done, Hetty!"

Before the war, Hetty the Humber had carried the family all over the south of England at weekends and on summer holidays, even venturing once or twice as far as those fabled parts of the Kingdom, Cornwall and Wales.

"Well, Brian knows a place up at the Elephant and Castle with a complete line in Austin spares and he's restored Gwen's old Austin Seven. Rebored, rewired, new tyres, lots of things; it's practically a new car. They don't actually need it, so it's in the garage here. I've kept it licensed, ready to go. We want to make it over to you as a homecoming present. It's all yours, Tom; if you want it after all your high life. Body still needs a bit of attention – pretty ropey – bit like mine," he added. "You might like to take her for a spin tomorrow. Keys are in the sideboard drawer."

Straight after breakfast the next morning Tom went outside to the lean-to garage. He tugged the door open and there stood the Austin. He prowled around it with delight. No Buick, Cadillac, Oldsmobile, Packard or Pontiac seemed as desirable at that moment as this modest little car, with the freedom it offered.

It was bright and sunny, and he was soon away from St Andrews, driving through the country lanes he knew so well. The lush green hedgerows were rampant with bindweed, frothy meadow-sweet and Queen Anne's lace. Ancient oaks and elms stretched their great branches overhead, creating a continuous dapple of shade and sunshine. Dazed butterflies kami-kazied on the windscreen. Terrified rabbits scuttered for cover. He passed the signpost pointing to Irons Bottom. As boys, he and Richard had found that name uproariously funny. He was reminded of other names that had amused him: Ponders End, Picketts Post, Sollers Hope. They suggested distant outposts where Pickett, Ponders or Sollers had staked their claims, raised the Flag, or, sadly, been eaten by cannibals.

Pity it's not an open tourer, he thought, especially when he caught sight of himself in the mirror, a loose strip of mildewed cloth from the headlining dangling in his hair. *Wonder if that pub in Brentdown is still there? Might pop over and see. Time for a quick one before lunch.* He stopped himself. *They won't be open – it's too early. And I've got a sodding report to write.* He turned for home.

He spent the rest of the day on his report and had it pretty well finished apart from polishing by the time he went to bed. He had said nothing of those magical, stolen moments with Marcie at Pinoñes, the rush of adrenalin as they pushed Bronski's Hillman into the ravine, the white-knuckle night drive through the mountains. And then the exhilaration of sailing to Baltimore on the *Dulcibelle Adams*, unconscious of Roger's fate. Tom remembered Roger speeding away from Hank's cabin that day. *Had it really been an accident?* Roger was an excellent driver; he could surely have found a way to stop the pursuers without hitting them. He imagined the corridors of the Chancery, hollow and empty without his friend.

The report contained no mention of the terror he had felt as he faced imminent death at the hands of the fanatical Dr Masudi. Above all, there was nothing to incriminate Sylvan. It was a bland, objective recitation of the facts. At least, those facts that he chose to include.

"Church at eleven tomorrow, dear," said his mother. "I expect you'd like to come?"

"Of course," he lied.

The church where his father had ministered for so many years was a late Victorian brick building, lacking, he had always felt, that sense of antiquity that older churches had. He had spent more Sundays of his childhood than he cared to remember staring at the stained-glass windows with their gaudy imitation Pre-Raphaelite angels and saints. Imitations of imitations.

The congregation launched into "Guide me Oh Thou Great Redeemer, pilgrim through this barren land". *That's me*, he thought with self-pity; then told himself sternly to chuck it. Flashes of the last four weeks (was that *all?*) kept distracting him. The strange little chapel with its damned souls and miracle offerings. Masudi prone on the deck with a dwarf hacking him to death. Roger in the wreckage of the car. *Oh God help us. Rest in peace, Roger.*

"Our Father, who art in heaven…" intoned the Minister.

Tom gave himself up to murmuring the familiar words. "Forgive us our trespasses, as we forgive those who trespass against us." *The Germans had certainly trespassed against us; do we forgive the Germans? It was a lot to ask. But if we don't, how can we leave the past behind and make the world anew. If thou, Lord, shouldest mark iniquities, O Lord, who shall stand? But there is forgiveness with thee.*

And what about Sylvan?

The congregation was small and largely elderly and most of them knew Tom from the years before the war. As they left the church they greeted him warmly but with a sense almost of wonderment.

Gwyneth – always known as Gwen – and Brian arrived soon after they got back to the house, and he got an unexpectedly affectionate greeting from his elder sister. "You look well," she said, "Washington must suit you."

He decided to ignore the probable implied criticism (*What did you do in the Great War, Tom? Well, I sat in a cushy office in America shovelling paper around*) and said, "It does. And you look pretty good yourself." Which is true, he thought, taking in her slight, neatly dressed figure, her tidy dark bob and her welcoming smile. In the sitting room, the tray with the sherry and accompanying tiny glasses was waiting on the sideboard.

"Hang on, while I nip upstairs," he said, "I've got a treat for you."

He returned with the bourbon and the small bottle of Angostura bitters. There would be sugar in the kitchen; he didn't have any orange slices, but the cherries would do. No ice, of course. *How did they manage without a fridge?* He had looked in the larder earlier and saw flies buzzing around the meat safe where today's joint had been reposing. The milk at breakfast had been suspiciously near turning.

"We're going to have an American-style – what – libation? To celebrate us all being here. Gwen, can you find me some glasses?"

She looked doubtful.

"What exactly do you want?"

"You won't have exactly what I want."

She produced some small water tumblers.

"Those will do." He prepared the cocktails and handed them out. "Where's Ma?"

"In the kitchen," said Gwen, "where do you think? Mother," she called, "Tom's prepared drinks! What's this, exactly?" She scrunched up her nose in disapproval as she accepted her glass. "Heavens, that's strong! Not sure I want to be drinking this at lunchtime." She set the glass down on a side table. "I'll just stick to a small sherry, thanks. Mother won't care for it," she added.

Tom had forgotten his sister's depressing tendency to take the fun out of any occasion.

Mrs Davis didn't care for it. "Very nice, Tom dear. What a nice thought. I'd better get back to the lamb."

"I'll come," said Gwen.

"Here's to you, Tom," said Brian, raising his glass. "We're both very pleased you're back, if only for a short time?"

"Oh I don't know at the moment." He changed the subject. "So how's life treating you and the blessed Gwyneth?" This was his own joke, and one the rest of the family disliked.

"A good deal better since the war ended, of course. It's still hard going but one just feels there's a bright future round the corner. Just seems to be taking a long time to get there."

A childhood bout of polio had weakened Brian's leg; he wore a metal brace for support and walked with a limp, making him ineligible for military service. He taught physics at a polytechnic, an institution that Tom's fellow students at Oxford had led him to believe was the absolute pits academically. Making conversation, Tom asked, in a rather desultory way, how the war had affected Brian's work there, but his brother-in-law was fairly reticent. Tom tried, "And Gwen?"

Her husband positively beamed. "She's been promoted to Deputy Head Mistress. Did you know?"

She would be, thought Tom unkindly. He noted that Brian seemed to be enjoying the cocktail.

"Another one?"

"Wouldn't say no," said Brian, beaming.

Gwen came back.

"Lunch is ready, let's sit down. Brian, you're not having another of those, are you?"

The Reverend Davis said grace, then carved the leg of lamb.

"I saved up all the coupons for it," said Mrs Davis with great satisfaction, "and Gwen gave me hers as well."

Gwen passed the plates and Tom poured wine, which she accepted with a good deal more enthusiasm.

"Oh, lovely. But just a small one – not used to it."

The conversation inevitably turned to the prolongation of rationing, a subject, Tom was coming to realise, that occupied most people in Britain.

"And last month bread went back on the ration," said his mother.

"It's the poor harvest," said Brian, "all that rain."

"You'd think that now the war is over, we would be able to get food from the Dominions like we used to."

Gwen said, "Well, a lot of the stuff we would have imported is now being diverted to Europe. They need it a lot more than we do. Goodness knows how long it will take them to recover."

Tom hoped they didn't know that America, in part unhappy with the post war Labour government, had somewhat reduced its financial support for Britain, diverting its effort to the reconstruction of Germany.

"All I know is, rationing is actually worse now than during the war," concluded Mrs Davis, adding, "but of course you are right, Gwen, *bach*; there are thousands in Europe far worse off than us, and it behoves us to be grateful and thank the good Lord for our blessings."

When Mrs Davis proudly brought in the small round cheese on a large plate much too big for it, Gwen exclaimed, "Oh I say, Camembert! Haven't had that since, when – gosh, must have been Toulouse in thirty-six."

Tom recalled that as a young woman, Gwen had travelled widely in Europe before the war, and her disbelief and then her devastation at the rise of the Nazis and the surrender of France still registered with him.

When he offered to help with the washing-up he was shooed out of the kitchen, but he couldn't face the thought of returning to the stuffy drawing room, and Brian was quite happy to accompany him out to the garden, while old Mr Davis dozed. Here Brian told him about what he had actually been doing during the war, which was working on the development of radar. He expressed his great personal admiration for President Roosevelt.

"What he achieved with such a handicap – far worse than mine. I try and remember that when I get a bit down – find it helpful."

By the time they went back inside, Tom had completely revised his opinion of his brother-in-law.

As they said their goodbyes, Gwen hugged Tom.

"Tommy, dear, it's been far too long. Now this beastly war is behind us, can we hope we'll be seeing more of you?"

"Yes, it has been too long," he said, and meant it.

After the guests had departed, Tom mentioned his conversation with Brian to his father.

"Yes, he did tell me something about that. Someone told me that the boffins thought him quite brilliant and he could have gone to work for the government after the war. But he loves teaching. I know someone else who works there and they tell me his students think the world of him." He glanced shrewdly at his son. "I had the impression you didn't used to have much time for him? Because he worked at a polytechnic and couldn't be in uniform?"

"I'm afraid that's true. In some ways, Oxford didn't do me a lot of good."

He had forgotten to thank his brother-in-law for the work he had done on the car. He would write to both of them and say how much he had enjoyed their company. It was true, he realised.

Chapter Thirty-Five

Tom was to report to Mr Clayton-Greene of the Foreign Office Personnel Department at 10 a.m. on Monday morning – if convenient. It was. On Sunday he had a minor panic; he'd need to look presentable, but he had expected to be in England for just a short time and had brought only his naval uniform and some casual clothes – uniform it would have to be, then.

It was an easy walk from Victoria Station along the side of St James Park to King Charles Street and the back entrance to the Foreign Office. An elderly porter led Tom up a flight of stairs and then around the gallery that overlooked a once-splendid central court which opened to a glazed roof high above. Now there was no roof, only a scanty web of scaffolding draped with flapping sheets of tarpaulin.

"Part of the Old India Office; not very high on the list of war-damage priorities," explained Tom's guide lugubriously.

Clayton-Greene gave him a cheerful welcome.

"John Portent rang to ask me to see you as soon as possible. He wants you back in Washington, but it seems you'll have to stay here for a while to see out the next phase of this astounding – I don't know – what do you call it?"

"Well, a security operation."

"Yes, that will do. He suggested that we might find you some departmental work for a bit. Everyone is screaming for extra hands, so that's not difficult. And he suggested that you might as well sit one of our entrance exams. Post-war special entry and all that. They'll be a piece of cake to someone like you."

Tom nodded with no show of enthusiasm as Clayton-Greene looked around the overcrowded room.

"Let's get out of here for a moment. There's something else."

He led Tom back to the India Office balcony through a maze of temporary offices, thrown up with hardboard partitions, festooned with telephone wire and cables, loud with the clacking of typewriters. They emerged into the cool, sad silence of the great ruin and stood at the marble rail, chipped and blasted by the bomb, as were the Corinthian pillars that rose to the gaping ceiling.

"Now, Lieutenant, I don't want to press you, but I want a quick word about Sylvan Ross. The *Queen Mary* docks on Wednesday. We will arrange to meet Ross. He's a very sick man, I gather."

Tom waited.

"I think you know the spooks are after him," Clayton-Greene went on, "but up to now they haven't told us a thing. American Central Intelligence – the CIA, I think they're calling it now – are convinced that the Foreign Office is a branch of the Kremlin. Can you believe? It appears they have passed a dossier on Sylvan Ross to MI5 and are baying for his blood. But my department has been told nothing. Nothing! MI5 – the spooks – have the papers. Philip Kimball, who liaises with them, you met him last week, tells us to stay calm and that it will all blow over. I believe he's already given us a report."

"What's the future for Sylvan?"

"Well, Personnel is somewhat peripheral to all this. As I said, we've been told to expect a pretty sick man. Various reports on him should be with us shortly, and when we've seen him we will discuss what to do next. Certainly sick leave, and, from what we hear so far, probably a spell in hospital, maybe even a mental ward. Perhaps later, a further assignment?" He frowned. "But of course, any misdemeanours will obviously have to be taken into account, and if criminal charges follow they will unfortunately have to take their course. But he's one of us, and naturally we will protect our own just as long as we can."

"I hope so," said Tom gloomily.

"Well, we must get weaving. I'm horrified that MI5 were on to you before we had the least sight of you in the Office here. *Mea culpa!* We really must tighten up the screws. Now I'd better take you to see what they've sorted out for you. By the way, if it's any help – others have been before the inquisitors at Leconfield House." He glanced around the empty vault and leant closer. "And here's a tip: just watch your rear mirror. They're likely to keep a tail on you; the spooks do that to our people. Unbelievable, isn't it, in our victorious democracy?"

He took Tom to meet the head of the Cyprus desk where he was to be attached for a while and introduced him to his new boss, a lanky, casually-dressed man called Maurice Pickett.

"Thanks, George," he said, "we're quite desperate for extra hands. Has our friend any useful expertise or experience?" Tom was about to declare his total ignorance when Clayton-Greene broke in: "You're the luckiest of men, Maurice: Lieutenant Davis has been doing secret work for us and I'll ask you not to probe him about it. He can't tell you anything; Official Secrets Act, Defence of the Realm, you know, all that sort of thing."

Tom warmed to Clayton-Greene. It may have been his way of selling a pup, but he had given him a face behind which to hide his confusion in this unknown world of Whitehall. He tried, "Well, I know a bit of Greek from school: Ancient Greek, though."

"Know anything about Cyprus?"

"The Minotaur?"

Pickett smirked.

"Sorry, old son, you're thinking of Crete. Cyprus is where we are trying to hold things together in the face of the government, the communists, the Orthodox Church and Uncle Tom Cobley and all."

"A thankless and probably vain task," said Clayton-Greene.

"That's as may be, George, but never forget that our task is to uphold the dignity of the British Empire, and ensure we are not driven out in a shower of rotten tomatoes."

"Do we have to be there at all?" Tom asked.

The other two looked across at each other with what he detected as gently mocking grimaces at his simplicity.

"We have important military installations on the island," said Pickett. "Vital for keeping tabs on the Palestine situation. The Greek Cypriots are agitating for reunification with Greece, to which the Turks are bitterly opposed. It's bound to lead to trouble sooner or later. We're engaged in a race between some sort of political patch-up, which this Office is set on, and MI5 who want to get in there and assassinate the ringleaders. Now there's a thought. With all this secret work you seem to have been doing you might be able to help us there. Frustrate their knavish tricks, you know." He fished around on his desk. "Here, take this file and read it through. It will put you in the picture."

"Thought you had an assignment lined up for the Lieutenant," said Clayton-Greene.

"Ah yes. The RAF are flying over some rabble-rousing priest. One of these bishops with the ridiculous chimney-pot hats, you know." Tom felt a twinge of annoyance at the arrogant attitude so many of the British displayed towards Johnny Foreigner. "You can arrange his reception; he's bound to be impressed by the uniform. As this is one of the PM's wheezes, we have to put on some sort of show."

Clayton-Greene said: "He's only a lieutenant. Don't you need someone more senior?"

"Perfectly adequate for this dubious bishop. Put a couple of extra stripes on his sleeve, if you like. Indeed, why the uniform anyway? I thought this was the Foreign Office?"

"He's only just arrived. No time to demobilise yet."

"Is everything in this file?" Tom asked, fed up with being talked over. "Can you give me a bit more to go on?"

"Oh yes," said Pickett. "Where were we? Yes. The prelate will arrive at RAF Blackbushe in Hampshire within the next week or two. You had better go down and see the commandant. We don't need a red carpet, but he might muster a small Guard of Honour. Just a little one. Then you bring him to London. Try and get a Rolls, or at least a Daimler. Then talk to the Government Hospitality people about some half-decent hotel. Fairly central, and a suite, I think. *Not* Claridges."

Clayton-Greene took Tom to his allocated office a few doors away, a small, windowless room minimally furnished with a desk, a couple of chairs and a filing cabinet. On the desk were a blotter and a telephone. "Sounded a bit like a Ruritanian farce to me, but I warn you, Pickett is tougher than he looks. He was in Greece a couple of years ago with the Underground there. You wouldn't know it, would you?"

"No, you wouldn't."

"Something funny?"

"No, not at all," said Tom, cheerfully. *Pickett's Post!* Those eminent Victorian adventurers, Pickett and Clayton-Greene!

Clayton-Greene turned to leave but put his hand on Tom's arm as he said, "Just take your time and settle in. Bit of advice. Try and forget Sylvan and all that happened. Not your problem any more." And, with an encouraging pat on the shoulder, he left.

"Hello, I'm Brenda, I'm Mr Clayton-Greene's PA. He's asked me to see that you get anything you want."

Brenda wore a smart summer dress, bright red lipstick, and had fair, naturally wavy hair, a nice contrast to the current fashion for frizzy permanents. She looked a good deal more elegant than most of the women Tom had seen in London so far.

They chatted a while, and she came back later with a packet of paper-clips, pencils, writing paper and a scribbling pad.

"Normally you'd get these things from Carole, your department secretary, but she's busy right now. Anyway, this lot should keep you out of trouble for a bit."

"Do I look like the sort of chap who gets into trouble?" he said, laughing, falling in easily with her banter.

She shrugged, smiling.

"Maybe. Who knows! Look, don't think I'm being forward, but I thought as it's your first day here, you might like to come and have lunch in the canteen behind Storeys Gate? Lots of us go there and I could introduce you to a few people."

"Why not," he said.

Brenda was quite a gossip and, as they ate, she filled him in amusingly on various members of the Foreign Office staff. She told him a little about herself; that she had joined the FO from Cambridge where she'd read English at Girton and had been in the ladies' rowing team.

"I did a bit of sculling myself at Oxford," said Tom, "was never good enough for the team, though. I just liked mucking about in boats."

At which point they were joined by a couple of young men, obviously friends of Brenda's.

"I was at Oxford," said one of them. "We always used to call it boating about in muck."

They roared with laughter.

Eventually, Brenda glanced at her watch.

"Heavens, is that the time already? I've got to run. It's been really nice chatting with you, Tom, we must do this again some time. And don't hesitate to ask me if there's anything else you want."

As he left the office that evening and headed towards Victoria Station, Tom thought about Clayton-Greene's advice: *Watch your rear mirror. They're likely to keep a tail on you.* Was it possible that the spooks were actually tailing him right now? He was about to glance over his shoulder, but stopped himself: don't let them know you're suspicious, and anyway, there were too many people on the pavement to know if there was someone taking a particular interest in him. What would Richard Hannay do? Tom turned abruptly on his heel and started walking briskly back in the direction from which he had just come, almost bumping into an elderly bowler-hatted gentleman who was directly behind him.

"Excuse me," said Tom. The man muttered under his breath but continued on his way.

Spotting a break in the traffic, Tom quickly cut across the road and paused on the other side. No-one else had crossed, and he started to feel very foolish. *There's no earthly reason why they would want to follow* you, he told himself, *you're not that important.* And he resumed his walk to the station. But he resolved in future to leave the office at different times and by different exits, and vary his route, just to be on the safe side. Be unpredictable, Hannay would say; keep them guessing.

Chapter Thirty-Six

Tom had made an appointment at RAF Blackbushe on the Wednesday to arrange for the arrival of the Cypriot priest. He had feared his welcome would be on the cool side: interfering young man from the FO telling chaps in uniform what to do. But there was an instant camaraderie, maybe because he was himself in uniform; and when he mentioned his brother, the wing commander said, "Richard Davis: I knew him! He was one of the bravest chaps in the wing. A real daredevil; nothing could stop him."

"Except a Messerschmitt," said Tom ruefully.

The commander looked agonised.

"Oh. Lord, I'm so sorry, I didn't mean…"

"Don't worry about it," said Tom. "We do what we have to."

"Hello, Tom, are you settling in all right?" asked Brenda when they bumped into each other at the tea trolley that afternoon. "What have you been up to?" They chatted for a while and then she asked, "What are you doing this weekend?"

"Hadn't thought about it, to be honest." He did now. The weekend in St Andrews gloomed before him. Yes, indeed. What was he going to do for the weekend?

Brenda said, "I'm going camping in the New Forest with some friends. We thought we'd take advantage of the Bank Holiday."

"Bank Holiday?" *Tom, you're doing it again,* hissed Marcie in his head. "What Bank Holiday?"

"August Bank Holiday, silly. On Monday. Do you mean to say you really didn't know?"

"Too long abroad," he said. "Thanks for reminding me. I think I'll get in touch with some old friends and get in a bit of sailing."

He found in his diary the telephone number of the old friends, who lived in Bosham, where his grandmother had come from. They were delighted, and he returned to his desk, the weekend now something to look forward to.

At three his phone went.

"Tom? It's Marcie."

"*Marcie.* Where are you? You're not in Washington, are you? What...?"

"No, I'm in London. I came with Sylvan on the *Queen Mary.* Sort of minder."

"How is he? How are *you*? I heard everything from John Portent. Oh god, Roger. Awful."

"Yes, it was. Sylvan is not in a good way, as John will have told you. Look, can you come to my flat this evening and we can catch up."

"Yes, yes, of course, where is it," he babbled, "I could come now..."

"No, after work is fine."

She gave him the address, and at six he was knocking on the door of the elegant little mews flat in Chelsea.

"Marcie."

She pulled him inside, slammed the door and they were in each other's arms. She was crying.

Eventually she stepped back, blew her nose inelegantly, took his hand and said, "Come upstairs to the living room. I'll fix us some drinks."

It was almost normal for a while. She poured them each a gin and tonic, they sat in separate chairs, he asked her about the flat.

"Had it for years. Closed it up when I went to DC, but the wonderful Mrs B has looked after it all through the war. And this bit of London missed the worst of the bombing."

"Who is Mrs B?"

"My cleaner. She's a treasure."

That's my Marcie, he thought. *Bet Mrs B lives in Whitechapel and got bombed*. But he didn't say it.

"Where's Sylvan?"

"In St Thomas' for evaluation. Then, if he's judged fit to be out in the big wide world, he can come here for a bit, until everybody decides what to do with him."

"You know the spooks are after him?"

She nodded.

He told her about what had happened on the *Orme Head*.

"Masudi," she said wonderingly, "he had us all fooled. Except Uncle Peter."

"MI5 thinks it may all be a fantasy. But a dangerous one. So they were pleased to have the information about him and they're going to follow it up."

She recounted the voyage on the *Queen Mary* with Sylvan. They talked a little about Roger, but the grief was still too raw. Later she said, "Stay to supper. Mrs B has left something in the oven, God knows what."

"Of course. I'll phone my parents and let them know I'll be late."

"Stay the night," she whispered.

When they got up on Friday morning she said, "There are some clothes of Gareth's still in that bottom drawer, never got round to clearing them out. Borrow a clean shirt and stuff if you want."

"Are you sure?"

She kissed him.

"I'm very sure. Can you come back tonight?"

He was about to say yes when he remembered his weekend arrangements.

"Oh, God, I don't think I can get out of it. I only fixed it up yesterday."

She almost smiled.

"Your face is a picture of misery."

"Then it's an accurate picture."

"No, go and enjoy your weekend. Anyway, I ought to make my presence known to various relatives I suppose."

"Anywhere in Sussex?" he asked hopefully.

"No, Norfolk, darling."

"Very flat, Norfolk," he said solemnly, and she pulled him back onto the bed, laughing.

Tom got off at the halt, slung his duffel-bag over his shoulder, crossed the traffic-less main road and set off the mile or so down the lane to the village. Bosham hadn't changed. Small cottages lined the street, the pub sign swung creaking in the breeze, the village shop was open and had set up a stall outside with local vegetables and eggs. He passed the squat little Saxon church with its helm roof, wild roses trailing over the low stone wall, and came out on the small village green which looked out over Bosham creek dotted with small boats gently riding at anchor. Gulls swung and mewed over the green-grey water, mallards fussed near the quay, and from the churchyard behind him he could hear the plaintive murmur of doves.

Eleanor and David were most apologetic: they were heavily involved in preparing for the church fête due to take place on the Bank Holiday Monday, but he had the use of their little sailing dinghy for as long as he wanted. He was guiltily pleased: he didn't much want to talk. Eleanor made him sandwiches for a picnic lunch and he walked down to the water.

He had the whole day to himself; the wind was in his favour, so he decided to sail all the way to the harbour mouth, working his way down the narrow channel in short tacks until the creek opened out and he could sail most of the way to the harbour bar on a comfortable broad reach. Sitting in the stern, sensing the wind on his face and continually adjusting the little boat to its whims, he recalled that last sail on the lovely *Dulcibelle Adams* in very different circumstances. *No*, he thought, *that first sail, with Roger, is the one I will always remember.*

He beached the dinghy on the sandy shore of East Head and walked a short way up into the dunes, where he ate his sandwiches. Then he flattened out the coarse marram grass, and lay back, staring peacefully at the high cirrus drifting far above. He could have slept, but knew he should keep an eye on the dinghy. His thoughts revolved around Marcie, Sylvan and Roger, but here they didn't hunt him down.

In the evening he went with his hosts to the pub; people recognised him and welcomed him back.

The next day the weather was cooler and there was a stiff breeze scudding across the creek. He took the dinghy out again and had an exhilarating sail as far as he dared towards the open sea. Eventually he came round reluctantly into the wind and settled into a fast run up the channel, the little boat planing, her bow lifting above the water.

He had promised his mother he would be home that evening; although she had said, "You go, *cariad,* and have a wonderful time," he knew how much she wanted him at home. And who knew how long he was going to be in the country? It was all still up in the air. And now Marcie was here.

On his way back to the cottage before catching the train, he stopped at the church, pushed open the heavy wooden door and entered its plain, cool interior. It was dressed in its Sunday best, tubs and vases full of flowers from the village gardens brightening the rough stone walls. He stood for a while by the massive stone font where villagers had been bringing their infants for baptism for hundreds of years. This building, which featured in the Bayeux Tapestry, was steeped in England's history, which it wore with lightness and grace. It was a comforting place. He was tempted to say a prayer for all of them but didn't know how to articulate it.

"How long are you in England for?" Eleanor asked as he prepared to set off for the station.

"No idea at the moment."

"We've hardly seen anything of you." She stood on tiptoe and kissed his cheek. "Make sure you come and visit us again as soon as you can, mind."

"I will."

The Bank Holiday Monday at his parents' turned out to less grisly than he had feared. He found it easier now to accept their obvious pleasure in his presence, their genuine interest in his American life.

"Tell you what," he said, in a moment of inspiration, "Why don't I take you out for a spin in the car? We could have lunch at that nice pub on the Downs – what's it called? – The Fox Runs Free. Come on, it'll be fun!"

And beyond expectation, it was.

Tuesday morning was grey and overcast, with a fine, cold mizzle that seemed to seep right through into his bones. He turned up the collar of his raincoat and walked quickly from the train station and into the office. He thought longingly of the clean, dry air of New Mexico, the luminous blue of the sky, the golden rays of the sun making Marcie's hair shine like spun silk…

The phone on his desk jangled.

"Tom, it's me."

"Marcie, how are you?"

"I'm sort of OK. Sylvan's here."

Bang goes tonight, then.

"Well, that's good, I suppose."

"I suppose. Tom, can you do lunch? One-ish? Mrs B recommends Lyons Corner House. The one in the Strand. On the corner."

He arrived at twelve forty-five. The huge restaurant was very crowded and noisy, but Tom's uniform, combined with Marcie's stylish New York clothes and her chic little hat, got them a table immediately. They sat down and, as Marcie drew off her gloves, Tom asked, "How was Norfolk? Apart from being flat?"

She shivered dramatically.

"Cold, actually, even at this time of year. Aunt Letty lives in a huge, draughty mansion on the edge of some desolate Broad; the wind comes straight from Siberia. And Aunt Letty's completely batty. It was all quite ghastly." She picked up the menu. "Lyons is very good value, according to Mrs B. Apparently her daughter works here as a Nippy."

At which point the aforesaid smiling waitress in her neat black dress with its white apron, collar and cuffs appeared to take their order. When she had gone, Marcie added, "Mrs B says don't believe the smiles. They get worked very hard, long hours, on their feet all day, and if they don't keep smiling they get sacked."

"You're making me feel bad already."

"Oh well, when you and Sylvan get to change the world I'm sure you'll sort it out between you."

"Talking of Sylvan, how is he?"

She shrugged. "Pretty awful."

You don't look too good yourself, he thought. *Must be difficult.*

"He wants to see you. Can you meet him Friday evening about five at the Reform Club. You know where that is, don't you?"

"Yes. I can leave a bit earlier. No-one seems especially bothered where you are. Marcie…"

"Ask for Mr Bowman, he's a member there. They'll be expecting you."

"What's this about?"

"Better let Sylvan tell you himself."

The rest of the conversation was desultory, and at one forty-five, Tom looked at his watch and said he must be getting back.

"Marcie, keep in touch, won't you?"

"Of course, darling," she said and pecked politely at his cheek as he stood to go.

Tom's new assignment involved contacting various Greek factions in London as well as the Orthodox hierarchy who, in fact, seemed remarkably cool about the forthcoming visit of the controversial priest. He was beginning to appreciate that the whole thing was highly political and he was not at all surprised that MI5 also had a finger in the Cyprus pie. He had just got back from a particularly trying meeting on Thursday and was quite ready for a distraction when Brenda came into his office.

"Tom, would you like to come to the pictures with me tonight?"

"Well, I…"

"It's just that my boyfriend bought two tickets already, but there's an emergency on at the hospital – he's a doctor at St Marys – and he has to work late. It's the last night that this film is on and I don't want to go on my own. My treat, of course."

"What's the film?"

"It's the latest Marx Brothers, *A Night in Casablanca*. Do come, you could probably use a good laugh,"

Yes, I could, he thought.

"Thanks, Brenda, that would be nice."

"Super. It's at the Gaumont in the Haymarket, the early showing, six o'clock, so we could get a bit of supper afterwards."

"Well, you were right," said Tom as they emerged from the cinema into the street, where it was only just starting to get dark, "that was a good laugh, and just what I needed. Thanks for the treat."

"Fancy some fish and chips? There's a great little place just round the corner."

"Yes, but my treat this time."

They were the only customers in the chip shop and took a table in a corner by the window. Unexpectedly, Brenda seemed ill at ease.

"Something wrong? You don't seem to be enjoying that."

She pushed her chips to the side of the plate, not looking at him.

"I think I told you I went to Cambridge? Well, that's where I met Sylvan Ross."

Tom's nerves jangled.

"Did you?"

"Yes. He was older than me, of course, final year and I had

only just come up. I was at Girton, reading English. Anyway, my brother was in Sylvan's year and the same college, and they used to take me out to parties and things. I fell totally in love with Sylvan. I still am in love with him, I think. I always saw him as one of the Romantic poets you know, Byron or Shelley. The radical ones, not Keats and Wordsworth, mooning around over nightingales and violets."

He relaxed a bit. If this was just going to be fond reminiscences it was probably safe.

"Think I remember from school that Wordsworth was pretty radical in his youth, wasn't he?" he said.

She smiled. "Yes, the French Revolution: 'Bliss it was that dawn to be alive, But to be young was very heaven'. Sylvan was so, so devil-may-care, extremely attractive in so many ways. The younger students were like moths at a flame." Nervously she straightened her knife and fork. "And I've had a peek at his files," she added, not meeting his eye. "I know what's going on."

"What's going on?"

"Come on, Tom, you know what's going on. Your name is in the file."

She leant forward and her voice dropped so low that he could hardly hear.

"I know he's back in England and he's pretty sick. What Sylvan was up to isn't yet generally known about the office but it soon will be. They think he's a double agent. Mr Clayton-Greene is holding off the spooks for the moment, but it looks as though they have Sylvan by the short hairs. But all the evidence so far comes from the Americans; even MI5 realise that isn't good enough. That's why they've been after you."

Tom could not help remembering that diner in Washington, where Marcie had first told him about Sylvan's covert associations. Brenda pushed her plate away and lit a cigarette, her hands shaking.

"They're all on edge. The MI5 spooks think the Russkis have some agents, pretty top people, in the Office. Did you see that

Russian film *Ivan the Terrible*? That sense of watchfulness, fear and – treachery - maybe I'm overdoing it, but…"

"Brenda, I sympathise. Truly."

"To be honest the Office hopes Sylvan will vanish, just *die* for God's sake! Mr Clayton-Greene said as much in my hearing."

She sniffed and rubbed her nose on the back of her hand, crossly, like a little girl.

"Why are you telling me all this?"

Her face was taut and pale.

"They still shoot traitors, don't they?"

"Only in wartime," he said gently, fearful where this was taking them.

"Hang them then, like that Lord Haw-Haw; probably worse." She shuddered. "Just think of it, Sylvan in the dock, sentenced as a traitor, being *hanged…* Christ, I couldn't…"

This time she rummaged in her bag for a handkerchief and wiped her eyes unashamedly.

"Oh God, Tom, isn't there something we can do to help him?"

He reached across the table and took her hand.

"Brenda, look, *if* he was a double agent, and *if* there was enough evidence against him, he'd be tried in a proper law court. He'd probably end up in prison. I don't see what… but obviously I'll do what I can, should the occasion arise. I can't say more than that. But I'm glad you've told me all this."

Tom took Brenda home in a taxi to a block of flats near Baker Street, careless of the extravagance. He felt it was the least he could do. There seemed no obvious way to help Sylvan. As they got out of the taxi she said, "Lie, cheat, swear black and blue for him if you must."

He took the bus back to Victoria, musing on the devotion that Sylvan seemed to inspire in these bright, strong women.

Chapter Thirty-Seven

Friday evening was mild but misty. Tom made his way down Lower Regent Street and through the Park to Pall Mall. He passed the Athenaeum, then the Travellers, then arrived at the imposing premises of the Reform Club, frowning over Pall Mall like an early Renaissance palace. He climbed the steps and gave his raincoat to the porter.

"Mr Bowman is expecting me," he told the frock-coated usher who appeared silently.

"Of course, sir. Right this way, please, sir."

Tom followed the usher up the broad staircase to the Gallery. At just on five in the afternoon, the Club was almost deserted and he immediately spotted Sylvan seated on one of the faded buttoned-leather chairs at a small round table behind the grand balustrade. The chair next to him was occupied by a vaguely familiar figure.

"Dear boy!" exclaimed Sylvan, "You are just the man we need."

"It's really good to see you, Sylvan. How are you?" said Tom, grasping Sylvan's hand. Still the rumpled suit, the bow tie, and the urgent need for a haircut. But Sylvan's face frightened him. The eyes seemed lifeless and deep sunken; the always prominent cheekbones stood out above hollow cheeks.

"Been better, to tell you the truth, but *san fairy ann*." He turned to his companion: "Guy, this is Tom Davis, I've been telling you about him – capital fellow. Tom, meet Guy Bowman."

"We've met," said Guy curtly

Tom frowned, then recognised him.

"Oh, yes, New York, that time with Bevin."

He had not taken to Bowman then, and now, irrationally, took against the socks Bowman was wearing: brightly patterned with mauve and mustard clocks. He wondered what on earth this man was doing with Sylvan.

"You naughty boy, why didn't you tell me you'd met Guy?"

"I didn't know you were acquainted, Sylvan."

"Oh, we go back a long way. We were at Cambridge together. Somehow we both got into the Diplomatic, but he now *big* man! Private Secretary to the SOS, the Secretary of State for Foreign Affairs, no less."

"SOS – SOB, son-of-a-bitch, more like," said Guy roughly, "can't stand the old bastard. Only stick it out because he's useful." He beckoned up a waiter from the dark recesses. "Drinks?"

"So, bring me up to date, Sylvan," said Tom when they had ordered.

"Well, you know Marcie and I landed last week. The Office met me with an ambulance if you please! So thoughtful, don't you think? I was quite expecting a police van. They took me to a clinic at St. Thomas', you know, across the river, for what they called *evaluation*." He rolled his eyes. "I ask you, dear boy. John Portent came to see me, and also that nice Clayton-Greene chap. After a few days in the penal colony I was released into Marcie's custody. I think those two both had a hand in arranging that. I'm staying at her flat in Chelsea, and the darling girl watches over me like a mother hen. I'm perfectly sane, as you see, but Marcie takes me to the clinic every day for more tests and treatments; never lets me out of her sight. Gave me a special dispensation to come here this evening to meet you, but woe betide me if I don't return to the flat within my curfew."

The drinks arrived and he was quiet for a while, sipping his Scotch and soda. Guy said nothing.

"John P filled me in on your somewhat eventful trip back to Blighty," Sylvan went on. "It seems that Dr Masudi managed to fall overboard. Wonder how *that* happened. Still, no great loss, in my opinion: *de mortuis nihil* of course, but I agree with Bronski. I always thought he was a shifty fellow. The ambassador would never hear a word against him, of course. He loves the Arabs."

Tom took a large swig of his own Scotch and said, "I rather hoped this chapter in my life was closed. I'm now under new instructions. But somehow I think you didn't want to meet me this evening just for the pleasure of my company."

"Guy, old son, make yourself useful and rustle up another round of drinks would you?" As Guy left he leant closer and said, "Tom, dear boy, you must have put two and two together by now?"

Tom nodded; no need to break Marcie's confidences.

"And I believe our charming MI5 gave you the going over. What a lot of wolves they are."

He sighed and drained his glass.

"So what is this all about?" Tom asked gently.

"So you know that I have worked for the Russians. Your kind heart may have refused the idea and – so far – so have the Foreign Office. Fact is that the goons of American Central Intelligence have got a pretty water-tight case against me and they are over here now to rub your public-school noses in it."

"I went to a grammar school."

"Lucky you."

Tom hesitated.

"So are you going to hand yourself in – make a confession?"

"Christ, no! If they want me they'll have to bloody well come and get me."

"Will *they* be the police?"

"Yes, but they aren't fully in the picture yet, and MI5 can't go about arresting people on spec, thank God, not in this country. Not yet."

Guy, who had returned as they spoke, said: "And the charge will be treason."

Tom took a deep breath, "Sylvan, you can still be hanged for treason."

"There might be worse fates."

"Nonsense," said Guy, "Think of the stink it would cause."

Tom knew what he meant: the shock to Anglo-American relations, suspicion that all was not yet revealed, witch-hunts, let alone all the personal and family grief.

"So how do you fit in?" he asked Guy.

"Me? Oh, I just want to change the world. I may not look like a social reformer, but nor did lots of them – Tolstoy, Bukharin and the rest – they just had the brains to understand that the system could not survive. Sylvan here is the romantic. I'm a pragmatist. And I recognise that the state of Britain, with its corrupt and parasitic upper class, is rotten, the City full of dirty tricks, and Parliament futile."

Tom had pegged Guy as a man of few words, but apparently not.

"Hush, Guy," said Sylvan, laying a calming hand on the other's arm, "You'll upset the waiter. Tom is loyal to the Foreign Office, and our plan – damage limitation, no more – is just what they want. Right, Tom?"

"But I don't know your plan."

The club was filling up. Tired civil servants drifted in; groups assembled at the bar in the court below. Some were coming up the staircase. Sylvan glanced around nervously.

"Look, let's finish our drinks and then we should get out of here. Tom, you go first. Meet me by the bridge in the Park in, say, fifteen minutes?"

Mists of light cotton-wool swirled over the lake. Tom looked towards the Mall and saw Sylvan, hurrying towards him. He propelled Tom by the elbow back along the lakeside towards the unkempt island at the head. A steep retaining wall above shuttered out the view from Buckingham Palace.

Pulling his companion down to a bench, Sylvan spoke quickly.

"Guy is watching for us. Tom, I am not going to wait for the police: I'm off. It's the only thing to do. It's best for everyone, best for the country too. If I don't go now, Tom, I will kill myself before they get me. It would be better than going to prison."

Tom was alarmed by Sylvan's intensity.

"You might get off. Look, I would testify that you're a patriot, not a traitor. So would John Portent. All your friends. We could get you the best lawyers. What about lifting Bronski? That was an act of patriotism – you said it yourself – an act of redemption," he added.

Sylvan smiled.

"Bless you, dear boy, but I've been too deep in this – this other thing – for the law ever to forgive me. But yes, the idea was to do something for this stupid old country of ours, and to break the hold the NKVD have had on me for all these years."

"You've broken with the Russians?"

"If only it were that easy. They don't let you do that. I'm no use to them now, but they will never let me go. I know too much, to start with."

"Blackmail?"

"Well, yes. They got hold of me at Cambridge. I wasn't the only one. I had done something, something that seemed rather… rather awful at the time. They found out and kept me on a string, but it was not until Washington that they pressed the button to activate me. Christ, I've been living a nightmare for years. Whatever comes now, that's past. I didn't really give them anything much, you know. The Russians were so far behind in terms of nuclear weapons development that I fooled myself into thinking if they caught up a bit there would be a sort of balance of power between East and West, and that might sort of be the best way to keep the peace. The Russkis know the strength of the Yanks and they wouldn't be so stupid as to start a fight. They wouldn't have a snowball's chance in hell."

He was quiet for a moment and Tom thought of the Hell that had been Hiroshima and Nagasaki. It wasn't only snowballs that hadn't had a chance.

Sylvan sighed and said vehemently. "Nobody now cares to remember that they were our allies and that without them we might well have lost the war!"

"But that's past, Sylvan. Now what? Are you telling me the Russians are going to rescue you, lift you, or whatever they do to save you from the *British?* Seems ironic, to say the least!"

"Something like that. You remember Captain Sodkin, the Soviet Naval Attaché in Washington?"

"Of course. You once warned me not to go to the Soviet Embassy, after he had invited me. Why did you do that?"

"Did I? Don't remember. Probably thought you shouldn't get too embroiled with the Russians. Good chap, Sodders. He's in London now, and in civvies, came over with Marcie and me on the *QM*. He will help us. If they hadn't got his wife and kids under their bloody thumbs he would defect; dozens of them have, you know. They know the whole system is rotten, that Stalin is a sick man who must surely die soon, and then it will begin to break up."

"How is Captain Sodkin going to help?"

Sylvan shook his head.

"I don't know. Sodkin and some of our friends at the Office are fixing it up."

"But where does Guy Bowman fit in to all this?"

"Oh, Guy's the one they want."

"The Russians?"

"Yes, *and* MI5. He's the big wheel, in cahoots I'm sorry to say with the NKVD and they want him back *tout de suite* before MI5 unmask him."

Tom took this in.

"But – Christ – he's the Private Secretary! Sylvan, is this true?"

Sylvan just nodded.

He felt fury rising in his chest. "Look Sylvan, risking everything for you is one thing, but I'm dammed if I'm prepared to do it for that bastard! Forget it!"

"Then I'm scuppered, dear boy. Bowman is the one they want. I'm only going along for the ride. Without him I have no way out. And is he any worse than me, after all?"

And to Tom's horror, Sylvan slumped forward, his head in

his hands, his body shaking. Tom patted him on the shoulder, trying, against all sense, to reassure him. Recovering his composure, Sylvan sat up straight again. In a small voice he said, "Well, we got Bronski."

"Look, Sylvan, with you two gone, will MI5 and all that lot be content?"

Sylvan laughed derisively. "Not likely. They'll be digging around for the others."

"Others? Do you mean communists in the public services?"

"Yes. Lots of brave men. You see, Uncle Joe Stalin may be the devil incarnate, but you've got to understand he is an aberration, he won't be there for ever."

As so often, Tom found himself half drawn into Sylvan's camp; his instinct was to share Sylvan's fears for the state of American or their own British democracy.

"But you still want to go there, even with Stalin in charge?"

"All the more reason. Perhaps there will be a chance of pushing things along a bit. From the inside."

Tom made a decision that he knew could change his life.

"All right, Sylvan, I'll do what I can to help."

Sylvan glanced around, He gripped Tom's arm and asked, quickly and nervously, "Marcie says you have a car?"

"Well, sort of, yes."

"That's what Sodkin wants. I really don't know much more. Give me your address and telephone number."

Tom rummaged in his pocket for a piece of paper and found an old receipt. Pulling out his pen, he scribbled the information on the back and handed it to Sylvan.

"Thank you. I'll tell Sodkin how to reach you. Here comes Guy."

Still angry, Tom faced Guy and said pugnaciously, "Just tell me why I shouldn't do my duty to my country and turn both of you clowns over to the authorities?"

Guy smirked and said, "Because you fancy Sylvan, I assume. Whoa!" he added, backing away as Tom leapt to his feet.

"That's a damn lie and you know it! Sylvan, tell him that's a filthy lie!"

"It's not true, Guy," said Sylvan, his voice steel. "Don't be ridiculous and apologise to Tom. We're not going to get very far without him."

Guy shrugged.

"Sorry. I think we ought to go now."

As he walked the short distance to Victoria Station, Tom wondered whether it was devotion to Marcie, the transference to Sylvan of his fraternal love for Richard or just plain cowardice that had prevented him from telling these two dangerous idiots where they got off, and reporting them at once to the authorities.

Chapter Thirty-Eight

"Cheer up, Tom," said his mother. "You look as if you'd dropped half a crown and found a sixpence!"

Tom looked up. It was his birthday but he didn't feel much like celebrating, however much his parents tried to make it special.

"Sorry! Not at all, just reflecting, you know, on getting older." Then, realising this might lead to the fraught topic of what he was to do with the rest of his life (what *was* he going to do with the rest of his life? Would Marcie be sharing it? Would he be in prison for aiding and abetting a traitor?), he added, "Wonderful cake. I don't know how you manage."

"Well, I saved the sugar and Mrs Brown keeps chickens and will usually let us have a few extra eggs… there are a lot of carrots in it."

His mother had given him half-a-dozen pocket handkerchiefs on which she had embroidered his initials.

"It's not much, *bach*, but it's not easy nowadays."

"Thank you so much, Ma. I do really appreciate all you're doing for me, you know."

He made himself useful in the garden, clearing away the pea haulms, lifting potatoes, mowing the lawn, clipping the hedge, cleaning and oiling all the garden tools, and felt a good deal better by Sunday evening. His father came out and sat with him on the old wooden bench in the evening sun.

"Thanks for doing all that work, son. It's beginning to get beyond me. Brian and Gwen help out a bit when they can, but they don't have much spare time and it's difficult for Brian with that gammy leg. Your mother does all the flowers, you know. Don't they look lovely?"

Tom looked around at the pink rambler roses tumbling over the wall, the catmint and lavender buzzing with bees, the blowsy hollyhocks, the little patch of mint and parsley. All of it was so redolent of the England he felt he was somehow betraying. He recalled the party at the Embassy where he had first met Marcie.

"Lovely. Must be a lot of hard work."

The conversation was banal, but he sensed the hidden currents and was content.

There was a hand-delivered envelope on his desk when he arrived in the office on Monday morning. The note paper was unheaded, the message typed. Lieutenant Davis was invited to be at the Mercury Restaurant, Wardour Street, Soho, that evening at seven o'clock. It was unsigned, but he didn't need a signature, he knew who it was from.

At night, Soho concealed its scars under winking neon signs and the glow of restaurants and honky-tonk joints. The shored-up buildings, the gaping ruin of St. Anne's church, the depressingly tawdry shop fronts and side alleys, were now masked behind the bright and restless foreground. Pubs, cafes and restaurants drew in and disgorged hosts of cheerful clients, taxis honked and the people in the narrow streets were out to enjoy themselves.

The Mercury proved to be a surprising survivor from pre-war days. Tom pushed open the door and looked around: a row of atrophied dishes set on glass stands under their glass covers; a few potted palms; square tables with chequered table-cloths and lit candles, mostly full. The air smelt of fried fat and cigarette smoke.

An elderly waiter in a faded tailcoat shuffled over to greet him. His thin, greying hair, drooping moustache and feet that flopped outwards reminded Tom of the Walrus in *Alice in Wonderland*. But a sharp eye had looked him over.

"Lieutenant Davis? This way, please."

He ushered Tom through a door at the rear of the dining room, and up a steep and narrow staircase to a smaller room upstairs. It was lit by shaded wall brackets and a lamp on the dining table, which was already laid. Further back in the shadows he could make out a low coffee table.

"What a pleasure to see you again, Lieutenant," said his host, emerging from the shadows to greet him. "When we met in Baltimore – was it only last month? – I thought we might not meet again, and certainly not so soon."

"The pleasure is all mine, sir," said Tom, accepting his handshake. As Naval Attaché, Captain Sodkin had had a neatly trimmed beard, but he was now clean-shaven and in civilian clothes.

"Let me introduce my, let me say, my companion: Boris, you may call him. He is really in charge of all our plans. His English is not good, so he prefers to stay in the background."

Boris was short and squat with a close-cropped, bullet-shaped head. He nodded and smiled politely at Tom, though a scar on the side of his face twisted his mouth into an unpleasant grin.

"First though," Sodkin continued, "a drink."

He led the way back to the coffee table where the vodka and caviar were waiting.

"*Za vashe zdaroviye!*"

"Cheers."

Tom threw back his head and let the cold spirit burn its way down his gullet. He gasped and set down his glass.

"You are quite the Russian," said Sodkin. "You will have a meal with us, yes? But first, sit down here for a word about this business."

If he were to make a stand, Tom knew that it was now or never. He ought to show these people the limits of his commitment, that he was still his own man. He was bothered by Sodkin's comment. With the recharging of glasses, he shaped his opening gambit, still clueless as to where it would lead.

"As to *this business*, Captain Sodkin, you are assuming a lot about my involvement. I must make it clear at the outset that I am not..."

he faltered for the second it took to ask himself what it was that he wasn't; not long enough to consider what he was or what he was doing here. "I am not," he concluded, defiantly, "I am not, shall I say, one of your people."

"My dear Tom," said Sodkin, "may I call you Tom? I feel we know each other well enough by now."

"Please do."

"And I am Alexei. As I was saying, my dear Tom, if you were, as you say, 'one of our people' you could not do this job. The police have files and profiles on everyone in this game, including myself, I'm sure. Boris here is perhaps different. He comes and goes."

He put a friendly arm on the shoulders of his silent companion, seated on the sofa beside him, and addressed him briefly in Russian. Boris made a self-deprecatory motion with his hands and shrugged his shoulders, the twisted smile curiously at odds with his equable demeanour.

"But I don't have a file?" *Not* yet, *anyway,* he thought miserably. "Is that why you want me for the job?"

Sodkin raised a conciliatory hand.

"Come, come! I will explain in a moment that you are invited to share in an act of great patriotism, a service to the United Kingdom. I am not alone among my countrymen in that I have developed a real love for your country, and for its way of life. Believe me. But first; why are you here? That is easy. We both want to help our mutual friend Sylvan Ross. He is now a broken man, but I have always trusted him, and it was he, of course, who sent you to me tonight."

He paused and poured each of them another shot of vodka.

"By the way, I was very sorry to hear about your friend Mr Roger Devereux. It was some of our NKVD people at the embassy, it was their idea. My assistant, Potemkin, he was NKVD too – damn fool went along with it, and he died. It was all a cock-up, as you say." He downed his vodka and leant back on the sofa. "Now. You may have realised that Sylvan planned the Bronski affair as an affirmation of his ultimate duty to Great Britain. Here was a man deeply compromised by his work for the Soviet authorities. He did it without pay, because he was caught in this malevolent web. Believe me, I hate it as much as you do. It has terror at its centre, its threads are made of fear. It cannot last. I and others hope it blows away before we die, even if, needs be, in its dungeons."

"We?"

"Like your Sylvan I am entangled in this web. So also is my friend Boris here. If we are caught with one foot wrong, then," – he drew the side of his hand across his throat – "and our families too."

Boris had clearly understood enough of what Sodkin had said to make the self-explanatory gesture as well.

"But you are going to sneak Sylvan and Guy Bowman out of Britain, presumably to some horrible fate in Moscow?" Tom protested.

"Oh yes. There we are just obeying orders."

"Obeying *orders*? Like the Nazis on trial at Nuremburg?"

Sodkin raised his hand again, perhaps defensively, this time.

"No, no, it won't be like that. And it's different. Look, what is best now for Britain? That Sylvan is brought to trial, a trial that will make Britain the laughing stock to her allies? To the Americans an ally they can no longer trust? You need them now as much as in the war. It's not only the atomic knowledge, but, as ever, her money. You know how, right now, she is still propping up your economy with her dollars."

"And Sylvan? He's the sacrifice?"

"No, no," insisted Sodkin again. "Think about it. First, he can never be readmitted to British society. Here, there is nothing but disgrace, almost certainly prison. Probably they would not hang him, except to make an example. But Sylvan would rather die than rot in captivity."

"But what better fate can be expected from Stalin? Prison, torture, third degree – we've all learned what you can do to people."

"Yes, Stalin is a monster. But he is seriously ill; he is never far from his doctors. He may be dying. It is hard to find out anything about him lately. But let me tell you, in the Russian House are many mansions. You think of us as a monolith and so we must appear. But believe me, all up and down the country there are cells of dissent, even in the highest places. When Stalin goes, you will see!" He nodded vigorously to emphasise his point. "I spoke to you before of these matters. Here in the security services we too have these cells – and perhaps you don't know this, but it will come out before long – dozens of our agents in the west have sought asylum. Military men, too. Anyway, take my word for it. Sylvan will be in the hands of one of our cells; a prisoner superficially, but in some quiet spot. A university perhaps, probably with his own dacha. He can write textbooks for us. He will be freer than he has been for years, in soul if not in body."

"Captain Sodkin – Alexei – just one thing, though, I must know," – *just reassure me*, Tom thought – "Lady Marcia…?"

The captain put a hand on Tom's arm.

"I know what you wish to ask. No, she never worked for us. But in her association with Sylvan she sometimes sailed pretty close to the wind, as we sailors might say, eh? She loves our Sylvan, and you, my dear Tom, you love him too, and that is why you are here and why you will help him now. And like us both, you have an ideal of justice and a fair deal for all, whatever we wish to call it – communism, socialism – ultimately these labels don't matter. More vodka?"

He poured and drank.

"For all its exciting charms I never really cared for the American free-for-all way of life, with devil take the hindmost. But in Great Britain I am sure that the goal of social justice still stands; perhaps it will be her last great contribution to show that social justice and capitalism can co-exist."

During the meal that followed, what had seemed yet another drift into an unplanned and unsought venture became a duty to perform. Tom began to feel that he was doing the right thing.

"All right, Alexei, you've persuaded me. What exactly do you need me to do?"

Sodkin produced a sheaf of notes and a map.

"Now then," he said briskly. "Our friends will cross to the continent from Newhaven. Your task is to drive them to a rendezvous quite near the harbour. The contact there will take them to Boris, who will have passports, tickets and everything that has been prepared for them."

Boris had still said nothing, but Tom thought he had been following their conversation in a way that suggested his command of the English language was not as rudimentary as Captain Sodkin had implied.

"Right. But where and when do I pick them up? At the Foreign Office, Downing Street entrance?" he couldn't help adding sarcastically.

"You will have your little joke, Tom," said Sodkin indulgently. "But, no. They will converge from different directions at Wimbledon Station."

Tom almost laughed aloud. How prosaic! He had expected something a bit more exotic than Wimbledon; some lonely moor, perhaps, a deserted airfield or haunted churchyard at dead of night.

"Guy Bowman will come by Underground, the District line," the captain went on, "and will be there to meet Sylvan off a train from Waterloo arriving at three-thirty in the afternoon."

Tom was to meet the two men in the concourse then conduct them to his car, which would be in the temporary car park adjoining the station. Only the day of the operation was missing.

"It will be soon. I will alert you the day before. One other thing; there is a telephone box about one hundred yards past the church in Little Topham, close to Reigate, on the Brighton road. You should reach it about thirty minutes after you leave Wimbledon Station. Ring me from there on this number in case there are last-minute instructions or any unforeseen difficulties."

He handed over a small, folded piece of paper, which Tom tucked carefully into his wallet, then stood up and held out his hand.

"Goodbye, *Tovarisch,* and good luck."

* * *

Tom had been in his office for no more than ten minutes the next morning when Carole, the departmental secretary, put her head around his door.

"Mr Pickett said to tell you that His Holiness is not coming this week after all. Technical hitch. Sometime next week is all they can promise." She looked disapprovingly at him. "Well, you don't need to look *that* pleased."

That was a stroke of luck. With a little bit more luck, this business with Sylvan would be over in a few days.

"Thanks, Carole. Would you ring up the hotel please? We've got a provisional booking for Thursday and Friday nights, better cancel it. Tell them we'll reschedule when we've got a definite date."

"Do you mean *rebook*?" she said tartly.

"Yes, sorry, of course. Rebook."

Even the language of America wouldn't release its grip on him.

Chapter Thirty-Nine

By ten past five on Wednesday, Tom was striding across the bridge heading to Waterloo Station, where he got the first train to Wimbledon for a reconnaissance of the meeting site. Climbing the stairs from the platform to the upper concourse, he found a position from where he would be able to spot Sylvan and Guy as they came through the ticket barrier, and then he went back down into the street and turned left into the car park.

It was a rough-and-ready sort of car park, separated from the tracks only by some huge advertising hoardings at the approach to the station. Just a piece of no man's land in front of a builders' supply yard where heaps of scrap were piled up against the fence. Although the first commuters were already starting to drive away, it appeared that almost every available space had been filled that day. *Good thing I checked it out,* thought Tom as he headed back into the station to get a train that would take him home, *it would be too ludicrous if Sylvan's escape were foiled because I couldn't find a place to park.*

"Brought you a nice cuppa tea, dear, and some squashed fly biscuits," said the tea-lady, setting them down on Tom's desk. "And there's Irish stew for lunch in the canteen. Don't touch the faggots. You never know what's in them."

"Thanks for the advice. You are indeed a pearl among women."

"Ooh, get away wiv you, ducks," she said as she shuffled out of his office.

The phone rang. He grabbed it quickly; it was already Thursday, three days since their meeting at the Mercury, and no call from Sodkin.

"Tom Davis speaking."

"Lieutenant Davis? Philip Kimball here. You may not remember me, we met a little while ago?"

"Yes, Mr Kimball, I do remember… it was just after I got back from the States."

"You gave us some information about Sylvan Ross. Just wanted to tell you there's nothing to worry about, we've got the rabbit in the bag, just about. Any day now."

"Oh. Well… well, thank you for telling me, that's… er… that's good news."

"Thought you would like to know. Well, cheerio."

That was strange, thought Tom. *I'm sure I told them at the meeting that I was a friend of Sylvan's, so why would he tell me they were going to nab him?* He tried to analyse Kimball's tone of voice; but could not tell if he had been pleased or giving Tom a warning.

He dialled Clayton-Greene's office number and asked what he could tell him about Philip Kimball.

"Kimball? Not a lot really. He's a big wheel in counter-intelligence, got an OBE in the New Year Honours. Why do you ask?"

"He just phoned me, about Sylvan Ross. Does he have any connection with Ross?"

"Not as far as I know. I think they both went to the same college in Cambridge – Trinity – but then, so did half the chaps in the Foreign Office. I wouldn't worry about it, if I were you; he's probably still helping to smooth out the waves caused by Ross's little – what did you call it? – 'security operation'. I gather the CIG got their knickers in a complete twist about it."

Now what? Should he phone Marcie, warn Sylvan? But Kimball "is a big wheel in counter-intelligence". It could be a trap of some sort. What did Charlie Weaver always say? *Simplest explanation's usually right.* That was the Occam's Razor principle that they had discussed in philosophy seminars at Oxford. *Clayton-Greene's probably right*, thought Tom, *you're reading too much into it.*

"Dear Sirs, in response to yours of the second inst," Tom dictated to Carole, "may I respectfully point out…"

The phone rang again. Tom picked it up and pressed it close to his ear, motioning to Carole to wait. Probably another false alarm. He heard the clicking sound as the call was put through.

"Tom? That you? Good. Tomorrow, three-thirty."

Frozen, he kept the phone close and said loudly, "Yes, yes! Will do. Half an hour then," and put down the receiver. He pulled out a handkerchief as though to stifle a sneeze.

"Nothing wrong, I hope?" asked Carole, with concern.

"No, no, really. Cold coming, I think, maybe flu." For dramatic effect he blew his nose rather forcefully. "Just a reminder that I'm wanted at a meeting in half an hour. Sorry about that. Thanks, Carole, just type up what you've got; we'll finish the others later."

Outside the building, he paused for a moment, then set off again towards Waterloo. He'd had an idea about the parking situation at Wimbledon.

There was still a handful of vacant spaces in the car park; he had to ensure that one would be available for him tomorrow. From the pile of builders' scrap, he took two discarded planks and two small oil drums and lugged them back to form a barricade in one of the few empty spots. As he did so he had a brief flashback of a similar barricade across a lonely mountain road, and of Roger's jest the last time he had seen him, just before he drove away… he shook his head to clear away the memories, then went quickly back to the station. At W.H. Smith's he bought a thick crayon and a large pad, as well as the early edition of the evening paper, making sure he got sufficient coins in his change that he could use for the telephone.

He propped the pad, on which he had written in large letters *RESERVED FOR AMBULANCE*, on his makeshift barricade.

"'Ere, watcha doin' of?" A watchman had come out from the

builders' yard and was eyeing him suspiciously. Without a qualm, Tom explained that a sick and disabled relative would be arriving tomorrow and that he was anxious to reserve a space. The half-crown he proffered as he spoke was gratefully accepted.

"All right, Guv. Just put that stuff back when you're done."

Tom felt chilled inside; it wasn't flu, it was fear: fear and excitement. He opened the door of the telephone box by the entrance to the station, then closed it again. There was no point ringing Marcie, she would be at the clinic with Sylvan this afternoon. He could do with a drink, but it was well after three and the pubs were closed. On the other side of the road he noticed a brightly-lit café. Suddenly feeling ravenous, he went in and ordered a pot of tea and two buttered crumpets with jam. He wolfed them down and felt better.

To prevent his mind wandering up other distracting channels, he ordered more tea and another crumpet, fished out his paper and folded it to the crossword. But it was no good. The very first clue he answered at once: "Revolutionary sets out – flyers." Answer: "Redstarts." He stared at it for a bit, wondering if this was an obscure message from MI5 letting him know they were on to him. Then, inevitably, the sluice-gate in his mind opened to release a flood of new concerns about Sodkin's plan. If the flyers got away – and he supposed that they would – where would that leave him? Was he playing the hero or was he a traitor too? Did commendation await him, or disgrace? But then another thought: if tomorrow was a success, there was no way in which his part could be made known. It would have to be *his* secret, to carry to his grave. There was only one person with whom he could share it: Marcie. Only she could say, "Well done."

But no, others knew: the Russians, of course. Could he trust Sodkin's word that he was not now one of "them", that he would be left alone? One interpretation of that had to be that he was quite unimportant. A useful pawn for this one move? A mere cog – no, no! screamed his memory. But if they thought he was of potential value they would come back at him, blackmail him, as they had Sylvan for all those years.

But couldn't the whole sorry farrago come to be of some good, and he could be instrumental in bringing it about? The prospect of nuclear conflict between the West and the USSR darkened the future of the world, but there was a chance of bridge-building. That insight Sodkin had given into the cracks of the Eastern monolith, and that young Tory MP who had said, "Why are we all so terrified of the Russians? They will break first – their system is so rotten."

And in the West, sometimes it seemed as though all the wonderful achievements in science and in industrial organisation were being used to turn the world into a hamburger heaven, watered by Coca-Cola. Someone had to give a lead to bring together the creators of seemingly unlimited wealth with the socialists, old communists, the religious community and all those who want the earth to blossom but also to ensure that its fruits are equitably shared.

So this is my destiny, he thought – *to Save the World? Me? Ha, bloody ha.*

Chapter Forty

"Another slice of pork pie, Tom?" asked Mrs Davis.

"No thanks, Ma; it's delicious, but I'm not really very hungry tonight."

The third crumpet was sitting heavily in his stomach.

"It's not like you to turn down pork pie," she said anxiously, "I hope you're not coming down with something."

"I do feel a bit tired…"

"Could be 'flu, there's a lot of it about. I'll make you a mug of hot lemon and honey, and you'd better get an early night."

The die was cast. As he got ready for bed his only thought should have been how best to accomplish his mission for Sylvan, and Guy Bowman, who in Tom's opinion was merely ballast; he was certainly not taking such a risk for *him*. But he tossed and turned half the night, going over in his head, as in a courtroom, the arguments for and against his involvement. Cold comfort came with the thought that he had merely a walk-on part in what was for the others a life-shattering drama, yet there he was, worrying about an entirely insignificant role – the messenger, the coachman – neither patriot nor traitor worthy of the hangman's rope. He finally dropped off to sleep rehearsing his checklist and timetable for the coming day's adventure.

Dawn was showing through the window when he woke with a start. Had he ever actually consented to this farce? Wasn't his duty now to end it, turn in Sylvan, reveal his Soviet contact? He could do it now, this morning. They would trap Sylvan, and much more importantly Guy, at Wimbledon as they arrived at three-thirty, while he was working conscientiously at his desk.

Cold and clammy and hating himself, he ran a hot bath. Through the comforting vapours he thought he could hear Marcie's voice inside his head: *Pull yourself together, Tom. You know what you have to do. In time they will all come to their senses. The atom bomb hangs like a dark cloud over the Russians just as much as over us. Russia will change, the way Sodkin hopes. Sylvan may even be able to help him. So think straight. Just call the office as soon as someone is there and say you have 'flu, bad back, anything. Nobody will care if you take a day off sick.*

That was the answer. *Thank you, dearest Marcie.* In fanciful mood – after all, wasn't he living in a fantasy? – he remembered again Homer's grey-eyed goddess. *Athene!* That was her! When Odysseus was in trouble, the goddess Athene appeared to him and told him what to do. Right. Back to the real world. He would wait until about nine when there was sure to be someone in the office.

When he went downstairs, his mother was already in the kitchen and had put the kettle on.

"You look awful, dear," she said in an affectionate tone that softened her words. "Did you sleep badly?"

Tom nodded.

"I think you might be right about me coming down with something."

He telephoned Pickett.

"Sorry, but I may have a touch of 'flu, don't want to spread it around. Mind if I take the day off?"

"Not a bit. You do that. Carole said you seemed a bit peaky yesterday."

"Why don't you go back to bed for a little while, catch up on your sleep?" said Mrs Davis.

Obediently he accepted a couple of aspirins, then sat up in bed, trying to read, staring out of the window, and fretting until she came up at noon with a bowl of soup.

"You're looking better. I was quite worried about you when you came downstairs this morning."

"I'm *feeling* much better," he said emphatically. "Don't think it's 'flu after all." He swung his legs out of the bed and stood up. "I've got the day off, Ma, be nice to make the best of it. Some friends of mine from Washington are over, staying in Chertsey. I'll call them and see if I can visit."

His mother was upstairs and well away from the hallway where the telephone was when he made his bogus call. She came down as he rang off.

"That's fixed!" he exclaimed in a voice that sounded falsely hearty even to him. "They suggest tea and then that I should stay for a local amateur dramatic do in the early evening and maybe stay the night – I think I might do that. Saturday tomorrow, after all."

He was early. He got out the car; he'd filled it with petrol yesterday, checked the oil, made sure there was an old oil-can full of water in the boot. But the lie nagged him. He returned indoors.

"Look, Ma, it really is all OK," and taking her by both elbows he kissed her forehead.

She looked up at him, puzzled.

"I didn't tell you the whole truth. But it's my cover story for an operation I'm involved with."

Her face fell.

"Oh dear, and we hoped you had given up all that secret stuff now the war is ended."

"This is the last chapter. It will all be over very soon, I promise."

It was time to go. He hugged her and made for the door.

"Take care, *bach* and wrap up well!" she called after him.

He was glad to have done that much. If all went wrong – if the evening news reported that the whole party was under arrest, this exchange would at least reduce the shock. The half-truth would be easier to live with than the crude lie.

It was barely twenty-five minutes' drive to Wimbledon station, allowing for average afternoon traffic. The weather was deteriorating:

it was windy, and short sharp showers rattled on the roof. He had time to turn aside at Morden Underground terminus where there used to be a café. It was still there. He bought three ham sandwiches and a bottle of cream soda; he had already stashed a bottle of whisky behind his seat. Some Dutch courage might be needed.

He was soon turning into the parking area. The barricade he had put up yesterday was still in place, but there were other spaces available today, better situated for a quick get-away, and he was able to park nose out right by the exit.

On the station concourse the clock showed that there were fifteen minutes before Sylvan's train was due. Guy had a choice of trains; the plan was for him to present himself only when Sylvan arrived. Feeling strangely calm, Tom bought an evening paper and waited at the spot he had found yesterday where he could watch the exits from the platforms below.

The concourse shook as the great expresses thundered through below. Doors slammed, guards whistled and unintelligible announcements bellowed from the loudspeakers as the stopping trains came and went. Passengers straggled up from the District Line. No sign of Guy. But at the stroke of three-thirty there was Sylvan, presenting his ticket at the barrier at the top of the stairs. The ticket collector squinted at it but did not look up.

Sylvan glanced around the concourse; their eyes met, but Tom carefully avoided looking at him again. Peering over the newspaper, he saw him go to the kiosk where he bought a magazine and some cigarettes.

Tom's instructions from Sodkin were that if only one of the travellers showed up at the station, he was to lead him to the car then return and wait for the other. A few minutes ticked by and he decided to move off. Sylvan followed him into the street and muttered urgently in his ear, "No Guy?"

"Not yet. I'll show you where the car is, then go back and wait for him."

But as they turned into the yard they stopped in their tracks. A small knot of people were gathered round his improvised barricade; with them, the watchman. He saw Tom and came quickly across. Tom's instinct was to run, but he stepped forward to meet him.

"Hey, what's going on?"

"Cor! 'orrible, it was! They shot 'im dead! The bloke shot first, though, I saw the flash, but that big train come through. Then, bang! Bang! – and they shot 'im!"

"What – *who?*"

"Secret police, I suppose. Plain clothes."

Two men were standing over a body thrown back over an upturned oil drum. From where Tom stood he could only see the legs, which ended in expensive shoes and garish socks. He recognised the design: brightly patterned with mauve and mustard clocks.

The men turned away.

"Better clear orf," said the watchman urgently, "before the rozzers show up!"

Tom returned to Sylvan, who was standing stock-still by the entrance as if struck by lightning. He propelled him quickly to the car and took off. As they turned into the street, the flashing lights of police cars were approaching. He accelerated away in the opposite direction.

Chapter Forty-One

They were soon back on the Morden Road heading for the Sutton by-pass leading to Reigate and the Brighton Road. Only then did he say, "It was Guy, of course."

"I knew it," said Sylvan.

They were clear of the built-up areas and humming along the bypass at a steady forty before Sylvan said, "Tom, do you want to give up?"

"It's your choice. It's just you now…"

He couldn't ask if the Russians would bother with the escape if they could only have Sylvan.

"Let's push on, if it's all the same to you."

It was. If Sylvan found himself in the dock, Tom would be beside him.

"Christ almighty, Sylvan, that was close. I guess they're still after you?" Remembering Clayton-Greene's warning about the security services, he glanced nervously in his rear-view mirror, uncertain what he should be looking for.

"Oddly, no, I think not. They have no reason to link me with Guy. Guy was their real quarry; he was a paid agent of the NKVD and MI5 had him clearly in their sights – without any help from the Yanks. He's – he *was* – the real pro. He's given Moscow the names of several of our agents. He also directed a raft of their agents here, and, sitting in the Minister of State's Office, gave his masters a running commentary on Foreign Office thinking. Such as it is."

"Bastard. *Bastard.*"

"Frankly, I agree. Sodkin was ordered to get Guy back to Moscow. It was his idea to put me in the same package for my own good."

"So you guess it was our spooks who got him, not the Russians?"

"Frankly again, yes. Not those fancy boys you meet in Leconfield House, of course. They'd never soil their lily-white hands, but they have their thugs in the basement; hoods, as our friends across the pond would say."

"But why kill him? What use is that?"

"Not a lot of use, no. But I think it quite possible that Guy may have shot first."

"That's what the watchman said."

"Well, in those circumstances the police, when armed, shoot to kill. They have no option. A wounded boar can still rend you."

In the close proximity of the little car, Tom sensed a growing tension in the man beside him. He had tried to emulate Sylvan's initial sang-froid, but now Tom shared this tension. Delayed shock, perhaps. He saw again Guy's sprawling body. His stomach churned, his hands on the wheel felt numb and cold.

"Let's pull in for a minute," he said, and bumped the car over the kerb into a gap in the furze-lined highway. They were high on the North Downs, where a crossing place linked two halves of a golf course split in two by the road. A rickety sign-post pointed to the tenth tee. Sylvan got out and vomited over the nearest gorse bush. Tom sat still, his head on the wheel, trying to breathe deeply and slowly. After a bit, he felt better and reached in the back for the whisky bottle. He took a swig, got out of the car and offered the bottle to Sylvan.

A fresh wind gave a clear view to the horizon. To the south they could see an ominous bank of dark cloud massing over the coast. Looking north towards London, Tom could pick out the dome of St. Paul's, Big Ben, and the chimneys of Battersea Power Station against a washed-out sky. He pointed out the familiar landmarks to Sylvan, and said gently, "A last look?" Sylvan threw a swift glance to where he was pointing and turned to get back in the car.

"If you think you can, Tom, we'd better push on." As they pulled away, he added, "There's another thing. So far it has been all MI5, but only yesterday the Yanks persuaded the Foreign Office that they have to make a move. The police will be briefed tomorrow and charges prepared. Hence the rush."

Tom swerved dangerously at this chill reminder that he was aiding and abetting the escape of a criminal.

"A man called Philip Kimball telephoned me yesterday and told me something like that," he said. "Did he *want* me to warn you? I was told he was in Intelligence. I thought it might be a trap."

"Philip Kimball wears many hats. You'd be wise to steer clear of him."

Still on the crest of the North Downs, they headed for Reigate Hill. Tom thought it better to talk, chat about anything, rather than dwell on the awful start to this adventure and what might happen next. But a nasty thought popped into his head.

"Sylvan, what baggage did Guy have – my God, tickets, passport?

"Just a light travel bag, same as me. Don't worry. We were told to have no documents on us at all. Sodkin's people are going to provide passports, money, tickets when we meet."

The telephone box in Little Topham was just where Alexei Sodkin had said it would be. Tom pulled into a lay-by and left Sylvan in the car while he dialled the number he had been given.

"Alexei?"

"Tom. Good. We know about Guy, we had men tailing both of you. He arrived at the station too early. He saw the opposition closing in on him. There were three of them. He seems to have panicked and bolted. They followed him into the station yard, fanned out and could not find him at first. Guy had holed up behind a sort of barricade. One of the hoods found him. It all happened very quickly. Our man thinks Guy drew his gun first, but they got him right between the eyes. Silencer perhaps, but with trains rushing through that station no-one would have heard."

"We must have got there just minutes after it happened."

"They emptied his pockets and one of them cleared off with his things."

"What happens now?"

"You have a little time, you are actually ahead of schedule. We had made an allowance for you to be held up in traffic. Let me speak to Sylvan, please."

Holding the receiver in one hand, Tom leant out of the door of the telephone box and called to Sylvan to come to the phone while he stepped out and lit a cigarette.

He had just taken his last puff and stepped on the stub when Sylvan called him back and handed him the phone.

"We go on," he said, walking back to the car.

"Hang on," said Tom to Sodkin, suppressing hysterical laughter at the bathos of the situation, "I need to feed more coins into this beastly machine. OK. Go ahead."

"Sylvan wants to continue," said Sodkin. "My orders, as I think you know, were to get Guy to Moscow. I was allowed to add Sylvan as part of the baggage, as it were. So now we have lost him, they may lose interest in Sylvan, may even put the blame for losing Guy onto him – and on me too," he added in a rueful tone.

Tom understood that in his low-key way Alexei was signalling that he was almost certainly for the chop.

Sodkin continued, "But for me, loyalty to friends is, I think, greater than loyalty to country, especially as my beloved homeland exists at present." The rueful tone changed to briskly efficient. "OK. So we go on. Same place as arranged, on the sea-front road, the promenade. Wait for the taxi that's coming to pick you up and take you to Boris. He will flash his lights twice as he passes. Good fellow – local man, and they all know him at the docks."

"Right."

They still had time. Tom was strangely reluctant to end the

conversation; he had a feeling that this really *would* be their last encounter.

"And when Sylvan finally makes it to Moscow?"

"Arrangements are in place, but the machine adjusts only slowly. Stalin is out of circulation, and, believe me, there is a ferment throughout the hierarchy. I know some of the men ready to take over, smash the system – and they will, in time – but right now the Berias, the secret police, with no clear political direction, just watch everything and everybody. I hope that our friends there will get hold of Sylvan, enlist him to prepare the tinder for the new revolution, help shed a little light over the desks of our powerless intellectuals. I know there are many, waiting to help."

"I just pray you're right, Alexei. I wish you all the best."

"*Do svidanya, Tovarisch.*"

"Goodbye, Alexei. Thanks for everything."

Now that the decision had been made, Sylvan appeared to relax. He had always responded to excitement. He had clearly enjoyed the Bronski exercise; perhaps he was even enjoying this last escape, though he was clearly no less shaken than Tom had been by Guy's death. Tom had to concentrate on the driving: the Austin brake mechanism tended to pull the car to one side and took some controlling, and the strong wind didn't help; they began to slither and slide down Reigate Hill. Sylvan grasped the dashboard in front of him with both hands.

"Keep her moving!" he yelled almost joyfully.

"You're quite mad" said Tom, with a feeble laugh. "But here we go!"

There was little traffic and they fairly bounced along what was now the Brighton Road proper. Suddenly Sylvan gripped his knee, tightly.

"Steady, old chap; police car behind."

Tom saw it, still way back, but with lights flashing.

"What do you want me to do?"

"Keep going. Just trundle along." Sylvan had slipped down as far as his long legs would allow and snatched the rug from the back to cover his head like a shawl. The police rushed by and were soon far ahead. Whoever they were after, it was not them.

Chapter Forty-Two

As the lights of the speeding police car disappeared down the road ahead of them Tom wiped the sweat from his forehead. Sylvan threw off the shawl, stretched and rearranged his cramped limbs. He was quite calm and even cheerful.

"As I thought when you re-emerged on the scene, the perfect car for the job! Even if they had been after us they would have passed us up in this little bus. Had you come up with a Maserati, or even a Jag, they'd certainly have stopped you, simply on principle."

The police car's appearance had set Tom's nerves twitching again.

"God's *sake*, Sylvan they probably *are* after us by now!"

"Probably not, as it turns out," said Sylvan in a satisfied tone. "I've calculated that no-one will have reason to miss me until Monday."

"I bloody well hope so. What makes you so confident?"

"Oh, they keep an eye on me – but only part time. Most weekdays I take a bus to attend this damn clinic. Marcie comes with me, and the MI5 blokes posted near her flat keep an eye on us going and coming. But I noticed that the watchers knock off early on a Friday, and I haven't spotted them at the weekend. I suppose they think Marcie is guarding me. Frightfully British, don't you think? They saw us set off this afternoon. It won't be before Monday that they realise I haven't come back. Then they may start to worry."

"What about Marcie?" Tom almost shouted, taking his eyes off the road for a moment and glaring at Sylvan. "Won't she get into trouble for letting you escape?"

"Steady, dear boy. Concentrate on the driving, please. She will dream up some cock-and-bull story that will satisfy them. She can be very inventive, and very persuasive."

"And what about me?" he asked more calmly. He was already resigned to whatever outcome lay ahead.

"Oh, there will be some dreary enquiry, and you may well be caught up in it. If things go wrong now – but they won't – Sodkin will fix you up. He was very taken with you, by the way."

Tom was not reassured. Yes, of course there would be an enquiry. No, of course he would not take Guy's place on the Russia run.

The Austin began to labour up the incline of the gap in the South Downs. In the old days, as the family car crested the rise between the rim of the Devil's Punchbowl and Ditchling Beacon, heading for a day by the sea at Brighton, he used to think they were almost there; but he knew there was quite a way to go yet. And now, for all the light traffic so far, there were two heavy vans labouring up the hill ahead of them. No chance of passing, and other cars were coming up behind. The car was down to bottom gear and the engine was running hot.

"I'll have to pull off when I get a chance."

"You can't stop now!"

"God, Sylvan, I have to or she'll blow up!"

They were at the steepest part of the rise, bare downland on either side of the road. Tom swung the car into a picnic spot, a small plateau with space for several cars to park and a viewing point for visitors. He got out, opened the boot, and took out a rag and a pair of thick gloves which he put on and then, holding the rag, he gingerly unscrewed the radiator cap. A plume of steam escaped with a hiss and he sighed. It would have to cool off before he refilled it. He stood staring out over the Downs where the evening light left shadows in the folds of the land, and glinted on the white scars of a chalk quarry and on the roofs and spires of the villages of the Sussex Weald. A brisk offshore wind spun streamers of cloud out to sea toward a darkening horizon.

When the radiator had cooled down sufficiently, Tom moved

towards the boot to get the can of water. He paused by Sylvan's open window and said, "Nearly done," when another police car pulled into the parking area.

"Sorry Tom," said Sylvan, "Maybe my calculations were wrong. Guess they've caught up with us." In his lap was a revolver.

"For God's sake put that damn thing away!"

A police officer was getting out of the car and was walking towards them.

Tom leant in to grab the gun, shoved it into the glove compartment and slammed it shut. Sylvan offered no resistance, just slumped back into his seat.

The policeman approached.

"Afternoon, sir," he said politely. "Noticed you were having a spot of bother with the engine. Anything I can help with?"

Tom turned towards him, praying that the officer hadn't seen him hiding the gun.

"Jolly kind of you, Officer. She just over-heated on this hill. Stopped to top up with water."

His heart was thumping so hard he was amazed that the policeman couldn't hear it.

"Righty-ho, then, as long as there's no problem…"

"No, there's no problem. Should be cooled down enough by now, we'll be on our way. Thanks for asking."

"No trouble at all, sir. Careful as you go now."

The policeman touched his cap and walked back to his vehicle.

Tom carefully poured the water into the radiator and screwed the cap back on. He waited until he was sure the police car was out of sight, slung the can in the boot, slammed it shut, then got back into the Austin.

"If they do stop us again, Sylvan, for Christ's sake, do *not* start shooting! Shoot a policeman and you'll get us both hanged."

"It's not for them, it's for me. I won't go back." He added almost brightly, "What about you, Tom? Do you want to come with me? I've six slugs in here. Shoot you first, if you wish."

"Don't be so bloody stupid." Tom changed up viciously, grinding the gears. "But you can damn well tell me where you got your information about Bronski, and how you were always able to stay one step ahead of the Russians."

"Haven't you worked it out by now? I had my own private secret agent among the Russians – Alexei Sodkin – but only for the Bronski affair. He told me about Bronski's meeting with the ballerinas at Moose Lodge and tipped me off that Potemkin was heading towards your rendezvous with Hank."

Tom swung out to avoid a bicycle that had emerged from a side road. The action gave him a little time to try to process this information. Eventually he said, "He's a good fellow, Alexei. He believes deeply in the ideal of communism, which Stalin has corrupted beyond recognition, so by helping you keep Viktor Bronski out of Soviet hands, he's thwarted Stalin's nuclear ambitions. All makes sense. He wouldn't have thought he was betraying his country, but saving the world from another megalomaniac dictator."

"That's about it."

"But how did they know where we were leaving from that morning? You didn't tell…"

"No, of course not. I told Alexei that we would be smuggling Bronski out by boat, but no details. We talked a lot while we were on the *Queen Mary* together and this is what he reckoned. His assistant, Grigori Potemkin, was NKVD, and the NKVD have big ears and long tentacles; it wouldn't have taken them long to work out that the four of us were all away from the embassy at the same time that Bronski disappeared, and that when we returned there was someone secreted in the residence. Alexei told me that on that Tuesday morning he overheard Potemkin on the telephone – to the Embassy, presumably – asking for Lieutenant Davis. Apparently he said something like, 'on leave… left this morning?' Alexei guessed that your going on leave was significant and that this was the day of departure. When he checked on Potemkin a little later, he was gone, and so was another chap called Ivanov, who was also NKVD.

He realised that they had reached the same conclusion as him, and he telephoned me immediately to warn us."

"Sounds plausible. But doesn't explain how they knew *where* we would be."

"Alexei suspects that Roger…" Sylvan stopped. He took several deep breaths before he was able to continue. "Alexei suspects that Roger may himself have inadvertently given away that information."

"*Roger?* How?"

"I didn't tell Alexei *where*, but I did say that you and Roger had been there before in the boat that was subsequently used for our operation. This Ivanov fellow was from Odessa, a keen yachtsman; he belonged to the same sailing club as Roger. Roger was too trusting…"

Again he paused, seemingly overcome with emotion. Tom nodded; yes, Roger had always seen the best in people.

Sylvan pulled himself together and went on.

"Alexei thinks it's quite likely that over a drink at the club he had chatted to Ivanov about your sailing weekend with Hank, before the information became important. Later, Potemkin and Ivanov could have worked out, as you did, that the safest way to smuggle Bronski out of the country was to embark him onto a smaller craft in an isolated location and then transfer him to an ocean-going vessel once it had left the harbour. They suspected that Roger was involved, and Ivanov remembered what he had told him about Hank's place and the *Dulcibelle Adams*. They put two and two together and came up with the right answer. This is pure speculation, obviously, but it does explain things."

"I suppose it does. Well, it doesn't really matter now, does it?" he said glumly.

They drove the rest of the way to Brighton in silence, Tom attempting to rehearse suitable phrases for their imminent parting. But no words came.

Chapter Forty-Three

It was still early evening, but the black storm-clouds that filled the sky made it seem like night as they crossed the river at Newhaven. A strong wind was blowing off the sea and squalls of raindrops spattered the windscreen. Tom caught a glimpse of the ferry in a pool of flood-light. A car was being hoisted aboard by crane. A few minutes further on they were out on the sea front. Tom found the spot where they were to wait and pulled the car over.

"We've done it. We're here. Minutes to spare." Sylvan straightened himself up in his seat.

"Tom," he said, and his voice was choking, "Tom, dearest boy, thank you for everything."

"Not a bit," Tom said awkwardly. "Here, let's have one for the road," and he reached for the whisky bottle.

Sylvan swallowed deeply, then took another swig. He wiped his mouth, sighed, and said, "Look out for the taxi fellow, will you. I'm going to have a pee. Long journey ahead."

He shut the door against a blast of wind and crossed over to the promenade.

Tom stayed in the Austin, the windows wound up tight against the wind and the rain. With its light springs, the little car shook to each gusty squall.

He could just make out Sylvan, leaning on the rail of the promenade, partly silhouetted against the white breakers that covered the nearer sea. Beyond that, sea and sky merged in total darkness. There was no horizon.

Then the flashing lights. He flicked on his headlights in return. The taxi-man was quickly with him.

"Any luggage? You're to give it to me. Where's the bloke?"

"Just having a pee. I'll get him."

He crossed over the sea front, bent against the gale and tripping on pebbles strewn across the promenade by a recent storm.

Sylvan was not there. Useless to call out his name against the roar of the wind and the rising tide. Tom glanced in both directions, then made for some concrete steps leading down to the beach a few yards to the right where there was a break in the rail.

He stumbled along the pebbled beach before he found him, spread-eagled, face down, under the sea wall.

The ugly bullet wound left no doubt that Sylvan was dead, but Tom fell on his knees and grasped him by the shoulders, turning the body this way and that to make sure. And then the taxi-driver was there at his side with a torch. He picked up the revolver, slipped on the safety catch and pocketed it.

"Come along, young feller, there's nothing you can do for him. He's gone."

Tom was still clinging to the lifeless body, and it was with some difficulty that the other man got him to let go and stand up.

"Just make sure we've left no tracks. Here, gimme a hand."

Together they pulled the corpse a few yards nearer the line of the surf, as close as they could get to where the incoming waves surged against the shingle.

"It's spring tides, the sea will take him away," said the taxi-man. "He'll be happier to go with the tide."

Soaked through with rain, spume and spray, they made their way back to the promenade.

"Now you git, young feller. I've got your man's bag in the taxi already. I'll get back to Boris. Now go home, mate – go on home."

Chapter Forty-Four

Tom drove like a zombie until he reached the telephone box at Little Topham from where he had rung Captain Sodkin that afternoon. He closed the door quickly to shut out the rain that beat against the glass, and dialled Marcie's number. She answered after the first ring.

"It's me. I have to see you – can I come now?

Mercifully, she asked no questions.

"Of course, I'll wait up for you."

"I'll be there within the hour."

Marcie drew Tom into the comforting warmth of her flat; she took in his wet clothing and the haunted expression on his face.

"My God, Tom, what happened?"

He tried breaking the news to her as gently as he could, but there was really no way he could soften the blow. He was sick at heart as he watched first disbelief then shock cross her face, before the tears came and she leant against his chest, her body heaving with sobs. He held her close, stroking her hair, saying nothing, until the initial spasm of grief had passed.

"Sorry about all the blubbing," she whispered, raising her tear-stained face, "must look an absolute fright."

"No, you look beautiful – you always look beautiful."

"I need to get a hankie – back in a jiffy."

She returned in about five minutes, her face washed and her hair brushed, though her cheeks were pale and her eyes red-rimmed. She was holding a bath towel and a knitted jersey.

"You'll catch your death of cold sitting around in those damp things. Give me that wet shirt and jacket, I'll hang them up in the kitchen to dry. Here's a towel and an old sweater of Gareth's."

Tom did not demur, guessing that she was using this minor fussing as a distraction from having to deal with the enormity of what had happened. She took his clothes into the kitchen; when she came back she was carrying a bottle of brandy and two glasses.

"I think we need this."

She poured them each a generous tot and handed one glass to Tom. She drained half her own drink, then sat on the sofa and patted the seat beside her. He sat down and saw that she was wearing the silver and turquoise earrings he had bought for her in New Mexico. *There's been a lot of water under the Rio Grande bridge since then,* he thought.

"You really loved Sylvan, didn't you, Marcie?"

"Yes, of course I did, but only as a sister might love a rather roguish brother. He wasn't interested in women in… well, you know, that way."

"That way? What way? You don't mean… what *do* you mean, Marcie?"

Her waspishness returned.

"You are such a naif, sometimes, Tom. Do I have to spell it out? Sylvan preferred men, young men, to women as sexual partners."

"Sylvan was a homosexual?"

"Can't understand why you never spotted it for yourself. I've known all along, of course. But women are always better at these things, I've found."

Tom was hardly a naif in these matters, having spent three years in the Royal Navy, part of the time below decks. And there had been quite an open cult at Oxford. Students used to joke about belonging to the Comintern or the Homintern. Cambridge's reputation was worse, and Sylvan, it appeared, had belonged to both. Marcie's revelation explained a lot. But he had missed all the clues; probably his affection for his friend had blinded him.

"Sylvan and I often went to concerts and plays and things together," she continued, "mutually advantageous: cover for him, a compatible and non-demanding companion for me. I'm afraid we rather enjoyed stirring up the rumour mill."

"I had sometimes thought that you and Sylvan…"

"No darling, it wasn't like that at all." She sipped some more of her brandy. "Last night, the night before he left, Sylvan told me everything; he knew that whatever happened today we would never see each other again."

Tom took both her hands in his.

"And can you…?"

"Yes, he wanted you to know. He and Roger were lovers."

Another shock. But again, when he thought about it… *Roger had said,* marriage not really an option; *perhaps he was trying to tell me.*

"Obviously it would have been fatal to both their careers if it became known," she went on, "so they had to keep the relationship secret. Worked pretty well; I don't think anyone at the embassy even suspected."

"I certainly didn't."

"He even fooled me, and I thought I knew him better than anyone." She disentangled their hands and took another sip. "That's one of the reasons why *you* got the dangerous assignment in New Mexico, and Sylvan made sure Roger was safe in Colorado; he couldn't bear to put him in harm's way."

"Great. So I was just cannon fodder?

"No, of course not!" She shifted on the sofa so her thigh lay along his. He put his glass down and laid his arm very gently on the back of the sofa, just touching her shoulders. "Sylvan thought very highly of you. He knew you were steadier than Roger and would do a good job – and so you did. When Roger was killed Sylvan was totally undone, went completely bonkers. He believed that Roger had deliberately driven into the Russian car so that Sylvan's operation was not put in jeopardy."

"Did he?"

"Who knows? But Sylvan blamed himself, of course. Roger's death was the last straw, on top of the strain of carrying not one but two oppressive secrets: Operation Roadrunner, and his involvement with the Russians."

"That's what Sir John said. But I assume *he* didn't know about Roger. Well, maybe he did… but the Russian thing, Marcie; do you know the whole story?"

She sighed.

"It started while he was still at Cambridge."

"Yes, he said as much."

"NKVD agents had caught him in an… indiscretion with another undergraduate. Male, of course. There were photos – pretty explicit ones, I gather – that they threatened to release to the gutter press. If they had, he would have been drummed out of the diplomatic corps, and probably arrested for gross indecency. His left-wing sympathies were quite genuine, so he chose the path of least resistance." She held out her empty glass. "Top-up, please?"

Tom refilled their glasses.

"They never asked him to do much," Marcie continued, "just enough to keep him dangling on their hook. I suppose they thought he might rebel if they pushed him too hard. And of course, in the end he *did* rebel."

She took two cigarettes from the box on the table and lit them. As she took one from between her lips and handed it to Tom, his heart turned over, remembering the first time she had done that, at Pinoñes.

"I know you always wondered where Sylvan got his information," she said, taking a deep drag on the cigarette. "It was from Captain Sodkin."

"Yes, he told me. And now I can see that when Alexei said he suspected that Roger had let slip a vital piece of information, that would have been devastating to Sylvan."

He drew on his own cigarette and sipped some more of the brandy; the chill that had gripped him since he had found Sylvan's body had mostly dissipated, and he was much calmer now.

"What an awful pile of bodies," he said mournfully. "Like the last act of Hamlet." *Goodnight, sweet Prince*, he remembered, *and flights of angels sing thee to thy rest.*

He sighed.

"Did Sylvan say anything about Patrick Marsden? Did he kill him to cover his own tracks?"

Marcie shook her head.

"He didn't mention Marsden, and I didn't ask."

"I don't suppose we'll ever know what really happened."

"Sylvan took to heart what you said about redemption. As he was telling me all this I got the feeling that he was making his Last Confession. He actually said, and he was in tears, 'Forgive me, Marcie, I have sinned. Have I atoned enough? Will I receive absolution?'"

The tears, which were still close to the surface, welled again in her own eyes. She stubbed out her cigarette and pulled out her handkerchief to wipe them away.

"And what did you say?"

"I gave him absolution," she whispered.

"Do you think he knew when he left this afternoon how it would end?" asked Tom. "Is that why he brought the gun?"

"Almost certainly. And without even Guy as a companion… well, in the end, what choices did he really have? To stay in England, where he would lose his job, his reputation, his future and at best receive a lengthy prison sentence? Or spend the rest of his life in a strange land, with no friends, no one who loved him, no one who even cared a fig about him? To a man like Sylvan that could be as much of a prison as an English one of bricks and mortar. When faced with two untenable options, he found a third way out."

They sat quietly, remembering their friend and all they had shared with him, until Tom heard Marcie murmur, "*Requiescat in pace*, Sylvan."

"Amen."

In the circumstances it seemed the only thing to say.

Then she took his hand and smiled. She relaxed visibly – perhaps by relating Sylvan's confession, she had also unburdened herself.

"So what happens now? What are you going to do?"

The time had come to answer this question.

"Well, I used to think I'd eventually join the diplomatic corps, like Sylvan, but not any more. Oddly enough, now I look back, I suppose it was at that meeting with Bevin a few months ago that my idealism began to falter. I was certainly carried along on the wave of Rooseveltian liberalism during the war years, even in the nest of self-seeking go-gettism that America's become."

"But you love living in America," she protested.

"I do. There's an energy and friendliness there that's missing here. But coming back to Britain now, in spite of all the privations and the insularity, and the snobbery – well, I don't know – there's something in my heart that still loves this wretched little island. Perhaps when I retire I shall live in Bosham and keep bees and go down the pub of an evening and be a frightful bore."

"Darling Tom, you could never be a frightful bore."

"But I won't go back to Washington, Marcie. I can see now that half-baked idealism is not the stuff of foreign policy. Bevin was right in a way: the role of the Foreign Office is the single-minded pursuit of the national interest." He shook his head. "I can't do that. I want to do something that will help people beyond just our own shores."

She turned his face gently towards his and kissed him. "Tom, you're still an idealist after all."

"Perhaps," he said with a smile. "I want to work for the United Nations in New York."

"'Tomorrow to fresh woods and pastures new'?"

"Not many woods and pastures in New York."

"Don't be so gloomy. There's Central Park. And with all your contacts there, you should have no problem getting a job."

"And you? What will you do now?"

"I don't really know. I thought I might go travelling."

She was still holding his hand; he put his other hand over hers. He remembered another thing that Roger had said on that last day: *You have a chance at a future with the person you love.*

"Come with me."

"Come with you?"

"Yes, come with me to New York."

He waited.

"There's one problem."

"What's that?" he asked anxiously.

"I can't cook."

He took her face in his hands and kissed her.

"But I can. Well, omelettes anyway. And macaroni-cheese."

She whispered: "then perhaps we might muddle through…"